Out of Darkness

Out of Darkness

A Novel

Keith C. Terry

Covenant Communications, Inc.

Published by Covenant Communications, Inc.
American Fork, Utah

Printed in the United States of America
First Printing: August 1995

01 00 99 98 97 96   10 9 8 7 6 5 4

ISBN 1-55503-867-0

Acknowledgments

Maurice R. Tanner for his careful insights into the Book of Mormon, his excellent ideas, and unflagging encouragement; and his wife, Hazel Tanner, who proofed and gave her support.

My wife, Ann, who proofed, corrected, and offered her expertise in structure and content. Joann Paget and Isaac Sefchovich for their editing skills.

The single most important group to lend scholarly support to this novel were key members of the Foundation for Ancient Research and Mormon Studies (F.A.R.M.S.). The results of their research in the past decade have opened up the exciting avenues that permeate this novel. Published studies by members of this committee opened my eyes to the possibility of focusing on this new information.

Specifically, I wish to express gratitude to Alvin Rencher, Wayne A. Larson, and Tim Layton for their pioneering studies in wordprints, and more recently to John Hilton, who has kept up the fire on the marvels of wordprints.

In addition, John W. Welch, who has made a major breakthrough in identifying the classic literary style of the Book of Mormon, which contains some of the world's finest chiasmus.

John Tvedtnes and his brilliant insights into Hebraisms has introduced the reader of the Book of Mormon to the richness of Near Eastern thought and language.

Stephen D. Ricks and William J. Hamblin for their work on warfare in the Book of Mormon. Daniel Peterson for his insights into the culture of the Hebrews.

Eric Boyle, vice president of Lindsay Olive Corporation, for arranging meetings with people in the Middle East olive oil industry. Also, to David Eitam for his cooperation in Haifa, Israel.

Contents

Characters

The Benefactor:

Thomas Kline—*Wealthy copper king of Phoenix, Arizona, who desires to interest the intellectual community in the Book of Mormon*

His Colleague:

Dr. Peter Polk—*Professor Emeritus, Brigham Young University*

The Unnatural Son:

Craig Kline—*Greedy, ruthless antagonist*

The Substitute Scholar:

Dr. Stephen Thorn—*Son-in-law to Robert Moore, faced with the decision of his life*

The Daughter/Wife:

Anney Thorn—*Stephen's lovely wife and Moore's dutiful daughter*

The Minister:

Robert Moore—*Bay Area Televangelist with questionable values*

The Scholars:

Dr. Henry Syman—*Chair, ancient studies, Purdue University*

Dr. Bernard Stein—*Author, ancient warfare, Yale University*

Dr. Frederick Shaw—*Professor, early nineteenth-century American studies, London University*

Dr. Martha Grain—*Professor, English literature, University of Missouri*

Dr. Judith Anderson—*Author, Bible as literature, Princeton University*

Dr. Palmer—*Professor, Egyptian documents and Near Eastern literature, Northwestern University, irate and intractable*

Dr. Calk—*Professor, Mesoamerican archeology, Texas A & M University*

The Presenters:

Colonel Rodney Kason—*Warfare*

Dr. Reuven Saul—*Chiasmus*

Conley Wilks—*Lehi's journey*

Characters

Dr. Raddai—*Hebraisms*

Lewis Granger—*Anti-Book of Mormon*

Three Professors—*Wordprints*

The Lawyers:

William Bennett—*Represents the project*

Matthew Sharp—*Represents Craig Kline*

The Graduate Student:

Roy Carver

The Bishops:

Martin Oren—*The former*

Jim Maxwell—*The present*

The Children:

Brenda Thorn

Todd Thorn

The Secretaries:

Mary Ellis—*Reluctant key to the financial threat*

Lois

June

The Investigators:

Daniel Knight

Mort Johnson

The Olive Growers:

Mr. Burger—*California*

Harvey Barak—*California*

David Rabin—*Haifa*

The husbandman—*Nablus*

And in that day shall the deaf hear the words of the book, and the eyes of the blind shall see out of obscurity, and out of darkness.

Isaiah 29:18

Chapter One
The Snag

Stephen bounded up the red brick steps to the tennis courts of the Pleasant Hill Country Club. At 43, Stephen was as vigorous and athletic as he had been at 25—or at least he felt he was. He stood on the walkway adjacent to the courts and watched the two older men complete their last set, both out of breath from so much exertion. Stephen caught the eye of the taller of the two men and waved. The man smiled and beckoned for Stephen to join them on the court.

A faint smile played around Stephen's mouth. He thought how much his congenial father-in-law, Bob Moore, loved the club sports. He rushed onto the tennis court as the two gray-haired men were about to shake hands.

"Dad," Stephen began, "I received a curious call from that professor this morning about ten—"

Robert Moore held up his hand to silence his eager son-in-law. He turned, shook hands with his opponent, and set a date for their next match. As he waved good-bye to his friend, Robert Moore, a popular televangelist in the Bay Area, picked up his can of balls and threw his arm around his son-in-law's shoulder.

"What did you find out?" Moore asked Stephen, grabbing a hand towel from the metal post as the two men walked down a brick path to the club's terrace. He made the question sound casual as he pressed the towel to his forehead and rubbed it across his full head of steel-gray hair.

"This may surprise you a little, Dad," Stephen replied, using the familiar term, as was his habit. "That project in San Diego has to do with the Book of Mormon."

Robert Moore showed no reaction. "Are you saying this changes things, son?" Moore seldom encountered surprises that altered his usual course of action. He merely worked around the unanticipated things in life. He was no friend of the Mormons, certainly not after his latest round of lectures, in which he exposed what he termed their ritualistic habits—but so what?

"Do you still want me to take the assignment?" Stephen asked.

"What has that got to do with it?"

Stephen glanced over at the older man. "Well, . . . I thought since the Mormons are anathema to your beliefs, you might have some objections. After all, need I remind you that just six months ago you gave those five lectures on the Mormons?"

Moore's eyes narrowed as he searched Stephen's face. "What did this coordinator say would be expected of you, Stephen?"

"Seven weeks holed up with some scholars—not Mormons. As a matter of fact, none of them know the nature of the project yet. Dr. Polk—you know, the coordinator—was actually reluctant to explain anything to me. I persisted in wanting to know some details, so he said he thought, since the project begins this Monday, that he could tell me briefly what it would be about. He told me that we'll be cloistered on an estate, taking apart the Book of Mormon."

"For what purpose?" the older man asked without surprise. "Did he tell you?" Moore's smooth voice reflected years of experience counseling his many followers.

"To discover whether the Book of Mormon is of antiquity."

"Did you ask this fellow—what's his name?"

"Polk. Dr. Peter Polk."

"Did he tell you what he intends to do with the information?"

"Actually, I felt like he thought I was probing him too much as it was. You spoke with him three months ago, Dad. Did he tell you anything then?"

Stephen followed his father-in-law into the locker room and sat down on the bench as the older man began to untie his shoes.

"I asked a lot of questions when I first talked to him, but three months ago he wouldn't tell me what the project was about. He wouldn't even tell *me* his name. At least you know the subject matter and his name. Wonder why he's been so close-mouthed?" Moore removed his shoes and let them drop to the floor.

"Yeah, I asked him that. He just said the project would have more validity if it were conducted by a nonbiased group. When I asked why he hadn't told you what the project would be, he said that he didn't want the participants to know the subject matter three months in advance, that if all the participants came without knowing beforehand, they would all begin on a somewhat equal stance."

"I guess that makes sense," Moore commented, pulling his white shirt over his head. "Then why did he tell you the subject matter this morning?"

"Well, he really didn't want to. But, as I said, he thought that at this point, just two days before we all meet to begin the project, it wouldn't make much difference. I wouldn't be able to do much research, anyway."

"He's right there," Moore reflected.

"He asked me not to say anything to the other participants about the project. He plans to introduce the subject Monday evening. How could I say anything when I don't know who the others are, anyway?"

"They sure are paying a high price for their nonbiased group," Moore interjected. "Did this coordinator tell you whether all the participants receive the same grant—of a hundred thousand dollars for just being there and doing the project?"

"I think they do, but I didn't ask him. At least that's what our contract says. He said I'll need to sign it Monday evening. Do you still want me to go?"

"Are you packed?"

"It's on, then? You know, I have some reservations, and I just thought that you—"

"Stephen, Stephen, my son. Of course I don't *want* you to go, but we have no viable alternative." Moore's eyes swept the small locker room. A lone attendant busily sorted towels in the caged-in booth near the entrance. Moore lowered his voice to a near whisper, "We need the money." And more hoarsely, "The money, Stephen, the money." There was a pause, and then the smooth voice said, "Oh, by the way, would you do me a favor?"

"What?"

"Have you mentioned to Anney what this project is about?"

"Not yet. I just found out when this coordinator called me at the office."

"Don't say anything to her about it, okay? It might upset her." *It might upset the whole signing of the contract Monday.* "The last thing you want is an upset wife. Just hold off telling her any of the details until you get down to San Diego and see what it is really all about."

"Sure, Dad, if that's what you want."

"That's what I want. I want to keep this between the two of us for a little while, okay?"

* * *

Peter Polk's thoughts raced with apprehension as the Mormon bishop dedicated the grave of Thomas B. Kline. The midday Phoenix sun blistered the white canopy. Under it gathered the overflow congregation of mourners made up of family and close friends. Peter's eyes narrowed as he scrutinized Craig, the deceased man's son, now sitting stoically beside his wife and two teenage sons.

Minutes before, Craig had brushed past Peter, asking to meet him in the limousine immediately after the services. *Asking? More of a command performance from the imperious tone of Craig's voice,* thought Peter. *What dire information does he want to impart to me? It can't be good, whatever it is.*

Religious man though he was, Peter heard few of the bishop's comforting words. His gaze continued along the rows of mourners. He recognized Craig's two older sisters with their husbands and families. Peter surmised, from his position standing at the back of the canopy, that the two rows of folding chairs were occupied by family. Behind the family stood some of Phoenix's most powerful and influential people. They had come to pay their respects to a community leader, a father, and a church member—a man that Peter had known as a friend, a partner in a complex project. Now he was dead. *Would the project die, too?*

Mary Ellis, Thomas's secretary of twenty-three years, stood to one side of the seated family, her wet eyes fixed on the casket. This faithful person had always been so efficient and quiet. He sensed that her loss was as great as his. Mary, with puffy lips and eyes red from crying, gave little heed to the hot breeze that capriciously played with her usually well-styled white hair. She had called Peter to inform him of Thomas's death and to confirm the time of burial. Even during that emotional moment, he and Mary had reviewed Peter's new responsibilities with the project now in his hands. Mary offered to help in any way she could, though she reminded him that all the correspondence and details of the project were in attorney Bill Bennett's office.

Still in all, Mary had cautioned Peter about her commitment. She had reminded him that all new assignments would now come from Craig Kline, the new chief executive officer. She still had a little over two years to go before retirement, and she wanted to maintain a good rapport with the new management. Nevertheless, whatever help she could give, within reason, she gladly offered, if it had the express consent of Craig Kline. Mary was part of the establishment.

Another bump in the road, Peter had thought, reflecting back on the call from Mary. At this moment, however, Peter was relieved to know that an account reserved for completing the project was already secured under the management of the accounting firm of Finley & Southam and that the remainder of the three-million-dollar trust was safely deposited at the California Bank and Trust in Beverly Hills. *Thank heavens the finances were taken care of before Thomas passed away.*

Thomas B. Kline had been a wealthy man who in some circles had been called "Arizona's copper king." In his lifetime he had garnered many millions of dollars and a few priceless possessions. Never stooping to dishonesty, he had the knack of getting what he went after.

He had a magnetic personality that had won Peter's friendship. More than that, his creative ideas had opened Peter's eyes to new ways to interest the world in the Book of Mormon. He had shown Peter how to push open the steel doors of his mind and usher in new thoughts and rich concepts—one of which was the new project. Peter needed no reminder that he would miss this special person.

A faint dry breeze wafted about the mourners, but it held no relief from the 105-degree afternoon heat. For Peter it merely acted as a furnace duct, focusing the heat on his exposed skin, skin he had inherited from his Irish progenitors who had immigrated to the Rocky Mountains after joining the Mormon faith. The genetic connection was evident: across his wide nose and over his plump cheeks, tiny blood vessels could be seen through the nearly transparent skin. His mother and grandfather had also had fragile Irish skin.

In sixty-six years of living, Peter had managed to increase his bulk steadily. But once a year, he often reflected wryly, he had the perfect physique—when he was in demand by the Church's organization for children, the Primary, to play Santa Claus. He would have welcomed the cool air of the Christmas season this afternoon.

For thirty of those sixty-six years Peter had taught Book of Mormon studies at Brigham Young University, and now he enjoyed the status of Professor Emeritus. He had raised his family of four children; loved his wife, who had died two years earlier; and continued to enjoy the roles of father and grandfather of nine grandchildren. He wished he were with them this very moment. This June day in Phoenix was as dry and hollow as the widening pit in his stomach. His sick feeling centered on Craig Kline.

In reality, Peter had felt just fine until Craig had sabotaged his equilibrium. With Thomas dead, there would be no father to rein in the son. *How could a man as magnanimous as Thomas produce the narrow, selfish bigot that was Craig?* Peter wondered angrily.

No more than a week ago, Peter had leaned across the slick black desk in Thomas Kline's office here in Phoenix and finalized the plans for the most ambitious project Peter had ever helped to create. That same day Thomas had stated that he was dying of cancer, but Peter had blocked the information from his mind. Such a short time from prediction to outcome.

The thought of his irreplaceable friend lying there in the closed casket so suddenly after their planning session stymied Peter. He had to remind himself that there are no guarantees in this life—the death of his Marian had convinced him of that. Frustration welled up in him for having no control of life. He needed Thomas more than Thomas needed him—much more.

He didn't want to be irreverent, but Peter could not control the direction of his thoughts. Face it. He was concerned about the project. The implementation of the "challenge" would now be in his hands. As long as the funds held out, he would have to make all the decisions and commitments necessary to see that this and future projects were carried out as he and Thomas had planned them. The burden of this new responsibility weighed heavily on Peter's mind.

Peter stirred from his reverie as the bishop ended his remarks. After the dedicatory prayer, he threaded his way through the gathering of mourners who surrounded the Kline family to express their condolences. He spoke to the bereaved daughters and then noticed a tall man with dark gray-streaked hair and a craggy face. It was Thomas's personal attorney, William Bennett. As Peter inched past the family, he wondered why he hadn't looked for Bennett earlier.

Bennett had been the real workhorse in setting up the project. Slowly, Peter edged his way toward William Bennett. He got close and extended his hand, bumping the arm of a lady in a white straw hat, the kind worn to fashionable garden parties.

"Dr. Polk, so nice to see you. Have you met my wife, Karen?"

The hat turned, and a strikingly beautiful blond woman in her early thirties smiled and extended her hand. It struck Peter that Bennett must be in his second marriage. He took the extended hand and expressed his delight at meeting her. Then he looked up at Bennett and said, "I called your office yesterday afternoon, but you were out. This whole thing is so sad. I thought Tom had at least ten more good years."

Others reached out and grabbed Bennett's hand, interrupting Peter's words. Peter could see that it was not an appropriate time to talk about vital subjects.

"Bill, I'll call you at your home this evening, if you don't mind. We need to discuss the project."

Bennett nodded.

Free of the group, Peter walked toward the black limousine that had been provided for his use. The limousine was fifth in a line of eight parked at the edge of the grass. Peter glanced back to study the scene before climbing into the back seat of the limousine. He noticed that Craig Kline had already freed himself from the group and was on his way toward the car. He appeared to be in a rush, neatly sidestepping a distinguished-looking couple who undoubtedly wanted to console him. The young driver held the door open for Peter, who got in and positioned himself in the center of the rear seat. The interior seemed dark, with heavy tinted glass blocking the direct sunlight. The car was idling, and the air conditioning flowed gently. Refreshingly cool though it was, it failed to soothe Peter's stirring thoughts. Something was about to happen; he felt certain of that.

A bright light flashed into the interior as the door opened again. It sliced across both sides of Craig's husky, broad-shouldered body, momentarily creating a faceless head shaded by the interior. Then the door closed, and Peter saw the serious expression on Craig's face—a face with a mean mouth.

Peter was the first to speak. Once again, he expressed his condolences and deep sorrow at the loss of Craig's father. The son remained solemn and respectful as he accepted the offered sympathy. Peter could detect annoyance in Craig's twitching eyebrows.

Amenities disposed of, Craig glowered intensely at Peter and said abruptly, "I must inform you, Dr. Polk, that your project has been canceled."

Craig's cold mouth did not further clarify the statement. Though unspoken, the words "I told you I would have the last say on this matter" rang through the air. The two men sat locked in a mutual stare. And for a moment the humming engine replaced all other sounds.

Peter hadn't expected such bluntness. He was certain he detected a gleam of satisfaction in Craig's dark eyes as the two men continued to stare at one another. *What does he mean, canceled? He can't just cancel this project. He doesn't have the authority to do that. Does he?* Peter studied the frozen face a moment longer and then blinked his eyes and spoke.

"Pardon me, Craig. I don't understand what you're saying."

"I'm merely telling you that I'm canceling the project. It's a dead issue. You have been stripped of authority to act as my father's agent in this matter. I have instructed my attorney to inform all concerned parties that there will be no meeting to carry out this crazy scheme you've cooked up. Oh, I'm sure you've already squandered part of the money, but I'll salvage the rest."

"What you're saying is that you want me to cancel the meeting of the participants. Is that right?" Peter asked quietly, not allowing himself to be provoked by the abruptness of this man.

"No, I'm not asking you to do any such thing. I'm telling you to stay out of it completely. My attorney will take over at this point. He will handle all the nasty little situations that this project created. You go back home. We have it well in hand, so don't worry about how this comes out. My attorney will be in touch with the bank to get the names, addresses, and phone numbers of the committed participants."

"Your attorney—you mean William Bennett?" Peter probed.

"Of course not. Except for a handshake today, I haven't had a word with that old fool in two years. He was my father's attorney—a bumbling idiot as far as I'm concerned. Dad would have gone broke long ago if Bennett had been his only legal counsel. He's nearly senile." Craig's cruel mouth turned up at the corners in a halfhearted smile. "I think he married that young blond to pump some life back into his tired old body. Bennett? Never."

The eyes were expressionless. They bothered Peter more than the mouth. Again Peter wondered how Thomas could have sired such a complete idiot. Craig fixed his shrewd eyes on Peter's face and said, "I understand from a phone conversation I overheard that you and he have never surfaced by name, that the two of you managed to put together the whole ridiculous scheme through agents. Is that true? Is it true that the participants don't even know who you are?"

Peter gave no reply. His thoughts may have been unsettled for a moment, but only a moment. Craig had tipped his hand. *What he is saying is that he really knows little about the whole project. He needs names and addresses even to know who is involved. How much can he tell his attorney so that immediate action can be taken to halt the project? He may not know the who, why, what, or where details of this thing. Did he have so little conversation with his father that he knows virtually nothing?*

"What I'm getting at, Dr. Polk," Craig's voice had a more conciliatory tone, "is the fact that this whole thing can be dissolved without anyone knowing that you and, more to the point, Dad had anything to do with it. To me that would be a plus. It certainly is so far as my father's reputation is concerned." Craig went on, "I think it would be acceptable to give each participant an additional five thousand for their inconvenience. They have all already received some sort of advance payment, I assume."

He assumes. Doesn't he know? Does he know anything about the project except the overall funding of three million dollars? Peter knew Thomas had told his son that much when Craig had sat in on their meeting a week ago. Does he know about the account in California Bank and Trust in Beverly Hills? Hasn't he been consulted since that meeting? Peter reminded himself that Thomas was no fool. Had he really shut out this arrogant son?

Peter stared at Craig's profile. Craig had stopped talking and, for a moment, was trying to form the right words for what he wanted to say.

"You know, I have to tell you something about Dad, Dr. Polk. You may be interested in knowing this." Craig stared out at the distant casket shielded by the artificial grass mound. "My dad never gave two hoots in hell about us kids while my sisters and I were growing up—that is, about what we thought, who we ran with, you know. He was always too busy. Mom was our only link with family as far as I'm concerned, and she had a lot of ideas that Dad never agreed with. She hated religion."

"No, I didn't know your mother; she died before I met your father." Peter was hoping by Craig's tone that he was softening in his approach to this whole issue.

"A strange thing happened to Dad," Craig sighed with his eyes still fixed on the casket. "When he started reading the Book of Mormon and decided to go back to church, like his mother always wanted him to do, he went a little bit nuts over the Mormon faith and got chummy with some of the members. I myself have never had any use for them. Some of them are big and powerful here in Phoenix. They act so high and holy."

Why is he telling me all of this? What is he driving at? Peter soon found out. Craig was not softening at all. He was leading up to something.

"Back to the canceled project." Craig stabbed away at the issue. "Perhaps a couple of those participants will start some sort of legal action. My attorney assured me this morning that, under the circumstances, my father's lingering illness may have clouded his judgment on several pet projects he was involved in. I have to agree with my attorney. Just *maybe* Dad wasn't in a sound state of mind when he funded your project with what anyone, especially a judge or jury, would think was a great amount of money. Too much money."

Peter sucked in the artificially cool air, but it did little to clear his mind. He tapped his fingers on his knees, turning his gaze from Craig to the jump seat directly in front of him, though not seeing it at all. He cleared his throat to speak. He began shaking his head before words came out of his mouth.

"Craig, you can't do this. You know as well as I that your father was clear thinking throughout all those months we planned this project. Just last week he *insisted* that the project move forward. He asked you personally, in my presence, to see that it was carried out. Surely you can't deny this."

"I don't deny it," Craig fired back. "If you recall, I didn't agree with my father. I have never agreed with my father on this matter, so I simply listened, but I did not agree." Craig's voice was emphatic on this point.

Peter's round face flushed with anger, "Craig, I can see that you're not listening to reason, so I'll tell you right here and now that if you try to stop this project, after all your father has put into it in time and money, I won't stand for it. Your father's wishes will be carried out as far as I'm concerned. You do realize that the money has already been placed in a trust account. As the trustee, I am authorized to disburse those funds."

Craig threw back his head and gave a sardonic laugh. "Dr. Polk, you people who sit in those stuffy classrooms fail to understand the real world. I have already secured the services of an attorney who specializes in breaking trusts. Surely you must know that there are ways of getting around something like this and that there are professionals available to make it happen."

Peter knew he was on unfamiliar ground when it came to challenging anyone on what was possible in breaking a trust. He also knew that he lacked a ready answer, except to insist that the project move forward.

"I'll fight you on this one, Craig! I'll fight you!" Peter's retort was fierce, but he instantly wished he had kept his cool.

"Come on, Dr. Polk, I don't think my father was in his right mind when he finalized the project. I think he was too ill to make a sound judgment. And I also think my attorney can convince a court of that fact, if we have to."

Peter didn't know law, but he knew enough to see that in an attempt to win, Craig would use his father's illness to prove that the elderly Kline had made faulty judgments. *How could a son accuse his father of being mentally incompetent when he knew in his heart that he wasn't?*

Peter sat in the cool, soft interior of the limousine with a sinking feeling in his stomach. It was the identical feeling he had experienced five days earlier when he heard Thomas had been hospitalized. How quickly things can change.

"Craig, I don't feel that you are being fair with me or your father in this matter. Please be reasonable."

"My father is dead. He's been dead for a long time as far as I'm concerned." Craig clenched his teeth together and slammed the palms of his hands down on his kneecaps. He was about to utter something more but decided against it. He fixed Peter with one more penetrating look, and then he reached for the door handle, stepped out into the searing heat, and walked back to his family.

Peter sat motionless, his mind on a steeplechase. His eyes tracked Craig's every move as he walked back to the grave and spoke with his wife and then with family members, young and old, who gathered around to talk.

The limousine driver opened the rear door and politely asked Peter if he was ready to leave.

"No . . . no, I would like to wait a few minutes more. But you may want to get inside. It's cooler in here."

Smiling his thanks, the driver closed the rear door, opened the door on the driver's side, and slid inside the car. He said nothing. Peter surveyed the scene a moment longer, and then he noticed William Bennett emerging from under the canopy. The Bennetts were leaving. Peter had kept his eye on Craig and was sure that the Bennetts had not spoken with Craig before walking across the grass to their car.

"Driver," Peter said in a louder than usual voice, "ah, what is your name?"

"Tony, sir."

"Tony, good. That's right, Tony. Do you see that silver Mercedes sedan over there?"

"You mean the one that the lady wearing the big white hat is just getting in?"

"That's right." Peter leaned back in the seat. "Would you mind following that car out of the cemetery? I need to talk to the driver, but I don't want to do it here. When we reach a stoplight, if possible, would you please pull up alongside their car so I can roll the window down and signal the driver?"

"No problem, sir."

Chapter Two
Money Problems

Saturday Afternoon

Stephen could see the white Mormon temple a block from where he parked his car in front of the Mormon bookstore. From the clubhouse in Pleasant Hill he had called information for the number, and with another quick call to the bookstore for directions, he was on his way. The girl in the bookstore had informed him that the easiest way to find their store was to go within a block of the Mormon temple in Oakland. Though he had never visited the temple, he had seen it for years high in the hills of Oakland, overlooking San Francisco Bay.

The bookstore was well stocked. One entire section displayed children's religious books and games. A long row of colorful books was classified *Fiction* by a small printed sign. Across the aisle there were tapes, kits, instructional aids, and other assorted materials. Along the wall shelf that led to the checkout counter was an array of what Stephen Thorn was certain were the doctrinal books. In front of this doctrinal section stood the only two other customers in the store.

Stephen stopped in front of the counter and spoke with the cheerful young lady who offered to help him.

"I'm looking for a copy of the Book of Mormon. Do you have one for sale?"

"Yes, we do. We have them in different sizes and bindings. What price range did you have in mind?"

"Oh, I want your least expensive copy, if you don't mind."

The sales girl stepped around the counter to the display shelf and picked up a navy blue-covered, hardbound book. On the cover, stamped in gold lettering, were the words, THE BOOK OF MORMON—Another Testament of Jesus Christ.

"Will this do? It's two-fifty."

"Two dollars and fifty cents?" Stephen asked, incredulous at the inexpensive price.

"Anything else?"

Stephen reached in his wallet and took out a five-dollar bill as the girl rang up the transaction.

"I would like to ask you one other thing, if you don't mind. Are you at all familiar with this book?"

"Yes, yes of course. What would you like to know? Maybe I can help you. Or maybe you would like to talk to Harold. He's kind of our resident scholar when it comes to Book of Mormon questions."

Harold turned out to be a thin-haired man somewhere between thirty and forty who was seated behind a desk beyond the book stacks. Stephen hadn't noticed him in an obscured corner of the shop. When Stephen asked his question, he didn't realize he was opening a floodgate.

"Thank you for taking a minute. Are you a Mormon?"

"Yes, I am. What can I do for you?"

"I would like to know if the Book of Mormon takes the place of the New Testament as scripture for the Mormons?"

"Not at all. It is a translation of sacred records about a people who lived in this hemisphere long before Columbus. Let me tell you something about this—"

"I'm sorry, I really don't have much time," Stephen interrupted, realizing that the man was ready to go into a lengthy discussion of the Book of Mormon. "I just needed to pick up this copy. . . . Ah, thank you." Stephen started to walk away and then returned to Harold's desk.

"Tell me in one word," Stephen asked, wanting the man to be brief, "do you people consider this book to be scripture for you?"

"Yes, we do."

"Thank you." Stephen had his answer, though it didn't clarify much. But for some reason he didn't want to know any more at this time. Not yet, not before he had a chance to thumb though the book. Stephen thanked the man and walked rapidly back to the front entrance and disappeared into the parking lot.

* * *

Stephen Thorn was three inches shorter than his father-in-law. He had to look up to meet the eyes of the Reverend Robert Moore as the two walked along the sidewalk of the older part of Lafayette, twelve miles east of San Francisco Bay. The homes were older, statelier than those that snaked about the hills of the town, but none were run-down. It was a middle-class bedroom community for busy commuters to San Francisco, and it looked it. Stephen and Anney had owned their home for ten years.

"I appreciate you taking a little stroll with me, Stephen," Moore said when they had gone half a block from the Thorn's modest two-story house.

Both men fit the late Saturday afternoon neighborhood scene. They were both wearing casual clothes—Stephen wore Levis, a T-shirt, and Reeboks with white socks, while Bob, more conservative in his dress, wore a blue-striped shirt, no tie, dress slacks, and shiny leather Torrines.

The father-in-law held his graying head high and walked with purpose. How many times did people, mostly older women, ask how it felt to sit in the presence of so great a man as Dr. Robert Moore? And Stephen would always respond, "Great, simply great."

Stephen had almost outgrown his boyish looks, though it had taken him forty-three years. His light brown hair had receded slightly since he had first met Anney during his senior year at Biola College. His face had a more mature appearance, and Anney liked it better. Stephen's body would always be slim, almost too thin, though of late he had noticed a slight spreading in the waist. "Not to worry," he had told Anney that very morning. He would continue to maintain a daily routine of exercise and jogging, and, he had added, they had better make time for him to keep in shape down there in San Diego.

All in all, for the last twenty years, Stephen's life had been smooth, almost tranquil. He had his job with his father-in-law, a good job for the most part, one that had given him public relations experience. Only in the past few months had he considered other employment.

"I wish I knew more about this so-called research project you're asking me to attend," Stephen asked.

"Hey, where's the ol' fire in my son? Cheer up." Moore took Stephen by the upper arm in a familiar grip, as he had done a thousand times before, and said, "I want to tell you once again what it means to me that you have accepted this mysterious assignment."

"Also," Moore continued, "I don't know if I already mentioned this to you, but I had my attorney check out the administrators of the funding. Two reputable firms, accounting and legal, are handling the agreement and the funding. My attorney tells me that those two firms would never get involved in some scam. They do their homework before they accept a client."

"I'm glad you did that because it occurred to me that it could be some promotional scheme where they use your name to sell who knows what to a religious audience," Stephen answered, reassured.

"No, that wouldn't be feasible. They would never have accepted you as my replacement if they were trying to promote something. They're paying too much money for me to believe that."

"Speaking of money, I appreciate you letting Anney and me keep twenty thousand of the hundred they're paying. We can use it—except, I think you can use it more." There was a slight query in his voice.

Stephen had been puzzled by how quickly the television ministry had plunged into financial straits. It seemed to him that six months earlier they had been mining a vein of gold. Stephen had launched a drive for funds wherein the listeners bought vials of water from the River Jordan, where Jesus had been baptized. That campaign alone brought in two hundred fifty thousand dollars. But suddenly, the funds had dried up. *I wish I could talk things over with Dad to my satisfaction. He keeps back so much.* He had discussed the financial situation with his father-in-law but not to his satisfaction.

"I met with my private lenders after leaving the club this morning," Moore went on. "They agreed to let us use the money you'll receive at the end of the project on a sort of accounts-receivable status to help secure a new loan. It was for three hundred and fifty thousand, which brings up the matter of mortgaging our homes." The venerable minister hesitated and then cleared his throat before continuing. "They want us to throw in the equity in our houses—my condo, your house. These people are serious lenders. You know, we've done this before. I have no doubt that things will work out to our benefit. Plus, I'm meeting with Clifford at the bank to get him to roll over the loan we have with them."

It was true, Stephen thought, *Anney and I have helped the ministry twice before by getting a second on our house. Everything has worked out fine in the past. Then why do I feel uneasy now?*

"Sure, sure. If we have to, let's do it."

"They'll take a direct lien on your place. I'll send you the papers when they're ready next week. You can sign them, get a notary down there to sign, and return them by express mail."

"Yeah, well, that ought to keep us going for a few months. But if I go to San Diego and participate in this project, we'll fall behind on our fall fund-raising kickoff."

"We may have that solved. I'm not going to the lectures in Australia this August. I'm staying here and putting my best foot forward to get out of this financial mess. So I want you to go down to that estate—and let me tell you, it must be *something,* judging by the photos we've got of it—and you enjoy yourself."

"Yeah, sure."

Stephen was about to tell his father-in-law that he had bought a Book of Mormon at a bookstore, but then he changed his mind.

Chapter Three
The Lawyer

Saturday Afternoon

"**I** couldn't believe someone was honking at me on the freeway," laughed Bill Bennett, unlocking the door to his plush office. "You must have a serious problem to be so agitated. Ever use a car phone?" he teased.

"So it looks like we've got to act fast if we're going to out-fox ol' Craig," Bennett surmised after listening to Peter describe the scene in the limousine. "I know you're worried about Craig and his lawyers invalidating the trust—and let me tell you it has been done—but it isn't as easy as Craig makes it sound. First of all, I don't think he knows that most of the funds are held by an accounting firm or that part of the money has been transferred to the California Bank and Trust in Beverly Hills." As Bennett talked, he pulled two cans of Diet Coke from an under-the-counter refrigerator and set them on the desk.

"Give me your summation of this whole situation, Bill. Frankly, I'm worried. I guess I'm not so much concerned about the money right now as I am about the participants in the project. I can just see them arriving Monday in California and Craig coming in with some kind of court order, shouting to all those professors that the project is off, that none of them will get paid. Do you follow me?"

"Yeah," Bennett nodded. He grabbed the back of his chair and straddled the seat, leaning his arms on the rim of the back. He seemed overly casual to Peter, who wanted Bennett's complete attention to this vital matter.

"Don't worry about him showing up on Monday with a court order. That takes time."

"But what if he just shows up without a legal document and scares the tar out of everybody? They could become so spooked about whether they'll receive their money that they may just jump right back on a plane and head home."

Bennett took a long swig of his soda and shook his head. "No, Peter, I don't think Craig knows where the project is being held. Unless Tom talked it over with him sometime before his death—which I doubt—ol' Craig knows next to nothing. Did you write a letter telling Tom about the estate we leased?"

Peter shook his head. "No, I told him everything over the phone. I don't recall writing any letters about any of this. We talked nearly daily by phone, so there was no need for letters."

"Good. But that doesn't mean Tom didn't write something to someone," Bennett said. "Mary would know."

Bennett punched Mary Ellis's home phone number. At length a recorded voice informed him that she was not available and asked that he please leave a message.

"Mary, this is Bill Bennett. If you're there, please call me at my office. I'll be here for the next hour." The two men looked at each other in silence. Peter was the first to speak.

"I think the only reason Craig confronted me this afternoon in the limousine was to scare me into caving in and canceling the project," he reasoned, wanting to make sense of the whole matter.

"You're probably right on that," Bennett mumbled, his mind seeming to race ahead of the conversation. "You realize, don't you, that I am the person who received the three million over the past two years. It was I who instructed Valley National to transfer one million of it to the Beverly Hills bank. They offered the best interest rate. And I might tell you that it is still there, receiving a good rate of return. The other two million was placed in trust with Finley & Southam. That was to fund you and that graduate student—getting your research equipment and lining up your scholars and whoever. As trustees, you and I are authorized to request those funds as we need them. You know how much you've spent for research and to get the computers set up, but three months ago I drew four hundred thousand for the estate rental deposit, the charter jet, and all those hotel reservations.

"Then a good part of the change, a thirty-thousand-dollar upfront deposit for each of the participating scholars, which, by the way, we paid already." Bennett kept rattling off the figures. He had a fair grasp of how the money had been disbursed. "The problem is that you and Tom made some expensive plans, what with bringing in those speakers and renting a lavish estate, not to mention paying for the staff to maintain it, plus all the travel to boot. The money's going fast. We're going to need some of the funds in that California account before this is over."

"Why don't we draw out the rest of the money in the Finley & Southam fund and deposit it in a bank with numbered accounts?" Peter asked.

"Because if Craig ever traced that move, he could charge us with fraud for sure," Bill responded with a snort.

"You don't think Craig knows about the bank in Beverly Hills? What about the bank deposit slips? Did you turn them over to Tom?" Peter's voice held a tone of apprehension.

"That's a good point, and I have them here in the files. I've never given Tom the receipts for anything. He asked me to keep everything here in my office, so I would have a ready reference." Bennett gripped the back of his chair and finished his statement. "I did send him a photocopy of the original deposits in the Valley National Bank, but that money has been moved. Craig will find those deposit slips in a hurry. But that is all he'll find. I have copies of the leases for the estate in North San Diego and the charter jet, and copies of receipts for everything else, including all the reservations at foreign hotels. I don't think he can locate the money in the bank in Beverly Hills." Bennett drank from the can of Diet Coke and set it down hard. "It doesn't matter. I will remind the bank manager at Valley National Monday morning that if anyone inquires about my deposit, he's to tell them nothing." Bennett stood for a moment in deep thought. The scowl on his face tightened his heavy jowls.

"Mary Ellis is our only hitch," he said at last. "As you know, she is a cosigner with me on the checking account in Beverly Hills."

"What are you saying?"

"Hey, if she decides to tell Craig where the funds are and that she's a signer, we're sunk. She sure could tie things up for us. I'll try to dissuade her from telling Craig," Bennett said, wondering if he had that much clout with Mary.

Bennett slid his chair back and stood up. His lined cheeks and chin creased even more as a mile-wide smile spread across his weathered face as he thought of a new angle. "It's pure luck that Tom never put his name to anything. This sure muddies the pond. Do you know that Craig is going to have to prove that the money sitting over in Beverly Hills is actually a trust fund his father created and not my own funds?"

Peter's brows came together in a concerned furrow. "What if he locates the account with Finley & Southam? Can he prove that the money wasn't yours or mine—that it's really his father's funds? And if so, can Craig get his hands on that money and stop payment to the participants in the project?"

Bennett didn't respond immediately to the question. He walked to the opposite side of the office to a book-lined wall containing case studies. "He may be able to do it, but the question is, how soon? What the two of us will have to do is stall everything we can. You need seven uninterrupted weeks, and I need to stonewall every dirty trick his lawyers can think up. This ought to be interesting."

Peter turned toward Bennett and said, "You've reassured me a little bit about the money. But you painted a true picture of Craig. I'm worried that he *will* find out the meeting location and come over and make a scene."

"The only way he would know that would be to ask one of us. All we need to do is stonewall this thing," Bennett repeated.

"Do you think we can get Mary on the phone now?" Peter asked.

Bennett whirled around and picked up the phone. He struck the redial button. It took three rings before Mary answered. She had just arrived home. In five minutes, Bennett explained the problem. Peter watched the attorney's face intently as he finished telling Mary about Craig's meeting in the limousine with Peter.

"Mary, we've got to block Craig from getting his hands on any information about the project, the name of the accounting firm, the location of the money, *anything* that might help him cut off the project." Bennett glanced at Peter and said into the phone, "Mary, is it okay with you if I turn on the speaker phone so Peter can talk to you as well?" Bennett motioned at Peter with his head as he pressed the button so both of them could listen and speak.

"Mary," Peter chimed in, "we appreciate any help you can give us at this time. We want to prevent Craig Kline from canceling the project."

"Yes," came the soft but precise voice. "But Dr. Polk, you must understand that I'm in an awkward position here. Much of the material Bill is asking me to conceal is on my computer." Mary's voice seemed stressed to Peter. "I don't think I have much, but I do know that I have typed letters to a few individuals for Mr. Kline where he mentioned the project. He loved to talk about it, you know. I think I even sent a letter or two to you on this matter."

"Mary, all we're asking you to do is stall somehow," said Peter. "Surely you don't believe for a minute that Tom wanted his son to cancel the project? Do you?"

"No, I don't. But I have to be careful how I involve myself in this whole affair. Keep in mind, I have another twenty-six months with the company before I retire." Mary's voice sounded wary.

Bennett interrupted, "I'm so sorry we have to pull you into this mess, Mary, but you know and I know that Tom would absolutely go through the ceiling if he knew what his son was doing."

Peter continued to speak to Mary. He explained to her how vital it was to him that the project not be stopped. Suddenly Bennett slapped his hands together and interrupted the conversation.

"Mary, can anyone in the office access material stored in your computer?"

"No. I have an access code that I use on all private correspondence. Why do you ask?"

"How would it be if you were to take a week off, starting now, and go somewhere that is difficult to reach . . . say, Mexico or the mountains? Somewhere that can't be reached by phone. We'll pay the expenses." Bill knew she had never married, so getting away would be easy.

"I don't know. I will have to admit that I thought I would stay home a couple of days, you know, just to sort out some things in my mind. I dread going back in Monday without Mr. Kline being there. You know what I mean."

Peter spoke, "Mary, I think I know what Bill is getting at. If you were out for a week, I would feel a little more secure about starting the project Monday, at least the project would get under—"

Bennett cut Peter off in mid-sentence. "If you can call in and tell them what you said to us," Bennett pleaded. "It's just a week, and a week would help us. Can you do that much? A week will also give you a little time to think over what we've asked you to do, which is not to help Craig get information that will indicate where the project is being held. Will you do that?"

There was silence on the other end of the phone.

Bennett shouted into the speaker, "Mary, you owe it to Tom to do us this little favor. We are not asking you to do anything illegal. Just leave town for a week." Bill pronounced his words succinctly, halting after each for emphasis. His voice became soft when he said, "Honey, will you do it?"

Another pause, and then, "Okay, but I want both of you to know that I have decided to take the week off on my own accord," she said testily. "You have not persuaded me to do this. I have a right to mourn the loss of someone so close to me."

Bennett grinned at Peter, whose face mirrored the same elation at Mary's comment. "One other thing," Bennett inserted, trying to restrain his delight that Mary had consented, "would you mind deciding on your own to go someplace where no one can reach you? Don't even tell me where. And if you do, would you please call me next weekend before you go back to work, or at least before you speak to anyone at your job? I need to know what's on your computer. Okay?"

"I'll think about that, William. Good evening."

The phone went dead.

For a moment Peter held back, and then he clapped his hands and grabbed Bennett by the arm in a victory grip. "She'll do it for a week!"

"More to the point, will she hang in there for seven weeks?" Peter wished he knew.

Waving away Bennett's suggestion that his wife pick them up and drive Peter to Sky Harbor Airport, Peter had called a cab. As the cab pulled away, Peter shot his left arm out to look at his watch. It was 6:10 in the evening. He still had to reschedule his flight plan to confuse Craig. He grinned inwardly at his ridiculous stealth tactics. *I should have worked for the CIA.* But the risk of losing the project was worth his efforts. He knew Craig was shrewd. *What if he should find out I'm going to San Diego?*

Peter worked out a new flight plan. The last place he wanted to go was directly back to the estate in North San Diego. He would buy a ticket to Salt Lake City and, at the last minute, take another flight to Los Angeles. Once there, he would rent a car, drive to the estate, then have his assistant take it back to Orange County and return on Amtrak. *It will work*, Peter reasoned in his mind. *But it will be late tonight when I arrive or maybe even tomorrow.*

Chapter Four
The Benefactor

Saturday Evening

Thomas, *Thomas, my dear friend, why did you have to die on me? I need you.* Peter sighed as he leaned back in the cab for the twenty-minute drive to the airport. He tried to reconstruct in his mind what had been said ten days ago when he and Thomas reviewed their plans and made final arrangements to commence the project.

* * *

Peter remembered the sweeping drama of the Remington painting that covered twelve square feet of wall space in Thomas Kline's executive office. Whenever he had been in Thomas's office, the canvas always struck him as a magnificent piece of art. The painting depicted a cowboy who appeared to be losing his grip on his saddle and was sliding from his startled horse as a dark grizzly, with mouth gaping open and both paws set to swat and destroy any intruder, seemed to have appeared from out of nowhere onto the winding trail along a stretch of a craggy mountain cliff.

It was classic Remington. Only an executive of Thomas Kline's means could have had such a work of art hanging in his office, a room four times the size of any normal office. Except for the Remington and other western art pieces, chrome and glass dominated the room. Most of the furnishings in the glass-walled office were of modern design, from the ivory leather swivel chairs to the curved, high-gloss black desk, swept clean of clutter.

Peter had always known that his longtime friend had a penchant for the ultramodern, and except for the Western art pieces of bronze and canvas, the Remington being the most imposing, much of the rest of the office had the sleek look of a Ferrari. Somehow the ornate, brown-stained frames and the dark, dull finish of the bronze figures—cowboys, Indians, and horses—complemented the chrome and glass. The designer had caught the enigma of Thomas himself, contrasting the two almost opposing art forms into a coordinated whole.

"Tell me, Tom," Peter had once asked, "what does a Remington painting like this one bring these days?"

"Don't exactly know," Thomas had replied. "Perhaps twelve million at the right auction. You know this kind of thing depends on who is bidding. But it's not for sale. I've donated it to the Southwestern Museum of Art for their Remington Room. My son, Craig, doesn't even know I've made that provision in my will. If I hadn't, Craig would find out in a hurry what it would bring at auction. It would be sold three months after I'm gone. You could place money on that little bit of information," he chuckled.

Thomas Kline might have been handsome once, but his features had looked painfully gaunt that day. In his prime he had been tall and wiry, but at the last his frame was bent, his body thin, his skin and bones partially shielded by his carefully tailored clothes.

Kline and Polk had known one another for over ten years. Peter had given a lecture in Phoenix on contemporary findings in the Book of Mormon, at a "Know Your Religion" series, when Thomas, who had been in the audience, remained behind and asked rather pointed questions about how the scholarly world outside the Church viewed the Book of Mormon. That brief conversation developed into an extended relationship of phone calls and occasional buzz sessions at Brigham Young University as well as in Thomas's executive office in Phoenix. Over the years, Peter had come to admire Thomas as a keen student of the Book of Mormon, one not content with simple explanations.

In time Thomas had confided in Peter that he wished he had

been active in the Mormon Church when he was raising his children. He wished his Elizabeth, who had died before he met Peter, had been a member of the Church. "Yes, Peter," he had said, "there is nothing so sad as an old man's lament for what he wished he had done differently."

"I don't know why," he had continued, "but one night my old bishop came to see me. He was a wonderful man, Bishop Jared Clayton. He died over ten years ago. Anyway, the evening he came to see me, he said he wanted me to buy twenty copies of the Book of Mormon so the ward could place them in some of the better motels in Phoenix. I straight out asked him how much it would cost; he said about fifty dollars. I gave him two hundred. He left me one of the giveaway copies of the Book of Mormon, and I read it. Not right at first, but one day I dusted it off and started to read. Well, I fell in love with the book instantly. That brought me back into the Church."

Peter painfully recalled the excitement in his friend's voice as their plans had unfolded: "Now here we are, Peter, with our little experiment ready to begin. Are we ready?"

Ready? Absolutely, thought Peter grimly. *Thomas deserves it—the Book of Mormon deserves to be opened to the best minds of the world! But ready for what? Ready for a fight with Craig?* Peter's mind leaped back to the meeting ten days before.

What excitement it had been for Peter to sit with Thomas Kline and finalize their plan involving a handpicked group of eight scholars, all English speaking and of Western culture—scholars who would spend seven isolated weeks in an intensive study of the Book of Mormon.

When they had first launched their plan some two years earlier, Thomas had said, "Peter, you work up all the details on how we can attract participants: the setting, the ground rules, etc. I'll fund the whole thing, including your time."

"Don't worry about paying me," Peter had replied. "This is a wish come true." But Thomas had insisted.

"How much should we offer them," Thomas had asked, "a hundred thousand dollars each?"

"They'll do it for much less," Peter had cautioned.

"Will they, Peter? Don't bet on it. Some may turn it down at that price. Pay them well, and demand great diligence. I would place a thirty thousand dollar up-front payment directly into their checking accounts before they even arrive. Tie them to you, Peter," Thomas had laughed. "That's a good American business tactic."

Thomas had been right—even high-level scholars had been interested when enough money was offered. But as they had expected, humans being what they are, some adjustments had to be made at the last minute.

"Let's go over your revised plans, Peter," Thomas had begun. "Tell me, what were you saying about one of the participants not being able to show up?"

Polk had moved his chair to the side of Tom's desk and then laid out a computer sheet with names and locations on it. Beside each name had been a red mark. One of the names had been circled with the same red ink.

"It's this fellow, here." Peter had pointed to the name, *Robert L. Moore.* "You know, he's the televangelist in the Bay Area. He called me last weekend to inform me that he could not participate. Then he proceeded to tell me that I should seriously consider using his executive assistant. I found out that he is a man in his forties, who happens to be this Robert Moore's son-in-law. This son-in-law has a master's in contemporary Christian philosophy and a doctorate in mass communications. He doesn't fit our scholar's profile at all."

"What about our backup scholars?"

"That's an interesting question. After all this planning, it seems that neither of the two backup people we had in place can come."

"Didn't we have them on some type of retainer?" Thomas had wanted to know. His voice had gone from kindly to demanding. It was the voice Thomas had employed for years in directing his mining empire. Peter had heard the tone on several occasions, but seldom had Thomas used it with him. Instantly Thomas had heard his tone and softened it. "I mean, what has happened to those fellows that neither of them can make it?"

"Do you recall that we agreed with the backups that if we

had not called them within two weeks of the actual commencement of the project they were free to commit themselves to other pursuits?"

"Umm," Thomas had mused.

"Well, one is already committed. The other is ill."

"And offering a hundred thousand dollars for their services didn't turn their heads?"

"I wouldn't say it didn't, but one of the two is not physically able to attend."

"Why?"

"His condition has recently taken a severe downturn, and he needs regular medical attention."

"What's wrong with him?"

"AIDS."

"You mean we got a man who's dying of AIDS?" Thomas had asked, incredulous. He had quickly waved his hand to indicate that the man wouldn't have suited the project in the first place. "I'm sorry he's dying of AIDS, but what about the second backup?"

"He's been offered a chance to accompany a dig in Central America with the possibility of taking over the project. Our offer pales by comparison. This is his dream of a lifetime."

"We still have our archeologist in place, don't we?"

"Yes, yes we do, but this leaves us with no backup," Peter had concluded.

"What do you want to do?"

Peter had known since the inception of the project that Thomas Kline was an executive who could make decisions quickly and bend them to conform to his desired ends, but most of the details of the project had been Peter's to complete. Now Peter had made his proposal. "I have checked out this son-in-law of the televangelist, Moore. He has a real handle on public communication, his work with his father-in-law is primarily publicity, but he is also likable, an even-tempered fellow with no great skills in research. But I've been thinking, what harm would there be in having a sort of nonscholar in the group?

"I know we haven't planned it this way, but it seems to me that the project has an overabundance of people who have academe oozing from their brains. What would it do to put a maverick in the group? Perhaps he would forge a certain commoner's view of the entire project." Resting his head on the high-backed leather chair, Peter had flashed his downward smile, his teeth protruding slightly, and said, "I think we should take him."

"What you're saying is we have no logical option."

"Not at all!" Peter had shot back. "I'm saying this man will offer a balance to an otherwise stilted group."

Thomas had rubbed his hands together as if he were in front of a fire on a cold winter morning, instead of twenty stories up in an air-conditioned room that kept out the 105-degree heat that would otherwise penetrate the office. "Okay, I think you're right about this young man—what did you say his name is?"

"I don't think I mentioned it. . . . I wrote it in right here," Peter had pushed his finger across the computer sheet to a penned-in name. "It's Stephen Thorn."

"But you haven't asked him. How do you know he's available and will accept the offer?"

"I think he will do it because his father-in-law has already assured me that he will see that he is available for the seven-week project."

"What next?" Thomas had liked to keep things moving. Peter had been about to speak when Thomas had continued, "By the way, my attorney called me. He suggested we certify that the funds I am setting aside for this project—the three million—are from a private party and not from any political, religious, business, or those types of organizations. If we don't, the group will think it's coming from the Mormon Church or Brigham Young University. The last thing I want is a lawsuit from a member of our group trying to extract money from the Church or trying to accuse the Church of sponsoring something it has nothing to do with."

Thomas had stopped rubbing his hands nervously. "Also, I think you need to know that my son has been giving me a hard time about this project. You know, he thinks this whole scheme is some kind of wild fantasy that old men have when they creep into senility."

Peter Polk had looked over at Thomas and reassured his friend and benefactor that the son was merely looking after the interests of his father. "Tom, he just doesn't understand what we're trying to achieve. Don't be too hard on the boy."

"Boy? He's forty-nine years old and just as cocky as the day he left Stanford. Well, anyway, I can just see him now. If a lawsuit were to come from this project of ours, he would certainly have the last word." Thomas had cleared his throat one more time. "Be sure that these scholars remain good, friendly people who enjoy a good game of chess and have none of the hostilities that seem to be prevalent today. You know, a gentle group of men."

"And women," Peter had reminded him.

Thomas Kline had abruptly said, "Oh, that's right. We still have at least two women in the group, don't we? You know the rules are changing these days, and we need to include the ladies. That is a fair ratio because, percentage-wise, there are still few women involved in scholarship on ancient studies or anything to do with antiquity in the Near East. Of course, not all the scholars we selected have a background in that field.

"The ladies are still on," Peter had assured him.

A knock on the solid white door leading into Thomas's office had interrupted their quiet discussion.

"Come! Come!" Thomas had shouted, glancing up from the paper laid out on his desk. The shout sounded like a repeating rifle. "That must be Craig."

Craig had opened the office door wide and let himself in. He was in shirt-sleeves, loose tie at the full neck, pants well pressed and cinched around an expanded middle. Dr. Polk hadn't seen Craig in over five years. He had put on some weight. Not that Peter hadn't. The top of Craig's head sported strands of graying hair, and his face was alert and intent.

"Come in, Craig. You've met Dr. Polk."

Craig's lips had stretched a smile across his white, straight teeth. Peter had thought how, as a boy, Craig Kline must have had the services of a good orthodontist. "It's good to see you again, Craig," Peter Polk had raised his bulk from the comfortable chair he had occupied and extended his hand.

"Both of you have a seat," Thomas had said. Peter had remembered that Thomas was a man who liked getting to the nub of the conversation and wasted little time on chitchat.

"Craig, as you know, I invited Dr. Polk to come down to Phoenix to bring me up to date on my . . . what did you call it, son, an old man's fantasy?"

Peter had turned his eyes to watch Craig's reaction to his father's little jab. *Not a flinch*, Peter had thought. *This fellow is a poker player.*

"Anyway, son, I have invited you in to hear, in the briefest terms, a review of what Dr. Polk will be doing to implement the project." Thomas had turned to Dr. Polk and nodded the cue. "Go ahead and tell him, Dr. Polk. I'll listen. You'll have to excuse me while I stand up. The doctor isn't sure what it is, but I get this numbness in my diaphragm. If I stand up for a while, it goes away."

Thomas had stood and walked slowly to the ledge of the window and leaned back against the double-paned glass, putting both hands on the ledge behind him. "Forgive me. I'm just an old man who likes to complain."

Peter had known even then it wasn't true. In the years he had known Thomas, he could not recall having heard a complaint leave his lips.

"I'll try not to belabor this explanation," Peter had said, casually placing one hand over the notes on Thomas's desk. "I understand that your father has told you something about the project."

"Yes, he has," the son had said in a crisp reply. "Please go on. I'm listening."

Are you? Dr. Polk had wondered. "Your father and I are of the opinion that the Book of Mormon has never been challenged by any heavyweight scholars. That is, scholars from major universities, professors in ancient studies, you know, Old and New Testament, Dead Sea Scrolls, and so forth. Such scholars have never seriously taken up the Book of Mormon as a work of antiquity for several reasons. Perhaps the most glaring is the issue of an angel delivering the record to Joseph Smith." Peter had paused. He knew Craig knew something about the Book of Mormon because for a decade his father had been trying to get him to read it. It was evident in Craig's demeanor that he was opposed to this project.

"We hope to encourage a group of recognized scholars to

take a good look at the contents of the Book of Mormon. This they will do in a cloistered setting where they can discuss its merits and failings over a period of seven weeks." Peter had looked at Thomas to see that his old friend had agreed so far with his explanation of the project.

"Go on, Peter," Thomas had said, nodding his head.

"The plan is," Peter had continued, "that I will act as the coordinator of the group, letting these eight scholars select a leader from among themselves. I will stipulate that they must read the Book of Mormon from cover to cover at least once in the first week, then assign them to specific areas of research and discussion. We will provide them with a non-Mormon graduate student, who will assist with the computers, and a charter jet to fly them to key Book of Mormon locations, such as Central America, Jerusalem, wherever, to check out their findings—but within the time constraints of the seven-week course. We think that if they do all this in a seminar setting, they will come away with a better understanding and a new respect for the Book of Mormon."

Finished, Peter had let his excitement abate. He had then interjected, "Oh, and at the end of the project, those several scholars will each write a well-documented, thirty-page report that we will have the rights to publish in scholarly journals. We think if we do all this, we will perhaps get some serious scholarship going at a few universities because the participants will see the merit of such a study. What do you think, Craig?" Peter had asked with a sincere smile.

"What do I think?" A smile had crossed Craig's broad face as well, though cynical and devoid of joy. "I think you have already made up your minds; the project is on, and from what I hear from Dad's banker, you two are already deeply committed to this little venture of yours. Isn't that right, Dad?"

"You might say so," Thomas had replied in a matter-of-fact tone.

"What do you want me to say?" The son had shrugged his shoulders. "Whatever I think doesn't really matter, does it?"

"That is not true. I really want your frank reaction." Peter's eyes had scrutinized the younger Kline.

"Well frankly, Dr. Polk," Craig had said, looking over at his father, "I . . . uh . . . I'd like to hit this lightly, because I know it's a pet thing with you and Dad." He had dragged out the word pet. The inference hadn't been lost on Peter. "My main concern, I suppose, is the outlay of money for this type of *experiment.* I have no qualms with leaving money to BYU. I would prefer that Dad establish a chair in their geology department, and I could respect his gift to the College of Religion if he were to do that, but this wild scheme has no merit whatsoever. Who cares if a handful of teachers find out there is more to the Book of Mormon than most can readily see? It is still the Book of Mormon." There had been a decided tone of contempt in Craig's voice. He had remained standing, as though sitting as requested would have made him party to the project.

"Well, Dad, I imagine you're committing a sizeable outlay of cash to play with the minds of a few scholars. It is not prudent." The son had paused to swallow hard. He seemed to be trying to control his anger.

"Fine, son," Thomas had said from his standing position at the window, "I appreciate your response. But just let me remind you of one thing: not all projects or investments have to have some grand scheme that will yield cash."

"Dad, I didn't come in here to argue with you. You asked me if I would like to come and listen to your plans for this project of yours. I have heard parts of it before. You are determined to carry it out. So what do you care what I think?"

Peter remembered that a faint hurt had crept into the father's eyes. Perhaps Thomas had felt anguish at his son's distance. It had been the look of a man misunderstood and incapable of explaining his full intent to a son he wanted to love, but the son would not allow it.

"Do you remember, Craig, when you were in college and you went to the art auction with me; what was that, thirty years ago? Remember what I bid on? And you thought I was insane to pay so much for that piece of art."

"Yes, Dad, I do." Craig had sighed, easing into the proffered chair as he glanced at the huge painting. "It was the Remington painting."

"Do you recall what I paid for it? Wasn't it a hundred and sixty-two thousand?"

"Dad, I don't want to get into an argument." Craig had not tried to keep the edge out of his voice as he responded to his father's question. "Yes, I know what you're leading up to. The thing is worth over ten million now. And for the life of me, I don't know why you have it hanging here when it needs to be in a more secure place . . . like a vault."

"I enjoy it, that's why," Thomas had shot back. "Anyway, if I want to try an experiment and it costs me three million to carry it out, then I figure I have made enough off of some of my *foolish* investments to play with an idea. If we can get one scholar convinced that the Book of Mormon has merit as a profound piece of religious litera—"

"Three million dollars!" Craig's body had shot out of his chair. "You can't be serious. That's plain foolhardy. Nobody in his right mind would spend that kind of money to research a hoax."

"Actually, Craig, the full amount in trust for Book of Mormon exploration is eighteen million dollars. Three million is for the first project. Other projects will follow." Kline's voice matched the powerful confidence in his demeanor.

Seeing his father's face, Craig had sat back down. He had sighed with resignation, "Like I said, Dad, your mind is made up, so why ask me?"

"Because I'm dying, and you're going to have to carry out my wishes!"

Peter closed his eyes, engulfed in sorrow. He remembered his disbelief as he had whirled around to look his old friend squarely in the face. *Did he say dying?*

The son had looked genuinely stunned, too. Thomas had let go of the window ledge and dropped to his chair.

"Dad, you don't really mean that?"

"I do. The doctor hasn't given me the results, but I know what is happening in my body. They'll find cancer. I have the same pain my mother had years ago when she died of cancer. I'm not afraid, though." Thomas had spoken in a near whisper. "Son, I'm sorry to blurt it out, but you surely know your father by now. I don't mince words. We've got a lot to go over, but I want to tell you right here, in front of Dr. Polk, that this project is on, and I want to see it completed. Don't disappoint an old man. Just humor me." Thomas had hesitated, sighed, and finally went on. "I guess I just want your blessing."

Anger? Hurt? Greed? What emotions had the hard look on Craig's face revealed? "Dad, I don't give blessings," he had retorted. "I think your bishop does."

* * *

Peter saw the offramp to Sky Harbor coming up. "What airline did you say?" the driver shouted over his shoulder.

"Southwest," Peter answered, gathering his belongings. He let the people mover at Sky Harbor send him along to the satellite gate where he would catch his flight to Los Angeles.

What am I going to do? What if he pulls the funds? How can I lead these people on when I know that there may not be any final payment for their seven weeks of intense work? What was that little tune that Mom used to sing, "Wishing Can Make It So?"

Wishing may not make it so, and if it doesn't, then what? First off, about half of the group will sue me, and the other half will hate me. I will not let this happen! I refuse to give in to this wicked man's plot to undermine our project. Wishing can *make it so.*

Peter bought a ticket to Salt Lake under his real name and a second ticket to Los Angeles using his first initials and his wife's maiden name. He shook his head, hardly believing what he had done. *Am I paranoid about Craig and his power to shut us down? This whole clandestine thing is not me.* Nevertheless, Peter boarded the flight to Los Angeles as P.J. Hanks.

Chapter Five
The Substitute Scholar

Week One—Monday Afternoon

Stephen and Anney rushed down the corridor together, stopping ten feet short of the metal detector checkpoint.

"Stephen, I miss you when you're gone just one night," Anney complained with her full lips turned down. "How am I going to stand seven weeks?" Her radiant blue eyes were alive and focused on the face she loved most. Anney was nearly as tall as Stephen. She touched his cheek softly with the palm of her hand.

Stephen looked at her a moment and then took hold of the hand on his cheek and pulled it to his lips. "I love you, Anney."

"I love you too. Call me every day, okay?"

"Honey, you know what the letter said," Stephen replied. "Friday afternoons from four to six o'clock and Sunday evenings from four to seven—except for emergencies. That's it. I hope they have more than one line into that place. I'd hate to get cut out of a call. Maybe they'll give me time off for good behavior," he quipped.

"Poor Stephen! I know you don't want to go. You're such a great support to Daddy. What would he do without you?" Anney hugged Stephen tight, oblivious of the crowd brushing past. She pulled back abruptly. "More to the point, how am I going to handle Todd without you? Was seventeen as painful for you?"

"Seventeen is no man's land for a kid, Anney. He just needs a little space. Don't be on him for every little thing. He's going to turn out all right. This is a tough time to be a teenager. You and Brenda do sort of gang up on him, as he says."

Anney's mouth tightened as she listened. "Well, this is not the time to discuss our differences over how to raise a boy. Be good, Stephen. I love you!"

Stephen gave his wife a quick hug and a smile, tossed his carry-on bag and briefcase onto the conveyor belt, and walked through the metal detector gate.

The late afternoon flight from Oakland to San Diego was scheduled for a stopover in Palm Springs. After buckling up, Stephen surreptitiously retrieved the Book of Mormon from his soft leather briefcase. As he replaced the briefcase on the floor under his seat, he was grateful no one else was seated in his row. He felt uncomfortable reading a book that some people—his father-in-law included—had claimed was false. The book didn't seem too strange. It looked more like the Bible. Still in all, he had not shown Anney nor his father-in-law the book. He had kept it out of sight until this moment.

Five hundred and thirty-one double-column pages. I'll never get through this. But I have to start if I'm to have any kind of chance with these people. He scanned the title page:

THE

BOOK OF MORMON

AN ACCOUNT WRITTEN BY
THE HAND OF MORMON

UPON PLATES

TAKEN FROM THE PLATES OF NEPHI

Stephen read a two-paragraph explanation that followed on the title page, then he noticed the words:

TRANSLATED BY JOSEPH SMITH, JUN.

He also saw that it was published by The Church of Jesus Christ of Latter-day Saints in Salt Lake City, Utah—1989. *Look at that*, he thought. *They've got a picture of Jesus Christ right here in the front of the book. In Dad's lectures on the Mormons, he tells his groups that the Mormons have twisted the real Christ into a resurrected man. Boy, am I ready for this?*

The commercial jet rose into the clear sky above the Bay and banked toward Palm Springs, while Stephen began reading the introduction on the following page: "The Book of Mormon is a volume of holy scripture comparable to the Bible." *This may be the longest book I've ever read.* He decided to skip the pages that looked like testimonials and turned to the beginning chapter, or more accurately, the first book within the Book of Mormon. Reluctant to begin, Stephen dropped the book into his lap. He leaned his head back and let his thoughts drift.

* * *

Stephen had never known his parents. His father had been killed in the Korean War, and his mother died two years later of injuries sustained in a head-on automobile accident on the recently completed Santa Ana Freeway at Downey.

His Uncle Ned, his father's older brother who owned a cattle ranch in Spring Valley, Nevada, had taken Stephen to raise him. Ned had two children: Julie and Hal. Julie was five years Stephen's senior, and Hal three. Hal was full of vim and vigor like so many of the ranchers' sons in the grass country that bordered the white, alkaline desert of western Utah.

Nearly all the ranchers owned some type of aircraft. They used them to fly over to Ely or down to Las Vegas. The Thorns were no different. Stephen and his cousin Hal, who both loved flying the Cessna, never flew near the commercial areas of Ely. They confined their air excitement to the open spaces along the Utah/Nevada border.

Neither boy had a pilot's license. But who really cared out

in the skies above the desert? Their fun spots in the sky were away from all air traffic, except the high-flying commercial jets that left a white vapor trail across Lehman Cave. Sometimes the two boys would take the Cessna up for an hour's spin. Ned didn't mind, just as long as the plane wasn't needed to run to Ely. Ever since they were small boys, Ned had let them take the controls, usually when he wanted to shoot game from the side window of the aircraft.

Though Stephen knew he was lacking in proper flight training, he had mastered the fundamentals, and that was all he cared about. He and Hal could take off and land on the graded airstrip near the barn as professionally as his Uncle Ned. Maneuvering the family Cessna around craggy cliffs where the rams climbed or across the desert to buzz mustangs had become second nature to the boys. Except for Stephen's love of horses, flying was the most enjoyable sport he knew.

One day sixteen-year-old Hal had run out of the house with a plastic freezer bag just as Stephen had finished unsaddling his horse after a Sunday morning ride. He had noticed his cousin stop by the corral where a couple of calves had stood, and he had watched curiously as Hal reached down and, with a flat piece of torn cardboard, scooped up a freshly plopped batch of dung. Stephen stood watching as Hal then filled a second bag with the same "pudding." Each bag contained about a quart of wet dung. Hal tied the bags shut with wire bands and shouted in Stephen's direction.

"Hey, Stephen. Let's hop in the Cessna and go to church."

"To church? What do you mean?"

"I mean let's fly over and visit some of those church people in the desert."

They were soon airborne and heading east, leaving the green grass region as they pointed the plane through Hope Canyon. In ten minutes they were out on the white, alkaline desert of western Utah. The sudden change in updraft sent the Cessna climbing, and then Hal steadied it and banked north by northeast. Off to the east in the distance, Stephen spied the tiny settlement of Creek Corner. It rested at the edge of the easternmost part of the White Mountain Range. There was a small creek that flowed east out of the mountains and left a green, well-watered trail of brush and scrub trees in its path. The inhabitants of the small settlement irrigated their wheat and hay by damming the creek and sending the water into their fields.

Hal lowered the Cessna into a gradual dive, aiming directly at the pitched-roof building in the center of the settlement. The settlement reminded Stephen of a mother hen and her chicks, with the common building surrounded by small cabins. The building served as school and church house for the breakaway colony of polygamists who had built the town.

"Now, listen to me," Hal shouted above the roar of the engine, which was deafening with the side window down. "I'm going to circle the church, then I'll come back in from the north and drop down to about sixty feet off the ground. That's when you take the controls. Then you keep this baby right on course so the wheels clear the two poplar trees in the play yard. That's all you have to worry about. You got it?"

Stephen nodded. "What are you gonna do, Hal?"

"See those kids down there in the church yard? We're gonna give 'em a little surprise." Hal laughed as he made a sweeping turn in the sky and brought the Cessna straight in like a World War II fighter pilot.

"You're not going to try to hit 'em, are you, Hal?"

"Naw, I just want the wet bags to hit the ground and splatter."

Stephen was nervous as he took the controls, though not about flying; he was concerned what would happen if someone reported them.

"Okay . . . ease this baby in." Hal had his arms out of the window, holding both bags at the ready. Stephen stalled the plane as much as possible, while gliding in at an altitude of no more than sixty feet. The youngsters on the ground—girls in long dresses and boys in bibbed overalls—had cupped their hands around their eyes to watch the Cessna sweep down. One of the girls, her long blond hair trailing behind, ran screaming for the church steps. Two older girls and five boys just stood looking up at the Cessna.

Allowing for a little lead, Hal dropped one bag and then the other. They plummeted to the ground. As they hit, the bags burst and splattered dung for twenty feet in all directions. Wet excrement hit eyes, hair, and clothes.

Stephen, not pleased with what Hal had done, banked the plane sharply and looked back. The biggest kid on the ground, whose back was dripping with dung, shook his fist in the air, and Stephen was sure that if he could have heard what that kid was saying, it would not have been sanctioned by the church leaders who were pouring out of the building to see what was happening.

The breakaway polygamists made life miserable for Hal and Stephen. Someone on the ground had the presence of mind to write down the call numbers on the fuselage.

Ned laid down the law: he restricted both boys from going to Ely or from flying for a month. Stephen had sensed that his Uncle Ned had found it amusing but had never let on.

* * *

On Stephen's seventeenth birthday, he sat in an attorney's office, listening to his Uncle Ned's last will and testament. His cousin, Mrs. Julie Thorn Harper, sat red-eyed and weeping. She got everything her parents left, except a simple trust that had been set up by Ned to see Stephen through college.

It had all happened so suddenly. Hal, Ned, and Mary were returning from the University of Nevada in Las Vegas, where Hal had just completed the spring semester of his junior year. No one knew for certain who had been flying the Cessna. It didn't matter.

Stephen had been too young to remember his parents before their deaths. But when the Nevada State Highway Patrol officer informed seventeen-year-old Stephen of the Cessna crash on Wheeler Peak that had taken the lives of his only remaining family except Julie—and she had her own family now—the news was almost more than Stephen could bear.

Often Stephen had wondered if the destruction of his family had anything to do with his enrollment in a Christian college. Was he looking for answers? Was his faith strong enough to see him through?

Stephen's life took on a new dimension when Anney slipped

into his lonely life. He knew she had been serious with a boy at Berkeley. It had been a traumatic involvement that Stephen never pressed her about. Whatever it was, it had brought her to him, and that was all he really cared about. Biola had been her father's recommendation.

The born-again Christian college in the Los Angeles area emphasized the teachings of Christ in the New Testament and persuaded its students and faculty to believe in the power of the Lord to save mankind. Stephen had become acquainted with Bob Moore, Anney's father, when Moore came to the campus as an invited speaker a couple of years in a row.

By the time Stephen graduated from Biola, he and Anney were engaged to be married in the fall. Fortunately, Uncle Ned's trust had another year's funds available. Biola had been less expensive than a major university would have been, so some money still remained. But it evaporated sooner than Stephen expected, leaving his master's program in jeopardy. Anney's father had come to the rescue.

During the second semester, Robert Moore approached his new son-in-law with a sort of grant. Moore had promised Stephen that he would underwrite his graduate program if Stephen would go into public communications and specialize in televangelism programming and fund raising so he could assist him in his ministry. He did. Stephen was grateful, and besides, being married to a popular minister's daughter appealed to Stephen.

Stephen and Anney had both their son and daughter by the time he received his doctor's degree. Since then, things had gone smoothly. He had a position at the ministry with his father-in-law at a reasonable salary, plus he was allowed to supplement his income doing promotional work for other ministries that were not television oriented. Stephen felt secure in his life with Anney.

* * *

Picking up the Book of Mormon, Stephen sighed and resumed reading. For some reason he felt like he was back in college, with the pressures of a graduate assignment weighing on his mind.

From his window seat, Stephen could see the sands of Palm Springs loom up as the jet glided quietly onto the landing strip. He placed his business card in page 13 of the Book of Mormon.

So far, so good. This book is a little awkward reading, but I do understand that this Lehi got his family out of Jerusalem because he was told to. Stephen thought the account so far would make poor copy as drama in a religious television series, but then so would the Bible if you took the straight text. *I can at least pretty much follow what's happening.*

Stephen sat in place and watched new passengers come on board the plane. In thirty minutes, the flight would continue on to San Diego, and a strange new experience that he could not hope to comprehend would begin. He opened the Book of Mormon and began reading once more.

Chapter Six
Ground Rules

Week One—Monday Evening

These are serious scholars. What am I doing in this place? Doesn't anybody know I don't belong here? Stephen Thorn looked across the elegant room from the open doors of the terrace. A faint breeze filtered through the palm trees that lined the walls of the estate. The lighted rectangular pool glowed a soft summer blue at Stephen's back. The entire estate exhibited the trappings of wealth.

Exactly what do I have to do to earn the money they will be paying me? I'm sure I'm not the only one here that is curious about what's expected for such a generous compensation. But I don't have to do any more than the agreement states. I probably lack the skills to do a good job on the research, anyway. Well, at least I was up front with the coordinator when he approved me to take Dad's place. I don't have to fake anything. I warned him that I was no scholar and certainly not in the same league with my father-in-law when it comes to scriptures.

I wonder how the others will respond when they learn this project has to do with the Book of Mormon? The little bit I read on the plane was certainly different from what I thought it would be. What did I think it would be, anyway?

I guess I ought to go in and join the group and find out what gives. Now, just remember what Anney said, "Keep your mouth shut, Thorn; take a low profile. That way they may never find out just how ignorant you really are."

Stephen took two steps across the threshold of the terrace doors and entered the spacious salon. He paused to glance around, not sure where he should sit or, for that matter, stand. He studied the group. Most were still standing. It looked like a small cocktail party with mostly men, though he did notice two women standing together, talking to a couple of men. They were clustered near the unlit, marble fireplace. Stephen guessed that everyone in the room was over forty. Two men who were seated together on a sofa were conversing nonstop. They spoke more with their hands than with their mouths. All the guests in the room had a certain air of confidence.

Again the reality of the whole affair came darting across Stephen's mind. He wondered for the thousandth time how the ministry ever got into such a financial mess that it had to resort to these types of schemes to acquire funds. *Was I asleep? Why haven't I given Dad more careful advice so we could have ridden out these past few months when the response from our listeners has been poor? Dad, I've let you down.*

Reluctantly, Stephen edged further into the enclave before him. The whole room held a distinct academic aura in spite of its opulent furnishings and rich tapestries, which stretched two stories up to a vaulted ceiling. Catching a glimpse of the one man he had met, a likable enough guy named Freddy something, Stephen turned to move in his direction.

"Dr. Thorn, sir." A young man approached as Stephen started across the room. Stephen paused and turned his head abruptly to the side to face the thin, angular man. "Yes?" Stephen asked.

"I just want to tell you, sir, that you'll find your place over there in the semicircle of chairs." A long finger attached to the young man's hand pointed to the center of the room. "Your place is the chair third from the right. We have left a folder on the cushion where you will be seated. It has your name on it. Enjoy the evening, sir."

Nodding to the young man, Stephen moved in the direction of the chairs. He would not interrupt Freddy just yet. After all, he had only met the man an hour or so ago. The word *sir* struck

Stephen as odd. He had not considered himself old enough to be called sir. *I guess maybe I am getting to that age*, he mused wryly.

Stephen bent down, picked up the black folder from the cushion, and sat down. His nose caught the masculine scent of leather from the folder—a pleasing scent that Stephen had enjoyed as a boy in the saddle on his uncle's ranch.

Centered on the front cover of the folder were embossed silver letters: DR. STEPHEN T. THORN. Stephen fingered the letters and then noticed that the folder was sealed. A carefully placed silver foil seal secured the front cover to the back. Small writing on the seal advised, "Please do not open until instructed to do so." He continued to stare down at the folder in his hands and couldn't help wondering if someone was enjoying watching him ponder the mystery of it all. *Keep your mood upbeat, Stephen, old boy.*

Earlier in the bedroom, while Stephen was dressing, his assigned roommate, Freddy, had mentioned several things about the house and rules. "You'll have to admit, Stephen, this house is a splendid shelter to while away a summer. Jolly good food, too. Of course, I'm not exactly pleased that our host favors the old temperance ideals. You know, don't you? No hard liquor allowed on the premises and wine only at meals."

"How do you know that?" Stephen had interjected, putting on his tie. "What about beer?"

"Read the little house rules sheet on your night stand. Beer I don't know. I don't think it's mentioned. By the by, how do you Americans interpret what constitutes strong spirits? That didn't come up. Another rule, which I wholeheartedly agree with, indicates that smoking is to be done outside on the grounds. It may not impact you, but the rules also mention that no participant is allowed to swear or use vulgar language. Pity. That part of the rules may be a bit of a strain for an old salt like me." Freddy had sighed as if he had glimpsed paradise but the zest of the experience had been stymied. "Well, I have to remember one very fundamental fact of life," he had philosophized.

"What is that?" Stephen had wanted to know.

"He who pays the piper calls the tune."

Stephen looked to his left and nodded with a smile at one of the two older men, the one with the round, abnormally puffy nose and a sort of W.C. Fields profile. He was standing to one side of the room, casually engaged in conversation. He caught Stephen's eye and gave him a knowing smile. Stephen was sure he had never met the man. No matter. He would get to know every one of the participants soon enough.

In a moment the mystery will be unraveled, Stephen thought, wondering how this Englishman would react to a study of the Book of Mormon. *It is just a job. I will get through this. I am here, after all, for the good of my family. I must hold that thought—pretty soon I'll believe it.*

The family. Sometimes he wondered how he ever got so involved with his wife's family. He loved them, but there were limits. Why had he allowed his father-in-law and Anney to so dominate his life? *I really should have stuck to my guns on taking another job. Anney was so adamant against leaving her Dad. But I never intended to stay with the ministry this long in the first place.* Stephen sighed. For some time he had felt dissatisfied with his job. For reasons of self-worth, he knew he needed to get out on his own—just take Anney and the two kids, go somewhere else, and get a job. *At forty-three—or am I forty-four?—forty-three, I have to get into what I really want to do in life.*

Stephen had read about midlife crisis. Was he actually experiencing such a thing? He had been offered a position with a large television ministry in Orange County but had declined it just six months ago. Anney had thrown a fit when he first mentioned it. He had made a show of trying to persuade her, but if the truth were known, he surely didn't want to be a toady for another minister, anyway. His had always been an unfulfilling assignment. He was just a step behind his father-in-law and always would be. Bob was too popular for Stephen ever to be considered his peer in the ministry.

And another thing was Anney. For the whole twenty years of their married life, she had been her father's greatest admirer. That was okay, but Stephen felt that he deserved as much of her respect and admiration as her father did. Frankly, it annoyed Stephen at times, and yet he loved the powerful minister of the air almost as much as Anney did.

Stephen knew that he owed his father-in-law a great deal. He had been a surrogate father after Stephen's uncle had died in the plane crash. He had financed Stephen's graduate studies. Stephen could never turn his back on such love and consideration. Was he any different from ten thousand other people who hung on every inspired word Bob Moore shouted from his magnificent pulpit? *Face it*, thought Stephen. *It has been exciting to be so close to a minor celebrity*. Every Sunday Bob tenderly, sometimes forcefully, reached out to the Bay Area and compelled his listeners to be all that they could be for Jesus.

Stephen stirred from his musings and smiled as Freddy lowered his sizable body into the upholstered chair beside him. His roommate was overweight, bald, somewhat red-faced and appeared to be somewhere in his mid-fifties—a professor of nineteenth-century American history from the University of London, a learned man holding a doctorate degree. Stephen had also learned that Dr. Frederick Shaw—Freddy, as he wanted to be called—was not currently married but had one daughter who was grown and on her own. Freddy exuded a decidedly fresh air of happiness at the thought of spending seven weeks surrounded by "the best this old world has to offer," meaning the opulent mansion with all the amenities of the Ritz, except hard spirits, of course.

Stephen had discovered all this about Freddy in the half-hour they had spent together in their spacious room while Stephen unpacked, freshened, and changed. Freddy had settled in earlier in the day. Having arrived that morning from London, he had spent much of the interim sleeping to overcome his jet lag.

As Freddy had explained the house rules, he had also interjected his observations of the mansion. Freddy guessed that it had at least twenty rooms, most with the same quality of expensive appointments that their bedroom displayed. He noted that the landscape paintings hanging on the walls of their bedroom were undoubtedly originals of some value. He speculated that the paintings and antique furnishings were collector's items.

The beds in their room were not merely twin-size sleepers; each was queen size with bold brass headboards with an enormous round ball atop each post. The walls were covered with hand-painted silk that matched the upholstered pieces in the room. Spacious was the word Stephen would use later to describe the rooms of the house to Anney. At least the accommodations for the next seven weeks were beyond anything he had hoped for. Perhaps too opulent. The service, he decided, was also beyond anything he had ever enjoyed.

"Jolly interesting group, wouldn't you say, Stephen, my friend?" the rotund, cheerful Englishman murmured into Stephen's right ear. Watching Freddy push the words from his mouth, Stephen couldn't help thinking how much he resembled the actor Peter Ustinov.

"I don't know, Freddy. You're the only person in the group I've met."

"Really, Stephen, you must get to know these people. After all, we are going to be like fellow freshmen cramming for an exam," Freddy advised, lowering his personalized leather folder onto his considerable lap. He patted the black cover and continued in a confidential voice, "Rather interesting folder, Stephen. Sealed. Why?" Stephen merely shrugged, glancing over to see that Freddy's was identical to his, the only difference being the embossed name.

"I get the impression that someone enjoys a bit of cat-and-mouse intrigue in this house. A true penchant for the mysterious, wouldn't you say?"

Eagerly, Freddy tried to guess who the guests were and what they represented. He whispered again to Stephen that he felt that the whole group was made up of Near Eastern scholars . . . well, not all, but most. He mentioned that he had mingled with the guests earlier in the afternoon and had purposely probed them to discover their fields of expertise. "It's my impression that we are about to embark on some ancient documents that have some meaning in the twentieth century but are definitely connected with the Near East. The only ones that don't compute are you and me. I'm in the nineteenth-century field of America. You, well . . . you are an enigma to the group."

"Why, thank you, Freddy. I appreciate the confidence you

show in me." *Should I tell him that I already know what the project is? Naw, not even to erase that little smirk off his mouth.* Stephen smiled in spite of himself, glad that he had one score for prior knowledge.

"I hate to break it to you, Stephen, my boy, but I have tried to fathom just why you are here and how you relate to this specialized research. Either you have not told me exactly what your talents are, or I have failed to understand the project. Perhaps it is a little of both. Let me just tell you that you are beyond an enigma. You are an aberration at this point in my calculations."

"What do you mean?" laughed Stephen.

"Oh, don't get me wrong, laddy. I meant it in the highest sense of the word. You are what I would call a contemporary scholar. Maybe you will offer a common touch to this lofty exercise. You see, I have to settle this thing in my mind. I'm an avid student of mysteries of all kinds." Freddy, about to make another observation, noticed a man in a dark suit approach the front of the room. Arching unkempt eyebrows, Freddy pursed his expressive lips in expectation.

Stephen's eyes followed Freddy's gaze. He saw an impeccably dressed man, about his own age, with sparse hair and a receding chin, stand quietly before the group. Immediately the voices in the room hushed. The man stood framed by the inert fireplace and silhouetted by a beam of late June sun. Stephen noticed speckled dust particles gliding along the beam of light between his vision and the face of the speaker. It was now 7:00 p.m., and the sun would move its beam of light toward the ceiling in a matter of minutes.

"I'm John Paul Osgood. I welcome you to Vista del Palma and hope you have found the accommodations to your liking." Stephen couldn't help noticing the speaker's inability to focus on anyone's eyes in the group. He seemed to be addressing a separate group in the rear, out of sight. Stephen had the strangest urge to turn around to see if there were other people behind him.

The piercing eyes of the speaker came back from studying the rear wall of the room to glance down at his notes, which were on three-by-five cards. His head bobbed up again as he spoke. "Each of you should have received directly into your bank account, or wherever you indicated we were to have transferred it, thirty thousand American dollars. As indicated in the agreement that each of you will sign this evening, additional money has already been deposited in a trust account with the accounting firm of Finley & Southam with instructions that at the end of the project each of you will receive an additional seventy thousand dollars—that is, of course, if all is in order. This shall represent payment in full for your services. At no time shall the firm or the party we represent be required to pay you any additional funds."

The man moved aside, and a tall, rugged man with gray-streaked hair took his place. He wore a dark suit as well.

"Ladies and gentlemen, I won't take but a minute to explain some of the pertinent information you need to know at this time, during the commencement of research. My name is William Bennett, and I am the senior partner in the law firm of Bennett and Associates. It was my firm that retained the accounting firm of Finley and Southam and their representative, Mr. Osgood, who just addressed you. I sent you a review copy of the agreement that you will be asked to sign at the conclusion of this meeting. I have requested the presence of a notary public, who is with a law firm in downtown San Diego. He will be along shortly."

The speaker pulled his left hand in front of him, revealing a black three-ring binder. He opened it to a white page of notes.

"I represent the confidential interests of the party that has created this rather unique research project, and I will explain only that which I have been instructed to deliver to you this evening.

"I wish to inform you at the outset that you are provided with all of these excellent accommodations at no personal expense to you, your family, or the institutions you are affiliated with. Food, lodging, and transportation, including a chartered jet at Lindbergh Field in San Diego, are to be complimentary. What is more, you will not be asked to repay the thirty thousand dollars, even if you should decide not to complete the research project. My client has been explicit in telling me that, under the conditions of the project, you participating researchers are to incur no out-of-pocket expenses, unless of course you wish to buy something of a personal nature or items for your family or friends." He cleared his throat.

"Speaking of family or friends, we indicated in the letter that you would have one weekend with your family or a guest during the course of the seven weeks. Accommodations have been arranged for you and your guests to stay at the beautiful Hotel Del Coronado three weeks from this Friday. The project will be put on hold Friday evening of that weekend until Sunday afternoon at six o'clock. You must place your request by tomorrow.

"Transportation is available while you are here at the estate. We have a large Dodge van, an Acura Legend sedan, and," Bennett commented as his blue-green eyes twinkled, "if you must, a Mercedes 500 SL—red, I think. You may use the vehicles when they are available. The van has a driver. We would expect you to arrange with the driver in advance so that everyone will have an equal opportunity to travel about. We do caution you on one thing. As we stated in the letter, you must be ready for study, discussion, and whatever else is part of the curriculum at eight each morning, except Sunday, when you may rest until noon. We expect you to have a two-hour lunch and to be ready for continuing research on into the afternoon until five o'clock. We realize that this is a rigorous schedule, but the nature of the research is such that it will require a sort of quasi-military regimen to facilitate the task.

"During at least one week you will be traveling to several countries. Perhaps one weekend you will travel within the United States. Most of you have verified that your passports are in order and visas secured for the countries previously indicated. Dr. Thorn, if you will see me after this meeting, I will make final arrangements to rush your paperwork.

"The chartered Gulf Stream jet will be your means of air travel. Next weekend, for example, you will be away for two days."

The speaker paused, folded the three-ring binder, placed it under his arm, and said, "I'm certain you have a host of questions to ask, but I will not be the person to answer them. I wish you well in your pursuit. I will return in seven weeks to sign off the project."

As an afterthought, the attorney paused and said, "There is one other matter I would like to express to you. You have not yet been told the nature of the project. Let me assure you that I have personally worked with the client who set up this project, and I know for a fact that it is a privately organized and funded research project. I have all the documentation on file in my office, and though I will not share with you my client's name or location, I can tell you that should a dispute arise regarding this matter, I have all the documentation to verify my statement." He moved two fingers in a kind of good-bye and moved to the back of the room.

The third speaker sauntered forward—the man with the W.C. Fields nose. Stephen noticed that he looked to be somewhere between sixty-five and seventy and that his suit was off the rack. The round face showed the ruddiness of the Irish, with tiny blood vessels encircling the nose and creeping out along the high cheekbones. This man had a jolly face. Stephen liked his demeanor— why, he couldn't exactly say. There was just something about the man that appealed to Stephen. He was wholesome.

Chapter Seven
The Scholars

Week One—Monday Evening

"Well, at last we meet, and what a pleasure it is to be here," the man said. "I am Doctor Peter Polk, Professor Emeritus of the College of Religion, Brigham Young University."

So this is Polk, thought Stephen in surprise. *So what did you expect?*

"I have a background in ancient scripture studies, but I have for thirty years, up to my retirement, taught and written about the Book of Mormon. I am your coordinator and will be with you for the full seven weeks of research." Peter said nothing more for a good thirty seconds. The information Peter divulged swept across the group. Whispered responses could be heard.

"I never guessed it would have anything to do with the Mormons," came Freddy's whisper to Stephen. "Maybe this little enterprise is not going to be as much fun as I thought. Although—" Freddy's voice silenced as Peter resumed speaking.

"I am very much aware that some of you have credentials that make mine appear insignificant by comparison. Nevertheless, I have been appointed as coordinator of the project. I will explain the project to you."

Stephen could not help noticing the contrasting manner and approach of this latest speaker. Incredibly, this man, with the round face and happy eyes, seemed to assume that everyone would be overjoyed to do some sort of Mormon study. "Yes, yes," he continued with excitement, "I have spent the past two years preparing for this seven-week course. Though I am certainly not the leading authority on the research at hand, I was nevertheless given full responsibility by our benefactor to arrange for the research that we will soon undertake. It is my task to direct you in your study, which is," the man paused to take a breath, "to determine if the Book of Mormon has sufficient evidence to qualify it as a work of antiquity."

The anticipated announcement caused momentary silence. An aura of tension could be sensed in the very air of the room.

Suddenly, a loud voice from the end of the semicircle startled Stephen and the others. A small, very thin man with a hawk-like nose had his hand up and his mouth open.

"Dr. Polk," roared the outraged voice, "if that is, in fact, a valid title with which to address you, are you saying that you are expecting this august group to delve into the Mormon Bible and try to show evidence of its antiquity?" The hawk's eyes narrowed, and he spat out "Mormon Bible" with disgust.

"Dr. Palmer," Peter Polk said in surprise, trying to soothe the situation, "I am merely asking that each of you do a reasonable study of the Book of Mormon, its origin, translation, and publication to determine whether it has sufficient evidence to be classified as a translation of antiquity."

Palmer shouted back, "Are you asking us to give our stamp of authenticity to the Mormon Bible by doing this kind of research?"

He was on his feet by now. Stephen noticed that he wasn't very tall, but he had a masculine, deep-pitched voice that rang with authority. "Is this group even aware that Joe Smith, its author, claimed to have received the book by the intervention of an angel?" Dr. Palmer turned to the group, and with his right hand outstretched, he asked them directly, "Do you people realize what a sham this whole affair can become? If you consent to delve into this nineteenth-century cult literature and give it some kind of credence by lending your names to such a research project, you will regret it. I for one will have nothing to do with this project."

"Dr. Palmer, if you will let me finish—" Peter tried to interrupt by raising his voice. *I was afraid of this. I should have told them the details of the research before they accepted the offer. Can this thing be coming apart before it's had a chance to begin?* Peter began to perspire.

"Sir, you know me. I've never heard of you. You hid behind this little game, enticing us with your money to come and be part of a scheme to add credibility to the works of your religion." Palmer's face went into a contortion as the words tumbled angrily from his mouth.

Stephen sat transfixed. He couldn't help but agree with this Palmer, but it was a crude way to approach the situation. *I don't want anything to do with this Mormon stuff, either, but do I have a choice?*

In the heat of the banter between Palmer and Polk, Freddy raised his hand to get the floor. "Sir," he said to Peter in a voice that commanded attention because it was more in the manner of a sergeant major in the British army than that of a history professor. Freddy's demeanor and voice were so aristocratic that everyone deferred to his demand to be heard.

"I, for one, fail to see what all this hubbub is about. Dr. Palmer insists that he does not want a sham, nor do any of us in the room." Freddy waited but a second, as if to make his point clear and unrushed. "Dr. Polk here has been kind enough to say that he is merely asking for evidence that the Book of Mormon is antiquity. I personally fail to see how the book can possibly meet the requirements. Nevertheless, it is a book that has generated countless converts to Mormonism. Does it really matter what position we take on this issue? All Dr. Polk is asking us to do is to try the water. Apparently, it is scalding my fellow participant, Dr. Palmer."

Peter came in on the heels of Freddy's intervention. "Please, please, I think perhaps you should wait until I explain what it is that we wish to accomplish. In no way would I or my colleague wish to compromise your beliefs or expertise. This is to be a bona fide study. I really hadn't thought that this project would cause such a negative response by scholars such as you."

"Obviously you didn't think this through very carefully not to have anticipated that some of us would have this kind of reaction," Dr. Palmer shouted back, seeming to ignore both Freddy's needling and Dr. Polk's entreaty. The group stirred, all expressing opinions in hushed tones.

Dr. Polk raised his hand as if he were waving to the group, but the sign meant silence. "May I have your attention? Please, ladies and gentle . . . please." In the ensuing silence, a dog could be heard barking somewhere on the estate.

"Thank you. I wish to continue with your instructions. Of course, all of you may have a number of questions." Stephen noticed the tiny beads of sweat on Dr. Polk's shiny, bald head. The track lights anchored high in the vaulted ceiling illuminated the dome of his head like a dentist's lamp does a patient's tooth.

"If you decide to see the project to its conclusion, please respect the terms that have been explained to you. I will not go over every detail of the research," Dr. Polk said, letting an uneasy smile creep into his round face. "The details will be supplied as they are needed. I will say this: the eight of you will be asked to select a chairman from within the group."

"Yes, Dr. Calk?" Peter asked reluctantly, acknowledging the hand that had sprung up.

Stephen shifted in his chair to get a better view of this Calk, who sat in the third chair to Stephen's right. He looked to be a man perhaps just fifty, tall, thin of face, and with a gray complexion.

"Frankly, sir, I'm concerned with this whole business. I have to say that Dr. Palmer has expressed some of my own feelings."

"Dr. Calk," Polk shot back, appearing a bit agitated with the turn of events, "may I just say that there will be time yet this evening to ask questions, either with the group or in private. Please hold them until after the orientation period of this project we—"

"Like Dr. Palmer, I am in no mood to wait for the right time slot for you to schedule me in to listen to the concerns that I wish to express," Dr. Calk interrupted with brows that seemed to sprout longer and more tangled as he spoke.

"I say, Stephen," Freddy whispered into Stephen's ear, "this little show is heating up a bit. Frankly, when the man said Book of Mormon, I thought it would be deadly dull around here, but it's shaping up quiet nicely, don't you think?"

Stephen started to reply, not sure how to take these sorts of comments from his roommate, but before he could open his mouth to whisper a reply, from Dr. Palmer's end of the row came the hawk's voice.

"I think Dr. . . . Dr. Calk is it?" Palmer asked, not waiting for a reply. "Dr. Calk is expressing the feelings of the whole group. I am deeply troubled by this turn of events." Palmer now sat stiffly, back straight and head erect, allowing his opinions to whirl from his lips with the sting of a swarm of yellow jackets. "I, for one, will not remain in this group for another minute," he said angrily. "I demand that my name be stricken from all correspondence, that all references to me—such as my name on this folder—" he said emphatically as he held up the folder, glanced at his embossed name, and tossed it to the floor, "be destroyed and that a letter from you, Dr. Polk, be sent to me, my dean, and the university president at Northwestern explaining that, upon learning of the subject matter, I immediately protested being brought here to do such devious research as you now propose."

Palmer rose as he continued to speak. "I will have my bank withdraw the thirty thousand dollars from my account and any interest that has been accrued and send it back to the accounting firm that issued it, accompanied by a letter specifically stating that I did not request the funds and they are not mine.

"Also, if I hear of any attachment of my name to this so-called Mormon Bible research, I will instruct my attorney to take appropriate action."

Palmer glowered down the row at the others of the group who regarded him with rapt attention. "Also, I happen to know a couple of you in this group, and I find it hard to understand why you would sit here and become part of this pseudo-research. Do you not know that your very reputations are on the line for even associating with this group? I am appalled at you. Does the money mean that much to you? Surely you are as repulsed as I am at the purpose of this gathering?"

"I beg to differ with you. Yeah, you down on the end, whatever your name is." The voice on Stephen's right sounded a great deal like Rocky Balboa, the bigger-than-life film boxer. The row of heads turned as one. Stephen saw at once that the comparison ended with the voice. Dr. Bernard Stein was a well-settled man in his forties with a jacket that draped about his slumped shoulders like the covers on an unmade bed. He had a classic nose and an intelligent look in his brown eyes.

Peter pointed his finger at Stein and nodded for him to proceed. "Please, Dr. Stein, do you have a word?"

"Well," Stein said, looking at Peter rather than addressing Dr. Palmer, "I came to research whatever subject is at hand. It is an honor to be in this rather illustrious body. If the subject happens to be the Book of Mormon, so be it. Actually, for me, so much the better. Someone once told me that it is not so much a religious work as it is a history of ancient warfare. My field is warfare, so I don't mind looking into what Joe Smith had to say about it."

Dr. Stein was about to sit down when he followed up with one more comment to seal his indignation. "I would appreciate it if the good doctor down on the end would not tell me what I should and should not do. I am an adult. If I decide to stay, what my colleagues at Yale think has absolutely no bearing." He nodded and sat down.

Before Peter could utter a word, Palmer bolted out of the room. Stephen's eyes tracked him to the foyer, where he confronted Osgood and Bennett. His arms were flailing about as he spoke nonstop. Stephen turned back to the front, sure that the proffered van would be on its way back to town immediately.

Chapter Eight
The Project Begins

Week One—Tuesday Morning

In the dimness of the typical morning overcast, which Southern Californians call "the June gloom," the group of scholars began to gather in the dining room. A Latino maid slowly moved around the room, switching on the lights. Several stations had been set up around the impressive dining table, with two spiral-bound books at each place. Since the table was large enough to seat sixteen dinner guests comfortably, the scholars had ample work space.

Stephen glanced at the small imprinted letters on the two books; both had the same title: Book of Mormon. He had already read twenty-six pages of the book on the flight the day before. Taking a breath, he brought his lips together in a straight line, recalling his resolve to get through this experience the best way possible.

For some reason, Stephen had a better outlook this morning. He felt refreshed after his run, topped by a shower and a buffet breakfast in the breakfast room of the kitchen. While waiting for Dr. Polk to enter, he fingered the two books. Soon Peter appeared at the head of the table. He was dressed casually in a long-sleeved sport shirt and trousers belted around his considerable middle. The atmosphere was relaxed; everyone had worn casual clothing. Somehow this made a difference.

"Good morning, everyone. I trust you had a good night's rest." Nods and good mornings were exchanged all around. Stephen felt that everyone was ready to get on with whatever it was they were to do. The black leather folder that Stephen had received the night before was open before him. On the right was a yellow note pad; to the left, the roster of participants, along with their credentials. The degrees and academic fields were impressive to Stephen. He had already scanned the list of names, trying to place names and faces as he studied each person around the table.

"Before I explain in any more detail what will be expected of you this week, I wish to express my sorrow that Dr. Palmer, a highly qualified authority on Egyptian documents and Near Eastern literary finds, has chosen not to remain with us on this project.

"He left rather suddenly last evening, and I for one am sorry he chose not to remain with us for the remainder of the project. His expertise on matters pertaining to Near Eastern documents would have greatly enhanced our study of the Book of Mormon."

Peter was standing as he spoke, the tips of his fingers touching the pad that had been placed on the table to protect it during its new use as a conference table. "I'm sure we are the losers in this sudden departure of Dr. Palmer; I'm also certain I need spend no more time explaining why he left. He made that clear last evening."

Freddy scribbled a quick note on his note pad and silently pushed the pad in front of Stephen. The two were seated at the opposite end of the table from Peter. Stephen glanced down at Freddy's chicken scratches: "Dr. Polk is smooth, very smooth. He makes it sound like Palmer was indispensable, when in reality he was a real pain."

Stephen caught Freddy's eye and gave him a knowing look, wondering if Peter saw the exchange. Peter had just picked up the black, spiral-bound book to his right.

"Now, you have in front of you two books. Each is a copy of the Book of Mormon. The one I'm holding in my hand is to your right—yes, good, that is correct." Peter nodded his head as he responded to the quiet queries as the participants picked up the books. "You now have in your hands a facsimile of the 1830 first edition of the Book of Mormon. There were five thousand copies of the first edition of this book. We have provided you with these special copies that are spiral bound and have wide margins to accommodate easy reading and note taking, should you wish. It is your copy to do with as you like."

Struck by an irresistible impulse, Stephen grabbed his own note pad and wrote, "How about burn it?" He shoved the pad under Freddy's nose. Freddy raised an eyebrow.

Stephen pulled the black, loose-leaf book toward him and began turning the pages. He noticed that the printing on the pages was formatted in a running text from the beginning to the end of the chapter. All chapters had the same running text format. He immediately saw the difference between the one he had been reading and the original version.

"Now," Peter continued, "to your left." He waited for the men and women to pick up the book. "Okay, yes. This is the latest edition of the Book of Mormon. If you will glance at the title page, you'll see that it is a 1989 edition. This, too, is your book. We have provided you with a wide-margin, spiral-bound copy to be used any way you like. It is your copy to keep. And by the way, for your information, we have in the library three copies each of the other editions that have been printed over the last one and three-quarter centuries. They are for your use should you wish to consult other editions and make notes of the changes that have been made since the first printing."

He has to be kidding, thought Stephen. *Who is going to get that involved before the end of seven weeks? If I get through one of these copies, it will be a major achievement for me. Does he really want us to wade through the Book of Mormon? Oh, joy. I can see this is going to be a boring experience. Yep, just as I figured, I'm going to earn every dime of that money before I get out of here.*

"Dr. Polk." The voice came from the center of the table; Judith Anderson was an attractive black professor from Princeton who taught Bible literature and had written a textbook entitled *Biblical Love and Hate*. She seemed out of place, dressed like the island girls in the Bahamas. She wore a sweeping floral outfit that emphasized her heavy makeup.

"Yes, Dr. Anderson?"

Anderson, that's her name. Stephen ran his finger down the list of participants, halting his finger on the name "Anderson,

Judith." *I've got to get every name down today.* In his field of public relations, it was Stephen's habit to know everyone in a small gathering within the first hour of a meeting.

"Are you asking us to read both of these works and do a comparative study in seven short weeks?" Judith Anderson asked. She seemed puzzled at what the assignment would be.

Others around the table also wondered in hushed voices about such a task. Peter held up his hand to stop what he felt would be an avalanche of questions from the group.

"Please." He smiled his characteristic downward grin and moved his head from side to side in gesture of saying wait. "No, no . . . please let me explain. You may read one or the other, or if you like, you may compare parts of each. Let me go on. The only specific instruction I will give you today, and maybe throughout the remainder of the project, is to ask each of you to spend three to four days this week reading the Book of Mormon. You may choose the version you wish to read, but I am sure that you will want to use both for reference. I would suggest you read the latest edition, though the choice is yours."

Does he really think I can read this in four days? Forget three—that isn't even an option. It means a hundred and fifty pages a day. How many pages an hour would that be? Stephen calculated, realizing that the task was even more challenging than he thought. *Maybe I can do it in four.*

Peter continued his explanation, "The reason you must read the Book of Mormon is obvious. In our initial planning, we came to the conclusion that the project would be less valid and, frankly, more confusing if you did not first read the Book of Mormon. We want you to do this prior to any in-depth study of the material and supporting data. Don't even think about delving into supplemental material; it may confuse you. I know you are adults, but on this one issue I must insist. Just follow Grandma's rule: 'Meat and carrots, then dessert.'" *Who is he kidding? I don't see any dessert*, Stephen thought.

Two voices spoke at once. Peter ignored them with a shake of his head. "I'll answer your questions in a moment, but let me finish these instructions. I'm aware also that two of you told me last evening that you had once read the Book of Mormon or at least perused it. Our distinguished Dr. Syman," Peter pointed down at the top of the balding head of a bifocaled man seated nearest him, "mentioned to me this morning that he had read the book twice. Perhaps others of you have as well." Peter shook his head as he continued, "Makes no difference. I would ask that you read it again."

"We have blocked out this week for a full reading of the document at hand, and that, my distinguished associates, is the Book of Mormon. We will give you no more information until you have all read the book on your own. It's imperative that you do this one assignment this week."

Peter's sternness quickly changed to a lighter tone as he said, "I assure you that this will be your only opportunity to lounge around. So I encourage you to find a corner or sit under a tree; go wherever you feel comfortable and are uninterrupted by chatter, music, or other distractions, and read every page. So that you do not get too discouraged with this task, I will tell you what you may anticipate. This coming Monday we will make a quick trip to western New York by charter jet. There you will see the area where the Book of Mormon was partly translated and printed. We will also visit other sites that you *must* see to fully appreciate this reading assignment.

"Before you launch into your reading of the book, I have asked my assistant, Roy Carver, to give you a brief explanation of the origin of the book. Roy comes to us from Harvard. His graduate studies are in Library Science. He is nearly finished with his doctoral work in original American documents and will accept a position with the Huntington Library at San Marino next year. Roy was good enough to spend one year working with me at Brigham Young University in an exhaustive study of documentation on the Book of Mormon. He is not affiliated with any religious denomination, but he is eminently qualified to assist any of you with your research and insight into the book." Peter turned to face the gangling young student and said, "Here is Roy."

Tall, thin, and with a mop of unruly, dark hair, Roy stepped from the rear of the dining room to the head of the table. He appeared to Stephen to be a shy person, not one given to addressing large gatherings. Roy placed his notes in front of him and began his presentation. He seemed to have the information memorized. Stephen noticed that he hardly glanced at his notes.

"Dr. Polk has asked me to present background on the nine-teenth-century origin of the Book of Mormon. I have taken my information from friendly documents, and, therefore, I am giving you, more or less, the official position of The Church of Jesus Christ of Latter-day Saints, the Mormons. When most scholars begin researching a subject, they assume that a document is what it purports to be. This is my position on the Book of Mormon at this time, though I must tell you that numerous studies refute the offi-cial claims of how the book came into existence." Roy turned a page of his notes.

"Joseph Smith and the Book of Mormon are inseparable. By that I mean he claimed to have translated the ancient writings and therefore is the principle figure in the origin of the book. He also supervised the book's printing.

"In 1820, at the age of fourteen, Smith claimed to have seen a vision in a grove of trees near his parents' farm in western New York. He wrote later that he had been visited by God the Father and Jesus Christ, who told him that the Church of Christ had been taken from the earth and that it would soon be restored." Roy looked up from his notes and then continued.

"Three years later, Smith claimed that an angel appeared to him in his bedroom during the night. The angel introduced himself as Moroni and said that he was a messenger sent from God. He gave a number of instructions during his visit, and he told Joseph about a book written on gold plates that gave an account of the ori-gin and history of the ancient inhabitants of this continent."

Freddy glanced at Stephen. Stephen's eyes rolled slightly in disbelief. Bernie lounged back in his chair with his arms folded, a smirk on his face.

Roy continued with his presentation. "This personage, Moroni, also said that the plates were buried in a nearby hill, which he showed Joseph in a vision. The angel warned him not to use the plates for profit. This would seem to be a natural thing for the boy to do with the gold plates since the Smith family was very poor.

"Joseph Smith went to the hidden location but was refused access to the plates. Each year he returned and met with the angel. After four years, Smith was allowed to retrieve the plates—strictly on loan—and an instrument prepared to assist him in translating. He was then given instructions to translate the words engraved on the plates. He was further told to show the plates to no one except by divine permission. The year was 1827. Smith was by this time twenty-two years of age and married.

"Smith carried the plates and the translators to a nearby wagon. Some speculate that the plates may have weighed close to one hundred pounds and that they may have been hardened by alloying gold with copper as is a practice currently. If that was the case, they were not pure gold but perhaps eight-carat gold, the metal hardened enough to preserve the inscriptions engraved on them."

Roy paused. All eyes were fixed on him. Though Stephen had never been curious about the Mormons, he nevertheless thought it was interesting to understand the background of how the book came into existence, or at least how Joseph Smith claimed it did.

Roy held up a sheet of paper and said, "Smith wrote a description of the plates; I'll read it.

The records were engraved on plates which had the appearance of gold; each plate was six inches wide and eight inches long, and not so thick as common tin. They were filled with engravings, in Egyptian characters, and bound together in a volume as the leaves of a book, with the rings running through the whole. The volume was something near six inches in thickness, a part of which was sealed.

"I'd like to pause here to make a comment," Roy said with little inflection to his voice. "A portion of the book was sealed. According to Joseph Smith's account, he was warned not to break the seal. He never translated the sealed part. He said that the sealed portion would one day be revealed to man, though according to the

Mormon church, this has not yet happened. Now, to continue with what I was quoting:

> Also, that there were two stones in silver bows—and these stones, fastened to a breastplate, constituted what is called the Urim and Thummim—deposited with the plates; and the possession and use of these stones constituted "seers" in ancient or former times; and that God had prepared them for the purpose of translating this book.

"Smith maintained that the characters upon the plates were written in reformed Egyptian. The book itself says so. You can study the details of how Smith claimed to translate the plates for yourselves.

"I will say this, however. Smith began immediately to translate. Throughout the course of translating, he used as scribes first one associate and then another. He would read the translation, and the scribe would write it down. His first scribe lost the first 116 pages of the manuscript. As a result, the angel took the plates for a period of time and later returned them with a warning that this sort of thing must not happen again. He told Joseph Smith not to retranslate the pages that had made up the entire first 116 pages of the manuscript. It was forbidden. When Joseph began to translate again, his wife, Emma, helped as scribe for a short period of time. Then in April of 1829, Oliver Cowdery, a traveling school teacher, happened along and became the scribe for the remainder of the translation.

"The book had its grammatical flaws. Some of the spelling was rather creative—not at all unusual for the times. In the same era, Andrew Jackson, soon to become President of the United States, once spelled the same word in the same letter four different ways."

Roy took pride in the fact that he had covered his subject clearly and in a short period of time. He then said, "One other note. Smith insisted that he translated most of the book between April and August of 1829." Roy cleared his throat, then said, "A little personal note. Of the events I have studied about the publication of the book, the claim that Joseph translated the plates in ninety days is almost too much for me to swallow. For those of us who study manuscripts and know how difficult it is to translate literary works, this claim is hard to believe. Putting such a complex document on paper in ninety days stretches credibility. With that, I thank you."

The response to Roy's remarks varied from person to person, from expressions of disbelief to outright belly laughs. But no one questioned his scholarship.

Peter resumed his position at the head of the table and said, "Thank you, Roy, for that excellent presentation on the background of the book. Now, as brief as it may seem, I will end this meeting and ask you to take your copies and begin the assignment. I'll remain here for a few minutes to answer questions pertinent to your immediate assignment. Of course, I'll be on the grounds, as will my young friend Roy, to help you since you are just getting acquainted with the estate and the routine. For relaxation, if you like, you may take advantage of the pool, the tennis courts, even the kitchen if you should wish to cook up something special. I repeat what I said before dismissing you last evening—please make yourselves at home. Go now, and find a pleasant spot for reading. Thank you." Peter swept his hands in front of him as if he were trying to scatter a flock of geese from the dooryard of a farmhouse.

"Well, Stephen, ol' boy, it looks like we have our week well scheduled," Freddy said, shaking his head at the whole project. He and Stephen got up from the table with books and folders in their arms and strolled toward their quarters.

"Do you think you can read this book in a week?" Stephen asked Freddy. "Did you notice that the latest edition is 531 pages in length? And that's without the 'lost' 116 pages," he laughed.

"So?"

"Hey man, we're not talking about a Ludlum novel. This is heavy stuff, major scriptures. I'm not sure I could read the New Testament in a week, and I've studied it."

"Cheer up, old chap. You'll make it. Motivate yourself. If all else fails, think of the money. Do you know what I keep saying to myself?"

"No, what?"

"Freddy, lad, you may have to walk through seven weeks of insufferable horror, but remember that at the end of these seven weeks you can spend an extra month on the beach at the Hotel Del Coronado. I already made reservations the minute I saw the flyer at the airport. It looks like such a nice place to sleep out the remainder of my summer in California."

"You know, I'm beginning to see that you really are a pleasure seeker."

"Did I ever deny it? But honestly, this little foray into the Book of Mormon may redeem me."

The statement kindled Stephen's interest. "Why do you say that?"

"You see—and this is confidential Stephen—while teaching about the Mormon movement in American history at the University of London, I stretched the truth a bit. From time to time—not often, mind you—one or two of my students would ask me if I had read Joseph Smith's Mormon book. I would assure them that I had and then go on to tell them that it is a hodgepodge of Old and New Testament ideas and writings, fashioned for the Mormon sect that followed Smith." Freddy's lips protruded and his large head moved from side to side as he spoke. He paused as they crossed the terrace to the outside entrance to their bedroom. "I never did, of course."

"Never did what?"

"Oh, never read the bloody thing. All I recall doing was thumbing through it. Now I can square myself on that issue. I won't have to fib any more. I detest liars."

"Why are you telling me this?"

"Because, Stephen, you seem to me to be like a father confessor." Freddy's chin went up as he spoke. "I need to bare my soul. You know it is very healthy to confess."

Stephen now shook his head, a little bewildered with his amusing roommate. In some ways, he seemed like a boy of ten.

For his part, Freddy tossed his books on his bed and flopped beside them, putting his hands behind his head while looking up at the ceiling. "By the by, Stephen," he said sleepily, "you may not believe me, but I am motivated to read that book, and I'm going to start as soon as I've had a little mid-morning snooze. And furthermore," Freddy patted the top book, which was the first edition, "just to make up for those occasional little fibs, I'm going to do old Joe Smith a favor: I'm going to read the first edition just like he wrote it. I like my history like my eggs—raw."

Stephen had already propped up two pillows on his bed, across from Freddy's. He kicked off his Reeboks and hoisted up the latest edition of the Book of Mormon. *Okay, here I go again.*

Chapter Nine
Computer Files

Week One—Tuesday Afternoon

She had searched the files in Mary's office: all letters, documents, receipts—in short, everything possible that would yield any information on funds and project location. Lois, Craig's personal secretary, who had been with him for a year, had also reviewed all the materials Thomas Kline's secretary had worked on or received in the past three years.

"Here is the breakdown of anything relating to your father's involvement in the project or anything remotely related to it," Lois indicated to Craig, who sat sulking at his desk. It was late Tuesday, and she had been rummaging Mary's files for thirty-six hours with meager results. "Keep in mind that I cannot access the personal letter files on the computer. Mary has the code to that."

"Did that girl who's supposed to be helping you find out anything about where Mary has been staying this week?" Craig barked.

"I'm sorry, Mr. Kline, Lindsay has checked with countless people who know Mary and has done a run-down on Mary's trips in the last five years: hotels, motels, restaurants, spas, you name it. She has pulled a blank in every case."

"I should have put a private investigator on it early Monday morning, instead of messing around with some amateur. See that it's done as soon as you get back to your desk. You might call Sharp to get a recommendation of a good investigative firm."

"Do you want me to read you the list of correspondence that mentions the project or at least alludes to it? Copies are all here in this folder. I see nothing to indicate where monies were transferred, except that we know Bennett first deposited the three million in Valley National Bank. He transferred the funds, but Valley won't divulge a thing about the transaction."

"How do you know he transferred them?"

"I found this note from Bennett in your father's desk file, telling him that he was transferring the money to California."

"Where is that note?" Craig showed excitement as his eyes darted to the folder she held out. He snatched it from her and rifled through the papers inside until he found the note.

Tom, I forgot to tell you in the meeting, I'm transferring the project funds to the California bank. As soon as it's completed, I'll give you the particulars. W.B.

Craig scowled with anger. *What California bank? I'm sure an investigator can find out.*

Lois remained hesitantly in front of Craig's desk. She flinched as Craig looked up in irritation. "What are you waiting for? Go get an investigator."

"Well, Mr. Kline, this doesn't relate to the project you indicated, but Mr. Bennett called. He didn't want to talk to you, but he asked me to give you a message."

"What message?" Craig snapped.

"He suggested that you might want to read your father's latest will before you and your sisters meet with him Thursday. He said you will find a copy in your father's safe deposit box. He believes that you have a key to it since it is a corporate safe deposit box." Message delivered, Lois quickly retreated to her desk.

Craig's whole body felt a sudden chill. *Bill Bennett thinks he's got me shut out. Well, he'll soon find out who holds the cards.* Craig mentally rearranged his schedule. He had agreed to take Mildred to lunch. Well, she would just have to wait until he read his father's will. "Oh, Lois, I'm going to my bank in an hour to go over my father's things. I may not be back this afternoon."

* * *

"I tell you, Mildred, I'm going after this Dr. Polk, and I'll sack him. Mark my words." Craig inserted the key into the lock of his father's safe deposit box. He had only opened his father's safe deposit box once before, when his father had asked him to retrieve a special broach that had belonged to his mother. It was when his mother died; his father had wanted to pin the broach on his wife's dress as she lay in the casket. Craig remembered the whispered scene after the mourners had viewed his mother's body and before they closed the casket.

"Dad," Craig had whispered in his father's ear, "Mother wouldn't want you to bury her with that broach. It has diamonds in it. Don't bury it with her. That's silly."

Thomas Kline had paused and turned to look into his son's eyes. He had deliberately closed the upper part of the casket without saying a word.

Craig opened the foot-long lid of the safe deposit box and looked at its contents. The first thing he pulled out was the will. He unfolded the pages and began to scan the first sheet; then, folding it over, his eyes raced down the second sheet and then the third.

"What is that you are reading, love?" Mildred asked from her seat across from him. Her pearl necklace alone could have bought ten of his mother's broaches. The well-tailored raw silk trouser suit she wore fit perfectly. Her hair was artfully swept to one side, and her face flawlessly made up——both had been done at her favorite salon that morning. Everything about Mildred looked professional and expensive.

"It's Dad's will. It's dated two weeks ago." Craig read on. He was silent, but there was bitterness in his eyes as they scanned the document impatiently. Suddenly, he stopped reading, looked up, and hit the table with his fist. "He's given away the Remington. He can't do that. He has left it to the Southwestern Museum of Art here in Phoenix. Mildred, do you know what that painting appraised for six months ago? I talked to the appraiser myself—twelve million dollars. Twelve million, and he has given it away," he whispered fiercely. "Dad can't do this. The painting is ours. It's ours, I tell you,

Mildred." Craig's face had turned a sickly gray.

"I'm not sure, but it seems to me your father had a right to will his things to anyone he liked," Mildred answered in a puzzled tone. "Besides, he has left all the stock in his company to you."

"Mildred, don't open your mouth in front of anyone about what my father had a right to do," Craig commanded. "I don't want anyone to hear you say anything. Just keep your mouth shut." Craig had scanned enough of his father's will to realize that he and his sisters had each been bequeathed roughly 2.2 million dollars in stocks and cash, plus equal shares of his father's real estate holdings. He knew that the copper empire his father had built belonged mostly to the stockholders and that his father had not held all that much stock in recent years. Of what he did hold, he had placed the lion's share in trust for Dr. Peter Polk's Book of Mormon projects. He carefully reread the will—fifteen million. Craig sat, bewildered. He knew that his father had set up that original grant of three million for Polk's project. But the will named Polk's group as the major beneficiary—to receive an additional fifteen million dollars.

"What was Dad thinking before he died? He left eighteen million dollars to study the Book of Mormon! It's insane. That's *our* money!"

"Oh well, we will still have a handsome living from the stocks he left you," Mildred soothed.

"Oh, will we?" Craig snarled, his voice heavy with sarcasm. "Has it occurred to you how much we spend a year just on clothing for you? Do you have any comprehension in that head of yours just what it costs a year to maintain our houses, cars, and extras, not to mention travel and entertainment? Try factoring in all your beauty and hair salon bills. Mildred, the money my father left us would not keep us five years at the rate we spend. I've got to invalidate that ridiculous Book of Mormon provision, or we'll soon have nothing." His jaw was as hard as steel.

Finally, Craig replaced the papers and shut the lid on the safe deposit box. He signaled for a bank officer to put it away and then, without speaking to a soul, took hold of Mildred's elbow with a firm grip and steered her to the parking lot. Once inside his BMW, he hit the button that set the cellular phone ringing in his attorney's office.

"Yes, tell him Craig Kline is on the line."

Soon Craig heard the booming voice. "Sharp here." Craig's voice cut off the amenities. "This mess is bigger than I thought. I just returned from reading my father's new will." Craig detailed the specifics, telling his attorney that he was not pleased with what he had read. "I want you to rally your forces and put a stop to the waste of money that is going on somewhere in California. That Mormon project has to stop now!"

"Do you have any suggestions on just how we can stop it?"

"That's what I pay *you* for." Craig swerved around a slower car that had braked in front of him. "What is that idiot trying to do? . . . No, no, I wasn't talking to you, Matt. Some old man stopped right in front of me."

Mildred tapped Craig's shoulder and suggested he let her drive so they would arrive in one piece. Craig waved her away.

"I know one thing. If I can locate that gathering, I intend to go in and cause a real stir. I'll tell them that they will not receive a red cent after attending the conference, or whatever Polk calls it."

"Just hold on, Craig. You don't want to do anything that will backfire on us and end in a lawsuit," the attorney cautioned. "There are ways to do it without hitting it head on. By the way, I have a great little investigative agency in L.A. that has taken up the assignment to locate the conference site. Based on what you overheard, we're pretty certain the conference is being held in Southern California."

"Oh, great! There are only about fifteen million people living in Southern California. It shouldn't be too hard to find them." Craig's mocking tone didn't help matters.

"Relax, Craig. There are ways. I think all we have to do is determine where some of the participants live and get information from their families."

"Good luck. Tell that fine little agency out in L.A. that if they haven't come up with something in a week, we'll fire them and get another group. I figure if we stop that project, we'll salvage roughly two and a half million. It's worth a try to squelch. Then we'll go after the main trust mentioned in the will."

* * *

A single light fixture hung above the kitchen table, illuminating the huddled group. They resembled poker players in a western saloon, but no cards were on the table, merely a couple of copies of the spiral-bound Book of Mormon and stale coffee in six mugs. The "rump" session had gone longer than usual.

There had been three days of near silence on the estate as the researchers moved from poolside to lawn to salon or bedroom. There had been little activity other than reading for most of each day. Stephen thought how like a monastery the house had become. At certain times, however, unexpected conversations erupted as the participants exchanged information or got to know one another.

Breakfast was fast becoming buzz-session time. The participants compared notes on how their reading was progressing and what they thought about what they had read. Some wished there was less warfare in the book; others would have preferred less preaching. However, all wished there were fewer pages to get through. They all had their little gripes, and some had found a few profound statements. All expressed opinions with the interplay of students rushing to complete a joint term assignment.

Lunch was usually more tranquil—not everyone ate at the same hour. Some snacked or ate at poolside, while others ignored eating altogether. Most read intently, knowing they had just four days to complete the assignment.

Dinner was more formal. Peter had insisted that everyone gather for the evening meal. At dinner he sat at the head of the long table, while the participants surrounded it. The first evening he had introduced "Polk's law at dinner," a rule that he hoped all would adhere to throughout the seven-week course, which was, "No discussion of the book."

Peter had told the group that he was interested in expanding his personal awareness of what each participant was doing in his or her life and field of study, and he requested that they suspend shop talk about the project during dinner. That could come earlier or later, he said. "Dinner time ought to be reserved for pleasant conversation, the way I've noticed the French so ably do it." For the most part they had followed his counsel, but that had not prevented the discussions that ensued at odd hours of the day and night. Late night sessions were becoming routine.

"It's a strange book. Can you imagine the mind of Joseph Smith, to weave such a fantasy, to actually sit down and write that many pages? He was either insane or possessed," Martha Grain interjected as she leaned back in her chair, full-breasted, her double chin pressed back to her neck. *She lacks the feminine qualities of Judith Anderson,* Stephen thought. True to his public relations training, Stephen caught himself evaluating their personalities.

"No, no, no," Bernard Stein protested. In his mid-forties, he was closest to Stephen's age. Some in the group had started calling him Bernie. He didn't mind. Stephen was certain he was the most surly person he had ever met. In just three days Bernie had managed to dump on the group his entire philosophy of life and complete disregard for anything sacred. Tonight was no exception.

Stephen was grateful that the house rules prevented swearing or open expressions of vulgarities. Bernie occasionally ignored the rules and blurted out obscenities, yet for the most part he was restrained. Stephen was certain that even for Bernie, the amount of money offered was too great to jeopardize for the pleasure of using a few well-chosen words.

Bernie had protested vociferously that Joseph Smith had not written the Book of Mormon. He concluded that it must have been someone with a good deal more understanding of ancient studies than Smith. "I tell you, before this course is over, every single one of you will be agreeing with me. Joseph Smith didn't write it. Whoever did write it had a wild imagination—poor grasp of English syntax—but a wild imagination."

"I'm sorry," Judith chimed in, giving no ground to Bernie's impressions, "but this is a hard book for me to read. My training in New Testament hasn't really prepared me for what I'm seeing here. I get the strangest sensation that when Joseph Smith wrote it he knew just enough about ancient scriptures to lead me on. But then

I run into some of the strangest names and foolish twists and turns."

Judith flipped through pages of her copy of the current edition of the Book of Mormon, which was open in front of her on the table. "Look at this. One of the largest books in the Book of Mormon is entitled *Alma*." She tapped the name with her well-manicured fingers. "Come on. This is a Latin name—*alma mater*—in Latin it could mean 'soul.' Of all the crazy names Joseph Smith could have come up with, he picks a Latin name. Latin? As a formal language, it wasn't even around when this Jewish family leaves Jerusalem. And it certainly isn't Near Eastern in origin." Judith shook her head as she spoke, "They want me to show evidence of Near Eastern antiquity when the book includes such a clearly Latin name as Alma and, in fact, it is the title of one of the books. Get serious, will ya?"

Freddy was about to squeeze in a comment when Judith pressed on with what she believed were flaws in the Book of Mormon's proper names. "Then this." She flipped the pages and found the red-lined name. "Here it is." She snickered to herself as she spoke, "Man, this guy—I guess it's Joseph Smith—lets his fancy run free. Listen, the name is 'Gidgiddoni.' Our author is a regular Dr. Seuss."

Judith looked up and chortled. "I'm telling you people, that it sounds like something you'd see on the label of a pair of designer shoes on Rodeo Drive." Judith's shoulders shook with laughter, though she held back from exploding out loud. "Where do you suppose Joseph Smith ran into folks from Italy out there in western New York?"

Others were searching for names to offer in jest; however, Henry Syman's voice dominated. He had not been laughing with the group. For the past hour, Stephen had noticed the silence of the Purdue professor, not that Stephen himself had said much either. He considered himself an observer, but not Henry Syman. He usually had a lot to contribute to the discussions.

"May I make an observation?" It was as if the board room had come to attention while the C.E.O. spoke. Stephen noticed that there was something about the persona of Dr. Syman that commanded respect and attention—no doubt a brilliant man with a whole lot more understanding of what they were reading than Stephen would ever acquire.

"I know some of you are quick to scorn Joseph Smith. He appears to be an easy target, but don't get too carried away before you've had a chance to take a better look at all these unusual names." Dr. Syman cleared his throat and spoke in a quiet, unassuming manner.

Henry did not seek the spotlight, but it focused on him by the very nature of his impressive credentials. "As some of you may know, I've already read the Book of Mormon, and I've studied some of its parts, though I am rereading it from cover to cover this week as I've been asked to do." He leaned into the group, the edge of the sleek, white kitchen table preventing him from getting any closer. "Surely you must know that I am not affiliated with the Mormons in any way, but I also know that we must carefully scrutinize this book. An off-handed opinion of contempt is the stuff of impatient scholarship, and it may come back to haunt you."

Stephen's eyes darted to Judith's face. She was stoic.

"Come on, Henry. You're too serious about this," Bernie chided.

"Am I?" Syman leaned back. "Every one of us here is intelligent, well informed in his own right. Each of us has done enough research to know better than to belittle or draw conclusions before the facts are in. So let me give you a little insight. Last night, I did a midnight research on several items in the Book of Mormon. One was a run-down of proper names in the Book of Mormon. I happened to be playing around on one of the computers in the library. By the way, do you realize that there are compact discs for the computer filled with research on the Book of Mormon? Those discs literally hold volumes. They're right in the library. Let me tell you, Mormon scholarship hasn't been sitting on its thumbs for the past century and a half. All you have to do is pull up whatever you want to learn in depth. It's all there."

Henry reached over to Judith's copy of the Book of Mormon, still open to the name "Gidgiddoni." He slid his fingertip along the strange name and said, "I'll bet we can go into the library right now and pull up that name and find out something about it. Shall we try?"

The participants scrambled to their feet and trailed one another down the wide marble-floored hall to the bleached oak double doors that opened into the library. *We must look like the cast of Clue*, Stephen chuckled to himself. Someone found the light switch and pressed it to reveal three computers and a Panasonic laser printer, which had been placed in front of the bookshelves that lined three walls. Henry led the pack to the center computer, its electrical cords snaking behind the tables, interconnected with the other computers and the printer.

He booted the set, waited until the list files directory flashed on the monitor, and then retrieved the Book of Mormon parent file. The screen flashed another menu. Three-quarters of the way down the screen, the file "PROPER NAMES" appeared. Henry highlighted the file and then punched number one to retrieve it. Onto the screen appeared the directions:

PLEASE ENTER NAME.

He entered "ALMA." Within seconds, the computer displayed information on the name.

Alma—Nephite prophet, founder of the church [c. 173-91 B.C.]
See, Book of Mormon, Mosiah 17 - Alma 5 for information on the first Alma.

Alma (the younger)—son of Alma, first chief judge, high priest [c. 100-73 B.C.]
See Alma under biographies.

The proper name has been viewed as being derived from Latin. It was also a Hebrew first name. The name Alma appears in the clay tablet letters discovered at Kokhba cave in 1954. The common translation, according to Yigel Yadine, an Israeli archeologist who has translated the letters, as stated in his book, *Discoveries of Bar Kokhba Cave,* is ALMA BAR JEHUDA, A.D. 160-180. The name Alma was used in an inscription on a tomb face for the son of Gid in an earlier period.

These translations are directly from Hebrew, and Dr. Yigel Yadine, who published his work in 1960, has adhered to the traditional method of interpretation employed by his contemporaries in Hebrew translations.

[Ricks]

Henry said nothing. He looked over his shoulder at Judith and asked, "Do you remember the spelling of that other name?"

Judith hesitated a moment, a little deflated by the discovery that the name Alma was very much Near Eastern. "Wait. I'll look it up again," Judith said as she opened her marked copy of the Book of Mormon. "G-i-d-g-i-d-d-o-n-i."

As Judith spoke, Henry punched in the letters and then hit Enter. The screen filled with information. Everyone crowded closer to see the words.

"I can't see it," complained Bernie from behind the others.

"Here, I'll read what it says," offered Henry.

Gidgiddoni—Nephite commander of army [c. A.D. 385]

3 Nephi 3:18 great commander of armies; 3:19 has spirit of revelation and prophecy . . .

3: 20-21 refuses people's petition for offensive campaign against robbers; 3:26 causes Nephites to make weapons; 4:13-14 defeats robbers; 4:24-26 cuts off robbers' retreat; 6:6 establishes great peace.

Related information: This name is an illustration of name formation in Nephite and Egyptian. The elaborate Nephite names of Gidgiddoni and Gidgidonah may be parallels to the Egyptian Djed-dihwti-iw-f and Died-djhwti-iw-a; in each case the stem is the same, sounding something like Jidjiddo-. To this the suffix -iw-f, and iw-s are added in Egyptian with the word ankh, signifying "he shall live" and "she shall live," respectively, and "thoth hath said she will live" and "she shall live," respectively; the two names meaning "Thoth hath said he shall live" and "Thoth hath said she will live." The suffixes in the two Nephite names are different, -iw-ni and iw-nah, but they are perfectly good Egyptian and indicate "I shall live" and "we shall live," respectively.

[Nibley]

The silence in the room shattered when Bernie said, "Isn't it interesting how scholars can make almost anything sound so brilliant? Come on. What connection does the Book of Mormon have to Egyptian? If anything, it would have to be associated with the Hebrews." Bernie's face became expansive as he scoffed at the screen. "I don't think for a minute that the Book of Mormon has anything to do with the Hebrews, but at least Joseph Smith could have kept his ancients straight."

"It's not that simple, Bernie," Henry cautioned. "While I was in here last night pulling up topics on the computer, I saw a couple of things that intrigued me, if for no other reason than it piqued my interest in some of these names and their roots in ancient Near Eastern language. You remember the two incorrigible sons at the beginning of the Book of Mormon?"

Stephen leaned in toward the group and said, "Do you mean the two brothers that gave Nephi such a hard time? I can't remember their names, but they're the ones who were cursed with a dark skin." Stephen remembered he was standing next to Judith and cringed at his words as he glanced down at her slender dark hands and delicate fingers.

"Yeah," Judith remarked, "and we're coming back to that bit of bigotry before this whole thing is over." She said no more. *At least she found out her so-called Italian name had Egyptian roots*, thought Stephen.

"Their names were Laman and Lemuel," Henry clarified. "They are what are known in Arabic as pendant names. Here, I'll show you what I discovered last night." He pulled up the name of Laman. The screen displayed the pertinent facts about Laman and told what a scoundrel he was. Further down on the screen the following information appeared:

LAMAN AND LEMUEL PENDANT NAMES

The two brothers' names go together in a musical fashion. These names follow the old Near Eastern custom of naming the first two sons in a family with rhyming twin names. S. Spiegel, author of *Ginzber Jubilee Volume*, pp. 349-350, called them "a pair of pendant names, such as Eldad and Medad, Hilleq and Billeq, or Jannes and Jambres."

The Arabs particularly seem to enjoy putting together such assonant names as Yagyg and Magyg (Gog and Magog), Harun and Quarun (Aaron and Korah), Qabil and Habil (Cain and Abel). Harut and Marut were the first two angels to fall from grace, like Laman and Lemuel.

These names never go in threes or fours but only in pairs, designating just the first two sons of a family with no reference to the rest. This 'Dioscuric' practice has a ritual significance, which has been discussed by Rendel Harris.
[Nibley]

"Harris's book, for your information, Freddy, was published at Cambridge, 1913."

"Well, that definitely disqualifies it. Only Oxford will do in these serious matters." Freddy laughed, holding his hand over his mouth since he was so close to the group that had crowded in to read the screen. The screen revealed more:

But of the actual practice itself, especially among the desert people, there can be no doubt, for we read in an ancient inscription: "N. Built this tomb for his sons Hatibat and Hamilat."

"I have to tell you folks," Henry concluded, tapping his index finger on the monitor screen, "you're not going to get a better example of pendant names than the two Joseph Smith dreamed up in the Book of Mormon. And, as it said, there was no real light shed on this custom of naming the first two sons with rhythmic-sounding names until Harris came out with his book—about eighty years after Joseph Smith printed the first edition of the Book of Mormon."

"He sure guessed those names right, didn't he?" Martha commented, a little bewildered at what they had just read.

"Guessed? I warned you about ignorance and how you may have to eat crow if you don't know the facts. I've shown you just a couple of examples. I stayed up half the night pulling up information like this. Do you know that there are over two hundred original proper names in the Book of Mormon? Two hundred. Why, we can't begin to research each one. They all have some kind of reference back to the Near East, like Laman and Lemuel," Henry hammered away. "I can show you some more if you're interested."

"Yeah, sure," Stephen agreed, far from sleepy now.

Bernie interjected, "Surely you're not going to buy their research without checking with an independent source, are you, Henry?"

"Of course not. I faxed a note this morning to my secretary and gave her several of these references to check out at Purdue's and BYU's libraries. She can do this very quickly with the modem in my office. I will probably get my hands slapped by Dr. Polk for doing it, but I had to learn through my own sources that this is not some kind of setup. She will send a Federal Express letter verifying these several documents."

"Good thinking, Henry," Stephen said, admiring the man's initiative.

"Did you say you want to see some more?"

"Yeah, sure. Why not?"

Henry pointed to the computer next to him and said, "Stephen, why don't you turn on that computer right there and follow along with—" The door opened behind the startled group.

A voice boomed over the heads of the pack. "Aha! I've caught you red-handed," Peter laughed. He stood in the wide doorway in his pajamas and robe, with his hands on his hips like a schoolmaster who had caught his students cribbing on an exam. They all turned to meet his gaze. It was true; they had not yet been given permission to use the computers.

"I'm sorry, Dr. Polk, if we have intruded where we were not to go," Henry volunteered in a subdued voice. "It's my fault; I encouraged it."

"Please, Dr. Syman. I'm not blaming any of you. If anyone can appreciate inquisitiveness, I certainly can." Peter had never been a bona fide taskmaster. It was a strange role for him to play. "I'm delighted that you are finding your studies interesting."

"Dr. Polk, may I ask a question?" Bernie Stein interrupted characteristically.

"Please do."

"Just how old was Joseph Smith when he allegedly wrote the Book of Mormon?"

"Joseph Smith insisted that he, in fact, *translated* the book."

"Okay, I'll go along with that for the time being. How old was he when he *translated* the Book of Mormon?"

"Joseph Smith received the plates, according to his word, when he was twenty-two. He said he returned the plates, from which he claimed to translate the document into English, when he was twenty-four."

"He was in his early twenties, and he maintained that he had the documents, or plates as you called them, from which he claimed he translated, for two years?"

"It's correct that he had them for two years, but remember that he said that most of the translation was done within the last three months of that time."

"But to be clear, he had two years in which to write roughly 530 pages?"

"That's right. Do you have any other questions?"

"No, but I'd like to make a comment." Bernie moved slightly in his chair before speaking. "Are you aware that I wrote the text of *Alexander's Wars*—it is a documented work of 478 pages—in thirty months? Granted, Joseph has a better track record at twenty-four months. But my work is of ancient records that I had to first interpret and then write."

Dr. Polk was the essence of patience. "Dr. Stein, I'm very much aware of your excellent work. In fact, I read it through, along with your other three texts that deal with ancient Middle Eastern warfare. Your keen insights into ancient battles prompted me to invite you to be in this study."

Bernie now felt a little embarrassed that he had brought it up, but he persisted with his point: "So wouldn't you say it is possible for a young man to have written the Book of Mormon in two years?"

"I think, Dr. Stein, you missed the point. I thought we—for the sake of this conversation—agreed that it was a *translation*."

"Okay, even better. Works can surely be translated in two years' time."

"Works of antiquity? Homer's *Odyssey*? Are you aware of how long that complex work took to translate into English?"

"I'm afraid I don't recall."

"It took twenty-two years of constant, daily effort to achieve the translation."

"Well, it is you who insists that the Book of Mormon is a translation. I say that Joseph Smith probably wrote it."

"Let me give you some stats." Peter swept the room with his eyes as he rifled in on his point. "All of you will learn this, but let me give you a slight preview of what you are dealing with in the Book of Mormon. He walked swiftly to the computer, tapped a few keys, and began to read from the text on the screen:

"Actual translation of the 1830 edition: 63 days.
"Number of typeset pages: 530.
"Written subject matter: the rise and fall of two major civilizations; a complex study of their governments, their wars, their methods of production of goods and services; a complex monetary system; a

detailed study of Mesoamerican warfare.

"Written phrases: consistent with a translation of Near Eastern syntax.

"Words: the book contains twice as many original English nouns as appear in the works of William Shakespeare."

Peter turned away from the computer and said, "All of this, mind you, in less than seventy days." Peter caught his breath, then remarked, "There is more—much, much, more—that you will uncover in this work.

"Now if you will kindly switch off the equipment and the lights when you're finished, I'm going back to bed."

Peter slowly climbed the wide staircase and returned to the luxurious master bedroom. He did not go to bed immediately; he remembered that he had not checked his voice mail in his home office. He dialed, punched in the correct code, and listened. The credit union wanted to know if he would like to take advantage of a new loan system. His daughter Emily had called to say she had not been able to get through to him. Had the phone been changed? Would he please call? His son Bret wanted to know where to reach him. His sister Shirley was having a family gathering in Salt Lake on Sunday; would he be able to make it? Then the dreaded voice came on the recorder: "Dr. Polk, I don't know where you have disappeared to, but I intend to find out. I want the Mormon project terminated. I will hold you personally responsible if you have not carried out my instructions to cancel. I get the feeling you haven't. Dire consequences will result. My attorney is certain that you are committing fraud."

Peter depressed the receiver and then redialed and played his voice mail through a second time. He again heard Craig's familiar voice—threatening him. Peter sat on the edge of his bed, the receiver dangling from his hand, and noted that Craig hadn't identified himself once.

Chapter Ten
Assignments

Week One—Thursday Afternoon

"What's all the excitement?" Stephen shouted to Judith as she darted past him in a white tennis dress, shouting for a phone.

"It's Ben! I have to call the paramedics. Get down to the court and help Bernie. He's with Ben right now. Hurry!"

Stephen followed Judith with his eyes from where he stood at poolside, and then he dashed for the tennis court, situated midway between the pool and the stables. A forest-green tarp that served as a windbreak lined the court's fence and prevented Stephen from seeing onto the court. Bounding around the corner post of the entrance to the enclosed court, Stephen saw Bernie bending over Ben, frantically trying mouth-to-mouth resuscitation to pump life into him.

Stephen had just begun to know Benjamin Calk, an archeologist from Texas A&M. In spite of the urgency of the moment, Stephen racked up the stats in his mind: Dr. Benjamin Calk—Rhodes scholar, Ph.D., full professor, Mesoamerican Archeology, Texas A&M. As Stephen got closer, Ben appeared to lie motionless in the late afternoon sun. His skin tone matched the gray-white concrete border of the court—a stark, lifeless appearance.

"Bernie! Bernie! Can I help?" Stephen shouted as he rushed up. Bernie took his lips from Dr. Calk's mouth and panted, "Here, Stephen, take my place for a minute. I can't get him to breathe on his own." Bernie leaned back, took a deep breath, sweat cascading down his nose and cheeks, and made room as Stephen quickly straddled the ashen form and put his lips to Dr. Calk's. "Do you know how to do this?" Bernie asked breathlessly.

"Yes, I'm trained in CPR," Stephen got out between breaths. True, although the only person he had practiced on was Anney. He could not recall putting his lips to another man's, ever. *No time for squeamishness*, thought Stephen as he applied what he had learned from the Red Cross course. He slowly breathed air into Ben's lungs. Calk's eyes were practically closed, and the pupils were fixed. *Is he dead?* Stephen wondered, in panic.

"I think he's had a coronary. Keep breathing. Not too much. Let it out easy. Just enough to keep him oxygenated. Keep it up, Stephen," Bernie encouraged. He looked about, bewildered. "Where in the world are the paramedics?"

It was a good five minutes before Fairbanks Ranch security officers were on the court to assist, and five minutes after that before the fire department arrived with life-sustaining equipment and a stretcher.

The efficient paramedics soon had Dr. Calk on the stretcher and off the court to a waiting Hartshorn paramedics ambulance. They whisked him to Scripps Memorial Hospital, where an alerted trauma team was standing by. It took a good half-hour after the fire department and security personnel left before some semblance of calm returned to the estate.

* * *

"I'm sorry to be late for this session. It appears that our numbers have dwindled to six," Peter announced to the group. "The cardiologist made it clear that Dr. Calk will not be returning to the project." Peter watched heads nod, affirming their concerns; most in the group had surmised as much. This meant that they would be without an archeologist.

The group of six had waited in the salon a half-hour for Peter's return, spending their time discussing the emergency earlier in the afternoon. It broke the routine, a routine now comfortably entrenched after only four days of being together. Henry had taken the time to share information from his secretary that he had received by Fed Ex earlier in the day. He informed the group that in the packet was a note that read: "Everything checks out. Elaine."

Roy, the lanky graduate student, entered the room and set Peter's wide leather briefcase at his feet. "Thanks, Roy," Peter's words trailed after the young man as he left quietly.

After answering a few more questions about Dr. Calk's condition and the course it would likely take, Peter glanced at his handwritten agenda and then moved quickly into the business at hand.

"First, oh yes, remind me to give you this brief quiz. It will only take a moment." Peter reached into his briefcase and retrieved a small stack of tests bundled with a rubber band.

He peered at the group above his half glasses and smiled. "What—no response?"

"I'll bite," Freddy volunteered from the center of the goosedown sofa. "Just what are we being quizzed on?"

"The Book of Mormon, of course." Peter tossed the subject aside with a sweep of his hand and set the bundle on a side table. "We'll get to this in a moment."

He returned to the agenda. "Here's what our coming week looks like—I told you there would be no more lounging about," Peter said good-naturedly. "I will turn over the project to the person you select as your chairperson. Then he or she will ask each of you to select a specific topic that focuses on an area of interest in the Book of Mormon. Then Sunday you must rest because Monday morning at 5:00 a.m. we'll be off to New York; Tuesday, back at the estate by nine in the evening; Wednesday through Saturday, doing intense work on your individual assignments on the book. It will be up to you how you wish to approach your topic of discussion. I will fade into the background and let you have at it.

"One bit of information: I hope that you will take advantage of the experts who are scheduled to arrive over the next couple of weeks. They will present forums on specific Book of Mormon topics."

Warming to his subject, Peter went on to inform the six that over the past six months he had hand-picked over a dozen authorities in selected fields of study to come and give two-hour presentations on their findings. The topics would range from Hebrew influences to depictions of ancient warfare in the Book of Mormon. He also made it clear to the group that none of the preselected presenters were affiliated with the Mormon Church. They were all independent researchers with one task—finding evidence of antiquity.

"Dr. Polk, can you tell us who some of these presenters are and the level of their expertise?" Judith asked.

"Certainly." Peter leaned on the edge of the leather-topped side table and folded his arms. "Colonel Rodney Kason, a retired colonel with impressive experience and a noted authority on ancient warfare in the Near East and Mesoamerica, will offer insights into how Mesoamerican warfare can be compared to the Israelite military heritage. In fact, Colonel Kason will be here bright and early tomorrow morning."

"How much did you pay him to slant his information, to make the Book of Mormon look good?" Bernie chuckled.

Peter smiled. "You do know him, don't you, Bernie?"

"He'll do," Bernie nodded, fully aware of Colonel Kason's impeccable integrity.

"One other example, then we'll proceed to the quiz. Dr. Reuven Saul, noted author and respected student of Hebrew from Hebrew University, Jerusalem, will speak on the subject of Hebrew influence in the Book of Mormon. Should be rather interesting. He, too, has spent six months—on top of his regular teaching load, of course—in preparation for a brief two-hour presentation. Pity the time is so short. The man could spend the full seven weeks discussing his topic alone. He has promised to entertain your questions afterwards, of course."

Peter cut off further discussion and handed out the quiz with one comment: "I hope you astute readers don't mind me evaluating your level of comprehension on your recent reading of the Book of Mormon. Each of you told me this afternoon that you had finished your assignment. Now let's see what you gleaned from your preliminary study."

I don't believe this. What do I know about what I read these last few days? It's all so jumbled in my mind that I'll never be able to answer questions on it. Stephen suddenly felt ill at ease. It had been so much reading in such a short period, and now a quiz. *What does Polk want, blood?*

The quiz consumed twenty minutes of the group's time. The questions on the first sheet were elementary and easy to answer for anyone who had seriously read the book. The second sheet dealt with the thrust and direction of the Book of Mormon and the rise and fall of the Nephite civilization and its civil, military, and religious culture.

Stephen felt that he was at a loss to give correct answers to the multiple-choice questions on the second page. He had to admit that he wasn't all that secure with his answers on the first page. After twenty minutes, he handed Peter back the test and shook his head, a little bewildered. The others in the group returned their papers with no response; they were better poker players, he decided.

"Now that we have the quiz behind us, let's relax," Polk declared. "Roy, are you here?" Peter looked behind him. The graduate student appeared from around the doorway to answer his call. "Ah, good. Roy, would you do us all a favor and put these tests through a shredder?"

Roy looked puzzled. "Dr. Polk, we don't have a shredder."

"Then would you please burn them?" Peter had a twinkle in his eye.

"Yes, sir." Roy left with the papers.

Peter turned back to the group, a smile spreading over his round face. The six visibly relaxed, whispering and laughing with each other.

"We need to lighten up around here," Peter chuckled. "I just wanted you to begin to focus on what you know and don't know. I hope this little quiz has shown each of you a need to constantly review what we're trying to understand about the Book of Mormon."

Henry Syman was the group's overwhelming choice for their leader. In fact, he was the only one they could all agree on. Syman accepted without fanfare.

"Now it's time to discuss your general impressions of the Book of Mormon," Peter suggested after Henry had been chosen to be the group's leader. "I don't want to lead you into a detailed discussion on any one aspect of the book—Dr. Syman will do that. But, since this will be my last time to direct you as a group, I thought I'd give you a chance to air some of your questions or concerns." Peter glanced over at Syman and smiled. "Thank you for accepting this job. I get to retire. Seriously, though, I would like to hear some of your impressions of what you've read up to now."

Nods and mumbling came from the group; some began flipping pages in search of marked passages. "I found the amount of warfare in the book surprising," Freddy said in all seriousness. "I didn't expect that. For years I have taught my students in England that the Book of Mormon was a religious framework for the foundation of Mormonism. It may be true, but there is so much blood and guts in this book. It's truly worse than the Old Testament when it comes to detailing gruesome tales of war."

"Yes, Freddy is absolutely right," Judith said. "Frankly, I wonder why all the wars were so carefully documented. It seems to me they could have written more about domestic and community life. Since, as one of the authors indicated, it was difficult to record on plates, they should have recorded information of a more universal interest—" Judith caught herself. "That is, if it *was* recorded on plates and then translated. Since I think Joseph Smith wrote it, he seems to be a frustrated military historian."

"Don't knock it," Bernie chimed in. "All that bloody fighting was the one aspect of the whole reading that kept my interest."

Freddy came in on the heels of Bernie: "You know, don't you, that Joseph Smith *was* a frustrated general of the militia in Illinois? He had visions of grandeur in his early years and was able to carry out those fantasies when he was empowered with considerable authority by the state. Oh, it doesn't surprise me at all that Joseph Smith wrote so much warfare into his little masterpiece. Not at all."

"May I pull this discussion back to center, please?" Peter asked in his kindest tone. He expected some type of feedback from the group but wasn't sure what path it would take. What he didn't want was a response that would end in a negative reaction to the reading of the Book of Mormon. So far, he detected no antagonism in the group. If anyone were to have spouted disparaging remarks, he thought it would have been Bernie, but none had surfaced so far.

Martha Grain sat at the back of the room, listening. She was stirring, Peter could see. She was not as verbal as the others. Since meeting her, Peter had wondered why she had accepted the offer to attend. She didn't seem at all interested in the project. *She is more like a typical college librarian who says little but carefully stores and retrieves. She would probably guard the special collections section of a library with suspicion and not even allow a dean to have access to documents unless certain basic requirements had been met. Her department chairman gave her a resounding recommendation. She seems a woman of simple tastes in dress and lifestyle. Why did she come? Does she need the hundred thousand dollars? It's possible. Maybe she has a hidden side that I haven't yet detected.* Martha stabbed the air with her hand, her lips set in a no-nonsense attitude.

"Yes, Dr. Grain," Peter acknowledged.

"Am I to understand that we are to make some sense of the Book of Mormon? I have read the book. The syntax is so atrocious that I actually threw the book down several times because of its writer's disregard for basic English word order." Martha stood, adjusted the glasses she wore on a gold chain, and proceeded to quote from some passages she had marked with color-coded lines. "I refer to this, but it hardly matters which phrase I choose; there are countless examples throughout the book. Here is a phrase that will serve to illustrate my point: 'because *that* my heart is broken.' Need I say that such a use of *that* in English is awkward and therefore smacks of an ignorant writer? If that form appeared once or twice in the book, I might understand that they could be simple errors, but it is used repeatedly. It is rather disconcerting to say the least."

Other hands went up in the group, but she refused to yield the floor. "Here is another example of poor sentence structure." She quickly thumbed the pages until she found the passage she sought. "Here it is: 'in all manner of wood, *and* of iron, *and* of copper, *and* of brass, *and* of steel, *and* of gold, *and* of silver, *and* of precious ores.' Goodness, what a misuse of the conjunction. Was this ignorant writer unaware of the proper use of the conjunction *and*? We all know that the conjunction *and* is normally used only before the last item in a series."

"May I say something, Dr. Polk?" Henry said, eager to be heard.

"Dr. Grain, do you have anything else to add?" Peter asked, wanting her to express herself fully, knowing that she was hanging herself.

"One more dreadful example, then I will have said my piece and Dr. Syman may have the floor." Martha found the page she was searching for and explained, "Here is a good example of unnecessary use of a pronoun. It is a case of using the pronoun as the direct object of the verb in one clause and a pronoun referring to the same person or thing in the following clause. This is done in a way that is redundant: 'I beheld, and saw the people of the seed of my brethren that *they* had overcome my seed.' Spare me this unnecessary extrapositional use of nouns and pronouns. I repeat what I said previously: the book has some sort of unusual word syntax or flawed structure throughout. There, that is all I have to say on the matter."

"Thank you, Dr. Grain. Dr. Syman, please," Peter pointed to Henry, who was about to come up out of his chair with agitation.

"May I say something about the word order in the Book of Mormon, and I'm sure you will agree with me, Dr. Polk." Henry took a deep breath and launched into a gentle attack on what had been said. "Dr. Grain brings up a very good point. She is right; the syntax is very bad English—but excellent Hebrew."

"Would you please clarify your statement?" Martha sniffed from the rear of the salon.

"Gladly," Henry nodded. "I am as aware as you that the syntax of the Book of Mormon makes poor English. But it is right on course were it a transliteration of Hebrew. Keep in mind everyone, the Book of Mormon claims to be a translation. Joseph Smith, even by the standards of his time, was an ignorant man. He must have translated what he saw."

"Are you saying you actually believe ol' Joe translated from those gold plates?" Bernie sighed.

"I didn't say that, Dr. Stein," Syman retorted. "I said that if it were a translation from a form of Hebrew, the book is more correct than not. Look at the use of cognates. Surely you're familiar with the biblical, 'I have dreamed a dream.' The same phrase is in the Book of Mormon. I'd have to look it up. I came across many uses of the cognate in the Book of Mormon. Let me tell you, the book is filled with Hebraisms preserved in this English translation. In other words, the unique characteristics of the original writings survived the translation process. I think it may very well be the strongest point in establishing whether this book has ancient roots."

Hands went up. Faces livened with interest. But Stephen felt suddenly ignorant and more adrift than at any point since leaving his house in Lafayette. Not only was the Book of Mormon dull history to him, but it seemed to have no sense of order. *Where is this Dr. Syman coming from, calling it good Hebrew? I don't know Hebrew. I can barely understand the book in English.*

* * *

"Now don't fuss at me over the limitation of subject matter," Dr. Syman cautioned. "We only have time for one topic each. In fact, we'll do well to cover that much material if we are to reach the depth I hope we will."

The assignments were neatly listed under subject categories, and the participants were asked to select a topic they felt most interested in or were at least comfortable with. As Peter promised, the topics ranged across the spectrum from literary styles to traces of Hebrew language and customs, war, politics, religion, and biblical findings. It was Henry Syman's duty to mediate the selections. Henry had discussed the details with Peter last night.

As the lunch hour neared, the scholars had selected their topics and were ready to begin. Some were a little disgruntled, finding it necessary to settle for their second choice.

Stephen had misgivings about his assignment. It was Henry who had suggested he take it. Most of the subjects had gone to one or the other of the participants who had a background of study in a related field. Stephen lacked a background in any of the areas, so Henry had kindly asked him to take the "Allegory of the Olive

Tree." Just what that entailed Stephen would soon learn. He knew he must have read it, but it had made no impact on his mind. *Surely he doesn't mean that strange section about pruning and dunging the olive trees while the master is preoccupied with his vineyard?*

Stephen sighed. He would have to review that part of the book and get it worked out in his mind. One saving grace—it covered only a couple of chapters in the book of Jacob. Most of the other subjects covered books within the book.

"Well, ladies and gentlemen, I think you have your work cut out for you. Go to it!" Henry said, as he shuffled his papers and stacked them in front of him. He arose to take the list of assigned topics to Peter as directed.

* * *

The master suite seemed to Henry more an apartment than a bedroom. He noticed a sitting room, a large bath with walk-in closets on either side, and an expansive view of the valley. In the distance he could see the Pacific Ocean.

"This is some bedroom."

"I feel foolish occupying it," Peter responded to Henry as he opened the door with a welcoming smile. "Have a seat over here. You know, it was not my idea to use an estate for this project. I was outvoted by the project's benefactor. It was his desire that the participants have plenty of room to move about, be isolated from community activities, and have all the creature comforts they could imagine. In this way, he hoped to entice them to stay with the project."

"For the most part, it seems to have worked. I love it here."

"Okay, let's see the assignments." Peter reached out for the sheets in Henry's hand and scanned the names on each.

Peter made several comments, surprised at some selections, pleased by others. "I see you have Stephen Thorn with the allegory."

"Yes, I persuaded him to take it. He seemed a little bewildered by what was left after our eager colleagues made their choices, so I strongly suggested this topic."

"Umm, it'll be interesting to see how he handles it. You know, of course, that it is perhaps the most challenging of all the topics?"

"No, I don't see it that way."

"It is. Believe me, it is."

"Dr. Polk—"

"Call me Peter. It's time we drop some of the formalities around here, don't you think?"

"Ah, Peter, during the selection of topics, several in the group asked why there were no presenters of opposing views. That is, why have we no person or persons on the list who make a practice of undermining the Book of Mormon? I'm sure there are those who lecture against your church—surely there are those who target the Book of Mormon."

"There are," Peter said, not surprised that this subject had arisen. It would make the project sticky. Peter stood for a moment in thought. Even Thomas had once suggested to Peter that the list of presenters "ought to include some individual who makes a living bashing the Book of Mormon or at least writes pseudo-scholarly articles that endeavor to expose the falsity of the Book of Mormon." And, after all, this was why the Reverend Robert Moore had been chosen to be a participant.

These scholars are definitely starting the project on the negative side. It will be interesting to see what happens. Finally, Peter had to agree that this factor would have to be addressed.

"All right," Peter nodded. "In fact, one minister who speaks out against the Mormons was originally scheduled to be one of our participants. He was unable to come. . . . Sent his son-in-law, Stephen Thorn, in his place at the last minute."

"Then, with your permission, we would like to invite in at least one."

"Yes, go ahead, though I think it will disappoint you."

"Why is that?" Henry probed.

"Because there are no real scholars among the lot."

"Do you mind if *we* make that judgment? I will be happy to coordinate the effort and help schedule the presenter."

"Please do. But with one request."

"Certainly."

"Would you schedule this or these anti-Book of Mormon presenters toward the conclusion of the project?"

"Are you concerned, Dr. . . . uh . . . Peter?"

"No, just cautious. Besides, I want you to get your money's worth from your anti-Mormon."

Chapter Eleven
Colonel Kason

Week One—Friday Morning

He had a military stature. The ramrod posture, the serious mouth, and the quick eyes indicated a man who understood war and how to employ it. Colonel Rodney Kason was a full-bird colonel who had served in the Vietnam War, the United States' involvements in Central America, and the Gulf War. Roy had whisked him from Lindbergh Field airport at 8:25 a.m. and brought him directly to the estate. Peter met him on the portico and ushered him into the dining room to meet the group that had been abuzz with anticipation. They were curious about the procedure that would be employed in the first of fifteen presentations.

The six scholars had been instructed for the past half-hour to cooperate in a little experiment. Peter had asked them, for the sake of objectivity, not to divulge in any way the nature of the project. He told them that the colonel was ignorant of the origin of the warfare document that he had been given six months earlier, and Peter wanted him to remain that way. The colonel had been told that the document was a copy of an original writing and that the only alteration was that proper names had been changed. "For instance," Peter illustrated the code, "Nephi has been changed to 'N,' Aaron is listed as 'AA,' the Lamanites are called the 'Ls,' and so forth. He has been informed that the document has to do with warfare in Mesoamerica, with some influences from the Near East. That gave the colonel some idea of the nature of the warfare but not its origin." Peter explained that the colonel had agreed to those terms.

"Actually, the colonel will leave here ignorant of the origin of the document unless one of you reveals what you know. He has been paid to study the document and to report on the period and the nature of the warfare."

"Are you saying, Peter, that this chap knows nothing of our intentions?" Freddy asked from the far end of the dining table, where he was seated next to Stephen. The pattern had been established. The participants, like members of a family, had staked out favorite spots at the table and sat there each time.

"That's right. Why should he need to know? You are not interested in whether he knows that it is the Book of Mormon. This way we get an unbiased impression." Peter smiled at Bernie, remembering his jab the night before.

"Are you afraid that he will give a negative report if he knows it is taken from the Book of Mormon?" Bernie asked, not to be put off.

Peter's eyes rolled up and he shook his head. "Let's just say that I want to see what his response is to a document he has been asked to research and expound on without knowledge of exactly what it is. Let's call it the Pepsi test, okay?"

The men and women mumbled to one another and, without any real objection, agreed to cooperate.

"In front of each of you is a document identical to his. It is titled *Document A*. You may peruse it, follow along with the colonel, do as you wish. Just remain silent on proper names and the origin."

Peter welcomed Colonel Kason to the dining room and introduced him to the group. Standing next to the colonel, Peter appeared slumped and physically dilapidated. Nevertheless, he spoke with ease and presented the colonel with pride in his voice.

"It's a privilege to introduce Colonel Rodney Kason. Group, this soldier is recently retired from active military duty. He is now a military consultant and often lectures at the United States Military Academy at West Point and at the Army's Command and General Staff College at Fort Leavenworth, Kansas. His field of study has been ancient warfare, and he has written three outstanding volumes on the concepts of Central American warfare, ancient and modern. They are textbooks currently being used in military classes." Peter caught his breath.

"Colonel Kason has agreed to come here this morning and present the subject of warfare in *Document A*. I might add," Peter said, about to retire to the rear of the room, "that Colonel Kason had never seen a copy of this document until six months ago. He has spent part of that time researching and analyzing the document to determine whether it does, in fact, accurately represent warfare in ancient Mesoamerica. Colonel Kason, the time is yours."

The group listened intently as Rodney Kason launched into his two-hour presentation on warfare. After his opening remarks, he moved directly to the subject at hand.

"First off," Kason began, "let me say that world history is long on warfare. In ancient times, war was considered inevitable; it was a way of life. You cannot compare twentieth century war with the fighting that was a constant occurrence two thousand years ago. As I have studied this document on warfare, it snugly fits the general pattern of what was common throughout the world at the time. The account recorded in this document took place at least a thousand years ago by my calculations, unless it is an obscure bit of isolated warfare on some island in our era.

"I do not know who the ancient historian was who wrote this document, but that is not my assignment. I merely need to substantiate that it was written about ancient warfare and that it meets the criteria for warfare of that period."

Intermittently, Bernie feverishly scribbled questions on his pad. He had respect for Colonel Kason, whose credentials Bernie knew well.

"By my count, there are over a hundred wars specifically mentioned in this account. I have labeled each, but time will not allow me to enumerate them. The reasons for these wars cover a wide range of disputes. The history covers a thousand-year period. First, let me say that this is not an inordinate number of wars for a thousand-year span. By comparison, there are 180 specific wars mentioned in a thousand-year period in Greek history, 140 in the Roman period, and 80 in the Hebrew span. So you see, this account indicates a condition that was common in that era. Most of the wars I've tallied in the document were conflicts centered on concerns over preserving the traditions of forebears; at least, that was a major issue."

Ten minutes into his lecture, Kason mentioned weapons. "You must remember that this account deals with premodern warfare; it is devoid of gunpowder, as, of course, were all conflicts in that era. Gunpowder came into play as an instrument of war in the fourteenth century, and the use of gunpowder weapons was in full force in Napoleon's time. The authors of this document knew nothing of modern methods of warfare. In this respect, the account is agreeable with its times. In other words, modern warfare is often dated to the rise of gunpowder. Therefore, premodern warfare would, of necessity, be quite different from the warfare we have known in the past three centuries."

After another half-hour, Kason was well immersed into weapons. Stephen was fascinated. *I've got to read those battle scenes again. I think I can stay awake if I understand what's going on.*

"There may be vast differences in how premodern armies fought, but they all tended to employ similar weapons. Face-to-face combat was conventional. They fought with swords, spears, and clubs, even axes. They also employed some types of missiles, such as javelins, spears, and arrows, all propelled by muscle power. In my study of the document, all of these methods were used. There is no violation of the ancient pattern of warfare here. However, there is some difference in this account and Near Eastern warfare.

"I bring this up because I am aware that the roots of this culture stemmed from Jerusalem, but my research shows there are some marked differences in the weapons and equipment used in Near Eastern combat and those employed by the people in this account. In the Bible, for example, chariots, cavalry, siege engines, helmets, and coats of mail are standard. Not so in this document. These warriors wore armor such as shields and bucklers, headplates, and the like, but not the type worn in the Near Eastern military during the same period.

"In one example, it tells about *staining* the sword. It is dif-

ficult to stain a steel sword, but not a wooden one. Early in the document, it tells of fashioning a sword after the sword owned by an
influential man in the old city of Jerusalem. Then, as the account
traverses years of time, there is no more mention of steel. True to
Mesoamerican technology, metal was rare.

"In Central America when the Spaniards arrived, the
Indians were armed with a unique sword. It was made of hardwood
with sharpened obsidian, a black, glass-like stone that the Indians
imbedded on either side of the flat wood. At the tip of the weapon
there was a point that could be thrust into an opponent.

"The sword is mentioned more than any other weapon in the
account I read. It is sometimes referred to metaphorically. For
example, 'fall by the sword,' or 'perish by the sword.' Then it is
used militarily as in, 'slaughter by the sword.' One other interesting
note: *Thrusting* or *stabbing* with swords is never written or even
alluded to in this account. The key word is *smite,* meaning a cutting
action, as is the case when the person my document calls "AA" cuts
off the arms of his attackers while he is defending the king's flock.
I don't have time to explain the power it would take to slice off an
adult's arm, though perhaps later I will mention this method of
using the sword.

"As near as I can detect—and I've only spent a few months
on this study—I have arrived at the conclusion that the armor in this
account is the type written about and depicted in Mayan art. It is
clearly not the heavy armor used in Near Eastern warfare, though
there are parallels. It is Mesoamerican, and yet the document never
explains in detail the kind of weapons and armor used; the authors
simply mention weapons in passing, and that is how I have derived
my information from the document.

"For example, if you will read with me on page 330, beginning about half a page down, you will note that armor is worn."
Kason paused a moment to allow the group to turn to the page in
the document placed before each participant. He began reading the
passage: "Now the leaders of the Ls had supposed, because of the
greatness of their numbers, yea, they supposed that they should be
privileged to come upon them as they had hitherto done; yea, and
they had also prepared themselves with shields, and with breast-

plates; and they had also prepared themselves with garments of skins, yea, very thick garments to cover their nakedness.'

"This armor covered only the torso." Kason used his hands in front of his chest to show the area. "As AA writes, it protected 'the vital parts of the body.' The legs were completely uncovered. And if you will notice a little later in the same chapter, the Ns suffered considerable leg wounds. Why didn't they cover their legs with greaves, a type of leg armor used in biblical battles? It seems that these armies were highly mobile. Theirs were battles of movement. If you follow the scenes, you can't help noticing how the armies pursued one another from one location to the next. They could not impair their method of fighting by restricting themselves with leg armor.

"A few weeks ago, Dr. Polk was good enough to fly me to Central America for a firsthand update on the latest findings on Mesoamerican warfare. I clearly lack sufficient time to tell you what I saw and learned on this trip, but it verifies to me that this document describes the kind of warfare used in Mesoamerica."

An hour and a half into his discussion of warfare, Kason had covered logistics, descriptions of battles, guerilla wars, and laws of warfare. Stephen glanced around at the faces of his fellow researchers. All were absorbed, taking notes, unaware of time passing.

"I'm impressed with the concept of oath-taking during battles in the account. It is here that the document reveals a strong Near Eastern flavor." Kason then stepped back from his electronic board, where he had shown graphically battle lines and tactics common to Mesoamerican warfare a thousand years ago.

"Personal oaths were a part of the battle scene," Kason elaborated. "In this respect, Near Eastern warfare and the warfare depicted in these documents are similar. Verbal oaths had all the binding effects that written contracts do for us today. They took oaths of surrender seriously. The document clearly exhibits the influence of ancient laws and customs of the Near East that carefully delineate the protocol of war."

Kason summarized: "There are patterns that I have uncovered in this document that reflect the dual heritage of the old Near

East and Mesoamerica. What more can I tell you?"

Bernie's voice rang out when Colonel Kason concluded his remarks and asked if there were any questions. "I have a whole list of questions I would like to ask."

"Please," Kason nodded to Bernie.

"First, do you think a person could have researched historical material in the early 1800s that would have given a writer the kind of background needed to fabricate these wars and remain premodern throughout the document?"

Kason looked down at his shiny black shoes and dusted invisible lint from his sleeve as he pondered the question. "I think with a careful writer, the book could have maintained a reasonable Near Eastern pattern of warfare. I'm not a great student of the Bible, but I think it would be possible to extract ancient warfare from its pages and write them into this account.

"But it's not that simple. If the writer had consulted the Bible, why would he leave out equipment that was standard in the Near East during the Old Testament era, such as coats of mail, helmets, and greaves? The very best example of armor in the Bible that deals with this level of warfare is David and Goliath. Goliath wore a coat of mail in the biblical description of that scene. Surely, if the writer were researching ancient warfare, he would have used the Old Testament model. There are no coats of mail in this document. A computer search helped me on that study."

Colonel Kason summarized his answer to Bernie's question when he said, "I have not done a detailed study of what type of books concerning ancient warfare were available in the U.S. in the early nineteenth century, but I do have an inventory of research material available at West Point covering the period around 1827. There were no treatises written in English specifically on ancient Near Eastern warfare, only books on battles that, in passing, mention tactics, logistics, armor, laws of war, and descriptions of battles. I suppose that if a dedicated scholar had spent ten years in the library at West Point in the 1820s, he could have pieced together a fairly accurate picture of ancient Near Eastern warfare, but it hadn't been done up to that time. As far as material available on Mesoamerican warfare goes, that is still being compiled. I hate to tell you this, but in the 1960s we did not have a detailed study of ancient Central American warfare. That came in the mid-seventies when there was a good deal of action taking place in and around Panama. The Pentagon needed information and assigned me to do the research."

Kason narrowed his wise eyes at the group and said in a near-hushed tone, "This document details warfare in Mesoamerica to the *nth* degree. It's uncanny."

Questions flew for another hour, and then Peter invited Colonel Kason to have lunch with the group. Over lunch on the terrace, the six researchers continued pressing for further clarification of points and comparisons of the military aspects of the document. At two in the afternoon, the colonel was shaking hands with the group in the foyer when Stephen approached.

"Thank you for coming, Colonel Kason," Stephen began. "I admire your knowledge. I have one more question. Maybe you can clear it up."

"I will if I can," Colonel Kason said with the sharp tone of a man used to being brief.

"Did you feel," Stephen asked, "as a military historian, that you were reading accounts that were really written by military officers of that period?"

"Absolutely. I read those accounts at least three different times and, of course, studied the battle scenes in detail. There is no question in my mind that the person, or more likely persons, who wrote the document had been ranking leaders in the military and had done extensive research of war documents. Frankly, it was the personal experiences that the writer or writers portrayed that lent it such credibility."

"Thank you, Colonel. You've answered my question."

* * *

Peter enjoyed dinner time. It was the time of day he had always reserved for family and friends to enjoy meaningful conversation. Since his early years with Marian, they had established the pattern of serving evening meals in the dining room. Often Marian would have a special arrangement of flowers as a centerpiece. She always used her good china and silverware. One major loss when Marian became ill, and later after her death, was the cessation of meals in the dining room. Now at the estate, Peter had revived this custom. At the commencement of the meal, he offered simple thanks to God for the food. Judith had commented that it reminded her of the way her grandmother and mother said grace before eating. No one objected.

"Judith, you seem to have an interesting background. How did you ever arrive at Princeton in the English Literature department?" Peter asked. He wanted to know everything he could about each participant, although he had dossiers that he had begun compiling as he selected them to be participants in the project.

"I'm sure this group wouldn't want me to sit here and tell my life history," Judith responded. "Let me say I wanted out of the south side of Chicago and into something that would give me the fulfillment my mind longed for. Actually, I had an interesting English literature teacher when I was in high school. She had been raised in England, though her parents were American. She pulled me aside and told me that I should consider applying for admission to a major university. She felt my writing was good enough to earn me a scholarship to a fine school. She helped me every step of the way, and I entered Occidental College in Los Angeles; then I did my advanced studies at Dartmouth, where I received my doctorate." Judith took a deep breath. "That's it. I got lucky. And two years ago I landed a job at Princeton in the English Lit. Department. I think they needed to even out the ethnic ratio, so I got the job."

"What about your book?" Martha asked from the opposite side of the table. "She showed me a copy in the room," she told the others. "I was impressed with all this lady has done."

"I'm a romantic," Judith volunteered, wishing the conversation would shift to another's career. "I pulled some love thoughts out of the Bible, spent about five years researching and organizing my findings, and found a New York publisher. I've left out my personal life, but that is for another day."

"Martha," Peter said, turning his attention to her, "it's ladies' night. So tell us about your academic background, or anything you wish to share with us."

"I'm just an old-fashioned English teacher," Martha replied, coloring slightly. "For twenty years I taught in a high school in St. Louis. Then the University of Missouri needed a no-nonsense grammarian and offered me the job. Meanwhile, I completed my doctorate at Northwestern. It took ten years of summers and one sabbatical from teaching high school to achieve it. I happen to enjoy the art of language. I don't know why I was selected to come here for the summer, but I'm enjoying every hour. I have no books to my credit—two papers only, dealing with the rapid alterations in the contemporary American usage of English. That's it. I'm a wife and the mother of a thirty-five-year-old daughter. I have two cats."

Moments before, Sergia, the maid, had served the soup, and it was cooling fast. Martha looked at her plate and reminded everyone that they should start eating. She felt that she had said enough.

Chapter Twelve
The Olive Tree

Week One—Friday Afternoon

Peter slipped into his spacious bedroom to make a call. He picked up his phone, a private line, and dialed William Bennett's home. It was a long time before Bill came on the line. He seemed out of breath. "I was on the tennis court. How are you doing, Peter?"

"I'm fine, but I'm wondering about our little problem with Craig. Since I called you the other night, I have received two more messages on my answering machine, both nearly identical to the first—rude and determined."

"Don't worry about those messages," Bill consoled. "I got a call from his attorney late yesterday afternoon. He is threatening me with a lawsuit if I don't explain to the bank that I'm merely acting as an agent for a private party concerning those funds at Finley & Southam. I do suspect that Craig's attorney, a fellow named Sharp, will file for an injunction against my using the funds, if he can find them.

"It looks like I'll have to run over to L.A. Monday and see what recourse I have to stop an injunction, should it happen. A friend of mine in L.A. will help me. He and I both graduated from U.S.C. law school."

Bill had his wind now. "All we can do is hang on at this point. You know our mutual friend Mary returns tomorrow from her little self-imposed exile. I'll try to convince her to sign a check with me to pull the money out of the Beverly Hills bank. Then we won't have to worry about the special funds at Finley & Southam."

"Our base financial needs may be a little less than we thought, Bill. We had another person drop out last night."

"What happened?"

"A heart attack. Would you believe it? Dr. Benjamin Calk had a heart attack yesterday afternoon on the tennis court. He's okay . . . may need surgery. He will definitely not be coming back. It's unfortunate, but in savings that's seventy thousand, plus some of his expenses around here. Maybe less than that, come to think of it. I plan to pay any medical expenses that his insurance doesn't cover—that is, if you agree."

"Sure, that's only fair."

* * *

It took Stephen two hours of walking and thinking before he felt like studying his new assignment in the Book of Mormon. He finally wandered into the stables and found a quiet spot to read, propped up against a saddle. He liked the scent of horses and saddle leather. It brought back great memories of his youth, living on his uncle's ranch.

When Stephen did open the book, he found *olive* in the index. As he found the page, he remembered that Henry had told him it was Jacob 5. *I read this the other day. I didn't understand it then, and I probably won't understand it now.* He was convinced that all he could hope to retain after five days of reading the Book of Mormon was an overabundance of wars, a lot of preaching, and some history.

Though, he had to admit, he had been impressed with a couple of areas of the book—particularly the writings of Alma, who spoke of faith with a compelling sincerity, and of Nephi, who wrote about the love of Christ. There were some discourses Stephen had found interesting, such as the one given by Christ when he appeared to the people after the destruction. *But if the book is a hoax, how can that be a true account?*

Stephen laboriously reread Jacob 5 and frankly wondered

what it meant. He had to think it through, and then he read the chapter again. It was still difficult to sort out after spending more than two hours on it.

Once more he read Jacob 5. This time, he could identify some methods of husbandry, but the story was still a mystery to him. *Well, I can't just sit here leaning on this saddle, rereading something that isn't coming to me. At least I need paper and pencil.*

He knew the story had something to do with a tame olive tree and a wild olive tree. The tame tree had become corrupted and required a rejuvenation from the wild olive tree that had been grafted in.

Stephen continued to ponder the allegory. *Let's see, the master of the vineyard . . . vineyard? I thought a vineyard was grapes, not olives. I'll have to check that one out; maybe I've caught Joseph Smith in an error. Vineyard.*

Stephen mulled over the chapter a moment longer and then decided he would go into the library and punch up *vineyard* on the computer. *It's probably not even on the computer,* he grumbled to himself.

* * *

Roy, the graduate student, slipped behind Stephen as the latter paused to study which computer he would tackle.

"May I help you, Dr. Thorn?"

Stephen turned around, startled by the deep voice at his back. He saw the thin, almost emaciated young man with a toothy smile and a friendly manner.

"I'm sorry if I startled you," Roy apologized.

In two minutes, with Roy's nimble fingers, Stephen came to understand that a vineyard was a term in the Near East to designate an orchard of olive or fig trees, or a field of grapevines. *So much for my theory that I had snagged an error in the Book of Mormon.*

He further read that the wild olive tree grows on primitive hillsides and in orchards in the eastern Mediterranean region from Greece to Egypt, including the Holy Land.

He learned that domestic olives grow exclusively in a Mediterranean-type climate. The areas where olives are produced dot the globe in a hop-skip fashion: the Near East, Southern Europe, California in the western United States, a region in Australia, and parts of the Orient.

Stephen pondered the regions where olives grow and said, "Roy, wasn't Joseph Smith from New York State?"

"That's right. He claimed to have translated the Book of Mormon in New York and in northern Pennsylvania."

"It says here that the only region where olive trees grow in the United States is California, or very close to it, but not in the eastern United States. Am I correct?"

"You can check it out, but that's what the computer says."

Roy continued pulling up information on the olive tree. They learned that the olive is prized for its oil and that only a fraction of the olives grown are cured for table olives. "What else do you want to know about olives, Dr. Thorn?" Roy asked.

"Let's look at the cultivation and horticulture of the olive tree. Pull up the records of the earliest known writings on the science of raising olives. Can you do that?"

"Absolutely." Roy was typing "olive horticulture" before Stephen could complete his request. It was as if Roy could read his mind.

"It says here, 1852. That was the first publication of an English translation of a hundred-page essay that was originally written in French in 1820."

"Are you sure there was no English publication on how to grow olives before 1852?" Stephen stared down at the screen as he spoke. "Umm, I believe that the Book of Mormon was published in 1830, right?"

"That's correct; March 22, 1830, to be exact."

"Why do you suppose it took over thirty years before a work on olive growing was published in English?"

"The English have no interest in the subject matter. There are no olive trees in England."

"Nor anywhere east of the Rocky Mountains in the United States." Stephen thought that there must be an answer that he hadn't uncovered.

"Does it strike you as odd that Joseph Smith would describe the cultivation and pruning of the olive tree, having never seen an olive tree? Where do you suppose he got his information?" *How do I know that what he wrote about dunging and pruning are all that accurate, anyway?*

Roy thought for a moment. "Well," he said, "you know there is a sketchy account in the New Testament and a few verses in Isaiah. You might want to check them out. Neither one is as detailed as the account in Jacob 5.

"Of course, there was that French publication in the 1820s and the slim possibility that Smith studied it," Roy suggested with no conviction.

"That's a possibility," Stephen surmised. "Could Joseph Smith read French?"

"No."

"Just wondering."

At Stephen's request, Roy pulled up the word *allegory* on the screen and read it aloud. "'Allegory—a literary dramatic or pictorial device in which each literal character, object, and event represents a symbol illustrating an idea or moral or religious principle. A symbolic representation.'"

Stephen studied the definition, reading it twice. He mused aloud, "Umm, then the olive tree represents something else. What? Do you know, Roy?"

"The House of Israel. Have you read the next chapter that gives the interpretation of the allegory?"

Stephen flushed, chagrined that he had not done his homework. *Why didn't I read on? Boy, that tells you how narrow I am. I know I read it the other day, but what I read then has little relationship to what I'm trying to digest now.*

"Let me play around with the computer, will you, Roy? If I have a problem, I'll call you. And thanks."

Stephen began typing into the computer all the words he could think of that were remotely connected to the allegory of the olive tree.

"Olive tree. The well-known *Olea europea*. It is extensively cultivated in Palestine for the sake of the oil. The olive requires being grafted; hence, Paul's allusion to the gentiles (Rom. 11:17-24); but he describes the reverse of the ordinary gardening operation, and it is therefore spoken of as "contrary to nature" (v. 24). Using the olive tree in an allegorical sense to illustrate Israel and the gentiles is also done by Zenos, as quoted by Jacob 5:6. Isaiah uses the illustration of the grapevine for the same purpose."

There was a complete bibliography of books, magazine articles, and symposium data about olive culture available. Stephen glanced down the list and realized that most detailed the olive-growing industry in California. One reference struck his attention as a source he would want to read: *An Essay on the History and Cultivation of the European Olive-Tree, Paris*: Printed by L.T. Cellot, 1820.

"Roy," Stephen called over his shoulder, getting the young man's attention. "Sorry to interrupt you, but how would I find this essay listed in the bibliography? You know, the French one that was translated and published in English in 1852?"

"We have a photocopy of the English translation of it here in the library. But I believe that it is also logged into the computer as a key reference to the Allegory of the Olive Tree in Jacob 5."

"I'd like a hard copy to mark up, Roy. Okay?"

Roy got up and leaned over Stephen to type in a few quick key strokes. Stephen could hear a laser printer hum into action. Within a few moments, he had a copy of the 1852 translation in his hands.

"Thanks," Stephen acknowledged. "By the way, how did you know how to find this essay on what I would consider a remote subject in the Book of Mormon?"

"Easy. I helped set up the complete system of reference materials we have here in this room."

"In the past year?"

"That's right. I have been researching and compiling information for a year on this project—of course, under Dr. Polk's direction. Because he did not want the research to be biased, Dr. Polk went to great lengths to include a variety of materials—many researched and written by non-Mormons. We have a rather impressive library on these computer compact discs." Roy pointed to a large case full of compact discs.

"How do they work?" Stephen asked, eyeing the CD player connected to the computers. "That looks a lot like my daughter's CD player, but her discs have music on them. You mean these can be pulled up on the computer screen?"

"Right," Roy answered. "You use the compact discs just like a floppy disk drive. Look." Roy inserted a disc, typed "d:" and pressed the Enter key. At the top of the screen, Stephen could see that instead of being at the C drive, he was now at the D drive.

"It's that easy?" Stephen asked.

"Sure," Roy replied. "Watch this." Roy typed "dir" and tapped the Enter key again. Immediately, the directory of documents on the compact disc appeared.

Stephen stood mesmerized as he read a long list of complete volumes, including the Talmud, the complete Jewish Quarterly Review, the Old Testament Pseudepigrapha, several Jewish and Hebrew apocryphal works, and the latest publication of the Compendium to the Dead Sea Scrolls. "All these complete books are on one compact disc?" he asked in wonder.

"That's right," Roy replied. "Amazing, isn't it?"

"And you pulled this together in one year? Am I right to assume that you are a walking reference to the Book of Mormon?" Stephen asked.

"Well, I don't know about that," the young man protested, looking uncomfortable. "But I have checked out a lot of material. The Allegory of the Olive Tree is just one."

"And am I also right to suppose that you have been instructed to withhold information until I ask?"

Roy's mouth widened in a telling grin. He leaned back in his chair and stretched as he spoke, avoiding a direct answer. "By the way, did you look up the name of the prophet in the Book of Mormon who is supposed to have written the Allegory of the Olive Tree?"

"No, I'm just getting started on this thing."

"You might find it interesting. It was the prophet Zenos."

"Spell that," Stephen asked.

"Z-e-n-o-s."

Stephen tapped a few keys and instantly read:

Zenos—Prophet of Israel

Then followed an outline of Zenos and what became of him. Stephen noted that he had given the parable of the olive tree, and because he stood firm on his religious convictions he had been martyred.

"I realize that I don't know all the prophets in the Old Testament, but I've never heard of Zenos."

"No, and you probably never will again unless you read about him in the Book of Mormon. The Mormons maintain that Zenos was an Old Testament prophet whose writings were once included in the books of the Old Testament but have since been removed. Zenos wasn't the only one, either. There is another prophet named Zenock, whose predictions appear in the Book of Mormon, but he is not to be found in the Bible."

"What do you make of this?" Stephen asked, realizing that he was covering some of the same research that Roy had already explored.

"I know only that the Book of Mormon is much more complex than I ever realized. Don't fool yourself as so many people do when they first read it. It may sound odd and not read as English should, but there are complex facets to the book that I have no explanations for; and without boasting, let me say that I have searched until I have found answers for much of what is there. But then, unusual writings are found in most cultures. I have been doing some work on the *Koran* in my spare time, and I find it fascinating and interestingly written."

Chapter Thirteen
The Daughter/Wife

Week One—Friday Afternoon

"Anney, it's your husband on line two," the receptionist's crisp voice announced on the speaker phone. The decor of Anney's small inner office was simple and inexpensive but reflected a mind that sought tranquility. Anney had decorated the walls with photographic reproductions, framed in chrome. Most were ocean scenes and sunsets—a decidedly serene element in an otherwise utilitarian office of blond oak wood with apricot-colored fabric on the chairs across from Anney's desk. She was alone, reviewing a flyer her father had asked her to proof for content and appearance.

"Oh, thanks, Rita." Anney tossed back her hair as she depressed the speaker button and picked up the receiver.

"Darling, how is everything going? I'm so glad you called."

"Hi, Anney. It's one minute past four; the rule is no calls until after four on Fridays. I couldn't wait to call you. Do you know how much I love you?"

"I love you too," Anney said softly. Delight spread across her attractive face and bright blue eyes.

"Bring me up to date, Anney. I miss you. I love you. Did you hear me? I l-o-v-e y-o-u!"

"Oh, it's great to hear your voice, darling. I miss you, too. I can't remember any time we've ever been apart when I have missed you more. I received your letter. Did you get my letters? I write you every day."

"Yeah, two letters. Thanks. I hate these phone restrictions. I feel like this is some kind of military academy. I'm glad you're getting my letters. I write every night."

"Yes, yes, I'm glad. It sounds so exciting," Anney bubbled.

"What does?" Stephen asked, a little bewildered.

"The mansion you're in—the rich setting and all."

"Oh, you must have received the letter I wrote Monday when I arrived here. Is that the only letter you have received?"

"Yes, and I'm dying to hear more. What is the research all about? Can you tell me now?"

Stephen hesitated and then stalled for a moment longer before explaining the project. "Hey, this place is incredible. I know that I tried to describe it in the letter, but let me tell you, it's even better than I thought."

Stephen had hoped Anney had received the letter he wrote Tuesday explaining about the Book of Mormon project. He had hoped that this call would not be her first encounter with the subject matter.

"I did tell you it's like living at the Ritz-Carlton without having to pick up the tab. Visualize the biggest house in Danville, then add two million dollars worth of extras, and you'll have some idea of what this place is like. It is fabulous. I mean, I have about everything I need or would ever want in the way of comforts . . . except you."

"You miss me, then?"

"Do I ever miss you! Hey, I room with a big teddy bear of a guy named Freddy. I think I mentioned him in that first letter. Does this guy ever snore. I mean he *really* snores. If you think I'm loud, you've got to hear Freddy. It's okay, though. When I hit the bed at night, I'm out until morning."

"Stephen, honey, I would love listening to you snore this evening, in our cozy bed. I wish you didn't have to be away seven long weeks."

"How are you and the kids doing?" Stephen asked brightly, hoping the conversation would not return to the project. "Does Brenda like it in Seattle?" Their eighteen-year-old daughter had finished high school the week before Stephen started the project and then had left for a three-week visit with her best friend, who had moved to Seattle the year before. "I'm calling her as soon as I get off the phone with you. How is Todd doing?"

"Yes, Brenda is having fun, and Todd is busy most of the day at Silvershine, detailing cars. He's making pretty good money. I'm afraid he has more of you in him than me. The gripe I have with him is his piggy room and the way he leaves the upstairs bathroom every morning. He just walks out of the house, leaving behind a trail of towels, socks, his aftershave, you name it."

"He's a kid, Anney. He'll grow up. I think I was worse."

"A kid?" Anney asked, shaking her head. "Stephen, he's seventeen years old and going into his senior year in high school. You call that a kid?" Anney caught herself and withdrew from discussing things that couldn't be resolved on the phone.

"Anyway, I miss you. The bed is so lonely at night. I can stand the days. I sort of like getting up without anyone disturbing me, taking my time in the bathroom, and not having to fix breakfast, but the nights are cold and lonely without you. It'll be so good to have you back."

"I'm ready. Boy, am I ready."

"You said you're tired every night? Working on the research project? Tell me, what is it?"

Stephen took a deep breath and let it out slowly. *Oh well, I might as well get it over with. I have to tell her sometime.* "I had no idea what this project would be, but it is a doozy," he said, laughing. "You'd never guess. No, it's too bizarre, at least for my temperament and training."

"Well, *tell* me," Anney said impatiently. "You *can* tell now, can't you?"

"Yeah, I can tell you. We're supposed to take apart the Book of Mormon and determine whether there is sufficient evidence to show that it is antiquity, or at least a translation of ancient writings."

Stephen heard Anney's quick breath. Then there was silence and then tension, ever so slight, but Stephen felt it through the phone. He knew the information came as a surprise to her. She hadn't expected the work to encompass the doctrine of a religious sect. He didn't know what she expected it would be, but it was definitely a shock. He could feel that. When she did manage a response, it came with a rush of words.

"You mean to tell me that the Mormons are behind this whole scheme? What are they trying to do, use you to promote their brand of religion? Face it, you know I don't like the Mormons." She hesitated again, trying to get hold of her feelings. "They have absolute control over their members. I think they're trying to take over America."

"Anney, calm down. I know you're not happy with this assignment. Neither am I," Stephen said, raising his voice, wishing he could have kept the conversation in a more congenial tone. "First of all, honey, it is not the church. The Mormon church has nothing to do with this thing. Maybe some wealthy members, but nothing official."

"How do you know that?" Anney could not hide the edge in her voice.

"Because two very reputable firms, one legal, the other accounting, verified last Monday night that the funds were not from any religious group. Those people have a national reputation; I'm sure they are not going to falsify their findings. The way they explained it, the people funding the project want us to determine if there is a strong influence of Near Eastern writing and some other criteria in the Book of Mormon. I frankly can't see how we can possibly finish this kind of study in six more weeks. But some seem to think we can. These other researchers are all business, I can tell you that."

Stephen enlivened his voice abruptly as he said, "Cheer up! Whatever the project, it's just another six weeks, then I'm home."

"Oh, that's great. . . . But Stephen, aren't you afraid to tamper with something like the Book of Mormon? How can you even handle the book, let alone study it?"

Stephen laughed. "Handle it? It's just paper and ink and a leather cover. There are no demons slithering through its pages—at least I haven't found any in mine."

"Don't trifle with me, Stephen Thorn, and don't patronize me." It was the stern, serious, no-funny-business Anney whom Stephen had known all his married life. "Oh, I wish we had turned down this project. I tell you, Stephen, no good will come of it. Does Dad know what you're doing?"

Stephen laughed for a moment before answering her jab. "Does Dad know? He sent me here, for heaven's sake. Does he *care* what I'm doing?"

"Don't be cynical with me. I just want to know if he knows about the Mormon connection in this project."

"Yes. He knew before I came. You act as if I were pushing drugs or something."

"I'm sorry, Stephen. I don't know. I do know it's not your fault that you have to study something as repugnant as this book. I certainly don't want to add to your burden."

Stephen felt like telling her that it wasn't all that bad, that he was being asked to find out some interesting things that he had not known before. After all, he had now read the entire book, and though it was hard reading, it did have some good points, false though they might be.

"Anney, I have to get off the line soon. Everybody else wants to call home, too. Why don't you let me talk to Dad for a minute?"

After a few more minutes of chat, Anney told Stephen to hold while she tried to ring her father's office. He was on a conference line and had asked not to be disturbed.

"Stephen, I can't get through right now; he's on another line. Why don't you call back when you can talk. I'll get off. Be sure you call Brenda, okay? I love you, Stephen. Do be careful. You're too good for that bunch down there."

"What a thought to leave me with. . . . I love you, too. I'll call back later. Bye."

The minutes slipped by. Anney couldn't focus on the layout. She kept thinking of Stephen and his new assignment. She would have spent her last breath trying to prevent his part in this Mormon scheme if she had known before he left. Why hadn't Daddy told her? But she knew why. Twenty years of seeing her bitterness— knowing that she blamed the Mormons for losing Chip—was why. *How could Daddy do such a thing? Did he need the money so much that he would risk letting Stephen be brainwashed?*

The door to her office stood ajar. Thirty minutes later it opened wide, and Anney's father, Bob, appeared in the doorway and said, "Sweetheart, Rita said you were trying to get me on the intercom a few minutes ago. I'm sorry. I was talking to Australia, Dr. Willey in Melbourne. He's so disappointed that I'm not going down to do the . . ."

Bob Moore stopped midsentence. He could see that his daughter was agitated, and he was sure he knew why. He quietly closed the door, sat down, and leaned back. It was nearly five o'clock. Moore sighed, knowing that this situation could not be handled swiftly. He would be late for his tennis game.

Haltingly, without looking up, Anney told her father about the call from Stephen. She was controlled—too controlled. He could see that she was angry with him. He waited until she could express herself.

At last she looked up, her mouth trembling. "Oh, Daddy, how could you do it? What if the Mormons get Stephen? Everyone knows they are aggressive in their recruiting efforts. The money is not worth it. Surely we don't need the money that desperately! I personally would give up whatever Stephen and I will get from it just to have him away from that group. Daddy, I want him home."

Bob stared uncomfortably up at the white squares on the lowered ceiling. He could never stand it when Anney cried, which, thankfully, wasn't often. He felt like he had betrayed his precious daughter. But why in heaven's name hadn't she given up this fierce resentment of the Mormons? That boy at Berkeley might have used his Mormon leader's counsel just to break up with her. He moved his lips in and out, rubbed his cheeks, and finally spoke: "I know you may have some concern about this odd assignment, honey, but frankly, I think it will do Stephen good to see just how phony this Book of Mormon really is."

Bob got up out of the chair and started back to the door. He turned and met Anney's eyes. "I have read the Book of Mormon. It lacks substance. Don't worry, Anney. Stephen will be fine. Besides, we need him there to improve our cash flow. I hate to say it, but we do need the money." He blew Anney a kiss with his fingertips. He looked at his watch to see if he had time to make the court by 5:30.

* * *

"Embedding is a formal characteristic in the book," Henry said, addressing the group on this Saturday morning session. Routine had set in. The session took on a classroom atmosphere. "If you recall, embedding is where each phrase in a series of phrases is grammatically or logically dependent upon the phrase just before it. In this way, phrases are linked together, making a chain. I got this out of a study by Perry—naturally, BYU again. Stay with me for a minute, and I'll explain this rather unique method of old Near Eastern writing. Turn to Alma 30:47; there's an excellent example of what I'm talking about in his writings."

While the rest turned pages, Henry walked to the imager, used his electronic pen, and drew a chain with five holes. He placed a number in each hole, and then he had Stephen read the verse while he wrote on the board.

"Now, if you read it on a five-line structure, let me show you what happens." The group followed Henry as he continued to write the phrases in parallel lines.

1. Therefore if thou shalt deny again,
2. behold God shall smite thee,
3.   that thou shalt become dumb,
4.   that thou shalt never open thy mouth any more,
5.   that thou shalt not deceive this people any more.

He stood back and pointed to each line. "Do you see it? It's here. Notice 'behold.' . . . Now the third line, 'that' . . . the fourth . . . 'that' . . . the fifth . . . 'that.' Do you see how each phrase is dependent on the phrase just before it? A beautiful example of what is called embedding. An ancient practice of phrasing."

"What did you say it's called, Henry?" Judith asked.

"Embedding," Henry replied with satisfaction. "It's an old Near Eastern practice. And I must say it is effectively used in the Book of Mormon from my limited observation."

"Have you found other examples?" Judith asked, intrigued.

"Oh, sure. Turn to . . ." With that, Henry continued to direct the group in locating examples of embedding in the Book of Mormon. Henry often led out with a group discussion of the Book of Mormon phrasing. He had the advantage over the others. His insight and research in Hebrew and his ability to find and secure documentation quickly allowed him to make the first presentation in his subject area.

What is he talking about? thought Stephen as he sat at the rear of the salon, trying to keep his mind on the topic at hand. It was comfortable in the down-filled chair. At this very moment, he frankly didn't care what the laborious Henry had to say about anything. Stephen had let his mind wander in and out of the topic of discussion. Stephen caught a phrase now and then, but his thoughts were of Anney. Lately, his wife had been on his mind.

It being Saturday, she was probably returning from her father's study, where she helped him by typing his notes for the Sunday sermon. He could see her svelte body sliding onto the seat of her BMW. He liked to watch her slide into the seat. He kept replaying the familiar scene in his mind.

"Ah, Stephen, you haven't queried me about the literary art of embedding," Henry said, not pleased with Stephen's lack of interest in the subject at hand.

"I'm sorry, Dr. Sy . . . I mean, Henry." Stephen jerked his head around to face Henry, a flush spreading over his face. "Were you speaking to me?"

"Yes, I was. I wanted to know if you needed a more elementary explanation of the ancient practice of embedding."

Stephen felt the barb but decided not to counter with an equally antagonistic statement. "I'm sorry, sir. My mind was on something else. I didn't catch all that you have been saying about the literary aspects of whatever it is you were trying to explain."

"Stephen," Henry blurted out, his irritation obvious from the tone in his voice, "we all need to apply ourselves to the task. We are, after all, receiving a handsome payment for our services. It is our job to dig up the facts to determine if there is a link here with antiquity. If you don't care to be part of this discussion, then please don't waste my time."

It had been years since Stephen had been brought up short

by a teacher. *Does he think he has the right to reprimand me?* "Just take it easy, Henry," Stephen said, unable to resist letting Henry know that everyone in the room was a peer. "I know you're fed up with me, but I'm just as much a part of this project as you. I just happened to let my mind wander, okay?"

"Quite right, old chap," Freddy said to Stephen. "You do have a bit of spunk. Hear, hear!" Henry stood silent, trying to compose himself.

Chapter Fourteen
The Minister

Week Two—Monday Morning

Dr. Polk moved to the front of the cabin of the Gulf Stream jet, standing behind the pilot and copilot as he spoke. He raised his voice to be heard above the swishing sound of air sliding off the skin of the aircraft.

"We'll soon be landing at Palmyra, New York. At 430 miles an hour, it doesn't take long. There will be two vans to meet us on the tarmac. One of the perks of going by charter is the extra service. No baggage check-in or pickup. The service takes care of those little extras. Besides, if we had come by commercial jet, we would have had to land at Rochester and drive over to Palmyra. As it is, we have been cleared to land at the small airport in Palmyra because our jet is within the range they can accommodate. Just thought you might like to know."

On his way forward in the plane, Peter had dropped into each lap a stapled packet of information entitled "Trip to Palmyra." It gave a description of the area around Palmyra, its history, and its importance in early Mormon history. On the last two sheets were photocopied a map of western New York and a regional map of the Palmyra area.

Peter raised his voice to be heard by all. "For your further information, we'll be staying at the Palmyra Inn; it's not exactly the Ritz, but it is comfortable. I stayed there last fall and thought their apple pie was as good as any my wife used to bake.

"First on our agenda is what Mormons call the sacred grove. It was in this grove that Joseph Smith claimed to have had the vision in which he said the Father and the Son appeared to him. From the grove we will go to the Smith home, which has been restored. It was there that he claimed the angel Moroni appeared to him. Yes, Dr. Stein?"

"Is the angel supposed to be the same person as the last scribe in the Book of Mormon?"

"Exactly. The account that Joseph Smith gave indicates that Moroni was a resurrected being who appeared to him as a glorified personage, a messenger from the Father—"

"Dr. Polk, are we supposed to keep a straight face while you explain this stuff? Don't get me wrong. I'm very much aware of religious shrines, but I hope you are not asking us to swallow this bullsh—" Bernie caught himself, not sure whether the word he was about to enunciate in its most crass, direct form was on Peter's no-no list.

Peter looked down at his copy of the agenda for a moment. As he looked up, a dozen wide eyes were fixed upon him, waiting for his response. "Dr. Stein, we will be visiting the Holy Land three weeks from now. I would hope that you will not be as irreverent there as you are here. I'm quite sure you won't be. May I ask all of you, wherever we happen to be—whether on the Mount of Olives or in a Catholic chapel in Yucatan—that you demonstrate by your demeanor a respect for all peoples' beliefs and traditions?" They got the message.

Peter then continued with the presentation that he had prepared. "Our next spot to visit will be the Hill Cumorah. If you recall, it was at that hill that Joseph Smith claimed he met the Angel Moroni, who had charge of the buried plates. The tour guide will give you a complete and detailed report of what transpired on that hill. Afterward, we'll return to our lodgings and rest. Tomorrow, we visit the printing press at Palymra. All in all, it should be beneficial and offer background information that I hope will help your study of the Book of Mormon."

* * *

"Anney, sweetheart, how are you?" Bob Moore purred as he rose to his feet to greet his tall, attractive daughter, who moved around the restaurant table to the place her father had reserved for her. Two of Moore's staff members also stood, while the two secretaries remained seated. Fred pulled out a chair for Anney.

"Daddy, I'm sorry I'm late, but I had to drop Todd off at the tune-up place to get his car." Anney returned her father's hug before sitting down. "How are you all?" She flashed a smile around the table, greeting each person by name. She knew her father's staff well.

"Have you had lunch, dear?" Moore asked.

"No . . . I mean, no, I'm not hungry. You people go right ahead. I'll just have coffee. Besides, it looks like you are about finished with your lunch, anyway."

Bob Moore raised his hand to the waiter to signal that his daughter would have coffee. "We've just asked for dessert; surely you'll try a little pie. I love Baker's Square pies. We've ordered our favorites: French Silk, Fresh Strawberry, Banana Cream Parfait, and Deep-dish Apple."

It never ceased to amaze Anney how her father had such perfect recall of so much trivia. He could give a minute description of every phase of yesterday's planning session or a complete rundown—names, addresses, and phone numbers—of several hundred key contributors to the television ministry. The slices of pie appeared on a large fiberglass tray, which the waiter placed in the center of the table. Besides the plates of pie, five additional dessert plates were also stacked on the tray as Moore had instructed.

"Just leave it right there. I'll hand them around the table," Moore instructed. The waiter left.

"Now then, let's all try each other's pies." With that, Bob Moore began to cut off small slices from each pie wedge with his table knife, placing them carefully on the empty dessert plates. It was a ritual Moore's staff had enjoyed as long as they had known him. Always during the serving of dessert, each person gave a portion to the others—whether it was pie, cake, or ice cream; it didn't matter. It was the variety that made the difference.

"Well now," Moore sighed. "Here, June . . . Fred . . . Rita . . ."

"Daddy, you do this so well. I've missed having lunch with you."

Anney had worked for her father part-time while the children were in elementary school. In those years, it was a different staff but the same ritual. Once a week he would take them to lunch. The day of the week varied, but it was Bob's way of saying, "Thanks for your help." He always picked up the tab.

Then, as Stephen's salary increased and the children's activities multiplied, they had agreed that family life was too hectic with both of them working. For several years, she had stayed home and been a full-time homemaker, chauffeur, and team mom. It seemed good to be back with the staff again.

Bob Moore flashed a smile at his daughter. His wide, handsome face had taken on a softer look in the past decade. Time had been kind to Bob. His hair was still full; the smooth lips and bright teeth gave off a wholesome, youthful appearance, belying his years. His eyes were piercing and direct. The camera crew filming his Sunday sermons would close in on those eyes whenever the Reverend Robert Moore's preaching became fervent. They loved his eyes and tried hard to reveal their natural intensity on camera. Bob had once been six feet three. Now, though it hardly showed, he had settled to six one.

At sixty-six, Bob showed no sign of slowing down. There was no time available in his life for getting old. He immersed himself in his activities with what appeared to be a rush to get finished. Golf: tee off at 6:10 a.m.; race through eighteen holes in 1 hour, 24 minutes, and 38 seconds. Tennis: on the court at 9:00 a.m.; three games and off. He played at sports like assembly line workers put together Fords. It was a go-go pace that few could match. Every evening at seven, if he did not have an appearance or a speaking engagement, Bob stopped in at the rest home in Pleasant Hill to see Nadia, his wife of forty years. She could no longer speak; the mishap during surgery had left her bedridden and helpless. When Bob couldn't make it to visit Nadia, Anney usually made an extra visit. Bob appreciated his only child, who had always been so devoted to him and the faith.

"I asked you to join us here so we could have a little chat with the staff. I don't think I mentioned it to you," Bob addressed the others, "though Anney already knows: this summer I will not be going to Australia; instead, I will remain right here and build the program. To do that, Anney has consented to come into the office and help me personally regain our former position as the number one Sunday gospel program in the Bay Area. I think you also know that our illustrious man, Anney's husband and my favorite son-in-law, Stephen, is taking my place at that seven-week conference. This is not convenient for Anney and me, but some sacrifices have to be made."

Bob took a bite of the strawberry pie, swallowed, and then continued. "Stephen was invited to participate in a research project in north San Diego. I'm sorry if I haven't been too clear on this project, but I understand our man is doing very well down there."

Bob related the information to the staff with a cheerfulness that belied his deep concern about the financial straits of the television ministry. "I just thought you would like to know what's happening over the next several weeks. Everyone will continue doing his or her best, and we'll get back on the charts."

This time Bob took a forkful of rich French Silk pie. The chocolate required a gulp of ice water to get it down. Bob smiled. "Great pie. Remember we like this one, June. . . . Well, this is not a meeting, so I will leave the details of what I have planned for our new image until I get back to the office at 3:30 this afternoon."

Everyone knew that was the signal for the lunch to break up. Bob retrieved his credit card after signing the slip. The staff members gathered their belongings and pushed their chairs back. June leaned over and whispered to Bob that he needed to stop by the bank on his way back to the office. As the group rose to leave, Moore took hold of Anney's arm and asked her to wait a moment. He signaled for the others to go on, that he wished to talk with Anney.

"Sweetheart," Bob began when the others had gone. He couldn't help noticing how charming and unpretentious his child was. "I need you to help me. I know you're not happy with the situation. I wanted to talk to you at the studio, but I didn't. If you are going to assist me these next few weeks, I need your wholehearted support. I know it's not easy for you to have Stephen off at that gathering. Don't think for a minute I don't miss him, too!"

"I'm puzzled, Daddy," Anney said. "In all honesty, I don't know why we are in a situation where Stephen is forced to endure something that is repulsive to him."

"Did he say that?"

"No. But it is. It has to be."

"Are you aware that this can be a great learning experience for Stephen? Think of the information on the fallacies of the Mormons he can amass. I intend to do another Mormon lecture series in the spring. Think of how we can script it with Stephen at my side, explaining in detail what he has uncovered."

"Daddy, are you aware that Stephen, right this very minute, is in western New York? He's traipsing about, being told all about the Mormons. Do you really think he is going to be told anything that you can use in an anti-Mormon lecture?"

"I don't like you to call my lectures 'anti-' anything. They are not that. I carefully research my material and lay out the facts. If the facts happen to be displeasing to those who would rather I not talk about them, then so be it."

"Please, Daddy. I don't know why I feel this way, but I sense that something is not right about this whole thing."

"It's the old Mormon boyfriend that keeps coming back to haunt us, isn't it, Anney?" Moore knew that he was tapping a raw nerve that had not numbed in over twenty years. He wished she had put that whole distressful affair behind her.

"You're not being fair, Daddy. That happened a long time ago."

"And you are still living with it. Honey, don't you think I understand? I said it then, and I'll say it now. That fellow, what was his name?"

"Chip."

"Yes, yes, Chip. He was wrong for you. Can you imagine your life now if you had married him?"

"Daddy, I love Stephen. This has nothing to do with Chip. I

was a child then." Anney realized her voice had raised in volume. She glanced over her shoulder to see if anyone was listening. No one was near their table. "I'm a responsible, loving wife and mother now. Do you think for a minute I'd pine for something that has nothing to do with my life now?"

"I'm sorry if I have upset you." Bob stirred in his chair. "I don't think this is going anywhere, not right now anyway. If I don't get to the bank, I'll be late for my appointment." Bob paused to study her face a moment. "My dear, dear, little Anney. Do you know you're everything to me? I love you so much that I can hardly stand to put you through these next six weeks, but I want you to know, I'm right here to help." Bob stood up, kissed Anney's forehead, and offered his hand to help her out of the chair.

"No, you go on. I just want to sit here awhile and finish my coffee."

"Fine." Bob left.

Anney closed her eyes and remembered it as if it had happened during lunch, just now.

* * *

Chip had parked his small MG in a loading zone. He didn't care if U.C. Berkeley campus security did give him a ticket. He had come to pick up Anney, the girl of his choice, and to rush her off to her parents' home in Walnut Creek so she could change for their date. Cat Stevens was appearing in concert, and he had tickets.

"We'll hurry," he assured her. The trip took fifteen minutes up through the lush hills of the East Bay region.

Chip waited downstairs for Anney. She would only be a minute. When Anney did come down ten minutes later, there was Chip in the living room, listening to the Reverend Moore.

"So you're one of those young men who go out to all the countries and instruct people in Mormonism."

"Well, sir, I was a missionary for two years in Germany, and I taught them about Christ."

"Hm . . . oh, here she is now, the lovely Anney Moore." Bob and Chip stood as Anney came in. "I was just getting to know a little something about your date, honey."

"Then you met Chip?" Anney said, caught off guard. "I think we'd better get going, or we'll lose our seats at the concert. Bye, Daddy."

Anney now recalled that her relationship with Chip had begun crumbling at that moment. A powerful televangelist speaking to a determined young Mormon. It wasn't the introduction she had planned for them to have. *What had I expected? What course could it otherwise have taken? I knew at the time they were worlds apart—worlds.*

"More coffee, ma'am?" the young waiter asked.

"No thanks, I'm late for work." Anney grabbed her bag and left.

*   *   *

Bob wished he could have stayed at the restaurant with Anney just a little longer. She hadn't expressed everything she needed to. *Maybe I don't want to hear all she's got to say.*

The San Francisco Trust and Fidelity Bank had been a trusted friend of the Reverend Robert Moore for almost three decades. Was the friendship ending? Bob wasn't sure. Had he come to the well too often? He dreaded this meeting with his long-time friend Clifford, a bank executive with whom Bob had an excellent rapport.

Bob entered the ornate lobby and saw Clifford in his office at the far end, door open, signaling for him to come in. The two friends conversed, and then Clifford went directly to the point: there would be a large principal-plus-interest payment due on the loan in three weeks—seventy-five thousand. Did Bob think he could make it?

Bob felt the easy, professional pressure being gently applied by his good friend and sometime tennis partner. At fifty, Clifford had thinning brown hair, drooping eyelids, and a pedantic manner that eased him about in the banking trade with uncommon agility.

"Cliff, you've got to give me an extension," Bob pleaded. "What if I pay the interest—say in three weeks—and you roll it over for another ninety days?"

"Actually, Bob, I don't make those decisions. They come from the board, and I'm not sure the board—"

"Listen, Cliff, you and I know that you have influence with the board. Now, all I want is for *you* to assure me that you will go to bat for me and get an extension—okay?"

Clifford sucked in air; his eyes narrowed on this man he admired, not so much as a businessman, but as a true motivator of other human beings, a man who could inspire one to achieve the impossible. So persuasive. Clifford studied Bob a moment longer and said, "Okay, I'll see what the board has to say."

Feeling defeated, Clifford leaned back in his leather chair and threw out a question. "Tell me, Bob, why is the ministry in more financial trouble than ever before? Oh, it has had its up and downs, but the swing up doesn't have the old momentum. Am I right?"

"It's the scandals surrounding televangelism. When you've got people like Bakker and Swaggart who have been slumming around in sleazy sex motels, or having affairs with some of their more vocal followers, the supermarket tabloids eat it up. When you come up with something that is totally unbelievable but true, their readership goes for it. People like to be wowed. You know, there's shock value to it. This has a negative impact on the rest of the ministries. People begin to say, 'Is ol' Robert Moore doing the same sleazy things?' Suddenly, a few contributors withhold their donations, and my ministry lands in the cellar."

"Let's hope, for our sake, that it isn't in the cellar. Just thought I would ask. Perhaps the board needs to know the reason for the downturn."

"Thanks for your help, Cliff. Are you free Saturday morning for a couple of sets?"

Chapter Fifteen
Palmyra

Week Two—Tuesday Evening

Palmyra had receded from the horizon thirty minutes earlier as the jet darted west into the glow of the late afternoon sun. Most of the group had settled in. Freddy had removed his seat belt and accepted the cup of tea offered by the steward. He felt it was relaxation time. The comfortable, well-designed interior allowed the passengers to swivel around to carry on a conversation facing each other. Judith was out of the circle but had turned about in her seat with her knees tucked under her and her chin on the headrest as she listened to Martha sum up her impressions of the Palmyra tour that they had concluded an hour earlier.

Martha mentioned how she had found it all rather interesting from a purely visual experience. The shrines were wholesome, the missionary guides were very friendly, and the replica of the Grandin press, which had printed the 1830 edition of the Book of Mormon, was fascinating. She was more impressed with the manner in which a printer worked to put together a book than she was with the intent of the visit, which she guessed was to allow the group to see firsthand the actual location where part of the translation had been made and the hill where the gold plates had been stored.

"I thought it was a very positive tour. I don't believe for a minute that Joseph Smith *translated* the book, you understand. But I'm satisfied he had his manuscript printed on an old press, like the one we saw," Martha concluded.

"Why don't you think he translated the Book of Mormon?" Judith asked with a tinge of sarcasm in her voice.

"Are you asking me? You of all people," Martha shot back with a huffy voice.

"All I'm asking is why *you* don't think he translated it."

"I not only don't think he translated the book," Martha stated with a voice of authority, "but I also seriously doubt that he wrote it."

"Why?" Judith persisted.

"Because if there is any truth to what those guides explained, Joseph Smith was too uneducated to write such a work."

"I disagree," Henry jumped in, ready to confront the issue. He had to turn his head far to the left in his front-facing seat to see the others in the rear. "I went to a performance at Purdue a couple of years ago, where they brought an unusual man on stage. It was one of those believe-it-or-not type situations. I had a hard time believing that he could really do what I saw him do, so after a while I just accepted what I saw and heard because I had no logical answer to explain it.

"You know what he did?" Henry went on without waiting for an answer. "He played the piano for us—very professionally. Then the guy who spoke for him said that this pianist could play anything he had ever heard. All he needed was to hear someone play it through once.

"A friend of mine on campus, who is a composer, wrote a piece that very day, took the music to the stage, played it from his score, picked up the score, and walked back to his seat. Only *he* had ever played that music. I believed him. Do you know what happened?

"This fellow, the pianist, sat at the same piano and played the music without a score. He played every note. He made a believer out of my musical friend, who kept telling me that he had given him nothing in advance. He had simply agreed to write and present an original piece of music at the performance. The master of ceremonies indicated that the man was an *autistic savant*. In most ways, he was severely retarded, but he had a gift for remembering and duplicating music, right down to the last grace note." Henry rubbed his right hand across the bald part of his high forehead, then said, "Perhaps Joseph Smith had some of those same traits. I think he read this document somewhere and repeated it back verbatim to his scribe, the last scribe . . . the one who did the ending—what was his name, Peter?"

Peter had been listening from the front of the aircraft, but had chosen not to involve himself in the chatter, except to clarify. "Oliver Cowdery."

"That's right, Oliver Cowdery."

"No, that isn't what happened. I disagree," Freddy said, pushing his body forward in the swivel seat. "I think Joseph Smith was a genius of the first water. He had to be. I've followed the man's interesting life from childhood up to his early death. He was an original genius on the American frontier. You do know, don't you, that he was only thirty-eight when the mob shot him. I have always said that the charm of the American frontier was its tolerance for new ideas, up to a point. Joseph Smith exceeded the limits of the frontier mentality."

They all got the distinct impression that Freddy was back in London, lecturing to his students, as he spoke. "But before they trapped him and shot him down in cold blood, he did some incredible things: he founded a religion, produced tomes of prophecy and scripture, built a beautiful city, established a military, and instituted a whole new set of mores for his people—including the practice of polygamy. Nauvoo was the envy of everyone traveling the Mississippi. Do you know what I think?" Freddy rushed on with his discourse. "As a student of nineteenth-century history, I'm convinced that with Mormonism growing at a sustained rate throughout the world, as it moves into the twenty-first century, it isn't going to be Lincoln they point to as the greatest man of the nineteenth century. He will be pushed aside. Joseph Smith will be the one. You have my word on that."

A snicker or two could be heard, but most listened to Freddy's insights. "With all that creative energy possessed by one incredible man," Freddy mused, "I think he could have written the Book of Mormon. I mean, Joseph was a great student of the Bible.

All he had to do was let his imagination run wild and give a variation on the Holy Scriptures. No, he wrote it—that's all there is to that."

"Then why didn't Joseph Smith take credit for the book?" Bernie asked. "You heard the guides back there. They insist that Joseph Smith said an *angel* gave him the plates and instructed him to translate them. The problem I have is why did he have to invent the angel? Now, as far as the use of those translating instruments he claimed to use on the plates . . . what were they called? I can't remember."

"Urim and Thummim . . . meaning interpreters or seer stones," Peter said, with no further comment.

"Thanks, Peter. You're right. Anyway, I understand why he would invent those. The use of those instruments gives the whole thing the mystic essence that would make it holy writ. But the angel, *never*. To me, that was not a good move on Smith's part."

"Oh, I think an angel gives great credibility to the whole scene, especially if you're creating a whole new religious sect," Judith interjected. "Remember, the angel came from God—he was a messenger. What more do you need to motivate people who are looking for the truth?"

Bernie had to have his say again. "Maybe we should accept the whole thing at face value. Angels appeared in the Old Testament. After all, Jacob wrestled with one as it states in the Old Testament."

"You don't really believe that, Bernie, not even about your kindred Jacob," Judith laughed.

"I didn't say I believed it; I simply said why not accept the account the way Joseph said he got the book? Then we drop it. Why do we have to worry about how the book got here? It's here, and we have to deal with that fact. We have to look at the book. Forget where it came from. This quick little trip here to New York has convinced me just how complex this whole thing is becoming. If we don't stick to our original goal, which is to show evidence that it is antiquity, then we're going to be in trouble timewise."

"But, Bernie," Stephen said, slightly reluctant to banter with these scholars, but not willing to sit and merely listen, "the angel is a factor in the whole account. He's not just any angel—he is General Moroni. He's the guardian of the plates. Do you know what I've been thinking? I'm frankly impressed with what we have uncovered so far in the Book of Mormon. The warfare alone indicates that the account is not as easy to set aside as I had hoped."

"Stephen," Bernie cautioned, "get back to reality. Remember, we don't have to believe anything; just look for evidence, that's all."

"I've been thinking about why great minds are not studying the Book of Mormon," Stephen persisted, no longer intimidated by Bernie. "For me, it's starting to get interesting; but for the intellectual, or even the bright ones, the biggest stumbling block is how Joseph Smith got the plates—an angel. In the twentieth century, it won't compute."

Stephen realized he was dominating the conversation, but he didn't care. "I say drop the angel bit. Wipe that story from the books. It might take the Mormons a generation to achieve total memory loss of the angel, but it would be worth it. Think of the minds that might take up a study of the Book of Mormon and join the religion. It would sweep the earth. Joseph should have only claimed he did it with divine instruments. In the age of electronics, those instruments don't sound half bad. They simply came with the record. That is not too farfetched. Do you get what I'm saying? But we're not yet into time travel. The Angel Moroni has to go."

"Spoken like a true public relations man," Freddy chuckled, eyeing the steward who was preparing food at the front of the cabin.

"Hey, don't laugh. I think I could pull it off," Stephen rejoined.

"Stephen makes a good point," Henry said. "We are now influenced by the story that Joseph got the plates from an angel. We can't conveniently drop that part. It is the one part that will cause us to have egg on our faces when we submit our reports after the project. We may substantiate internal evidences, but our peers will always say, 'But you surely don't buy the angel bit.'

"Another thing in response to Stephen's comment," Henry said. "It may be difficult to sell the world on angels appearing and so forth, but don't forget that in the traditional Judeo-Christian belief, angels have appeared to prophets. Look in the New Testament. When Peter, James, and John accompanied Christ to the Mount of Transfiguration, Elijah appeared with a host of other angels.

"No, Stephen," Henry concluded with a look of disapproval, "you may be right about eliminating the angel story from a public relations viewpoint, but there are an awful lot of Christians who are not ready to give up the account of what may have occurred on the Mount of Transfiguration. There is strong precedence for what Joseph Smith claims happened to him. The belief that God, the framer of heaven and earth, can jolly well appear to whomever He wants is deeply embedded in the Christian faith. Scripturally, God has done so before, and so have his angels. So, if Christians *really* knew the Bible, they would see nothing strange in Joseph Smith's experience. It seems to me that they would think it is blasphemy to suppose that God is bound by man's dictates, whether He can or cannot send heavenly messengers to earth."

Stephen wondered about Henry. He seemed to come on strong with firm convictions. *Does he really believe the Joseph Smith account?*

Henry, realizing he had been a little too serious, turned to Peter, who held an intense gaze after listening to Henry defend the appearance of angels, and commented, "Peter, tell us again, if Joseph Smith had the plates in his possession, why didn't he keep them? He could have displayed them for the whole world to see. Just think of the credibility it would have lent to the whole account. Why didn't he?" Henry disguised mockery in his voice as he toyed with Peter.

"Surely," Peter responded, "you have worked with the stern angels in Special Collections at Purdue enough to know that they do not let historical documents and books out of their sight, not for a minute. If you go to a table to use them, you must return them or suffer their wrath. It's all very simple: the plates were on loan from the special collections guardian angel, and so Joseph Smith had to return them."

They all laughed, realizing they had come full circle. It was time for the delicious-looking snack that the steward was setting up at the front of the cabin.

Chapter Sixteen
Chiasmus

Week Two—Thursday

Craig sat across from his attorney, gleeful that his father's secretary, Mary, had pulled up information that led to the monies that Bennett had placed with Finley & Southam, a Los Angeles accounting firm.

When Mary returned Monday from her brief mourning leave, Craig had instructed her to pull up all information, correspondence, and memos that his father had written over the past two years. He wanted anything that in any way mentioned the "Mormon project." Though uneasy, Mary had gleaned the files and found only one letter to Bennett acknowledging information about where the funds would be placed in reserve to pay all expenses of the project: estate, travel, and participants. No amount was listed, but the firm of Finley & Southam was. The other documents, letters, and materials yielded nothing of significance.

"How much is in that reserve account?" Matthew Sharp, Craig's attorney, wanted to know.

"It doesn't say in the letter. I'm sure it's a sizable amount—maybe a million. The only thing we have is what you see there," Craig leaned out of his chair and pointed his finger at the photocopy of the letter to Bennett.

"Well, this isn't going to be easy, but we'll try to get an injunction. I'll call a firm that I do business with in Los Angeles and tell them to get on it today. I think we can secure an injunction on those funds."

"How fast can an injunction take effect and what will it do?"

"It depends on the judge. But once Finley & Southam is slapped with an injunction, those funds are frozen until we get a judgment on the project. If we win the case, then those funds will come back to your father's estate. But it could take two weeks to get that injunction."

"Two weeks! I want it sooner than that!" Craig shouted.

"Listen, Craig, I will do my best. I'll even fly over there tomorrow morning, but first we have to file in California, and that takes time. I'll give you every ounce of energy I have, but I don't make the laws," Sharp said as he picked up the phone to call the law office in California.

* * *

Since Stephen had arrived in the exclusive suburb of San Diego over a week ago, the morning sun had not yet shone on Stephen while he jogged. It was the same refreshing, early morning marine layer that the Bay Area enjoyed. Stephen had just completed the gradual climb to the top of a hill where incredible homes graced the winding street. They were beyond anything he had ever seen. Someone had told him that the lady who lived in the sprawling home behind the walls to his left was the widow of the man who created the fast-food chain, McDonald's—the estate was valued at thirty million dollars.

There are homes of lesser value, Stephen thought as he pushed his body over the crest and started down the opposite side. *The one over here couldn't be more than a mere three million. Just a nice, comfortable little estate tucked away in these manicured hills. A little something for Anney. She'd go for that one.* Stephen reached the cul-de-sac, made a wide turn, and headed back toward *his* estate.

"Good morning," came a shout from Stephen's side.

"Oh . . . hi . . . ," Stephen blurted out, catching his breath. The man, Stephen surmised, must have just begun his jog from his driveway.

"I'm Martin Oren."

"Stephen Thorn." Stephen nodded a greeting to Oren. The two jogged for the length of the estate on their left when Oren said, "Do you live in the neighborhood?"

"Not really . . . ," Stephen panted. He hadn't done much talking while jogging. It interfered with his breathing, and he disliked anything that interfered with breathing.

"I'm just staying here at Fairbanks for . . . part of the summer."

"Oh, are you part of the group I heard about over at the Claybourn place?"

Stephen had heard the estate called Vista del Palma. He didn't know who owned the estate, and he frankly didn't care, but this friendly fellow seemed to know more than he.

"I don't know any Claybourns, but I am staying at the place at the far end of this street . . . the one with the black wrought-iron gates."

"Yeah, that's the one. I heard you guys are doing some kind of study."

Stephen continued to respond as his newly acquired, inquisitive companion kept probing. Where the road made a Y, Stephen jogged to the left to head directly for the estate; Martin Oren took the right.

"Hey," Martin shouted as he moved down the asphalt road away from Stephen, "I may see you again. Nice meeting you."

* * *

Henry ushered the six participants into the room and took the front chair usually reserved for Peter, who had not yet arrived. He had asked that Henry introduce the presenter from Columbia University.

Stephen felt refreshed. He knew, as did all serious joggers, that he experienced a high five minutes after completing his run, and it remained with him for the next hour.

"Tell me, Stephen, my boy, how was your little sprint around the ghetto?" Freddy asked.

"I don't *sprint*—I jog."

"Semantics, merely semantics."

"Who's up this morning?" Stephen asked, glancing down at the day's agenda.

Freddy looked over his shoulder and saw the man who would be the presenter talking with Peter in the foyer. "That fellow over there. He's steeped in Hebrew literature. He doesn't look too intelligent. Tiny little chap, don't you think? But I understand from Henry that he is a leading scholar on chiasmus."

"Ky . . . what?"

"You remember. Martha was mentioning it the other day on the terrace. Come to think of it, you may not have heard her tell us about this little literary gem she came across in the computer. She was impressed. Anyway, it has to do with a poetic form that Martha insists is in the Book of Mormon. It fits into her assigned subject, you know."

Henry introduced the speaker: Reuven Saul, Professor Emeritus, Hebrew Studies, Columbia University, and author of two volumes on poetic forms in Hebrew literature. The small professor eased himself into his subject, caressing his words—a man accustomed to taking his time and measuring every thought. Stephen could see that here was a scholar with a personal passion for the world of Hebrew writings.

Dr. Saul stood before the group with full knowledge that he was appraising the Book of Mormon. "Since my subject is chiasmus in the Book of Mormon, perhaps I should lead into it with something that you are all familiar with that borders on the literary form of chiasmus: 'Old King Cole was a merry old soul, and a merry old soul was he.' Dr. Saul's smile seemed canned. "Do you hear the rhythm in that little piece? It is easy to memorize and fun to recite. It is an inverted type of parallelism. It is simple to diagram: a b, b a." He wrote the letters on the electronic board and pointed to the X arrangement.

"Here's another example of the literary form that may be easy to follow." Dr. Saul wrote the following on the board and pointed out the pattern:

a. O **God,**
   b. **Break**
      c. Their **teeth** in their mouth;
      c. The great **teeth** of the young lions
   b. **Break** out
a. O **Yahweh.**

(Psalm 58)

Dr. Saul turned from the board back to the group and said, "Chiasmus, essentially, is the arranging of a series of words or ideas in one order and then repeating them in reverse order, in this manner." He pointed to the board again. "O *God* is **a**—then, *Break* is **b**—then, Their *teeth* in their mouth is **c**—then, The great *teeth* of the young lions is **c**—notice that it is at this point that we begin the reverse order. This second **c** is followed by *Break out*, and it is **b**—we continue reversing the order. The next is O *Yahweh*, which is **a**—and it completes the reverse order."

Saul paused to let this new concept take effect on the participants. Then he said, "This is chiasmus in its most elementary form; nevertheless, there is power in this little segment of Psalm 58."

Dr. Saul then asked that everyone look at the sheet he had passed out to the group. On the second page was typed a biblical passage from Genesis.

"You do see it?" he asked with a touch of excitement. Heads nodded.

"Here is a short one from the Book of Mormon in the book called 2 Nephi 29:13:

a. The **Jews**
   b. shall have the **words**
      c. of the **Nephites,**
      c. and the **Nephites**
   b. shall have the **words**
a. of the **Jews.**

"I think you have it now," Dr. Saul nodded approvingly as

his astute "pupils" compared their discoveries. "We can go on to some more complex works," he said, turning a page of his outline. Martha rapidly placed markers in passage after passage. *She could have taught this session*, Stephen thought, watching her.

"Now, there were several good reasons for the creation of chiasmus as a literary form of writing. One, it made it easier to memorize passages expressed in this form. The Hebrew tradition relied heavily upon oral presentations. Stories and messages were passed along by word of mouth. If you recall, long passages of the Torah were committed to memory. Chiastic groupings aided the transmission to memory. Also, it has a pleasing, aesthetic sound— don't you think? Notice this one taken from the Old Testament:

a. And all flesh **died that moved upon the earth,**
   b. Both **birds,**
      c. And **cattle,**
         d. and **beasts,**
            e. And every **creeping thing** that creepeth upon the earth,
               f. And every **man:**
                  g. All in whose **nostrils** was the breath of the spirit of life
                     h. Of all that was on the **dry land**
                        I. Died
                        I. And **was destroyed;**
                     h. Every **living thing**
                  g. That was upon the **face of the ground,**
               f. Both **man,**
            e. And **creeping things,**
         d. (And **beasts),**
      c. And **cattle,**
   b. And **birds** of the heavens;
a. And they were **destroyed from the earth**.

(Genesis 7:21-23)

Stephen looked down at his paper again. *What an interesting concept,* he thought. *I've read that passage a dozen times and never analyzed the structure.*

"Perhaps you are already aware," Saul went on, "that in ancient writings, the element of internal organization required some type of word structure; paragraphs, punctuation, capitalization, and other devices that modern man uses had not yet been created for the written language."

Dr. Saul stretched his neck and peered at Peter, who sat to the rear of the dining room, and said, "Is it true, Dr. Polk, that when the Book of Mormon was first submitted for printing, it lacked punctuation? A colleague suggested this when I told her I was flying out here to lecture on chiasmus in the Book of Mormon."

"That is not entirely true, but nearly so. Each chapter was one long paragraph with scant punctuation," Peter responded.

"There you have it—a form of antiquity."

Dr. Saul then had the group examine several examples taken from the Old and New Testament. He indicated that there were many more. He then asked them to turn to the next page of the handout to a Book of Mormon example: Mosiah 5:10-12.

a. Whosoever shall not take upon him **the name of Christ**
    b. must be **called** by some other name;
        c. therefore, he findeth himself **on the left hand of God.**
            d. And I would that ye should **remember** also, that this is the **name . . .**
                e. that **never should be blotted out,**
                    f. except it be through **transgression;** therefore,
                    f. take heed that ye do not **transgress,**
                e. that the name **be not blotted out** of your hearts. . .
            d. I would that ye should **remember** to retain the name . . .
        c. that ye are not found **on the left hand of God,**
    b. but that ye hear and know the voice by which ye shall **be called,**
a. and also, **the name** by which he shall call you.

Stephen heard the words as they flowed meaningfully from Dr. Saul's lips. They sounded so right. For a brief moment, something about the passage sounded familiar, beautiful, full of wonder.

Do I know Christ's voice? The thought faded as Dr. Saul began to comment on that passage.

"So as you see, the pattern is: a b c d e f—reverse order—f e d c b a. You may be interested to know that this passage is only one example of the more complex chiastic structure of the entire, several-chapters-long speech given by King Benjamin in the section or 'book' of Mosiah in the Book of Mormon."

Stephen turned his eyes abruptly to Bernie, and Bernie nodded. Then Stephen leaned over and whispered, "Freddy, may I look at your Book of Mormon?"

Freddy shoved it across the table for Stephen to thumb through. He had not actually looked at the first edition since he had been given his copy the first day. *How stupid of me not to take the time to compare the two versions,* he thought. *I'm always playing "catch-up." I've got to pour on the oil—Peter deserves better from me.*

An hour later, Dr. Saul had graphically shown the group that chiasmus was a literary form that spread throughout the writings of Nephi, Mosiah, Alma, and Mormon, with some samples in other writings in the Book of Mormon as well.

"For those of you who are Christian, you will find one of the best examples of chiasmus in the writings of Alma. Do you recall that Alma was suffering under the great pain of having committed wrongs? Then he has an awareness of Christ and comes out of his depressed state and moves to a joyful state. This is on page 8 of your handout. We will only look at the inverted part beginning with 'k' back to 'k.'

"I might add that this chiasmus encompasses the entire chapter of Alma 36. It is what I would consider a classic. Among the Mormon scholars at Brigham Young University, there are those who consider this the finest example of the poetic form of chiasmus. You would have to read the entire chapter and diagram it out to get the full impact. Here it is in a condensed form. Only key phrases are presented. You may compare it with the full text:

k. Born of God
　　l. I sought to destroy the church
　　　　m. My limbs were paralyzed
　　　　　　n. Fear of being in the **presence of God**
　　　　　　　　o. Pains of a damned soul
　　　　　　　　　　p. Harrowed up by the memory of sins
　　　　　　　　　　　　q. I remembered **Jesus Christ, a son of God**
　　　　　　　　　　　　q. I cried, **Jesus, son of God**
　　　　　　　　　　p. Harrowed up by the memory of sins no more
　　　　　　　　o. Joy as exceeding as was the **pain**
　　　　　　n. Long to be in the **presence of God**
　　　　m. My limbs received strength again
　　l. I labored to bring souls to repentance
k. Born of God

Stephen had read that before but had not noticed the great turning point in Alma's life. He saw clearly now that Alma had come to Christ. He had cried out the name Christ. *If a Mormon prays sincerely to Christ, would he receive an answer to his prayer? Of course he would, or God would not be just.* Stephen shook his head to bring his thoughts back to the technicalities being discussed. *No, don't let yourself get emotionally involved; stick with the agenda. Forget what the scripture says. The agenda is chiasmus. I'll have to admit this chiasmus stuff is pretty impressive.* Stephen pulled his thoughts back to the issue at hand—the technical literary form of chiasmus.

Martha stirred in her place at the table, agitated by the discussion. Unable to wait for a formal question-answer period, she continually questioned the whole concept and whether the Book of Mormon chiasmus had the same lyrical quality as, say that in the Old Testament. Did it seem to Dr. Saul that it was of the same level of sophistication as that in Old Testament or, for that matter, in the Greek and Hebrew?

"I have to be candid with you," Saul said, pulling his tiny body to its maximum height. "The chiasmus I studied in the Book of Mormon comprises perhaps the most intricate selections of this literary art form that I have ever seen. I took the liberty of meeting a month ago with the leading authorities on Book of Mormon chiasmus, Welch being the most astute—he's at Brigham Young University. This gracious man spent five hours with me, showing me literary forms that I have not even expressed to you because of time constraints and complexities of the form, but I have come to appreciate what is found inside the Book of Mormon. Without being too technical, may I quote Welch on what he explained to me about 1 Nephi 17:36-39?" Fingers flipped through pages to find Nephi.

"Listen to me first. Don't worry about following me yet," Saul cautioned the group. "You asked me how sophisticated chiasmus is in the Book of Mormon. I'll tell you what I learned from Welch about 1 Nephi 17:36-39. According to Welch—and by the way, I rechecked everything that he told me—Nephi masterfully combines direct parallelisms with inverted parallelisms. Parts A and A', as we designate the reverse line, each contain two directly parallel thoughts. Parts B and B' are built of four poetical lines, each containing three parts. They are inverted when they reappear the second time."

Stephen mentally dropped out of the discussion. His mind could not grasp what Dr. Saul was explaining. The man might as well have been explaining some mathematical problem. Then he realized that Saul wanted to demonstrate the complexities of the passage, so he had purposely gone zipping over the heads of most. Stephen got the distinct impression that Martha didn't really understand what he was explaining, either.

Five minutes later, Dr. Saul concluded by finishing a detailed diagram of Alma 41: 13-15. "Alma here gives a clever twist by not only reversing the order, or, as Welch says, 'Alma pairs two lists of four terms and reverses their order at the same time. Alma writes a list of pairs and then a pair of lists.' A clever fellow, this Alma. He is among the finest writers of chiasmus that I have ever studied. Madam," Saul said, looking directly at Martha, "I hope I have answered your question."

She nodded, a little bewildered with all that he had expounded.

"Yes?" Dr. Saul pointed at Bernie.

"How difficult is it to write chiasmus?" Bernie wanted to know, his tone giving the impression that anyone, given proper training, could do it.

"I should warn you that even the most technically skilled writers have difficulty giving it the lilt and rhythm that is so vital to the form. If someone has been properly schooled, and this would require enmeshing oneself in the literary culture where it is recited—something we in this country do not have access to—then I suppose with some degree of talent one could write chiasmus. Yet there is more usage of chiastic form in the book of Alma than in all the book of Isaiah in the Old Testament, though I admit that Isaiah has tradition on his side. For example, look at this passage:

For my thoughts are not your thoughts,
Neither are your ways my ways, saith the Lord.
(Isaiah 55:8)

"This is a simple Isaiah classic. And, of course, he has others that are much longer. But none of his is any more complex than I have found in the Book of Mormon."

Martha raised her voice, "I have sat here fascinated by this whole presentation, and I'm not easily fascinated by anything."

Freddy scribbled for Stephen: "No truer words were ever spoken."

"It seems to me," Martha said, "you are saying that this ancient literary form was in vogue in the nineteenth century."

"No, I didn't say that. It has never been in vogue in Western literature. It is predominantly a Near Eastern literary form, though it is found in the Orient. In fact, the Western world knew little about this literary form until the mid-nineteenth century, and even then it was confined to Europe. Of course, it was in the Bible, but there is no evidence that anyone in America understood chiasmus in 1830, the year the Book of Mormon was published. Is that not correct, Dr. Polk?"

"1830 is correct." Peter beamed, listening to this man who had nothing to gain from explaining that Joseph Smith could not have known the literary form.

"Then how do you explain the presence of this chiasmus in the Book of Mormon?" Henry asked, caught up in the moment.

Dr. Saul made a slight squeak of laughter and said, "Oh, my goodness, I can't explain that. That wasn't part of my assignment. All I know is that it enhances interpretation of Mormon scriptures and is expertly executed in that book. It is excellent chiasmus."

"Yes, please," Saul said, pointing to Freddy, who had politely raised his hand.

"Considering your impression that the Book of Mormon has excellent chiasmus, would you use it in your curriculum at Columbia while teaching this form of literary expression?" Freddy knew the answer before asking the question.

"You do understand that I have retired from active teaching," Saul reminded Freddy.

"Yes, but you do appear as a guest lecturer, do you not?" Freddy pressed the issue.

"I hesitate to give you a definitive answer to your question. I . . . uh . . . have given this some thought because, as I indicated, the chiastic form in the Book of Mormon is outstanding, but . . . well . . . I would have a problem presenting these insights in a formal classroom setting, say at Columbia."

"Why?"

"Ah . . . the source of the material would trouble me," Dr. Saul stumbled about in his answer. "I cannot substantiate who wrote them and where they came from, so I feel that it would place me in a rather awkward position to teach them in a classroom."

"Are you saying that it matters a great deal where certain literary forms originate to decide whether to teach them?"

"I'm sorry, but I really didn't come here to debate the issue of whether I would teach these as examples of good chiasmus."

"Dr. Saul, you have come from praising chiasmus in the Book of Mormon by using the terms *excellent* to *outstanding* to *good*." Freddy bore home with his statements. "Are we to assume that you are vacillating on your opinion of just how laudable the chiasmus is in the Book of Mormon, say, in relationship to the Old Testament?"

"I have not changed my opinion about the excellent work that has been done in the Book of Mormon. My chief reason for not wanting to teach it in an academic setting on the university level has more to do with the Book of Mormon's origin."

"And what is its origin?"

"Why, anyone who has studied the history of the book knows that Joseph Smith claimed to have translated it from gold documents he received from an angel."

"Gold plates. He definitely called them gold plates, not gold documents. They were the type commonly used in Mesoamerica as a material on which to record a history of a civilization, that is, before the Spaniards melted them down into bullion and shipped them back to Spain," Freddy retorted with scorn in his voice.

"I see, gold plates. At any rate, one can hardly take seriously a document that has come to us in such an unorthodox manner," Dr. Saul persisted. "Wouldn't you say?"

Freddy threw up both hands and bowed his head slightly toward Dr. Saul at the other end of the long table. "I just wanted to know your reason. Thank you ever so kindly, doctor."

Chapter Seventeen
Day Trip

Week Three—Tuesday

The olive orchards stretched out for miles on either side of the highway as Stephen pointed the Toyota Camry toward the city limits of Lindsay, California, situated at the foot of the Sierra Nevada Mountains, where groves of citrus, olives, almonds, and vineyards of grapes crowded the valley floor. Someone had recently told Stephen that the San Joaquin Valley produced enough fruit to supply the entire United States. It was verdant with growth.

The approaching highway sign on Stephen's right declared LINDSAY, CALIFORNIA—World's Biggest Olive Producer.

Good. I only want to deal with the big-league players. Now, if the map is right, I go about a quarter of a mile, turn west a half a mile, then I should be at the Lindsay plant.

The plant was exactly where the map Stephen had picked up at the rental office said it would be. It had taken him three hours to go from the estate to Lindbergh Field, LAX, and Visalia. Not too bad, Stephen figured.

The receptionist asked Stephen to go into Mr. Burger's office; he was expecting him. Burger was ten years older than Stephen and somewhat thick in the waist. He was friendly and helpful.

"Now then," Burger began, after offering Stephen coffee or juice—he'd had enough coffee on the plane, so he took apple juice—"I have never been asked to share my interest in the history of the olive, except once in my daughter's fifth-grade class. As I told you on the phone, if I can't answer your questions, perhaps someone else can because we have men working here from Europe and the Near East."

"That's why I'm here. I would like to get your understanding of raising olives and maybe talk to one of your men from the Near East."

"How can I help you, Dr. Thorn? What can I tell you about the background of the olive tree?"

"This may sound a little far-fetched, but I need to know about the horticulture of olives to complete an assignment I'm compiling for a group. Specifically, I have to learn about the propagation, cultivation, pruning, and harvesting of the olive tree. I'm sure you are qualified to explain the European olive tree, which I understand is the most common here in Lindsay. First, are olives grown in any part of the United States other than California?"

"Virtually none. Maybe in the Yuma area of Arizona, but that would be it. It's strictly a matter of climate. We have the ideal Mediterranean climate for raising olives."

"It's the Mediterranean area that I want to talk about."

With that, Stephen took Burger through a brief explanation of the challenge he faced of trying to determine whether the Allegory of the Olive Tree was accurate in its description of pruning, grafting, dunging, and harvesting. Burger listened to Stephen retell the account in Jacob 5. He was engrossed in the account and noted the ancient problems of raising olive trees.

"Interesting account about how the master of the vineyard goes out, gets the wild olive branches, and grafts them into the main trunk." Burger leaned forward with his elbows on the desk and twirled his yellow pencil as he spoke. "We don't do that, of course, but I have read about that method. It is usually done in the Mideast, from what I hear.

"Dr. Thorn, the person who could really answer your questions is out in the plant. You need to meet Harvey, Harvey Barak from Lebanon. He's the fellow I told you about on the phone. He has worked here for the past twenty years. He'd love to return to his country, but he says they are killing each other and he can't take his family back. Would you like to meet him?" Burger stood up and looked through a window into the processing room. Spotting the man he was looking for, he moved toward the door, motioning for Stephen to follow.

They sat together among shiny vats, pipes, and the scent of damp salt. It was not yet processing season, so the employees were refitting parts and cleaning the stainless steel riggings, pipes, and vats that would soon be fired up to process table olives.

Harvey Barak, a man in his mid-fifties, listened to Stephen explain about the grafting, pruning, and burning of dead branches of the olive trees in the allegory. His head nodded as Stephen read the verses. When Stephen concluded reading the account, he asked, "Is there any place that you know of where they raise olive trees in this manner?"

Barak nodded eagerly, "Yes, yes, I do know of places where the people still work the trees as you have read to me. In my country."

"You mean in Lebanon? Do they farm the olive vineyards the way it is described in this book?"

"Yes, oh yes. Not in my country only; in Syria they do it the same as the book says. And when I was a soldier and we were at the border—you know, the border of Israel—there, too, the Palestinians do also."

"Are you sure they farm olive trees this way in Israel?" Stephen probed, knowing he would be in Israel in a week.

"They did when I was there. Maybe no longer now." The man's leathery face brightened as he revealed what he thought Stephen wanted to hear.

Stephen definitely wanted to know everything the man could remember about the old way of farming olives.

"In my country and other countries, the olive farmers still go out to the hills and bring back wild olive branches to—what is your word—when you put the branch in the mother tree?"

"Graft," Burger volunteered.

"Yes, yes, that is the word. They still graft in the wild olive branches. The old farmers say that it adds life and causes the fruit to be big and full of oil. It is done this way in the old villages that never change."

* * *

When Stephen pulled back onto the highway in the rented Camry, he knew his next major step was to locate a village in Israel that farmed olive orchards the way he had just heard Harvey Barak explain.

He settled back in the seat and flipped the radio to a San Francisco station. The disc jockey was telling his listeners what a glorious afternoon it was beside the bay. *I'd love to go home, if only for an hour.*

* * *

Stephen drove out of the airport in Oakland at 4:20, elated that he had been able to change his flight plan. The traffic on Freeway 24 had started to congest, but shortly after he left the tunnel near Orinda, it was seventy miles an hour all the way to Lafayette and home. He rationalized that he probably wouldn't have taken the flight from Visalia to Oakland if he had found a direct flight from there to San Diego. Had he taken his planned flight, he would have had a two-and-a-half-hour layover at LAX before boarding a flight to San Diego. Here in Oakland he could catch a direct flight at 9:30 and still be back at the estate by 11:30. *Who are you kidding, Thorn? You'd have come home no matter what. It was just too tempting. . . . I can't wait to have Anney's warm body next to me.*

Stephen felt like a kid out of school as he sped toward home. He had not called Anney or Todd to tell them he was coming. He would surprise them.

* * *

"I don't like the way this investigation is going," Craig grumbled to Sharp. The attorney had dropped in to give Kline a full briefing on the slow progress of the injunction and the difficulty in locating either the estate or the bank account that held the remainder of the funds.

The lawyers in Los Angeles had filed the lawsuit and requested of the judge an injunction on the funds at Finley & Southam. Now Sharp was telling Craig the judge would not hear the case for at least two weeks. Sharp summarized the realities of the predicament with a shrug.

"Are you telling me we have to sit around and wait for some stupid judge to move on this thing?" Craig demanded. "Why?"

"Because that is the soonest any judge is going to act on something like this. When he reads the case, he'll see that most of the funds will not be paid until the project is over. The project has at least another four weeks to go. So the judge will want to know why the rush. It'll take a couple of weeks, but I think we can block Finley & Southam from issuing checks on those funds, or however they plan to do it." Sharp looked at his pad, then said, "Now, as far as the location of the group is concerned, investigators are certain they are in the Southern California area. We know that much from Polk's sister in Salt Lake, who went on and on about her exciting brother. They haven't made a breakthrough yet."

"Then maybe we need to get some fresh investigators on this."

"Don't rush it. These people in L.A. are good. I did as you requested: I offered a bonus of ten thousand dollars if they come up with the location within the next two weeks." Sharp was obviously frustrated with the entire situation. "They are working their tails off out there, okay? Those people are using the best systems available. They have a computer search going on—checking out all instructors at Brigham Young University who teach anything related to the Book of Mormon. They are tracking down everyone who is out of town, anywhere, and asking family and friends where they have gone."

"Do you think only Brigham Young professors are going to be at the project? What about others? Maybe there are professors from other universities who will be there." Craig wished he had paid more attention to the details when Dr. Polk explained it that day in his father's office. He had been too concerned about getting his father out of it to listen to the details.

"That's a thought. I thought it was a Mormon project and

only Mormons would be in it."

"Did I tell you that?"

Sharp shook his head as he mulled that over and thought. *Of course others could be involved.* Then he said, as he continued to make his report, "The third thing: We haven't a clue as to where Bennett deposited the rest of the money. But I doubt if he has dipped into that account, especially if your father was a signer." Sharp tossed his pad on the desk and looked up at Craig, "So somewhere in Southern California there is a tidy little account that only Bennett knows about."

"And Bennett—I *hate* Bennett—isn't it highly irregular for one lawyer to control three million dollars of a client's funds?"

"It's not the norm, but it happens. Remember, Bennett was your daddy's fair-haired boy."

* * *

The key slipped familiarly into the lock. Stephen pushed the door open as he had done so often before. "Anyone home?" he shouted in the cozy entrance hall. Suddenly he had the impression that he had lived most of his life in a cramped space. The entire downstairs of his house would fit into the entrance hall and salon of the estate. Still, it was home.

"Dad! Dad! Is that you?" The voice came from the kitchen. It was so friendly and sounded so mellow and rich. From around the corner came a six-foot-two, blond, athletic-looking seventeen-year-old. The mouth was one large grin. "Hey, hey, Dad. All right!"

Stephen felt a surge of emotion. He hadn't realized how much he had missed his son. With arms wide open, Stephen grabbed his son and held him tight. He had his mother's coloring and easy smile.

"Wow, what a great surprise. Does Mom know you're home?"

"No. I thought I'd surprise her."

"Well, you sure surprised me. Did you quit that nerdy assignment? Mom is hoping you will."

"Naw, I'm just home for a few hours. I was lucky and

caught a flight here. When is your mother due home?"

"I don't know. Probably in half an hour. I was about to leave. Jim and John and me are going to the all-star game tonight, . . . but if you are only going to be here a couple hours, I can call 'em and tell 'em I can't make it."

The two walked into the living room arm in arm. Stephen let go of his tall son and leaned on the back of the sofa that faced the fireplace.

"Are you kidding? I don't want to spoil your plans. I wish I could go with you. Golly, you're a good-looking kid." Stephen reached over and lightly pinched Todd's cheek. "No way—you go on. I'll wait here for your mother. Hey, though, . . . are you going to come down in two weeks and stay at the Hotel Del Coronado with the family? They say it's the best."

"Yeah, I think so. Mom says it's all paid for and we can really live it up. A limo at the airport, all we can eat, room service, the beach, chicks everywhere—sure, I'll be there, Dad."

In another five minutes, Stephen had Todd out the door and on his way to his friends and the all-star game at Candlestick Park. He then went up to the bedroom, showered and shaved, threw on the cotton, short-sleeved shirt that Todd had given him for Father's Day, and felt like he was in paradise.

"Todd?" came Anney's voice from the hall downstairs.

"It's me, honey." Stephen appeared at the top of the stairs and saw the most beautiful person he had ever known, her face showing a mixture of shock and joy. In three bounding steps, they were in each other's arms.

* * *

The late afternoon breeze coming through the bedroom window puffed the curtains out like sails. Stephen felt warm and satisfied as he cradled Anney's body close to his. "What luck ol' Todd had plans tonight," he murmured in her ear. "I mean, I love him to pieces, but I *needed* you . . . all to myself. . . . Mmm . . . you smell sooo good. I've missed you, sweetheart."

Anney was proud of herself. In the two precious hours that

they were together—in the bedroom and later during dinner—she said nothing about the project. Not until Stephen said he had fifteen minutes before leaving for the airport did she fall apart on the issue of his staying in San Diego another four weeks.

"I'm so concerned. What must they be drilling into you, Stephen? Aren't you concerned about your beliefs? Have you evaluated your feelings and what this thing could be doing to you?" Her anxieties poured out, unchecked.

"Whoa, you sound like the Mormons have their hooks into me. There is only one Mormon down there; the rest of us are scholars. Well, I may not be a scholar, but I'm associating with people whose faith ranges from no faith to a Jew to a Unitarian to a . . . Sweetheart, don't you have any confidence in my ability to carry out something like this without letting it get personal?"

"I hope so. Oh, how I hope so." Anney stood by the kitchen counter, slipping some chocolate chip cookies she had baked the night before into a plastic bag for Stephen. He reached around her and grabbed a cookie, along with her hand. He lifted her hand to his cheek, then kissed it gently. Hungrily, he pulled her close and kissed the full lips, now devoid of lipstick.

Anney responded as she had earlier, with full feelings of love and physical passion for this wonderful man. They embraced a long time under the glaring lights of the kitchen ceiling. Finally, Anney rested her head on Stephen's shoulder and said, "You know, Stephen, you just might be in trouble with that leader down there for slipping home for a couple of hours. . . . What's his name?"

"Peter, Dr. Peter Polk. You don't really care if I am in trouble," Stephen grinned. "As a matter of fact, if I understand what I'm hearing, you'd like me to get kicked out of the project, anyway. True, I have violated the rules by coming here. But you made me do it—you and your sexy body."

"Well, Daddy sure doesn't want you to get kicked out of the project. He's really counting on that money coming in." Anney moved away from Stephen's embrace, zipped the plastic bag shut, and handed the cookies to Stephen. "I don't know when I've seen him so agitated over money. So you'd better get, for Daddy's sake. But I'll be so glad when this project is over and we're back together again as a family." She turned, and with her back to the counter, reached out to Stephen one more time. "Don't forget how much I love you."

* * *

"We meet again." Stephen was breathing hard as he pulled alongside Martin Oren, who was gliding downhill toward the guard gate. Stephen remembered that he was a friendly fellow. Although he didn't like jogging and talking at the same time, he decided to make an effort to greet the man. This probably would be the last time he would run into Oren, since he planned to start jogging an hour earlier, beginning tomorrow. He felt he was crowding the time he had allotted for showering and getting ready to attend sessions on the project.

As the two joggers reached the guard gate, they whirled around and started back toward the Y in the road. They soon overtook two teenage girls who were struggling up the slope.

"Think they have their hearts into jogging?" Stephen smiled, jerking his thumb toward the girls.

Glancing at the girls, Martin shouted, "Hey, Victoria, who's your friend?" The dark-haired, shorter girl on the right turned her head as she continued to jog with her friend.

"Hi, Bishop Oren," her musical, young voice rang out. "How are you this morning? This is Chrissi, my best friend."

Bishop Oren? What does she mean by the title bishop? Is he some kind of church official? . . . Bishop?

"Hi," Chrissi managed, flushed and obviously out of breath but very attractive.

"When you girls finish your run, you can come over to my house and lift weights," Oren taunted. "Have you seen the weight room in my garage?"

"Sorry, we're not into lifting weights."

The girls peeled off two houses later and stumbled up the driveway to Victoria's metal gate, which opened electronically as they neared.

"So you have weights at your place?"

"That's right. Why don't you come over and work out on them when you have time?"

"Hey, I'll think about that. Thanks." Stephen had reached his turnoff.

"See ya," came Martin's farewell.

Chapter Eighteen
Impressions

Week Four—Monday

The Daniel Knight Investigative Service on Beverly Drive in Los Angeles had taken on the case of what the chief investigator, Knight himself, called the Mormon Project investigation. Knight had put one of his best investigators on the case when he first received it ten days earlier. Sharp, the lawyer from Arizona, had personally called to say that his client had offered a ten-thousand-dollar bonus to his firm if he could locate either the estate where the research conference was in progress or the bank that held the Mormon funds—more than a million dollars—within the next ten days. That kind of incentive sent the project to the top of their investigative cases, with what Knight called "red priority." The staff knew that meant it was a hot item and that everyone would be expected to help whenever needed. It meant late-night strategy sessions and lots of overtime without much extra pay.

"Give me everything you've uncovered so far," Knight asked Mort Johnson, the investigator he had assigned to the case. Knight and Johnson were both seasoned detectives who had been with the LAPD for over twenty-five years each. Dan Knight had built his agency mostly on marriage problems, some corporate crimes, and, occasionally, a serious insurance case or some silk-stocking affair among the truly well-heeled in Beverly Hills, Bel Air, or Westwood. He assured his clients that his services were "professional and confidential."

Knight perused the Mormon Project file, closed the cover, and demanded, "Is this everything you've got on the case after two weeks?"

"Hey, Dan, this is a tough nut to crack. You've got a guy who is covering his tracks. Notice that our phone bill ploy backfired. Boy, did that gal at USWest give me a hard time when I called and told her I was Polk and wanted a photocopy of my calls for the last three months. She must have checked with Polk or something. Anyway, it blew up in my face. And what's more, Polk's married children won't talk to nobody. The old man must have called the whole bunch. I can't get anywhere. You know these Mormons are as tight-lipped as the Mafia."

Mort leaned back and lit a cigarette before he continued his explanation of the case. "I am flying up to Salt Lake City tomorrow to talk with Polk's sister. I know you hate the flying expenses, but the guy does live in Utah."

"I didn't say that," Knight said defensively. "All I ask is that you come up with something we can get our teeth into. You know what I mean. And I want it soon. These people are willing to pay for top-notch service, and we can give it to 'em—if we work smart."

"What about the BYU professors who might be part of the project, besides Polk?" Knight asked.

"I've chased down, by phone, everybody on the religion faculty. This summer, they are all over the globe, and those that are around have never heard of the project. Maybe I should take an extra day and go down to BYU while I'm in Salt Lake. If you want me to, I will."

"I think you should. Yes, do that," Knight agreed.

"As far as that phantom bank account that's supposed to have at least a million in it," Mort continued dragging on his Marlboro, "I'll need some direction on that one. It isn't easy to get into that circle of people; they love frustrating little guys like me, if you know what I mean."

"Yeah, I'll give that some thought. I'll probably put Heidi on it. Last year she found some money stashed away in an account that a husband was holding out on his wife in a divorce thing. I'll talk to her. You keep bird-dogging the location of that estate, and she can try her hand at finding the hidden account."

"You're positive that account exists?"

"Mort," Knight sighed, tired of talking, "I only know what they tell me." He shrugged and then said, "By the way, this attorney, Sharp—he thinks there may be some professors that have nothing to do with the Mormon school who might be part of the group. I asked him if he wanted to spend megabucks to do a computer search of major campuses across the nation and phone to see if anyone pops up who might be involved in the Mormon project."

"What'd he say?"

"He said that he would talk it over with his client and let me know. Can you imagine how many names you'd have to sift through to find one person who is at that project?"

* * *

The building's interior was Spanish, with brown tile and heavy, dark-stained beams in the ceiling. Club meetings, weddings, and parties of all kinds were held here almost nightly. Use of this center was one of the perks of life at Fairbanks Ranch. The afternoon sun glistened on the man-made lake that stretched from the bay windows to a grass-covered mound fifty yards to the west.

"Tell me again why we came over here to listen to this guy talk about the Arabian desert," Stephen asked Bernie while the two sat watching a muscular man in his thirties adjust the lighting.

"Do I look like I know anything?" Bernie replied, slouched in a large wooden chair. Three rows of matching chairs had been set up in front of a large-screen television set.

Stephen paid little attention to Bernie's caustic reply. It was purely show. Stephen had come to admire this professor of war.

"You know, Bernie, you really ought to take up jogging. It would improve your disposition."

"Do I have to put up with this suburban health advice? Save me the lecture."

The desert presentation thrust the group into a poignant

view of ancient travel and human endurance. The speaker Henry introduced had been in the Arabian desert during the fall months the previous year. He had gone by way of Land Rover with a group of rugged adventurers on a grueling trip through the most forbidding regions of the south-central Arabian desert and had returned to report his experiences.

Stephen wondered how Polk ever got hold of this young fellow, whose blond beard and coarse, tanned skin witnessed his penchant for the out-of-doors. His name was Conley Wilks, and his background was world geography, University of Arizona, Tucson. There was a rugged charm and earnestness about the man that put everyone at ease.

While the VCR projected images onto the oversized screen, Wilks narrated the scenes. First he explained that he had taken a route in his Range Rover from downtown Jerusalem to the northern tip of the Red Sea. Since it was a few months after the Gulf War, he had to go through several road-blocks. At each barricade he had been required to explain that he was on a photographic journey to *Sayhut* in Yemen.

His conditions had improved at the northern tip of the Red Sea, when he joined others, which included an Arabian interpreter. Together, they set out, all traveling in three Land Rovers.

Wilks explained to the six scholars that his assignment from Dr. Polk had been to traverse the region from Jerusalem south along the Red Sea to a point about twenty-five miles north of the capital city of San'a'. Polk had given him the Book of Mormon and had marked the description of Lehi's exodus from Jerusalem with his family, which was found at the beginning of 1 Nephi.

He paused the VCR to show a hilly, desert region—a typical Palm Springs appearance without the palm trees, condos, and swimming pools. "The first map of this region was done by the French cartographer Jean Bourguignon D'Anville. This location has retained its name since before the rise of Islam. As you see, the copy of the map depicted on the screen indicates that the name of this region was called Nehem on this first-known map, printed in 1767. I tell you this because, if you will look in your Book of Mormon and read with me in 1 Nephi, you will see, as I did, that

Lehi, the father of the group that is mentioned in this passage, may have stopped with his family at what today is Nehem.

"Notice what it says in Chapter 16, verse 17, that they pitched their tents and prepared to 'tarry for the space of a time.' Nehem was a fertile region, so they probably planted crops while they stayed there. But during this time a sad event took place. According to Nephi, Ishmael, whose daughters married Lehi's sons, died, and I quote, 'was buried in the place which was called Nahom.' This is significant. Today it is called Nehem, which is very similar to Lehi's Nahom.

"I'm not qualified to give you the variations of spelling on that name, Nehem, but my research indicates that it is *NHM* in Hebrew. The Arabic is *Nahama,* referring to a soft groan or moan, and is related to consoling.

"The point is, and you can see the data on this in several sources that I have here photocopied, that the word means *place of burial and mourning.* In other words, the meaning of the word Nahom, as Lehi called it, indicates that it was a traditional burial site in the hills near present-day Nehem."

The tanned face turned away from the screen to view the group. "Now, have I confused you? In 1936, Philby, the British explorer, described the remains there of one of the largest burial sites in Arabia. This certainly could have been where Lehi and his family buried Ishmael, as I said, the father of the daughters they had brought with them to marry.

"It was here also that Lehi and his family indicated that they had turned east in their trek to the sea. Look at 1 Nephi 17—it says that Lehi and his family, 'did travel nearly eastward from that time forth.' This would have lead them across the mountains and valleys where the old incense trade routes were located. There seem to have been few time constraints on their travel, so they must have traveled along the valleys where there were wells and perhaps grass for their camels.

"First Nephi tells that their travels took them through 'the more fertile parts' of the desert. It took eight long, hard years to get to the sea. The normal time for the incense caravans to traverse the same region was, on average, three months. To me, this means they took their time and must have stopped for months or years at a time. Also, according to the record, they ate a good deal of raw meat during this period while they were on the route eastward, because, as Nephi said in his writings, they could not have a fire. They were warned against it. Again, according to what Nephi wrote, they were probably hiding from those who might have robbed them or harmed them in some way along the route."

The video, which was still running at the front of the room, displayed the scenes graphically. They showed a valley and mountains that were as bleak as any Stephen had seen in the Southern California desert. Then the film came to a lush, green region in present-day Oman. Wilks said, "Here we have a rich, verdant region with forests, a river, and ultimately a very inviting, white, sandy beach, with the blue Indian Ocean beyond."

It was obvious to all that a ship large enough to take the family across the ocean could have been built from wood taken from the tall trees that appeared to be plentiful in the area.

As the presentation ended, the usual questions from the group followed about Lehi's travels. It may have been interesting to some, but the fact that a group of determined people in the year 600 B.C. could have left Jerusalem and arrived in the Americas was not such an astounding feat to Stephen. He felt confident that he and Anney could have done it. True, it was interesting that the Book of Mormon described the region so well and that the geographer could pinpoint his route as he traversed the Arabian peninsula. It was notable that Joseph Smith, as he wrote the account in the Book of Mormon, was generally on the mark, considering that an accurate map of Arabia was not a common thing in 1830 in western New York. Still, he could have obtained his information somewhere during that time. Stephen wasn't all that impressed.

* * *

"Mary. Bill Bennett here. I'm sorry to bother you this evening. I'm sure you just got home from work. But I need to talk about the funds that you and I control." Bennett spoke in his most conciliatory manner. Not easy for a man of his innate impatience.

"Bill, I don't wish to be rude, but you have interrupted me at a most inopportune time."

"I just need you to do a couple of things," Bennett said.

"Well, I didn't do what you asked me to do last time, did I? What makes you think I will this time?"

Bill let the rebuke roll over his head and across the room. He was no stranger to insults. He could take the caustic remarks from her—all he wanted was cooperation. True, he had called her the Sunday evening she had returned from "mourning" and asked her to review her material on the computer to see if there was anything damaging to the project. She had refused. She did tell him that evening when he called back that she had found a letter that indicated that Finley & Southam was holding some funds that had been earmarked as final payment to the participants for their part in the project, plus other expenses, though there were no specific names or amounts listed for them. The letter had been addressed to Peter Polk.

Bennett realized that a judge could force Finley & Southam to turn over their records to the court and could freeze the funds with an injunction. There again, it would take time.

He also understood that he could be served with a subpoena. He was aware that it had already been filed. Such a document is public in Los Angeles County. Bennett was tense. The pressure was on.

"All I need, Mary, is for you to fly out to California with me and sign a check. Surely you know I would be prudent with the money. I want to get it out of that account and placed in another, where Craig can't get his hands on it."

"And I say no. Bill, I mean no. How much clearer can I be?" Mary's voice rose with impatience as she spoke. "Those are not our funds to be willy-nilly moving around. Please don't call me again. I'm so exasperated with this whole mess. I didn't ask to be in the middle of this thing. I want to be—"

"I get the point, Mary. I do." For a moment both stopped long enough to hear the void, then Bennett said, "Have you told Craig that you are a cosigner on that account?"

The silence became more intense as Bennett gripped the

phone with his viselike hand and hoped she would say no.

"I haven't gotten around to telling him, yet," came Mary's prissy reply.

"Thank you, Mary. You're a sweetheart. I'll make it up to you someday."

* * *

The garage door on the end folded up after Stephen pressed button four. He and Freddy stood back as the bright red 500 SL exposed her sleek lines and sassy style—just waiting to be driven. This was the first time the two men felt relaxed enough to ask for the Mercedes convertible that had come with the lease arrangement. Someone had already removed the roof, revealing the soft, brown leather seats and no-nonsense instrument panel.

"I just hope you know your way around the countryside, Stephen, old boy. I would hate to be late for dinner," Freddy cautioned as they surveyed the expensive, immaculately detailed sports car. The license plate frame sported the cryptic phrase: "Get in, sit down, shut up, and hang on."

Both men chuckled as they read it.

"My sentiments to you exactly, Freddy. I couldn't have said it more eloquently."

The car roared to life as Stephen maneuvered it onto the suburban street and headed for the main gate and an hour's relaxation in the late afternoon sun. Fifty yards from the gate, Stephen slowed and waved to a young lady who was walking a tiny Pomeranian dog. Stephen saw the friendly face and braked.

"Hi there!" he called. "Let me think . . ." Stephen idled the car as the young lady approached from the left. "Victoria, that's the name. Hi, Victoria."

"Hi, Steve."

"No, it's Stephen."

"I like Steve better."

Stephen introduced Freddy, who gave Stephen that what-you-already-know-some-of-the-beauties-in-the-neighborhood look. Stephen asked Victoria if the dog was hers.

"No, actually she's my aunt's. I have an aunt who is in Europe for the summer, and she left Taffy with us. Cute, isn't she? Isn't this the Claybourn's car? Why didn't I see you jogging this morning?"

"Freddy and I are going for a spin in this hot little car. . . . I guess it does belong to the Claybourns. And by the way, I was jogging this morning, but I didn't see *you.*"

"Maybe it was because I was still asleep."

"Well, don't let it happen again. I'll be looking for you tomorrow. Hey, where is your friend?"

"Chrissi? She was just sleeping over. She lives in Carmel Valley."

Stephen waved good-bye, and Freddy mentioned how much he enjoyed meeting her. Then Stephen started to accelerate but hit the brake instead, tossing Freddy slightly forward.

"By the way, Victoria," Stephen said as he turned his head around to catch her eyes ten feet back from the car. "Martin—the guy I was jogging with when I met you—he seems to be a good friend of yours. Why did you call him *Bishop* Oren?"

"Oh, he used to be my bishop. We're Mormons, you know. Even though he is no longer the bishop, that's a title we sort of keep using."

* * *

Stephen listened to the faint sound of a lonely coyote off in the nearby hills and then the distant sound of a dog guarding somebody's treasure up the street. The moon was full, its brilliance creeping along the edge of the beveled glass that reached to the vaulted bedroom ceiling.

"Freddy, are you awake? I know you are. You're not snoring yet."

Freddy said nothing.

"As I think of what we're doing—the bunch of us—I get a little squeamish inside. You know, kinda like kids playing a parlor game, but this is not a game and we're not kids. I'm beginning to get strange vibes from all the reading I have been doing in the Book of Mormon, feelings I can't begin to explain. Every time I go in and sit at the computer with Roy or pick up a document or reread the book, I see a new and inexplicable view of the Book of Mormon. Do you know what I mean?"

Still no stir, though Stephen knew Freddy was listening.

"These feelings—more like sensations—that I'm having are starting to get to me. I never knew that there was so much to discover about things. This is the first time in my life I have spent every breathing minute of the day thinking about only one thing—in this case, the Book of Mormon. Maybe I'm the susceptible type. Kinda like a person with poor immune defenses. What do you think? Are you having some of these same feelings, or am I imagining things?"

Stephen didn't expect a response now. He wanted Freddy to hear him out.

"My Anncy has warned me. She warned me the other night while I was at home."

"You were home?" Freddy's startled voice sounded with alarm and curiosity in the dim light of the bedroom.

"Oops. Okay, I admit it. I was up in the San Joaquin Valley and decided to take a direct flight from Oakland back here." Stephen knew Freddy didn't understand that he had left out one or two vital points of travel. "So, me being me, I got two precious hours with the most beautiful lady in the world. And believe me, I made the most of them."

"You devil. You low-down varmint, as they say out here in this country. You never cease to amaze me," Freddy said in a pseudo-chiding tone.

Stephen knew this was Freddy's way of getting out of an awkward discussion that he did not initiate.

Suddenly, Stephen felt a pillow smash across his face and knew that Freddy felt capricious and wanted to have a good old-fashioned pillow fight, the kind he had with Todd when he was just a kid. Two grown men in a pillow fight. Why not?

Chapter Nineteen
The Garden

The group had been in the air for two hours. In two more hours the flight was scheduled to refuel in Newark, New Jersey, before crossing the Atlantic to Spain, where a second refueling would be necessary, and then on to Tel Aviv. Henry felt that part of the time in the cabin would be well spent discussing several points of the Book of Mormon and comparing notes on research the group had done over the past week. He called on Bernie to lead out with a discussion of what he termed "minor research" on the book of Ether that was "wedged," as Bernie had described it, into the main body of the Book of Mormon.

"Okay," Bernie agreed, gathering his thoughts. "I came across some interesting research on the book of Ether. As I mentioned, it is—as the Mormon scholar Nibley said—an ancient epic milieu. There are some interesting aspects to the book. It is so sweeping and yet so compact in information that the book is over almost before you have a chance to understand what is going on."

"Yeah, Henry," Stephen agreed, "it seemed like there was so much left out. But I will say this much, I found the part where their leader, whatever his name is—"

"He's not named," Bernie corrected. "They simply called him the Brother of Jared . . . an interesting mystery in itself."

"Anyway," Stephen continued, "as I was saying, I thought when he went up on the mountain and the Lord chewed him out for three solid hours—can you imagine being bawled out by the Lord for three hours?—that he was a totally different person after that experience. Do you remember when he takes the stones up and wants the Lord to touch them with his finger and make them shine in the dark? He said things like, 'Please, Lord,' 'Thank you, Lord,' 'Don't be angry with thy servant, dear Lord.'" Stephen chuckled. "I mean, this leader of the group—whatever his name was—became one humble dude."

"I found out a little bit of trivia while I was researching this book," Bernie said. "It's somewhere here in my notes." Bernie reached down and pulled up a black canvas cloth bag and took out a legal-size, yellow note pad. He thumbed through a few pages until he came to some handwritten notes that were labeled at the top of the page: "Ether Notes."

"Here it is. Nibley says—and by the way, if any of you have consulted Nibley among the books in the library at the estate, you know that he rambles all over the place as he tells his interesting little tidbits. Some call him the Mormon apologist. Anyway, I didn't know that in the Palestinian Talmud it tells about the legend of the stone that shone in the dark. Listen to this: 'Moreover, that particular hero was in possession of a life-giving talisman which in many legends is a stone that shines in the dark—a reminder that the Zohar itself was, according to the Palestinian Talmud, a shining stone with which'—get this—'none other than Noah had to illuminate the ark.' So, according to legend, at least, there was light in the ark, emanating from a glowing stone."

Bernie was about to turn the discussion over to Henry when he said, "Oh, one other little thing on the book of Ether that I found interesting. The book tells about rebellion after rebellion against the established government, the coup leader being a strong man, often a military leader. When the rebels took over, did you notice that time after time they put the overthrown king under house arrest? Some of those arrested rulers remained as prisoners their entire lives. They raised children to adulthood while they were prisoners. Do you want to know something? This concept of house prisoners is right out of the steppe regions of Central Asia. Old Joe Smith couldn't have been more accurate if he had researched the Central

Asian culture, which, by the way, has been detailed only in the last couple of decades. So much for that bit of trivia."

Bernie swirled around in his chair and then turned back to give one last summary remark. "I'm not overly impressed with the book of Ether; it lacks detail and enrichment for me. One other little matter, then I'll shut up. Did you notice in the book that when the huge civilization was annihilated by war, the two remaining persons were the two opposing leaders? After everyone is killed off, the two leaders remain standing, and then they go for each other in hand-to-hand combat until one of them falls and is killed. This, too, is typical of ancient warfare in the steppe region of Central Asia. The last guy to go is the leader. When any battle began, a cadre of guards moved into place to protect the leader. All the warriors expected to die before the leader could be attacked. Here again, Smith was right on the money. He called that one exactly right when the civilization was wiped out in the end. What stymies me is where on earth he got his information in the 1820s. The fact is that much of the Central Asian history was not published until the twentieth century."

Henry thanked Bernie for his insights and then called on Martha to give her evaluation of the use of consonants in the proper names of the Jaredites in the book of Ether. The discussion continued on the topic of the book of Ether for another hour.

* * *

"Since I can remember, I've wanted to visit Israel and especially Jerusalem. . . . And here I am, riding into the very streets I have read about," Stephen said to Peter, who was seated next to him. The excitement of being in the Holy Land was nearly overpowering. There had been several surprises in the appearance of the land. The fields of cotton growing adjacent to the airport and the pine trees on the hillsides had been unexpected. Stephen had supposed that the whole country was a bleak desert.

From the window of the van, he and his traveling companions could see casual soldiers patrolling the streets. "They don't look like the fierce Israeli army the news makes them out to be. But

I'll bet that if the least little thing happened, we'd see the military go into high alert. These uniformed kids would, no doubt, stop playing around with the pretty girls and become real soldiers," Bernie said above the noise of the bus.

Dozens of tour buses inched along the crowded streets. Tourism sustained Jerusalem. All Western and many Near Eastern religions laid claim to the city and took special heed whenever anything upset the normal flow of life.

"We'll be staying here at the King David Hotel," Peter announced. "They have every service usual to an international hotel, and our rooms are overlooking the Old City. You might keep your eyes open for famous travelers. I understand that some heads of state stay here when they are in Jerusalem. I suggest you all take a nap, then join me for lunch in the main dining room."

Peter wanted to shower and shave, as did the others. Their plane had touched the tarmac at 6:00 a.m., Jerusalem time, two hours earlier. Clearing customs had been smooth, especially for a party coming in on a chartered jet.

The van ride from the airport had taken less than an hour, and now it was 8:10 in the morning. All in the group were exhausted. The flight had taken four hours from the refueling stop in Spain and had required a crew of three officers and two stewards. After being suspended in the air for so many hours, Stephen had come to realize that even executive travel wasn't all he had imagined it to be.

In their room, while Freddy showered, Stephen sat on his bed with the phone to his ear, holding for a Mr. David Rabin to pick up the line. Rabin spoke five languages, English included, and was director of the Olive Oil Museum in Haifa, which was a part of Shemen Industries. *Shemen means oil in Hebrew*, Stephen remembered. He was glad he had done his homework. He had learned that there was an olive growers organization, a support group for the home industry that was dominated by the Palestinians.

"Hello, hello," an impatient voice spoke through the receiver.

"Yes, hello. This is Stephen Thorn. I believe I spoke with you last week from California about olive orchards in Israel."

"Oh, yes, yes, yes. Nice to talk to you."

"Well, sir, I just arrived here in Jerusalem this morning and would like to meet with you when you have time. As I indicated to you when I called from California, I would like to see firsthand the old olive trees and see how the growers work with them."

"I have already arranged for us to visit a grove near Nablus in Samaria. But before we go over to Nablus, I'd very much like for you to see our olive museum here in Haifa. Perhaps this is not possible if you have a crowded schedule." Stephen heard Rabin pronounce *schedule* with same shussh sound that Freddy used.

"I'm afraid our schedule won't allow for a trip to Haifa, but I intend to rent a car and would like to meet you near the olive grove. Can you tell me how to get there?" Stephen asked.

"That would be fine, of course. Drive to Nablus, which is about forty miles north of Jerusalem. Come directly into the center of the city, into the bazaar. I will find you. But a little word of caution: The Arabs sometimes throw stones at rental cars. As you travel through the occupied region, be careful."

Stephen expressed his thanks and hung up. Freddy was emerging from the shower. He had already agreed to accompany Stephen on his little foray into the countryside. Stephen wondered for a moment whether to mention to Freddy the warning he had received from David Rabin, then he thought better of it.

* * *

Stephen slept through lunch. He had showered and stretched out on the bed and didn't wake up until Freddy shook him forcefully.

"Stephen, lad, we're due at the Hebrew University in an hour, and you haven't eaten. How can you survive if you don't eat?" Freddy was a man who had never missed a meal.

Stephen was groggy, barely aware of Freddy shaking him. He turned over on his side, longing to slip back into oblivion.

"No, no," Freddy persisted. "I can't let you go back to sleep. You will miss out on the lecture, be up all night, and blame me for the whole thing. Up, up, up. Henry has issued a command. He wants everyone in the conference room at three o'clock. That gives you half an hour to get down there with me."

Stephen realized that it was useless to try to put him off. "Okay, okay, okay. You win, Freddy."

* * *

"I've asked you to come here before we leave by van to attend Professor Raddai's lecture," Henry said to the participants in the conference room of the elegant old hotel. He felt comfortable in his role as chairperson and took the job seriously. Also, he coordinated well with Peter. The two made a good team.

Henry went on to explain who Professor Raddai was. "He is an impeccable scholar, eminently qualified to talk on the subject of ancient Hebrew influences in the Book of Mormon." Henry indicated that he had known of Professor Raddai since graduate school and vouched for his scholarship in Hebrew and Near Eastern languages. At Henry's signal, each participant was handed a copy of the document identical to the one that Raddai had been sent six months earlier.

Henry cleared his throat and explained the situation and what would be expected. "This is another of those blind presentations. I've just handed you a computer printout of the first edition of the Book of Mormon. The computer was programmed to remove all punctuation and capitalization except proper names, and all proper names have been changed to make it more difficult for Professor Raddai to trace this document to the Book of Mormon. He is aware that the document is intended as a blind study and has accepted this arrangement. Truly a congenial man, except that, at first, he was offended by the heavy stress on Christ in the document. Mr. Bennett, who contacted him, smoothed over that rough spot and convinced Professor Raddai to accept this challenge."

Henry went on, "We will presently see what he has made of this document. Keep in mind that you will be in the presence of a linguistic genius, for whom I have the highest regard. I can assure you that he will give an unbiased opinion. . . . I'm certain of that. It should be interesting."

Stephen now felt comfortable with the other participants. In fact, he had grown in self-confidence. He had gradually become aware that the participants were, after all, human, and that, although they were brilliant within the parameters of their particular disciplines, they sometimes seemed almost illiterate in other areas.

"The material I shall review this evening was sent to me several months ago, with an accompanying letter, by a Mr. William Bennett in Phoenix, Arizona, who is an attorney. He asked that I accept a fee for reading the document and preparing myself to present my findings to this illustrious body. My treatise was to encompass the following question: 'What indications are there that this material is a translation of an original Hebrew document?' I do not know the origin of this document, nor how Mr. Bennett acquired it," Raddai said, as he addressed the group. "You understand that this document has a heavy emphasis on Jesus Christ . . . and I am a Jew. I agreed to make the presentation with the clear understanding that I do not endorse any of the material as my personal beliefs."

Stephen had the impression that Raddai spoke with a German accent, and he looked to be seventy years of age. Stephen reviewed the printed sheet in front of him. It offered a brief sketch of Professor Raddai's background and education. He was right about the accent, he noted. Raddai was born in Augsburg, Germany, attended the Federal University in Stuttgart, and then took two degrees, one in Hebrew etymology at Frankfurt and the other in Hebrew translations at Oxford. He was currently on the faculty at the University of Jerusalem as a full professor, where he chaired the Department of Etymology. He pursued dual hobbies, one in the scholarship of ancient scripture, the other in Hebrew. *A bright guy*, Stephen thought, as he looked up from the sheet on the lift-top desk where he was seated.

Professor Raddai told the group, in passing, that he had called Bennett and felt better about the project when he learned that the reason for not disclosing the origin of the document was to allow for greater objectivity. He had accepted Bennett's reason and the fee that had been paid to him by a respected American accounting firm.

"So, shall we get on with this? You've come a long way for such a brief discussion of a very complex matter."

With a nod of the head, Professor Raddai said, "I have related this to you so that you may know that I am dealing with a blind study, unaware of any other ongoing research—only what is in front me. For my fee, I have devoted considerable time and effort to this task. One other note: I have not involved others in this research, here or anywhere in the world, in accordance with my agreement with Mr. Bennett. I'm sure he feared that I would find someone who could tell me the origin of the document." Raddai grinned like a child who had outfoxed his parents.

"So here I am, ready to give you the benefit of my analysis of the document. I presume that each of you knows the origin of the document, so we won't have to play any games. I will simply give you what I have discovered. Keep in mind, I could be wrong in my point of view, but as the document touches on Hebrew, I have the background and training to feel comfortable in making certain assumptions and conclusions."

Professor Raddai covered the same ground the group had already delved into at the estate. Every member of the group had perused Nibley's *Since Cumorah*, which presented a detailed discussion of what he titled "Strange Things Strangely Told" and the more refined scholarship of such writers as Tvedtnes on the subject of Hebrew influences.

But seated in an amphitheater classroom at the Hebrew University within the confines of Jerusalem, Stephen had a sense of uncovering a hidden treasure. It was an overwhelming experience—he was moved beyond the point of gaining mere knowledge. He listened intently to Raddai explain the Near Eastern influences of the document he had been given.

"Need I tell you people, such as the distinguished Professor Syman, who must know more about this subject than I, that this document has many characteristics of the Hebrew language and, may I add, traditions. It is filled with Hebraisms; therefore, I must conclude that the authors—and undoubtedly there were over a dozen writers who participated in its formation—were Hebrew. The signs are everywhere. I believe that it was originally written in

Hebrew, with some Egyptian influences before it was translated. The document I have been given is hardly what I would term a good translation into English.

"In fact, it is poor English. But the best of the Hebrew form has been applied, as if the translator wanted to retain the flavor of its Hebrew origins but utilize English words.

"I see also that those who did the writing in Hebrew used ancient phrases that were common at least five hundred years before Christ and maybe earlier."

He highlighted several examples, beginning with the repetitious use of the phrase "and it came to pass." Stephen couldn't resist a glance at Martha, remembering her comment over three weeks earlier that if they edited out the phrase "and it came to pass," the Book of Mormon could be reduced to half its size, and it would somewhat improve the grammar.

"'And it came to pass' is Egyptian more than Hebrew. It certainly isn't good English," Raddai said.

Martha nodded her head. Since her first faux pas, she had done her homework on Hebraisms in the estate's library and had reconsidered the Hebrew in the Book of Mormon. "If an ignorant man translated it," she had told Roy one evening, "then it would not be a well-written translation." She now kept her mouth shut. Still in all, she was now curious to hear what Raddai would have to say about the other Hebraisms in the book.

"The phrase was used as a technique of punctuation in ancient writings. Phrases often began with an introductory remark such as, 'It happened that,' or 'It came to pass.' This is so common I shan't belabor the point.

"Other phrases that are common construction in Hebrew would be contrary to normal English syntax. Where one would use the possessive or descriptive relationship between two nouns, Hebrew usually puts the possessive or descriptive noun last: 'plates brass' rather than the preferred English usage 'brass plates,' or 'night darkness' rather than the English usage 'dark night.' In translating to English, the word *of* has been added for clarity—'plates *of* brass' and 'night *of* darkness.' There are also relatively few adverbs in Hebrew; 'with joy' is used, instead of 'joyfully.'"

Professor Raddai continued to give one example after another, showing where the Book of Mormon was loaded with Hebraisms. There was hardly a part of speech that he didn't highlight: the subordinate clause, the relative clause, the extrapositional nouns and pronouns, comparisons in a unique English construction. Professor Raddai simply pushed aside the unimportant.

For two hours Raddai lectured, backing up his statement that the document was more Hebrew in origin than any other language. After a short break, followed by an additional hour, Professor Raddai had covered his subject well.

"Here you have my understanding and brief analysis of the document," he summarized. "I defy anyone who understands ancient Hebrew words and structure to tell me that most of this document is anything but a Hebrew document, with other Near Eastern influences scattered throughout it. It is not Western, though it happens to be translated into English. As the document progresses, it exhibits less Hebrew influence and garners a unique expression of its own. This is because the civilization that it depicts has, by then, distanced itself so far from its origins that, like any civilization, it has taken on a character of its own. Obviously, the one factor that keeps the continuity of the Hebrew language is the record, or the brass plates of which it speaks.

"These plates became their schoolmaster in the best tradition of remaining committed for generations to a single written form. This was a stroke of genius; without those brass plates, the civilization would have lost a vital link to a sophisticated language."

When Raddai concluded his prepared remarks, he made himself available for discussion and questions.

"Professor Raddai," Judith asked, "one review I read on the subject of the authenticity of this document suggests that the author mimicked Hebrew. That is, that he or she possessed a rich mind for creative expression and may have copied some Hebrew phrasing extracted from the Bible, for example. Is this premise remotely valid?"

"I sense you have serious doubts about the origin of this document," Raddai probed.

Judith merely returned his gaze.

"May I go back to several excellent examples in the document?" the Hebrew scholar answered patiently.

"I mentioned one evidence in passing, but perhaps I should remind you of this Hebraism. The document employs colophons."

"Would you clarify what those are, sir?" Stephen asked. "I didn't quite understand what you meant." He was driven with a desire to learn and did not care if he sounded ignorant. He knew he was striking down his pose as an intellectual. But if he had to report on all this information, he wanted to be certain he understood what was being discussed. Never mind the others. He was going to do the best job he could.

"Of course. Colophons are introductions and conclusions. The writers of this document wish to acquaint us with background and material that will lay a foundation as to authorship. This was a popular form of Egyptian writing. All the major writers in this document use the traditional form of colophons, which in itself is not new, since the English Bible employs a wide use of colophons as various authors introduce their writings. At the commencement of their writings, they tell who they are and what has happened to them up to that point in their writings. Then, as they conclude, they explain why they have written what they have written. As I said, it is not unique, but Document A certainly depicts writers who were very familiar with that form of writing."

Professor Raddai moved to a table that stood to one side of the lecture hall and leaned on the edge as he spoke, his well-worn manuscript in his hands. "Notice the beginning of the document. In the first book, the first words are 'An account of L and his wife S, and his four sons,' then . . ." Raddai flipped pages rapidly, "the writer finishes that statement with, 'This is according to the account of N; or in other words, I, N, wrote this record.' Notice how this writer wrote in the ancient form, but that is not all. As you read the entire first book of the document, you see the pattern of colophons well established. Writer N wrote his own titles, prefaces, summaries, and conclusions. In the entire chapter nine of this book, writer N is telling us about what he has recorded in the previous eight chapters and what he intends yet to write. Throughout the document there is a complicated set of prefaces and summaries."

Raddai carefully reiterated his conclusion that the document he had studied was an authentic Hebrew account that had been translated into English in such a manner that the Hebrew form of writing was preserved. "May I conclude by saying that this document was done by ancient writers working with written materials over an extended period. If it was not, then the group that actually composed this in modern times had to be extremely skilled at Hebrew writings. It would have taken many years to fabricate such a document correctly."

No one wanted the session to end, but Henry knew they had a tight schedule, so he stood to thank Professor Raddai. "For those who still have questions, Professor Raddai will be available for the next forty-eight hours to give private or small-group sessions to further clarify his findings," he concluded. Peter hastened forward to ask Raddai if he would care to join the group at the King David for dinner two evenings hence. The professor graciously accepted the invitation.

* * *

Bernie had relatives in Jerusalem. He had been close-mouthed about the fact because he wasn't sure his fellow travelers would be interested in his family. He made a few calls during a lull in the group's activities and, to his surprise, not only found them quickly but was greeted with warmth and excitement. Bernie's aunt, Irina Dubrovski, a sister to his mother, spoke rapidly to him in Yiddish. Upon learning about his companions, she invited the whole group to a dinner party in their apartment in a newer section of Jerusalem. Only four of the group attended: Bernie, Peter, Judith, and Stephen. The others had made prior commitments. All family members in the area gathered at the Dubrovskis' to meet Anna's nephew from America. The space was cramped, yet Stephen felt welcome. He and Judith had gone together to buy two bottles of red wine for the meal. Bernie had assured them that red would do.

It seemed that everyone was talking at once when the four guests arrived. Bernie was smothered with love from his relatives.

The uncle, Boleslav, a powerfully built man who spoke only Yiddish, kissed Bernie squarely on the lips and patted him on the back. The short, round aunt did likewise. All the cousins, men and women, crowded around for more kisses. Their children hung back, a little shy but curious. This side of the family had lived in Jerusalem since 1974, when they had miraculously escaped Russia.

"My relatives think this country is paradise. I tell them that things are better in America, but they don't listen. To them, this is the height of successful living. Sure there are soldiers everywhere, but they know that they must protect the land. Natalie, their youngest daughter," Bernie gestured toward a thin, dark-haired girl with a lovely oval face who stood near her father, "has just been accepted by Columbia University. She will come to New York in the fall and live with my family."

"Yes," Natalie said in fluent English, "and Bernard has promised to pay for my education."

Bernie shrugged.

Natalie spoke English and translated for her parents throughout the meal. The conversation was lively, interspersed with laughter. The meal began with borsch, a soup made of beets served cold, with a dab of sour cream in the center. Natalie told the American group that they might find the same soup called "borscht" in ethnic recipe books, but that the Russian version is called "borsch." Then came a hot dish that Judith loved—called kugel, a pudding of noodles with raisins, eggs, green apples, brown sugar, cinnamon, and butter—followed by boiled chicken and a fresh green salad with black olives and tomatoes. They enjoyed their meal with the red wine and beer.

For dessert the aunt served Pirozhney. To Stephen, it resembled apple pie, with a thicker crust than Anney made. Tea followed and continuous, enthusiastic conversation.

"They want you to know that Israel is here to stay," Bernie translated in a loud voice to be heard above the din. "They believe that God is bringing all the Jews here who want to come. He will make it a strong nation that can never be destroyed." Bernie smiled. "I'm just translating. Draw your own conclusions."

Irina said something in Yiddish to Stephen and Peter as she

pointed to a plaque on the wall behind the sofa. Stephen stood up and peered over the shoulders of the two male cousins who were seated on it. The words were written in a language Stephen couldn't understand, though it seemed to him to be Hebrew.

Bernie touched Stephen's shoulder and said, "It's a biblical quote in Hebrew."

"What does it say?"

Bernie shrugged. "I can't translate Hebrew verbatim, but it says something about the Lord bringing his people out of captivity."

"Natalie, can you translate this for Stephen?" Bernie asked.

She nodded that she could. She left the room for a moment and when she returned, she was holding a book of scriptures. She pointed to a page and told Stephen to read the verses aloud. Stephen could see the words were in English.

> For lo, the days come, saith the Lord, that I will bring again the captivity of my people Israel and Judah, saith the Lord: and I will cause them to return to the land that I gave to their fathers, and they shall possess it.

> I will even gather you from the people, and assemble you out of the countries where ye have been scattered, and I will give you the land of Israel.

Stephen reread the verses in silence and pondered them with the whole family looking on. They had suddenly become quiet as he read, respecting his desire to study it a moment longer.

When Stephen concluded his brief study, he looked at Boleslav, the uncle, bowed slightly, and said, "This is my first encounter with the direct fulfillment of that prophecy. You are the people the Lord has brought here. I don't understand the meaning entirely, but I believe it is so." Bernie translated Stephen's comments into Yiddish. The family in the room nodded and murmured their agreement, as they smiled and clapped Stephen on the back.

Stephen basked in their approval. *How marvelous this evening has been. You can't begin to know Jerusalem until you know its people.* Stephen wished Anney could have been here to meet this wonderful family.

* * *

Stephen had never thought he would stand next to the Garden of Gethsemane on the Mount of Olives. To him it was the center point of this trip. When he thought what had happened here, the great sacrifice of the savior of mankind, he felt a swelling within.

The hawkers, selling their souvenirs, and the eager would-be guides distracted from the serenity of the moment. Most of their group had emerged from the Church of All Nations after seeing the rock that tradition said Christ had knelt upon. Outside, as Stephen stood along the wrought-iron fence, Martha moved in beside him to talk a moment. She was a puzzle to him. Stephen had wondered at times just what Martha believed and what motivated her.

"Stephen, you, being a fundamentalist, may not appreciate what Bernie and I have been talking about, but I think you need to hear it. I personally have no religion, so this whole scene is empty for me. It is just so much earth, olive trees, and rocks." Martha's eyes scanned the panoramic view of the wall of the Old City, with the sealed Golden Gate in the center. Then, fixing Stephen with an intense glare, she said, "I would like to point out one thing that has troubled me in the Book of Mormon, among many things. Have you noticed how the name of Christ appears centuries before his birth? Why do you suppose Joseph Smith, a bright fellow, would make that mistake? Did he think we would not notice it?"

"Why are you buttonholing me?" Stephen protested. "Martha, I may have been showing an interest in the Book of Mormon this last week, but I sure don't believe in or care if it has some flaws. That's not my assignment."

She went on, not to be put off by Stephen's pseudo-disinterest. "The Book of Mormon prophets seem to know when Christ is coming, where he will be born, and exactly what his name will be." Martha sat on the edge of the two-foot wall that ran below the fence and wiped the perspiration from her face as she continued to press her point. "The Bible doesn't even tell us the name of Christ until the event happens. Yet in the Book of Mormon, they are conversing with him, and he's talking to them, and they know him as Jesus Christ. Major flaw, Stephen . . . a major flaw. This clouds the research for me."

"So what do you want me to do, hang it up? Not go through with the project? Give up my seventy thousand and go home, simply because we can't explain this mix-up in the book? Is that what you want me to do?"

"Well, you don't need to get so testy about it. I thought you would be willing to discuss a matter that sheds a whole different light on the Book of Mormon."

She's such a bitchy woman. I don't like her. I don't like her telling me where the flaws are in this book. I don't want to hear them. . . . Whoa, Stephen, old boy. Why don't you want to hear them? Because you want to believe in what the Book of Mormon is teaching? How can you let yourself go and fall into this trap? Pull out before it's too late.

"Martha," Stephen took a long breath, uncomfortable with the exchange. "I'm too new at this to understand all the ramifications about what it says and what it doesn't. You know I'm not steeped in this antiquity stuff like the rest of you."

"Hmmpf," was Martha's only reply.

Judith quietly approached and sat next to Martha.

"What are you two so engrossed in?" Judith asked. She looked radiant, even in the heat, in her powder-blue silk blouse and white pants.

Martha studied Judith for a moment. They had shared the same room for four weeks and had developed a guarded respect for one another. "I'm just trying to tell Stephen that some things are not adding up right in the Book of Mormon, and he snaps my head off."

"Stephen, how could you?" Judith laughed, trying to lighten the situation.

Martha continued, "Yesterday, no problems. I listened and learned from Professor Raddai. I love a brilliant mind like that. He could have been discussing the pros and cons of why Jack and Jill went up the hill, and it would most likely have been eloquent and insightful. But I'm concerned about the name of Christ appearing in the Book of Mormon over five hundred years before his birth. Something's wrong. Judith, are you aware of this flaw?"

"That's interesting, Martha, that you saw that in the book; it was Bernie who mentioned it to me."

"Well, for your information, I put Bernie onto it last week."

"Anyway," Judith persisted, "I read the other day that a group has done a time line on a compendium to the Dead Sea Scrolls. It seems that the scrolls' references to Christ and other phrases previously regarded as having originated with the New Testament actually date back six hundred years before the birth of Christ. I understand that Christian scholars have been keeping the lid on those Dead Sea Scrolls for upwards of twenty years. Besides, I brought that up with Peter the other day and he directed me to specific chapters in the book of Nephi and explained to me that Nephi received the name in a vision. His father, Lehi, never seemed to know the name Jesus Christ."

Martha's eyes rolled upward at the last explanation, "Oh, great, Judith. That explains everything. That is too convenient for my mind to accept. And as to the group working over the Dead Sea Scrolls, they're probably Mormons," Martha said with finality. "At any rate, I intend to see the Dead Sea Scrolls at the Shrine of the Book. Who knows what I'll find out?"

"Martha, Martha, the day is too beautiful and the setting too historical to be talking shop like this. I just feel like relaxing," Judith said.

"Same here."

Martha arose and wandered off to talk to Bernie. She knew he would agree with almost any criticism she raised, even if he did tend to use her insights as if they were his. To Martha, Bernie was beginning to feel as comfortable as an old shoe.

Judith let her eyes sweep the ancient olive trees. "Stephen, I so wish my mother were here. She deserves this more than me."

"Your mother? Why?"

"Oh, yes, my mother. A true believer in the simple gospel of Christ—south side of Chicago, the old chapel on the corner of the block. Our people bought it from the white Baptists when I was a little girl, and the whites were pouring out of the neighborhood like a plague had struck. What a neat old church. You know, the kind with the steeple in front and the wide stairs leading up to big, white doors. It was always fun to go to church. We mostly sang hymns and listened to our stirring preacher, the Reverend Billy. Amen, brother, amen. Oh, I loved it when he'd get fired up over some point of religion, and then there would be this rhythmic sound through-out the church, as various members would echo their agreement with Billy. It was a true, dramatic art form. I loved it." The scene came into Judith's mind like a video that played only the beautiful parts, as if there had been no poverty and hardship in the run-down neighborhood and its dilapidated church house.

"Then, when I went to college, I thought of it as part of my past that I needed to bury. So I buried it. But let me tell you, Stephen, it is difficult to bury your past." Judith stretched her arms, feeling a little groggy from jet lag. "No, it's still with me. I feel it strongly here today. As Billy would say if he were here, 'Praise the Lord Jesus.'"

"I wasn't brought up on religion of any kind," Stephen mused. "I can't remember ever attending church with my aunt and uncle, who raised me. But I certainly have been in church every Sunday since I started college. That's why this means so much to me. If only Anney, my wife, were here." Stephen felt suddenly homesick and a long way from family. "Anney would love it here."

Chapter Twenty
The Old Way

Stephen saw that many areas of the countryside appeared more fertile than he had expected—the miles of wheat and grass, the Jordan Valley with citrus groves, grapevines, and banana groves.

"Nobody ever told me that there were groves and groves of banana trees, loaded with small bananas, here in Israel. Nor that the western side of the hill country leading up from Tel Aviv to Jerusalem is covered with pine trees. Why don't they tell you these things? I just assumed that most of the countryside looked stark, like Bethlehem," Stephen said to Freddy, who was half asleep with the seat reclining to Stephen's left. Freddy nodded as Stephen sped along in the rented car.

They had picked up the car at eight o'clock that morning around the corner from the King David Hotel. Stephen and Freddy had not gone three blocks when they realized the car they were in was not air-conditioned. They abruptly circled the block, returned to Eldan Rent-A-Car, and exchanged the car for a small four-door Fiat with air. It had taken a half-hour tour of the narrow streets before Stephen and Freddy found the main highway to Jericho. They drove to the ancient city and proceeded north up the Jordan Valley toward the Sea of Galilee. They knew that they would always be sorry if they came so close and did not make the effort to visit the Jordan River and the Sea of Galilee before turning south again to the Palestinian city of Nablus.

When the bright blue water of the Sea of Galilee appeared at the resort town of Deganya, Stephen shook Freddy awake. "Hey, Freddy, you've got to see this beautiful Sea of Galilee." Freddy came to life. There were fishing boats out plying the waters and three water-skiers skimming over the surface of the sea. "Somehow I never thought of the Sea of Galilee as a resort lake for teenagers. They seem out of place," Stephen said, a little bewildered at the sight. "Let's drive up the coast a few miles and see if there isn't an unspoiled stretch of beach." Soon Stephen found a quiet, rocky beach, not far from Tiberias. He picked up a few stones for Anney. How he wished she were here.

With little time to spare if they planned to make the twelve o'clock appointment with David Rabin, the oil museum director, the hasty tourists sped past the lake and pointed the car west at Tiberias, where they were soon in the high plateau region of Galilee. They traveled over the hills, through Nazareth, and on to Nablus, midway between the Sea of Galilee and Jerusalem. They had two hours to make the bazaar in Nablus and meet the director.

"Tell me again why it's so important for us to learn about the olive culture of this country? Will it alter our souls?" Freddy asked.

"It has to do with my assignment, smart aleck. You didn't have to come. Remember, I'm supposed to figure out the Allegory of the Olive Tree. I'm doing my homework, and you agreed to come along," Stephen reminded Freddy. "I don't think you will ever appreciate this allegory as I am coming to appreciate it."

"Tut tut," Freddy scoffed.

"No, I'm serious, Freddy. It is uncanny what I have learned about this bit of writing that has been wedged into the book of Jacob."

"Personally, I thought the lot of it was rather boring. I can't actually remember any of it, though I did read it."

"It may seem boring because you haven't studied it. I have come to realize after getting into all available commentaries that the whole chapter is telling the religious history of the world. Zenos, the prophet who told the allegory, explains in great detail every little aspect of olive horticulture. I mean he explains in the most *minute* detail exactly how the master of the vineyard dispatches his servant to prune, dung, graft, and harvest the fruit of the tree."

"So, what makes that so interesting?" Freddy asked obliquely.

"Because it is not only interesting for those of us who want to know how the Lord continually strives with his people, but I thought it was interesting simply because Joseph Smith had never seen an olive tree in his life." Stephen swerved around an army vehicle that was traveling half his speed. "Do you realize how hard it would be to explain in detail the growing and harvesting of olives if you had never seen an olive tree?"

"Stephen, you've a few rough edges, one can see. Don't be naive. Smith could have read it in a book. Some of this is rubbish."

"What book, Freddy? The earliest writings about the olive culture in Europe were published in French in the 1820s, and I'm convinced that Joseph Smith had not learned French. I've read everything Roy and I could dig up on the subject. Not until this century do you have anything in English that comes close to explaining how to graft olive branches into the mother tree. Oh, it's mentioned in the New Testament about the wild olive tree, but it does not go into detail about the methods of cultivation and propagation as the allegory does." Stephen insisted on driving his point home to Freddy.

"Do you know that each point of Jacob 5, which deals with the olive tree, has been subjected to the scrutiny of horticulturists who understand every facet of the olive tree and its production of fruit? They have taken Jacob 5 verse by verse to show how proper pruning, dunging, and grafting affect the outcome of the fruit. They explain how trees grown from seed are stronger and live longer than those grown from cuttings. All this is in Jacob 5. Freddy, I tell you there is no way an ignorant man like Joseph Smith could have known the details of olive tree horticulture that are presented in Jacob 5."

"Why do you say that, Stephen? Smith was raised on a farm. I think he knew a good deal about fruit trees. There was soaring imagination in the man."

"Maybe fruit trees, Freddy, but not olive trees. The olive

tree produces fruit in a very confined climate. I read where it can only produce fruit in a Mediterranean climate with warm, wet winters and hot, dry summers. It will not tolerate temperatures below 34 degrees Fahrenheit. Joseph Smith never knew a climate so warm. The farthest he traveled toward a warm climate was to Washington, D.C. It snows and freezes in Washington. I tell you, Freddy, Joseph Smith did not write Jacob 5. A guy can't fake the details that are in the Allegory of the Olive Tree."

Stephen eased the Fiat into a parking slot along the center square in the crowded downtown section of Nablus. The swarthy Arab vendors were out in full force. Alongside the car stood a cart laden with small, ripe bananas; next to that cart was a flat-bedded cart heaped with bread and dry pastries; further on, a cart with trays of nuts and dates.

Stephen and Freddy emerged from the car and glanced about. They had no idea what David Rabin would look like. They hoped he would spot them. "I say, Stephen, how about a few bananas and some nuts? Are you game?"

"Sure," Stephen said, continuing to crane his neck around, looking for anyone that appeared to be educated and sophisticated. Freddy moved among the sellers and began bargaining for food. He brought back a clear plastic bag of bananas, some hazelnuts, a few dark dates, and two huge, elongated bagels with sesame seeds scattered over the crust.

"Strange thing, Stephen," Freddy observed as he bit into the large date and spit out the pit. "Do you notice that there are no flies or bugs of any description?"

"You're right," Stephen agreed in surprise. He continued to search the scene and then saw a man walking toward them, smiling.

"Professor Thorn," the man said in clear, precise English.

"David Rabin?" Stephen asked, relieved that their eminent guide had found them.

"Yes, yes. I spotted you as soon as I got out of my car. You do stand out, I must say," he laughed.

Stephen shook hands with Rabin and introduced him to Freddy.

"Well, I see you are partakers of some of our better home-grown products," Rabin observed. "And I suppose you are ready to follow me in your car to the olive farm I have to show you. I say follow because you should not leave your rented car here. I must tell you that this community is a hotbed of Palestinian resistance to Israeli rule. Are you ready?" Freddy raised his eyebrows and exchanged a glance with Stephen.

* * *

The soil felt sandy and dry as the group walked out to the vineyard. The man speaking Arabic had difficulty making himself understood, even by Rabin. He had lived in the region of Samaria all his life, as had his parents before him. The man was a Palestinian whose life had been spent among the olive trees. Rabin spoke Arabic also, but it was not his native tongue. He said something to the Arab farmer and then turned to Stephen and Freddy to comment.

"You know, Professor Thorn—"

"Call me Stephen," the American interrupted. "I'm not really a professor, though I do have a doctorate degree. Feel free to call Professor Frederick Shaw here a professor. He is familiar with that title. I'm not." Freddy remained silent. "Forgive me," Stephen apologized. "I interrupted you. What were you about to say?"

"I wanted to mention that the olives that are processed here are pressed into oil. Olive oil is the single greatest food oil in the Near East. It is also used for medicine and remedies. You may not know it, but each day many mothers here take a small amount of olive oil, rub it on the heads of their children, then take the children out into the bright sunlight and, for a few minutes, allow the sun to shine down on the children's foreheads. This, they believe, pours strength and good health into their little bodies."

Stephen nodded with some interest. They continued to follow the Palestinian farmer to the edge of the vineyard, where he spoke as Rabin interpreted.

"He said that they do the pruning in the late fall and the grafting of young branches in the spring. You asked about the grafting in of the wild olive branches. He wants us to come with him to the end of the vineyard and see the new spring grafts."

Stephen walked alongside the farmer. The man spoke to Stephen as if he could understand every word. Stephen turned to Rabin. Rabin tried to keep up with what the old farmer was saying in Arabic. He began translating only the main thread of his conversation.

"He is telling you that the large olive trees, the ones over there along the crest, are eight hundred years old. He insists that his family has been tending these trees since before armies invaded with chariots. I think he means the Crusades. Don't quote me on that. These people out here have many traditions that have been in their families for hundreds of years. But you can believe that these trees are hundreds of years old."

Another fifty yards, and the farmer stopped abruptly in front of a gnarled olive tree that was covered with small, oblong olives. The husbandman took hold of one branch and then another and another. He tugged on one, patted the spindle-like branch, and then, through Rabin, told Stephen that this was a good example of wild olive branches grafted into an ancient, living, tame olive tree.

"He says," Rabin told Stephen, "that this grand old mother tree has supplied oil for his family for over five hundred years. She just recently began to have weak rootstock. The wild olive branches will stimulate the rootstock and cause the mother tree to become strong and hearty again. He is telling me more, but I think I have given you the gist of the reason for grafting."

Stephen could sense that there was a deep-seated relationship between the farmer and his living trees. He needed no interpreter to translate the feelings of love and respect this husbandman held for his ancient orchard.

They studied the root system, the bark, and the new wild olive grafts. Some of the old trees were laden with green, growing olives.

"Freddy, have you ever tasted an olive picked right from the tree?"

"Can't recall ever having seen an olive tree, let alone the fruit, except in the can, of course."

"Here, try one." Stephen plucked one small olive from a branch, wiped it on his shirt, and handed it to Freddy. "It may be a little firmer than the canned, but it has plenty of meat. Just don't break your tooth on the pit inside."

Stephen couldn't resist the temptation, and Rabin watched the interplay with amusement.

Freddy took the small green olive, placed it in his mouth, and bit down. The bitter juice spread across the taste buds on Freddy's tongue and up the sides of his inner cheeks.

With a startled look, Freddy turned and spat out the raw olive. He continued to spit and wipe at his mouth with the back of his hand, all the while cursing Stephen.

"You bloody little . . . you set me up," he spat out the words as he tried to spit out the bad taste in his mouth. "I'll get you for this."

Stephen was laughing too hard to answer. "I couldn't help myself." When he finally controlled his laughter, Stephen continued, "Freddy, you're so eager to try any food, I thought you might enjoy a freshly picked olive. Actually, though, the devil made me do it."

"Despicable," Freddy finally said after another minute of spitting and wiping.

The others smiled but were not keen on laughing at this large, powerful-looking Englishman, who looked capable of causing bodily harm if one were not careful.

When the commotion settled and the frivolity was put aside, Stephen asked the farmer if they could see a wild olive tree from which the grafts had been taken.

"But before that, David, would you ask the man how he fertilizes the olive trees here in his vineyard?"

After a lengthy explanation by the husbandman, who all the while gestured with his hands, Rabin interpreted: "The way he and his family have always done it. They use the dung from the stables. It is a well-rotted farmyard manure. He says he applies the manure in the autumn and other decomposed materials for nutrients. It is not good for the taste to use only manure; he has other organic material, such as leaves, to dung the trees without impairing the quality of the fruit. He says he first spreads the manure over the surface, then digs about the trees, exposing the roots but not harming them. Then he turns the composition evenly in the soil. He insists that the warm, moist dung gives energy to the roots, but you must dig down so that the tops of the roots are well covered with a proper mix of soil and dung."

"Another question before we leave here. I would like him to tell us what he does with the dead branches when he prunes the mother tree. And ask him the purpose of removing the dead branches."

More words passed back and forth, then Rabin said, "He burns the dead branches."

"Ask him why."

The answer was quick and to the point. "Because," Rabin clarified, "of the evil insects that infect the dry branches with their poison. The insects can kill the mother tree if they are not burned. Also, fruit grows only on new branches each season. If the old branches are not removed, the tree will soon stop producing fruit."

The only place I have read anywhere that the branches are burned is in the Book of Mormon. Paul does not mention anything so detailed as this in the New Testament. Everything is correct to the letter. How could Joseph Smith have known so much about the details of olive husbandry? How? How? How?

The group followed the farmer to the edge of the vineyard, where no shade gave relief from the afternoon summer sun. They tramped to a hill overlooking the olive orchard, where the ground was dry and rocky. With no irrigation, the eroded cliffs could sustain only brush. Along a dusty, seldom-trodden path, near the top of the hill, the husbandman stopped beside a large, spindly bush that grew out of the side of the hill, among the rocks. Its leaves were similar to the mother olive, but the branches were slender and tiny fruit dotted the plant.

"He says this is the wild olive. It is more a bush than a tree, but he insists that the branches have life to give to the mother tree," Rabin said, peering closely at a branch.

Stephen asked if he could pick a small branch to take back with him to the United States. The farmer must have understood Stephen's hand movement. He quickly reached over, broke off a small branch, handed it to Stephen, and nodded with a friendly smile, devoid of front teeth. "A gift to you," he said in Arabic.

While Rabin and his host walked quickly back toward the husbandman's house and the cars, Stephen and Freddy followed at a slower pace, with dust puffing up about their feet.

"I could use a bloody beer about this time," Freddy said.

"Seriously, though," Stephen said, getting back to the olive trees, "you have not read the Allegory of the Olive Tree as I have. I don't mean that in a boastful way. I'm just stating a fact.

"I've studied every angle as requested," Stephen said, kicking a stick in his path and sending it twirling through the air. "I say it again: It is uncanny. I have been overwhelmed with the simple knowledge that I have gained here this afternoon. Not Paul, not Isaiah, nor any of the Old or New Testament prophets spoke of dunging deep around the roots and burning the discarded dead branches. This information is not in the writings of the known prophets."

"I'm waiting for my intellect to overtake my emotions at this point. Clearly, you have made an interesting find." Freddy had no other response to Stephen's amazement at what he had learned this late afternoon.

"Whoever wrote the Book of Mormon," Stephen said, "received the information some other way than simply sitting down and putting pen to paper. I intend to base my entire report around this experience we've had this afternoon. It is the single greatest personal example I have had up to this moment. I tell you, Freddy, we are about something that is not to be taken lightly."

* * *

"He's leaving Jerusalem late this afternoon and driving up near the Sea of Galilee to visit an olive vineyard, then he will return to Jerusalem tonight to get ready to catch his flight back tomorrow morning." Anney related Stephen's status to her father from the office doorway. Bob had been about to make a second call when Anney popped in to bring him up to date on Stephen's latest adventures.

"You mean orchard," Bob corrected, still holding his finger

on the phone button, ready to dial.

Anney laughed with that good-natured manner that was so infectious, a little puzzled at what she had said. "Orchard? Oh, yeah, that's just what I said to Stephen, and he said, 'Anney,'" Anney made her voice deep and her lips protrude, "'the correct word for the location of growing old-world olive trees is *vineyard*.'

"Anyway, he starts for home later tonight, which will be early morning there. By late tomorrow he'll be back in San Diego. Then the kids and I are flying down to have a wonderful family weekend, all expenses paid, at that fabulous old hotel, the Hotel Del Coronado." Anney almost squeaked with excitement. "I'll leave you alone; just thought you wanted to know."

"I do, I do," Bob said, realizing he must have appeared impatient. "Oh, Anney, would you mind closing the door behind you as you leave? It's one of those private things that I . . . you know."

Anney thought he meant a private session counseling someone who needed comforting. She closed the door and Bob dialed the bank, then the extension. "Cliff, Bob Moore—I'm sorry I didn't return your call yesterday, but I've been flooded with people and requests to speak. You know my life—how are you?"

Cliff went directly to the issue. "Bob, I can't stall the board any longer. They absolutely have to have the interest payment by next week, or they will call in the loan." Clifford had an edge to his voice that Bob had dreaded hearing.

Bob wanted to be lighthearted about the whole situation and kid with his good friend, but the moment was not right. *What can I say?*

"I'll come up with it, Cliff. Trust me on this one." The two spoke a moment longer and then said good-bye.

How can I come up with twenty-five thousand by next Wednesday? This is asking too much. What am I going to do? Who do I know that will lend me that kind of unsecured money? Think, man, think.

* * *

The Knight Investigative Agency hadn't gotten any closer to solving the whereabouts of the project than two weeks earlier. Through Craig's attorney, Sharp, the investigative agency had gotten word that unless there was a breakthrough by Saturday morning, they were pulling the case and going with another firm. It had taken too long.

The two investigators sat with somber expressions. "We've already lost the ten thousand bonus, and we could have used it, too. Now let's just save ourselves and make a decent fee out of this rat trap," Dan Knight said, knowing he was a man close with a dollar, and that he had already spent more man-hours than he should have. He would be relieved when the whole thing ended. "Let's review all that we know right now."

For two hours, the veteran investigators pored over what they had done and who they had seen. The names began to melt together until none had any real meaning. All the information was on the office computer system, and the investigators' color-coded names, family connections, places, and travel destinations were on their copies of the printout. After drilling one another from every possible angle, Knight pulled up Peter's known travel route—until the time he dropped out of existence. They had already pieced together the flight from Phoenix to Los Angeles following the funeral.

"Wait, wait!" Knight said, startled at his discovery. "Polk arrived in Phoenix the evening before the funeral. Is that correct?"

"Yes, we already knew that; he spent the night at his sister's home in Mesa. So?" Mort Johnson asked.

"How do we *know* that he spent the night at his sister's?"

"Because our research shows that that's where he usually stayed when he visited his friend Kline in Phoenix."

"But it's an assumption. We don't know, for a fact, that he stayed at her place, do we?"

"No, I guess not. But since he usually did, it's a safe assumption that he did. It saves us running down every hotel and motel in Phoenix to see if he was a guest. And even if we did try to run down his name, we're not detectives paid by the City of Phoenix. It's a tough job to deal with motels and hotels that don't like to give information out on their guests. They all say it's bad for business."

"I have a hunch. It may lead us to where we want to go," Knight said as he punched "Craig Kline" into the computer. The monitor immediately flashed the words of the interview with Kline, where Kline gave detailed information of everything he knew about Polk and all that he knew Polk had done the day of the funeral. "I walked over to the limo that we had rented for Polk and got in. We had a nice little chat about me stopping the project."

Dan Knight had read that transcript dozens of times to determine times, dates, people—those who might have information as to Peter's whereabouts. But he had never noticed that the limo at the funeral, the one Craig got into, was actually hired for Peter.

In one adroit move, Knight picked up the phone and got through to Craig Kline at his office in Phoenix.

"Mr. Kline, Dan Knight here. We may have a lead. Do you know the name of the leasing firm that provided all those limos for your father's funeral?"

In five minutes, Knight had the leasing manager on the phone, hunting through his dispatches to determine which one of his drivers took Dr. Polk to the cemetery.

Chapter Twenty-One
The Overwhelming Truth

Week Five—Early Friday Morning

All craving for sleep had fled Stephen's body. He had stayed at his reading long after everyone in the cabin had dozed off. Near silence prevailed inside the Gulf Stream jet as the plane drifted through the atmosphere at 30,000 feet over the Atlantic. It was California bound. The comfortable leather seats reclined to allow the occupants to stretch out full length and sleep.

The small side panel light beamed down on the pages as Stephen eagerly turned them, reading key parts of the book. No longer was he interested in showing evidence of antiquity in the Book of Mormon. Oh, he would do it because he had to. But it was no longer an issue with him. He also knew that his report would wait until after this evening. He had a much more involved personal agenda to keep.

During the three days in Israel, and even for several days prior to that, he had felt strange, new feelings—penetrating and insightful. These were more personal disclosures that transcended the mere study of documents. Stephen knew that his whole being was undergoing some sort of transformation. He could not explain it to himself because he had never before experienced such feelings. He probed his inner self for an explanation, and none sprang forward. No longer was he concerned about the project as he once had been. He was beyond the point of merely satisfying the demands of the job. His motivation welled up from a new, more compelling source now. His soul was hungry for spiritual nourishment. *I am like a starving man*, Stephen thought. *I can't get enough. This is food to me, food to my soul.*

Stephen desperately desired to know what was in the book that would be satisfying to his mental cravings. He had read and reread the appearance of Christ to the Nephites. The words were mellow and soothing to him—more than that, they rang true. It was as if somewhere he had experienced this feeling of ecstasy before, somewhere in a dim past, a distant but still very real past.

Reading the account a second time, Stephen studied the scene where Christ appeared to the Nephites. It described how he had come down and had reached out lovingly to the surviving people of the Nephites. He had come as a resurrected being, having been with the Father. He had come to comfort the people and let them thrust their hands into his side and feel the nail prints. *He has come to comfort me*, Stephen marveled.

Stephen let his eyes flow down the pages as he read the account. *How did I miss this the first time I read it? I read it, but I didn't understand what I was reading. Now I see that the Savior came to those people and he taught them.*

Stephen read from 3 Nephi 11, where the Father introduced the Son, and Christ began to speak to the surviving Nephite people who had gone through such upheaval:

> And it came to pass that he stretched forth his hand and spake unto the people, saying: Behold, I am Jesus Christ, whom the prophets testified shall come into the world. And behold, I am the light and the life of the world; and I have drunk out of that bitter cup which the Father hath given me, and have glorified the Father in taking upon me the sins of the world, in the which I have suffered the will of the Father in all things from the beginning. And it came to pass that when Jesus had spoken these words the whole multitude fell to the earth; for they remembered that it had been prophesied among them that Christ should show himself unto them after his ascension into heaven.

The words flowed with warmth across Stephen's thirsty mind. They generated thoughts of knowing the Savior personally, of being one of those whom the Savior had retrieved from the human heap of despair—this knowledge gave Stephen a calm sense of worth. These tender words played over his senses as naturally as a mother's hum soothes her child. Joy encompassed his thoughts and enfolded his mind with blissful peace. Never before had his comprehension of the goodness of the Savior reached such heights.

Even as his spirit was uplifted, an uneasy realization invaded his thoughts. On the one hand, he was discovering the real message of the Book of Mormon—but on the other, he cringed inwardly at the thought of telling his family and friends about his newly discovered belief. *How can I face Anney, Bob, the children? What must I be thinking?* The ecstasy was slipping.

The book lay open on his lap. Stephen picked up the book again to finish reading the account. The ecstasy returned. His eyes scanned the words of 3 Nephi 11, where the people filing by bowed down and kissed the Savior's feet.

Oh, to be Nephi and be allowed to bow down and kiss the feet of the Lord! I would do that. I would adore him. Oh, to have that experience. What a joy. How can I retain that same joy? What must I do? Why do I feel the way I feel? The words are as brilliant to my eyes as if Christ himself were speaking to me. Can this be me? Am I having an encounter with the Lord? All these years that I have been involved in helping Bob with the ministry; not once did I have the sensations that I'm experiencing now. Is it right? Should I let myself indulge in these feelings of ecstasy? What is happening to me?

Startled at his own thoughts, for a moment Stephen wondered if he had uttered the words aloud. His eyes quickly scanned the cabin, fearful that someone had heard his thoughts, that he may have given utterance out loud. He wasn't certain.

Freddy hadn't stirred, so it didn't startle him, but then what did? Stephen was grateful that everyone continued to doze while he grappled with his inner feelings. Besides, he was growing weary of the group's verbal fencing on every issue.

Stephen plunged back into his study of 3 Nephi. He read Chapter 11 and then 12, 13 . . . all the way to the end of the book.

He read it chapter by chapter, then reread those chapters. He was discovering the simple good news of Christ. *How often Bob has begged his congregation to feed upon the good news of Christ. Has Bob ever really fed upon it?*

Up to now, Stephen had not experienced that. When he had read the words of Christ in the New Testament, somehow he had never felt fulfilled. Never was it this rich and gratifying to the taste. *This is almost paradise,* he thought. *What is there about this account that speaks to my spirit? Lord, Lord God Almighty, help me to understand what's happening inside my very soul. It's new and unfamiliar, and I have to know if it's right.*

Stephen's mind suddenly felt a peaceful assurance that things would be okay. Somehow he would find this experience to be acceptable, not only to him but to Anney as well. *Oh, Anney, how will I ever explain it to you? You surely were forewarned that I would be touched by what I was reading. But you must come to see it as I see it. You* must. *If you could only realize it, your spirit is sensitive, too.*

* * *

Tony, the limo driver, obligingly called Knight Investigative Agency and left the name of the Caravan Inn where Peter had stayed the night before the funeral. Dan Knight was exultant as he asked Mort to fly over to Phoenix for the day and secure a log of the calls Peter had made.

"Try to persuade a night clerk at the Caravan Inn to help you, and don't spend more than two hundred bucks on the guy to get the information we need. Why am I telling you what to do? Just do it, Mort."

* * *

Bennett pulled his car into the parking terrace alongside Mary's Toyota. She was just getting out when she saw him.

She shook her head in frustration. "Bill, what have I done to deserve this?"

"Listen, Mary." Bennett looked around to make certain no one else was within earshot. "I learned an hour ago that Craig has already obtained a preliminary injunction on the escrow account for the participants. We can't touch it now. Peter is going to be disheartened when he learns this turn of events. Now I feel he has a right to use the money in the Beverly Hills bank to fulfill Thomas Kline's obligation to the participants who are expecting to be paid." Bennett paused and scrutinized Mary's face.

"Do the people who committed themselves to that project know that they're not getting paid the balance due them?" Mary asked the question with the same contemptuous attitude she had maintained since the funeral.

"No, they do not. Because I still hope there's a chance that you will change your mind and help pull the funds from the account." Bennett changed his tone and asked beseechingly, "Is there a chance? It would make my job so much easier if you would just say yes."

"I have told you before and I'll tell you again. No, no, and no! You have no right to do this to me. I am merely an employee who wants to do what is right."

"Okay." Bill tried to control his frustration at what he considered a stubborn woman. "All I can do is ask."

"Well, I would appreciate it if you wouldn't ask again. Now, I don't want to be late."

"I still think you are entertaining the thought of cooperating with us; otherwise, why haven't you told Craig where the funds are and that you are a cosigner on the account?"

Mary had already started toward the elevator that led directly to the main offices. She said over her shoulder as she continued to walk away from Bennett, "I may tell him about it this morning. If he finds out from some other person, he may be very displeased that I haven't come forth with the information. Goodbye, Bill."

Mary rode the elevator to the twentieth floor, got out, and started toward Craig's office with a determination to tell him everything.

"Just go on in," Lois said to Mary. "He's on the phone with his attorney. I'm sure he won't mind you waiting to speak to him."

Mary stepped into the familiar office that had been Thomas Kline's and felt a twinge of nostalgia and regret. Craig looked up from making a note and motioned for Mary to take a seat.

"Yeah, now that you finally have the injunction, I want you to stop the transfer of the Remington. . . . I know my father wanted it to go to the Southwestern Museum, but I say he wasn't thinking clearly when he gave it to the museum. You got it, man; he was simply not himself. Have you heard the latest appraisal? It's over twelve million and, the piece belongs to the heirs, not to some stuffy, poorly lit, back wall of a museum. . . . Right. . . . Let me know." Craig hung up the receiver.

"Mary, have you got some news for me? I haven't seen you in this office for days. You belong in here, you know, as my secretary. I'm thinking I could use a girl who knows her way around."

"I couldn't help overhearing you talk about the Remington," Mary began, a small frown creasing her forehead.

"Yes, as you know, Dad left it to a small museum here in Phoenix, but I don't want to give it up just yet, so I'm contesting that part of the will, plus a couple of other things."

"Your father's pet project?"

"Do you know anything that is happening with that project out in California? You were kinda tight with Dr. Polk, weren't you?"

"I was never *tight* with anyone," Mary said tartly, her mouth forming a straight line.

"Well, anyway, I think I have 'em trapped," Craig said. "I have a preliminary injunction on the funds that are earmarked for those people he has pulled in to participate. Let Polk try to get his hands on that money. He is going to have a tough time explaining to the people why they are not going to get paid. I'm not too concerned about the other funds; I think Dad's signature is required to access the account. And my attorney said that whoever touches that money may find himself in a lawsuit for misappropriation of funds."

Craig seemed happier than he had been in days. "Now, how

can I help you this morning, besides offering you a job doing what you did so well for Dad?"

Mary sat for a brief moment not speaking, aware that this bully in front of her would undermine Thomas Kline's wishes, given enough sharp legal minds. *What right does he have to interfere? He is a greedy, arrogant man. Those were his father's funds, not his. Thomas Kline was ten times the man his son is. His possessions should go to whomever he wished.*

"I . . . I just wanted to know if you wanted me to search further for any information on the whereabouts of that project." Mary had changed her mind about telling Craig about her signature on the other account. She guessed it was his effort to steal the Remington, because that was how she viewed it. She felt that there was something immoral in that kind of behavior—especially by a son.

"We're getting so close to closing Polk down that I doubt if I need any more rummaging through files for notes or a slip of paper. No, you go on about your job. If you decide to be my secretary, the job is open. I could use a certified secretary. You certainly made my father look good. I could use a little of your class, too."

With no emotion and no fear, Mary stood up to leave but first said, "May I remind you that your father wanted the Remington to be placed in a public facility so the whole world could enjoy it?"

Craig heard the barb in Mary's voice and chose to ignore it.

Chapter Twenty-Two
The Bishop

It was 8 a.m. by the time Stephen laced his Reeboks and did his warm-ups. Freddy emerged from a long shower, saw Stephen in his jogging shorts and T-shirt, and told him he was insane. For Freddy, there would be nothing this weekend but relaxation at the Hotel Del Coronado. "I'm going to lounge at the pool and have a drink, then maybe another; then I'll perhaps wander into the dining room and order something scrumptious; from there I'll catch up on sleep, go back—"

"Sorry, Freddy. I haven't time to listen to your scenario on gluttonous living. I have to jog."

Freddy stood with hands on his hips and a bath towel around his considerable middle, cocked his head sideways, and gaped in wonderment at this strange animal he roomed with.

Stephen quickly rounded the corner of the estate and moved up the hill toward the Orens' place. He jogged faster than usual. He hoped he wasn't too late. Coming down the opposite side of the hill, he saw Oren's Mercedes idling in the cobblestone driveway. *Good, good, good. He hasn't left for work.*

When Stephen got to the car, he moved his legs up and down in a hopping movement to cool down while he waited for Oren's return. He was still panting harder than he normally did from the dart up the hill. It was okay to dash when it was only a few yards, but half a mile seemed excessive. In two minutes the front door opened and Martin stepped out of the house—white shirt and tie and a just-showered appearance. He looked ready for the office.

"Well, well, well," Oren said effusively, "how's my favorite jogging buddy? I'm not dressed for action, as you can see."

"Hi, Martin." Stephen dropped his arms from their extended position, where he had stretched them in a rotating movement, which he had been told kept blood circulating rapidly. Continuing to move from side to side, he flashed Oren a quick smile. "I didn't come to go jogging. I just need to talk with you for a couple of minutes, but I see you're on your way to work. Maybe I can catch you some other time," Stephen said, not really wanting to leave without talking.

"No, no. It's my company. I can be late if I want. I'd like to talk. What can I do to help?"

"Do you mind if we step into your garage?" Stephen asked, pointing toward the four-car garage to the left of the circular drive. "I would like to ask you some questions."

Oren reached into the car, turned off the ignition, and punched the garage door opener. The two men entered the garage, and Oren asked Stephen to take a seat on the weight bench. Oren pulled up a plastic case and sat down.

"So, what is it?"

Still breathing raggedly, Stephen began to tell Martin Oren about the project, his involvement, the group, and the fact that he had returned at midnight from a research trip to Israel to check out some aspects of the Book of Mormon.

"No one told me that it was a Book of Mormon study down there. You mean, I've been this close to a group of sharp guys who have been digging into the Book of Mormon, and I didn't know? That is amazing."

"Be that as it may, it's true. I personally have read the entire Book of Mormon once and some parts as much as four times." Stephen took the terry-cloth towel Oren handed him and wiped his forehead where salty beads of sweat were running into his eyes. "The thing I need help with is my inner self. No one else in the group has indicated in any way that this study has had any personal impact on them. I even tried to be detached from what I was studying. I have arrived at the point where I feel that the Book of Mormon is exactly what it says it is. I'm convinced that the teachings in that book will lead a person closer to God than any other literary work. I guess you might say the Spirit has hit me. I'm ready to commit myself to Mormonism, and I've never even been in a Mormon church."

Oren ignored the clock and focused on Stephen. The thought of this man coming to understand the Spirit without any outside help, no instruction, no plan of conversion—simply by catching the spirit of the Book of Mormon—held Oren in awe. A tingling sensation moved down his spine.

In half an hour, Oren had the full story of the project, how Stephen became a participant in his father-in-law's place, and, finally, Stephen's conversion to the truth of the writings in the Book of Mormon. When Stephen concluded his account, Oren called his office to tell them he would be late arriving at the office, if he came in at all.

"My wife, Anney, is coming in this afternoon, with the kids, to spend the weekend at the Hotel Del Coronado. I've never hidden my feelings from Anney, but at this time, I doubt if she can take it," Stephen said, getting up off the bench for the fifth time. It was difficult for him to sit still very long.

"I don't know your Anney, but she sounds like a reasonable person," Martin said. "You know, you have to tell her of your new feelings. It isn't fair for her not to enjoy the same spirit," Oren urged, a sensitive tone to his voice.

Stephen pressed both hands hard to the sides of his head. "I know that. My mind is whirling, trying to work out a way of breaking it to her. You have to understand we are not talking about a woman who may attend church a dozen times a year, who thinks it is good for the children, and who volunteers to serve coffee and donuts once every six months. Anney is such a part of her father's ministry that the very foundation of our lives will be shaken when she hears what I have to tell her."

"When do you want to tell her, then?" Oren persisted, firmly convinced that it must be soon. "This evening, tomorrow, Sunday?

You know you do need to explain it before she goes back home."

"I guess . . . Sunday," Stephen finally answered, with hesitation in his voice. "I can't spoil the weekend for the family. I just can't."

The two spoke like old friends for another half-hour, and then Stephen realized he needed sleep, but how he would manage it was a puzzle. His mind was racing far too fast to quiet down, but he had to sleep. He had slept little since leaving Jerusalem. His body would collapse in a heap if he didn't take time to rest. Oren closed the garage door behind him and walked to his car. He opened the door, turned and held out his hand, and gazed deeply into Stephen's tired but intense eyes.

"This is a great moment in your life. You may not understand the full impact right now, but you have achieved something few men ever do. You have found the gospel of Jesus Christ through searching. Now you can't let this feeling die. If you do, the Spirit of the Holy Ghost may never touch your mind and heart again. It is propitious, Stephen; make the most of it." He held Stephen's hand and squeezed it for an extra moment. Then he released it and stepped into his car.

"Thank you for taking the time to talk to me," said Stephen. "I won't say I feel better, but you have given me reassurance that I'm moving in the only possible direction at this time."

"Hey, I'd love to meet your family while they're here. If you want to drop over . . ."

"Thanks, we'll see how the time goes."

* * *

Midnight on a Friday was often busy, but it being midsummer in Phoenix, the tourist trade was slow, and there was nothing special happening in Scottsdale, particularly at the Caravan Inn. Mike Conkin had the night shift. He hated working at the desk through the night. The hardest part was staying alert and acting like he enjoyed what he was doing. He had resolved to quit this job as soon as he could and get back to school. He should never have left school in the first place.

Mike glanced up at the large man approaching the desk.

"May I help you, sir?" Mike asked, glad to have a break in the monotony.

"Perhaps." Mort sized up Mike. Young, college age, no money, maybe needs to make a car payment and can't meet it this weekend. *I think I'll just hit him with what I want and see if he responds. I think he will.*

"I'd like to look at the phone calls that a Peter Polk made while he was here on June twenty-first. Have you received back the billings? And if so, can I look at 'em?"

"Oh, I can't let you . . . ah . . . sir, the management would have to approve . . ."

Mort held out a hundred dollar bill. Mike studied the money. He looked around, then shook his head, "I don't think I could. . . ."

Mort laid down a second hundred dollar bill. "Kid, this is my limit. I don't need the information any more than two hundred bucks' worth."

When Mort left through the front door of the Caravan Inn, he was folding a photocopy of the phone calls Peter Polk had made from his room Friday evening and Saturday morning, the day of Thomas Kline's funeral. Mike watched Mort leave and felt like a louse. There was something about this business that ran against his moral grain. He wished he hadn't needed the money. But two hundred dollars in his college savings would help. *So what if the management finds out? Let them fire me.*

"Dan, I hate to wake you, but I think we're onto something. I got Polk's calls, and I'm checking them out."

Mort waited a second for Dan to shake off the effects of deep slumber, then he continued: "He made three calls, one to his home number—I recognize that number—probably to check his messages, the next one to a Mesa number. I checked that with information. It's his sister. The third may be what we're looking for. He called a number in the 415 area code. That's in the Bay Area. Our person may be from San Francisco or thereabouts. I called the number, just to check it out. When I checked out the number, I got a recording telling me all about how I should attend church on Sunday at the *Hour of Christian Joy*. Here, I wrote it down. It says that the Reverend Moore will be addressing the vital subject of summer awakenings, whatever that means. Anyway, we'll have to wait until morning to find out about this preacher and his connection with the Mormon Project."

* * *

The rooms were turn-of-the-century Victorian. It was the sort of hotel where guests could drop back a century and relive the atmosphere of that era, when San Diego was young and the Hotel Del Coronado was reached only by ferry. It was a grand hotel, and Anney loved every part of it, from the dark-stained walls in the lobby to the legend of the ghost in the room on the top floor—purported to be the ghost of a woman who was killed by her husband on their honeymoon. Besides, it was good to be with the whole family; this outing was much like the ones they had enjoyed on dozens of short vacations when the children were little.

"Wasn't that a delicious Sunday brunch?" Stephen commented as he and Anney walked along the shoreline, half a mile from the hotel. A few people were around, but the beach was not crowded. It was just ten in the morning.

They had been up late the night before. A small band in the ballroom played favorites from the sixties and seventies. Stephen and Anney danced until one, had a little nightcap, and turned in. The suite had two bedrooms. Todd had already fallen asleep on the roll-out couch in the living room, leaving the movie channel playing, and Brenda was asleep in the smaller bedroom. Quietly, Anney and Stephen had slipped into their room and each other's arms as they had done the previous evening.

The waves lapped at Anney's bare toes and the sand whirled about her feet as the water receded. The air was balmy. "I wish you were going home with us," Anney said with a wistful voice.

"Two more weeks—not even that if you knock off Saturday and Sunday. We finish Friday of the seventh week." Stephen kicked at the sand as he spoke, "I know I've told you a dozen times, but you don't know how I longed for you to be with me in Israel."

"Yeah, tell me about it," Anney said for the tenth time as well. "You really got to see all the places that Daddy has talked about for years? Daddy told me, while you were in Jerusalem this last week, that if he had it to do over, he would have taken mother and me to the Holy Land. He says that's one big regret of his life."

"Well, it is something to see."

"What *I* really wish is that I could have been with you at the dinner with your friend's Russian relatives. Someday, I want to find Mother's family in Ukraine, at least my aunt in Prague. She always wanted to go back, you know, to see for herself that they were all right."

"Umm," Stephen responded absently.

"Stephen, is something wrong? You are acting sort of funny. What did you discover there that has caused a change in you?" Anney, always direct, probed Stephen as if he were on a witness stand.

"What?" Stephen asked with an incredulous voice.

"You heard me. A change."

Stephen tossed up his arms and said with disbelief, "Is it that obvious?"

"All I know is that during this entire little vacation, you have acted like you wanted to tell me something. I don't know what, but it is right on the edge of your thoughts, and you seem ready to burst out with it."

Am I ready to tell her? Is she ready to listen? I am ready, but is she? I don't know if I can say the right words. What kind of introduction does something like this require?

"Well, your silence tells me you are trying to figure out a way to break something to me. Stephen, just tell me." Anney looked worried, but determined.

"Anney, I don't think you want to hear what I have to say." Her face remained determined. "But I have to say it, either here or on the phone. Sometime you have to hear it from me."

Anney's face paled, such dreaded words. She took hold of Stephen's arm and pulled him around to face her. She searched his face, and still he couldn't speak. "So *tell* me," she pleaded in anguish.

"It has to do with the project. . . . Ah . . . I came down here with a strong resolve to be objective, even negative, about this research. Ask Dr. Polk; he'll confirm it."

"I don't care about Dr. Polk. He has nothing to do with us," Anney said impatiently.

"You may not care about Dr. Polk, but you need to know that he has had nothing to with what's happened to me. I am the one who got these feelings, by myself."

"What are you trying to tell me, Stephen? Stephen, what?"

Stephen knew Anney could already formulate his next words. "I have come to realize that the Book of Mormon is really true." *There, it's out; at last it's out!*

The world whirled around Anney. She gasped for air, sank to her knees, and pressed her hands to the sides of her head, unaware of the water surging over her legs. She could not have been in more agony if Stephen had taken a gun and shot her right there on the beach. Her hands trembled, and her mouth moved, but no words came out, at least not at first. Then she caught her breath, and with lips curled into the fierce snarl of a mother lioness, she exploded. "No! You cannot do this to me and our children! No, no, no, no!"

Stephen tried to put his arms around Anney's shoulders, but she whirled away and struggled to her feet. She began to cry great heaving sobs. Then, raising her right hand as if she were trying to stop an onrushing freight train, she repeated incoherently again and again, "This is not right. This is not right. This is not right."

Stephen took one step toward her, and Anney shouted, "Stop! Don't come near me. I don't want you to touch me. Do you hear me? I don't want you near me. Leave me alone."

She dropped the sandals she had been carrying, turned, and staggered back to the hotel.

Stephen stood a long while watching Anney fade into the distant mist. When she had disappeared behind the hotel's enclosure wall, he took a few steps, picked up the sandals, and followed after her with a heavy heart, knowing that it would be futile to try to speak with her for the next hour or two. *Oh, God, what have I done? What am I going to do?*

* * *

The receptionist had asked Mort Johnson to follow the ushers into the studio. He was cautioned not to make a sound because Dr. Moore was just concluding the taping of a broadcast that would be shown on next Sunday's *Hour of Christian Joy*. Mort nodded that he understood.

The studio was nearly filled with people, Mort guessed over three hundred. He had never been to a Sunday morning gospel broadcast, but he had been to many other types of meetings. This was just another experience for a man who had experienced far too much for one life. He took the seat in the back that had been shown to him by a young usher. The only sound was the voice of Bob Moore pleading with the people of the Bay Area to follow Jesus Christ in their daily lives.

"Take comfort, find hope, and let the light of the Almighty lift up your souls. Enjoy peace from Jesus Christ, be a true and loving person who is willing to give, and thus you will enjoy the great and wonderful feelings of knowing that God loves you. He does love you," Bob concluded. He waited for the camera to move forward as he had instructed the director, and then he said, "Yes, yes, oh yes, He does in fact love all of us. We are His, and He is ours. Amen."

A resounding amen came spontaneously from the audience, who, with few exceptions, loved this man who showed them the way to reach heaven with joy in their hearts.

Most of the congregation had left, and only a handful of admirers lingered to compliment Bob on "one of the finest sermons ever given." One older lady pressed a ten-dollar bill into Bob's hand and told him, "May God bless you for your goodness. Maybe this will help. I don't have much, but it is my blessing to you that you will prosper."

I need a blessing. If I don't get some cash into the bank by Wednesday, there will be no ministry—there will be no Bob Moore to preach to you. The need for money crowded Bob's every thought. The bank directors had threatened to call in the loan by five o'clock Wednesday if the interest was not paid. There was nothing more Clifford could do.

"Dr. Moore, there is a gentleman up in the last row who would like to have a word with you," the young usher whispered into Bob's right ear.

Bob invited Mort into the studio office, asked him to sit down, and offered him coffee. From a coffee pot resting on a hot plate on a side table, Bob poured coffee and handed a cup to Mort, who took a sip, realizing it was nearly boiling hot.

"Now, how can I help you, Mr. . . . ?"

"Just call me Mort." Mort cleared his throat from the effects of the hot coffee. "I called your office yesterday and got the recording telling about your television gospel show. What little I heard sounded encouraging. I'm always amazed at how easy it looks for you people who have such a gift."

Never one to hurry a compliment, Bob thanked Mort.

"I do this every Sunday. It is then carried by station KQTV all over this area the following Sunday. I love the work of the Lord."

"I'm sure you do." Mort put down his coffee on the metal desk in front of him and said, "I really called yesterday to talk with your son-in-law, but the receptionist tells me he's in the San Diego area attending a meeting that is lasting seven weeks. Is that so?"

"Yes. He was invited, with some other scholars, to participate in a religious study. Why do you ask? Has something happened that I need to know about?"

"No," Mort said reassuringly. *At last I've found them!* "Would it be possible for you to give me the address and phone number of your son-in-law so I can talk with him? It's a rather confidential matter that I'm sure he would want to know about."

"Well, my son-in-law and I work together here in the ministry. If I can be of help," Bob queried.

"No, I need to speak with him." Mort was beginning to get nervous with this inquisitive preacher. *Is he going to stonewall me like all the others?*

"People normally leave a donation after one of your sermons. Isn't that right, Reverend?" Mort was reaching for his wallet as he spoke.

"No, no, you needn't feel an obligation to pay." Bob was startled by the implications of the offer of money. "If I can help you, I will help you; that is, if I feel it's that important. My only dilemma is locating the card with Stephen's address and phone number. His wife and children are down there now, enjoying a weekend together." Bob volunteered generalities, beginning to wonder who the man was. "Who do you represent?" Bob asked bluntly.

Mort shook his head. "I just need some information; that's all."

Bob decided to be direct. "You have been deliberately vague with me on this matter. Is something happening at this gathering that is not right? Does it have anything to do with the fees that are yet to be paid?" Bob was gripped with panic.

Mort turned his eyes to the floor, rather than go eyeball to eyeball with this minister who could stare down an elephant.

"I think you know what you are after. Something is not right here. I would suggest you go back to whoever sent you and tell them I would like to speak with that person myself before I divulge anything about my son-in-law."

Mort quickly left the office, telling Moore that he would be back in touch with him. He had let himself get suckered in by a pro. Bob had Mort out of the office in two minutes, with the hot coffee still steaming on the desk. Mort knew he had to call in for instructions. At the entrance to the building, he noticed a pay phone and called Knight.

* * *

There was silence in the rented limousine all the way to the airport. Todd had innocently asked if something was wrong when the family first took their seats in the plush automobile. Brenda, a glowing, attractive blonde, with a nose too pointed to be really beautiful, put her finger to her lips. Todd got the message.

The driver helped them with their luggage check-in. No one spoke unless it was for baggage instructions. Not until they came up to the detector screen, where Stephen could go no further, did

Anney say without any hint of her thoughts, "Stephen, I want you to get on the plane with us now."

"Anney, be reasonable."

"Reasonable? *You* want *me* to be reasonable?" Anney asked, barely able to keep her voice low.

Stephen was at a loss. For a moment he said nothing. Brenda glanced around at the stream of people waiting to pass through the metal detector. She and Todd were both embarrassed. But they did not move away from their parents. They clustered as a family, each awaiting the outcome.

Todd could only remember one other time when his mother had been this upset with his father in front of him. Six months ago, he remembered standing in the kitchen when his father happened to mention something about taking a job in Southern California with a popular televangelist. He remembered his mother shouting at his father about how good Grandfather had been to the family and how could he leave him. Now that same wave of intensity seemed to prevail here on the main ramp to Southwest's Flight 347.

Stephen gave a slight laugh and said with palms open, "I don't have a ticket."

Anney turned to Todd and said, "Give your father your ticket." Anney began rummaging through her purse for her wallet. "Todd, you catch the next flight. I'll give you two hundred dollars to buy another ticket. With the rest you can have dinner while you wait for the next flight." Anney continued to search for money. Several Kleenexes fell on the floor. Brenda quickly scooped them into her hand. Anney was flustered, not able to locate the cash inside her wallet.

"Mom," Todd said quietly, "come on. . . . This isn't cool. Not here, not right now. This is—"

"Did you hear me? Don't sass me. Give him your ticket." Anney stopped searching for the cash, reached over, and grabbed the envelope containing Todd's airline ticket from his hand. She shoved it at Stephen, crushing the ticket folder into his chest. "Here! Here, take it, and get on this flight with me, or I'll never believe you truly love us." Tears were beginning to race down her bright pink cheeks as she stood firm in her decision to force

Stephen to go with her.

Stephen clasped both hands over the wadded ticket and stood dumfounded at Anney's near-insane reaction to what he had told her on the beach.

"I see. You are not going to come with me. Okay, okay, you have turned on us. You are so insensitive to our needs that you would let this thing tear us apart," Anney cried out, trying to wipe her tears with the back of her hand.

Brenda handed the tissues to her mother. People had stopped to stare. Even the security people at the detection screen were eyeing the scene, not sure whether it was a ploy to distract them or a good old-fashioned family fight. Either way, it was interesting to all who passed by.

Anney pressed her lips together, turned sharply on her white heels, and then plunked her purse onto the conveyor belt. Without another word, she stalked through the detection screen. The alarm sounded, but she paid no attention to it.

"Ma'am," a six-foot-four black security guard said, sidling up beside her as she started up the ramp, "you'll have to return and take out whatever metal you are carrying, then pass through the detector again. I'm sorry, very sorry, ma'am."

Anney felt confused for a minute, and then she reversed her steps, took out the car keys she had put in her skirt pocket, and walked back through the detector. Barely able to see through her tears, she picked up the keys and purse and started up the ramp again with her head held high and her back ramrod straight.

The children stood watching her, wondering what had gotten into their mother. Stephen knew. He said, "Here, Todd," as he returned the crumpled airline ticket to his son. "Go comfort your mother. She needs understanding right now. I'll explain later."

"Sure, Dad."

Still bewildered at what she had just seen, Brenda reached up and kissed Stephen on the cheek and quickly followed Todd through the detector.

Chapter Twenty-Three
Opposing Views

Week Six—Monday Morning

"Who do these people think they are?" Craig asked Knight on the phone. He sat alone at the breakfast table, drinking coffee and studying a letter from the Southwestern Museum of Art. They were requesting the Remington painting. Sharp had received the letter Friday and had delivered it to Craig's sprawling home in Paradise Valley this morning. It was a formal reminder by the museum curator that the Remington, with other artworks, had been bequeathed to the museum. They asked that Craig please consider the matter and act appropriately. They also noted that they were aware that the estate had not yet been settled but appealed to Mr. Kline to cooperate.

Craig scoffed at the letter. He had told Sharp that there would have to be a court fight before he released that painting or any of the dozen other western paintings of a more modest value that his father had left to the museum. Besides, he had the paintings in a safe place—a vault at the bank.

Now he listened to Knight tell him that some evangelist clown wanted to talk to him personally before the man would give out information on his son-in-law's whereabouts.

Craig had agreed to a meeting with Bob Moore. "This evangelist better have some information, or I'll throw him out. What do you think he has in mind? Why can't he simply tell us where his son-in-law is? Why such a big deal?"

Knight didn't know. "He'll be in your office at ten this morning. Is that okay?"

"Yeah, I'll talk to him, but I don't make deals. Have you found out any more about the bank account? I didn't think so." Craig hung up the phone, sick to death of the whole mess his father had left behind.

* * *

Stephen sat on the grass with his hands on his knees, listening to Bishop Oren console him. The two had jogged a mile and then plopped down on the recently cut lawn of the greenbelt. Stopping during a jog was highly irregular for the two men but very necessary this morning. Stephen yearned for advice about his new, inexplicable feelings toward what he had always thought was a good way of life. Suddenly his former understanding of life and the hereafter was no longer enough. He eagerly sought a higher level of spiritual involvement.

"Sometimes, just when you think you've got it down, you find that you need to make some changes. It will always be that way," Oren said, as he sensed Stephen's desperate need for correct answers.

Stephen had rehearsed the events of the weekend to Oren, including the airport scene. "Can't you see? My heart is in pieces right now. I desperately want to arrange things to include my family, but I'm still groping for answers so that I can point my soul in the best possible direction. I do think I'm approaching a point at which the old way will never do." Stephen's brow wrinkled as he stared off to his left into the brightness of the morning glow edging through the overcast sky.

Oren chewed on a blade of grass as he spoke, "Stephen, you have a wife who cares about you. You know she really cares. She feels threatened by this sudden change in you. *You* know why you feel the need to change, but she doesn't. This thing could take time. You asked me what you should do. I say, why not endure the remaining days of the project? You're so close. And as you told me the other day, at least you would be helping your family moneywise.

"So, if you want to know my counsel to you, have a little patience with Anney. Get her on your side. You convinced her to marry you, didn't you? Try ways of appealing to her that you used then. It is never too late. Get her to read the Book of Mormon with you. She ought to experience what you've experienced." Oren spit out the grass. "Does that make sense?"

Stephen wiped sweat from his cheeks with the back of his hand. "It makes sense. . . . Except I don't think I can get her to even touch the book, let alone read it. You should have seen her yesterday. But I guess I'll leave that between the two of us."

"Yes, I understand. I think I have the picture, but I also know that time is a great healer of wounded hearts." Oren reached over and patted Stephen's hand and said, "You will have to allow for the healing process. There may be no short cuts. What more can I tell you?"

"You've been super about taking time to listen to my distresses."

"So, are you still in agreement that I invite the missionaries to come over to my place tomorrow night and explain more about the gospel to you?"

"Sure, I haven't changed my mind about going forward with this thing. I believe it's right for me, more now than before." Stephen rose to his feet; his muscles had cooled. He felt a slight stiffness and knew that it was because he had violated his cardinal rule of never stopping in the middle of a good jog. "I hope I haven't given you the impression that I've changed my mind at all. My feelings about the Book of Mormon have not changed. As for the missionary presentation, I'll be there."

* * *

Anney was too emotionally distraught to call her father last evening. She had needed a little space—time to think. She was grateful he hadn't called. The kids had cooperated by hurrying off to see their friends shortly after they got home from the airport. She had spent the evening with her thoughts and had reviewed her emotional experience and the impact it must have had on Brenda and

Todd. She had dismissed that by rationalizing that the children were nearly adults and would have to face the real world as she was certainly doing. She knew they would get over it. It wasn't as traumatic for them as for her. They were unaware of the reason for the blowup in the first place.

The thing that had bothered her last evening, and even now as she pulled into her reserved parking space at the office of the ministry, was her confusion about what Stephen had told her—that he had found something wonderful, something that offered him hope, or whatever it was he had told her. She sat for a moment with her forehead pressed against the steering wheel.

Chip, the boy she had loved so fervently, had expressed some of these same feelings. *Do they teach all the men the same method of gaining some mysterious spirit or what?*

Now it was time to talk this over with her father. *Why do I have to talk it over with my father?* She knew the reason as she asked the question. Why? Because she had always done it that way. He had always been there for her needs. It was his magnanimous way of helping her through life.

Anney stopped by her father's office before walking to her own. He was not there. It appeared that he had not been in yet this morning—the familiar coffee cup and newspaper were missing.

In her office, Anney asked by intercom if June knew where her father was.

"Oh, he left you a message early this morning, Anney. He said he had to be out of the office all day. He is meeting with a person who may be a big donor to the ministry. He'll call you when he gets in this evening."

It's just as well I don't have to discuss this with anyone right now. I'm not up to it.

* * *

"Yes, send him in," Craig replied when his secretary announced that the Reverend Robert Moore was waiting in the outer office.

No one could be more gracious than Bob when meeting

someone he deemed important to know, or vital to his financial interests. They shook hands, and then Craig asked if Bob would care for coffee. Bob sat down and began to comment on the spectacular view of the city.

"Yes, it is quite impressive," Craig agreed, pouring two cups of coffee and handing one to Bob. "Actually, until recently this was my father's office. He died a few weeks ago—he was along in years—so I moved in. My old office is down the hall, but it's not nearly as spacious as this one."

Craig sat down and placed both hands together, fingertips touching. "I hope I don't seem too blunt, but I have interrupted my schedule to allow time for you this morning. Frankly, I want to know the location of your son-in-law. To set your mind at ease, it is not your son-in-law I want to talk to, but I do need to know the location of the group he is working with."

Craig shifted in his soft, executive chair and came to the point. "I would like that information. I'm not an unreasonable man. I'm sure your organization accepts contributions, so I would like to donate, say . . . five thousand dollars in exchange for your son-in-law's location."

"Did I ask for money?" Bob said, disturbed by the directness of the man.

"No, no you didn't. But I think that a donation is in order. After all, you have come all this way for some reason, so I hope that a few thousand will compensate." Craig kept an amiable tone to his voice. Inside he was irritated with this smooth operator. Craig had already sensed that the minister had come for money.

He must want to know the location pretty desperately to casually offer me five thousand dollars, Bob thought. He knew that desperate men did desperate things. *This thing must be important and worth more. It must be worth a lot more than he is letting on.*

Bob probed to learn a little more. "I understand you have been trying to locate this project since it started. Isn't that so?" Bob guessed.

"Who told you that?"

"It is true, isn't it?" Bob said without expression. He had no way of knowing, but it couldn't hurt to send out feelers to learn the reason this Craig Kline wanted Bob's bit of information.

Craig said nothing, his eyes narrowing as he searched Moore's face.

Clearly Bob could see that this man would pay more than five thousand. *If he voluntarily offered five, would he make a deal on twenty-five thousand in a cashier's check made out to the ministry? That would pay the interest on the loan. I'll press for it. But will he go for it? That's a lot of money for information.* "The donation must be twenty-five thousand," Bob blurted out.

"What?" Craig came up out of his chair, spilling his coffee. "Are you insane?"

Bob got a firsthand view of the real Craig—the Craig whose violence only those closest to him truly understood. He hit the desk with his fist and said, "No. This is extortion, and I'll not be a party to it."

Bob knew that he must remain in control; it meant keeping a cool head. He would prevail. He felt confident about that.

"A moment ago, you were willing to donate five thousand," Bob continued. "I am at the head of a ministry that happens to lack funds. If you want my information, I also want the best for my congregation, and we need twenty-five thousand dollars. Furthermore, I would like it in a cashier's check, personally delivered to me tomorrow by two o'clock. I will remain here in Phoenix until the transaction is completed. You will receive the location and phone number you want in return for the donation, of course." Bob realized he didn't know just what this man wanted to do with the information once he got it, but he seemed to require it badly.

Craig walked to the window and stared out. He took an extra minute and then turned around to scrutinize this stone-faced minister. "Okay, I'll do it," he said finally. "What assurance do I have that the information you give me is current to this very hour?"

"I will give you *my* assurance."

"What do you mean?" Craig asked with a sneer on his unpleasant mouth.

"I mean I am a man of God, so when I give my word, it is sound."

"Yeah, sure," Craig said sarcastically.

* * *

Bob Moore had made two calls from his hotel room at the Hyatt Regency in downtown Phoenix. He called June, his secretary, Monday afternoon to reassure her that he was fine. He gave her the extension number to his room and then told her he would be home the next afternoon. He also told her that he had been with a man who wanted to make a sizable donation to the ministry, so he needed to wait until he had the check in hand before returning home.

The second call was to Anney. He knew Anney would understand and not be concerned with his absence. In a casual, offhanded way, he asked Anney how he could get in touch with Stephen. He told her he couldn't recall the phone number or the address, though Stephen had given him both.

"Well, Daddy, the address is a post office box. But he is in the locked community at a place called Fairbanks Ranch. They have an eight hundred number." She gave him the number, told him she missed him, and said good-bye. Moore wrote the information on a piece of paper and settled down to wait. The ball was in Craig's court.

When the knock came, a serious man of prodigious girth and brown teeth stepped in and asked to see the information Bob had for Mr. Kline. Bob looked over the gorilla-like man and then handed him the paper with the location and phone number he had received from Anney written on it. The gorilla asked if he could use the phone. He called Craig's office and read off the information he had been handed. "Yeah, sure, no . . . okay, I'll wait." He hung up the phone.

The man waited without uttering another word. He sat by the window and looked out on the city.

In an hour the phone rang. Bob answered it, but it was for George. George, the gorilla, took the receiver. He grunted a few times and then hung up. George pulled a legal-sized envelope from his inside jacket pocket and handed it to Moore. Bob opened the envelope, and there it was—a certified check for $25,000.

"Mr. Kline says everything checks out with his people in

California. I'll be leaving."

Bob closed the door behind George with a sweeping sense of relief. *What was that mob routine all about? Is there something illegal about this whole thing?*

He was ready to leave. He needed to get back home and to the bank by tomorrow morning. At least he had the money in hand to stall the bank from calling in the entire loan.

* * *

Through dogged persistence, Henry was successful in reaching a publisher who dealt with anti-Mormon literature. His name was Lewis Granger, and he had been lecturing for fifteen years about what he termed the *problems* with the Book of Mormon. Henry had learned that Granger's publishing house grossed over a million dollars a year in books, tapes, and publications, including a quarterly magazine entitled *Mormonism Unveiled*. Henry had told the group at breakfast about Granger coming to present his findings, mentioning the man's annual income as well. The group had wondered how popular anti-Mormonism really was to garner that kind of money.

Stephen was late entering the dining room for the presentation. He had hung up the phone with his secretary in Pleasant Hill a few minutes before. She had given him the name of Dr. Barry Ross, a Brigham Young University professor who had written to Bob Moore after his series of exposé lectures on the Mormons. The letter had taken Bob to task, point by point, for his comments made during the lecture. Bob had given the letter to Stephen the day he received it and had asked that Stephen answer it. Stephen remembered that he had struggled with the reply.

Ten minutes before the current presentation, it had occurred to Stephen that if Ross at Brigham Young University kept tabs on persons who lectured about the Mormon "cult," perhaps he would have some information on this fellow Granger. Stephen wanted to know more about the man.

In the library, Stephen had pressed Roy into service. He had given Roy brief instructions about securing any information Dr.

Ross had on the presenter. "If Ross has anything he can share, ask him to please fax the information in the next few minutes. Oh, and by the way, Roy," Stephen had instructed, "tell Dr. Ross that you are part of Dr. Polk's project and that we need the information pronto. Thanks." Stephen wasn't sure he would come up with anything, but he had a hunch about this man. Stephen slipped into his chair beside Freddy. Their eyes met. Freddy's seemed to ask what Stephen was up to.

The exposé lecturer, Lewis Granger, had assured Henry that he could easily present his material before a group of scholars. He welcomed the opportunity to enlighten the group about the contradictions in the Book of Mormon. With Peter's full approval, Henry had arranged for the presentation two weeks earlier. Due to the injunction on the project funds, Peter had used his dwindling personal savings to fly the man in from Salt Lake City, the site of his thriving publishing company.

Roy had picked up the publisher at Lindbergh Field, and now Granger stood before the group, ready to enlighten them.

"I understand from Dr. Syman that each of you has focused on a part of the Book of Mormon," the publisher said. "He also tells me that you have had other presentations on various aspects of the book. Let me say it is an honor to be here."

He was a tall, impressive-looking man of fifty whose credentials were not academic, but he had experience in research, writing, and publishing. He appeared to know his subject well.

He had brought to the dining table a stack of nine books. He began by hoisting up each book and making a comment about it. "I have only assembled authors whom I consider to be researchers of the highest stature. Each has studied parts of the Book of Mormon; therefore, I have read their writings, discussed with them their particular areas of interest, and feel confident that their conclusions are adequate for my presentation here. Their judgment is that the book is, without a doubt, a nineteenth-century writing."

He picked up the top book. "For example, here is Vogel's work, *Indian Origins in the Book of Mormon*. Very enlightening. You will find that he shows clearly that there were many books in the western New York area on the theme of the American Indian being part of the lost tribes of Israel. This, of course, influenced Joseph Smith in his writings.

"Next is Michael Coe's study, *Central American Archaeology*. He was an eminent archaeologist from Yale who put to bed, once and for all, Mormon claims that the ruins in Central America are part of a civilization of early inhabitants on this continent who ostensibly emigrated from the Holy Land."

"May I ask a question?" Bernie said, unable to resist a clarification of what the speaker was saying.

"Well, I usually have a question-and-answer period after my discussion. But one question will be all right, if you would make it brief."

Bernie proceeded without allowing Granger to finish his comment. "It is my understanding that the Mormons, or more specifically, the Church of Jesus Christ of Latter-day Saints, has never made an official statement as to geographical locations in the Book of Mormon. I personally checked that out with some officials in Salt Lake City, and they faxed me a statement of policy. The Mormons have never taken an official stand on the location of the people who migrated from the Holy Land."

"Well, surely you know what I meant by *Mormons.*"

"No, I'm afraid I don't." Bernie look puzzled.

"I mean the scholars and researchers," Granger said, quickly moving ahead with his presentation.

"Wait a minute," Bernie inserted. "Don't be so quick to gloss over this little matter about what is official and what isn't. In my mind it makes *a lot* of difference whether something is officially sanctioned by an organization or merely accepted by a segment of its members."

"I'm sorry; I don't think I follow what you are getting at."

"I'm getting at what is hearsay and what is fact. Don't confuse the two."

Granger looked at his watch, cleared his throat, and then looked down at Bernie with a businesslike gaze and said, "Now, if we can go on, perhaps we can come back to your question later, after I have had a chance to present what I've come to present. Perhaps I will cover your concerns at some point during my lecture." Bernie nodded approval. He knew this man had been handling objections for fifteen-plus years and could see that he was an expert at his trade. *He has to be*, thought Bernie, *to make the kind of money he is making doing what he is doing.* It was precisely the money that disturbed Bernie the most.

"Next," Granger continued, "is the *Spaulding Manuscript Rediscovered* by Harvey Lewis. He shows in his work that Joseph Smith had access to the Spaulding manuscript and used the theme as the core of his Nephite and Lamanite tribal conflicts. And so on. Now, if you will allow me, I would like to present my findings."

The six were reserved but courteous. They took notes and listened for the next hour to the publisher explain how he had uncovered, with outstanding researchers, a complete framework from which he showed the Book of Mormon to be a nineteenth-century writing, in part due to the use of phrases and words of that era. Whether Joseph Smith wrote the book or someone close to him did was not the key issue in the presenter's mind. His focus was simply that the book was nineteenth-century writing.

Granger took a sip of water from the glass Roy had provided. He had been speaking so long that his mouth was dry.

Judith spoke first during the question-and-answer period. She was soft-spoken and charming. "Then it is your contention that the Book of Mormon is a fictional account from the mind of a nineteenth-century author?"

Bernie stared at Judith. He could not understand how she could have let so much of the information the publisher had presented as fact slip past her.

"Oh, yes," Lewis Granger said, with the confidence of a man who has won over his audience.

"May I ask another question, Mr. Granger? Is it your opinion that much of the writing of the Book of Mormon is poor, with imaginative spelling and grammar? Would you say it has structural and linguistic flaws that cast a long shadow over the book?"

Bernie let a faint smile cross his lips. He knew Judith was warming up for the kill.

"I feel that the book is so poorly written that it has taken the Mormon Church nearly a century and three quarters to clean it up."

Judith asked one more question: "Why do you think Joseph Smith, as you insist, 'wrote' the book with very little punctuation?"

"Because he was an ignorant frontiersman. He didn't understand the basic rules of English grammar. It is as simple as that."

Bernie was too excited to wait for Judith to make her point. "I have a couple of questions to ask you," he blurted angrily. "And no more putting me off!"

Granger wore a wounded expression. He merely shook his head as if he had done nothing to warrant Bernie's wrath. "You mentioned very forcefully from . . ." Bernie glanced down at his notes, "Melrose that there were many source books on Hebrew writings in style and form that may have influenced Joseph Smith in western New York. Tell me, when do you think Joseph Smith gained an education in Hebraisms so he could incorporate them into his work? And how long do you think it would take to gain a sufficient knowledge of Hebrew to mimic so accurately the Hebrew style of writing?" Bernie disallowed Granger's rebuttal and followed up with, "I understand you think Joseph Smith simply copied the Hebrew method of composition from available Hebrew works and the Bible, and this gave the book the flavor of a Near Eastern influence, specifically Hebrew."

"I think you have the point," Granger said, "but I think you are oversimplifying what I said. You must understand that Joseph Smith was a very cunning man and went to great lengths to deceive his followers."

Just then, Roy quietly entered the room from the rear, walked over, and cupped his hands to Stephen's ear. Stephen arose and followed Roy to the hall.

In the hall, the gangling graduate student, who was four inches taller than Stephen, leaned over slightly to say in a hushed voice, "I have here some information for you. Five minutes ago Ross's office faxed me the dossier they have on this Granger fellow. They were very cooperative. Anyway, you may want to look it over." Roy handed Stephen a folder containing the faxed material.

With the adroitness of a speed reader, Stephen perused the material. He handed back the folder and quietly instructed, "Roy, would you make copies of these letters for the participants and

Granger? He may be interested in what we have uncovered."

Roy agreed with a nod of his head and whirled around to reenter the library at the far end of the hall. Stephen returned to the presentation just as Bernie was making what sounded like a summation.

"I don't enjoy playing games with an ignorant man, Mr. Granger," Bernie said, relishing the moment, "but you, I understand, make a handsome living publishing and lecturing on anti-Mormon topics. Isn't that right?"

"Much of what I make goes back into my ministry to uncover more of the deception of Mormonism. I want you to know that I have recently been to Russia with a busy itinerary to meet with leading religious Russians to warn them about the Mormons making a strong impact on the Russian people. We spoke to many pastors and Bible students and warned them about the Mormons."

"I don't care whether the Mormons or you or the Hindus are making inroads into Russia. We are here discussing the antiquity and possible authenticity of the Book of Mormon. . . ."

Henry signaled with three fingers lifted toward Bernie and said, "Bernie, Mr. Granger is our guest. I think we owe him the courtesy of refraining from any personal references or belittling his work."

"Henry, get serious. This guy is nothing but a sham. He goes around as some kind of 'Christian authority' and bashes the Mormons. I don't care that he does that. He came to give us some sound insights into the flaws of the Book of Mormon. I haven't heard a single thing that indicates that he has done his homework on the critical issues of the book. So far as I'm concerned, he deserves my response."

"I'm sorry, ah, I don't think I understand what you—"

"Maybe I can make it simple." Bernie leaned forward in his chair at the dining table. "I am twice the age Joseph Smith was when he finished his work on the Book of Mormon. I am Jewish; I speak English." Bernie caught Martha's eye and winked. "There are those here who would challenge that statement. I speak Russian, and I can understand Yiddish. I have spent a lifetime trying to master Hebrew, and I'm *still* trying to learn it."

Bernie continued, "Are you telling me that a young man in his early twenties could take the Hebrew books that were supposed to have been available in western New York—and I doubt that there were all that many—and this young man, Joseph Smith, without tutoring, working all day on the farm, had the luxury of studying and mastering Hebrew? I have had the luxury of time to study, and I still have severe deficits in Hebrew." Bernie looked around at his colleagues and said, "For us to sit here and listen to you tell us that Joseph Smith got his Hebrew from some crash course at the local library—"

"I didn't say he got his information at the local library."

"After the in-depth research of the Hebrew influences we've discovered in the Book of Mormon," Bernie went on as if Granger had said nothing, "we can see that your position is ludicrous."

"Well, I, I don't know your name, but I think you have overlooked the extraordinary abilities of Joseph Smith," Granger said in rebuttal.

"Make up your mind!" roared Bernie. "On the one hand you tell us that he submitted the original manuscript with little punctuation and poor grammar because he lacked the education and basic skills to do any better. Then you turn around and tell us how truly bright the man was by inserting Hebraisms that would choke twenty mules—not just a few Hebraisms, but many, throughout the book. I'm sorry; your presentation is as leaky as a rusty bucket."

"Now, Bernie," Freddy interjected, as if he were coming to the presenter's rescue. "I think you are being entirely too hard on this man who, after all, is our guest." Freddy smiled at the presenter, but Bernie knew by Freddy's tone that he was ready to attack the man as well.

Freddy addressed Granger. "May I ask you one thing? I didn't hear you bring it up, and I'm as curious as the next person. It seems to me that Joseph Smith claimed to have taken his writings from gold plates. Do you believe they were actually gold or some type of metal in the form of plates that he copied from?"

"No, certainly not. It is a part of the whole scheme that is easily dismissed. He claimed to have them, but that is too preposterous to believe."

"Why do you say that?" Freddy asked, his tone as friendly as a kitten.

"It is too hard for logical, thinking people to accept."

"Would you say he had some kind of document, maybe not gold, but brass?" Freddy asked.

"I don't think there were any plates or metal of any type. The words came from Smith's imagination."

Freddy tapped his pencil on the table for a moment, staring at the presenter. "I'm terribly sorry you feel that way, because, quite frankly, I have gone to a great deal of trouble to research that particular issue of the framework of the project. Are you at all aware of the number of people, ordinary people, like you and me, who recorded in journals, made signed statements, and in dozens of ways said they saw or felt the plates? Some actually lifted them, and others claimed to turn the pages. Joseph Smith's own wife, Emma, had to move the eighty- or ninety-pound pile of plates to dust the dining table. Are you aware of that?"

Freddy paused, but Granger made no response. Freddy continued. "Joseph Smith's own mother felt the plates through some light cloth. She rubbed the metal together and expressed the fact that she absolutely couldn't wait to physically *see* the plates. All told, I believe the latest count of those who affirmed that they knew Joseph Smith definitely had the plates comes to sixteen. Mind you, these were law-abiding, reputable people living in New York. Dependable people, salt of the earth. They left no doubt whatsoever as to their witness because, in the case of eleven of them, their specific assignment was to see the plates and testify to what they had seen by signing a document to that particular effect. Now, how do we get around the plates?"

"I'm afraid I don't follow your reasoning," Granger said in a huff.

"What do you mean, you don't follow my reasoning? You've preached against this book for fifteen years. I'm saying that many people, on separate occasions, claimed that Joseph Smith had these gold plates in his possession for a period of months. Would that many ordinary people lie? In a court of law, it takes but two witnesses to prove a man guilty of murder." Freddy pounded the table with his fist and shouted, "The plates, sir, the plates. What do you do with the fact that there were plates?"

Stephen's eyebrows lifted. *Can this be Freddy I'm hearing? He has been so noncommittal. Maybe he is beginning to see the truths in the Book of Mormon, too.*

"What would you have me say? I can't see where it is important whether he had plates or not," Granger said.

"It's very important. And why does a chap in the 1820s, whilst he can barely keep food on the table, walk around with gold plates, guarding them with his life? We have excellent testimony that he did."

"I say there were no gold plates," Granger concluded.

Stephen had been uneasy throughout Granger's presentation. *I've watched Bob give lectures like this. He has a touch of the same theatrics this man displays. It's a show, isn't it? This guy doesn't care whether he is correct or not. All he wants to do is discredit the Mormons.*

Finally acknowledging to himself that to say nothing would be tantamount to supporting the man's anti-Mormon beliefs, Stephen jumped into the arena with a question about the olive tree in Jacob 5. When Granger said that Joseph Smith could have copied that from several sources in the Bible, Stephen asked, "Have you read the allegory, or better, have you *studied* the complexities of the Allegory of the Olive Tree and the horticultural science involved? I don't intend to get into a discussion with you about the allegory. Fragments of the Allegory of the Olive Tree are scattered throughout the Bible, but so much is missing. Joseph Smith would have been required to go to outside source material. There was none available then."

Stephen paused to make his point. "I agree with my esteemed colleagues. I think before you give another one of your Book-of-Mormon-bashing lectures, you ought to do your homework. For a critic to disprove a book's authenticity, he must analyze the religious, cultural, historical, and social elements of the book. Then he must show how such a work fails to represent the society it claims to depict. It is my opinion that the Book of Mormon clearly portrays the Near Eastern world." Stephen looked over his shoulder at the rear door. *What is taking Roy so long? I need those copies!*

Granger was not an easy man to stifle. He stood and took all that the group had to fire at him. He countered and brought up the issue of mistakes in word usage, such as the French term *adieu,* the reference to dragons, and several other words that his research had uncovered. None of the group of six, including Henry, was impressed with his presentation. It contained too many areas that the man could not address.

It was Martha who asked him to give a brief account of how chiasmus could be so prevalent in the Book of Mormon, while Joseph Smith lacked knowledge of that method of literary writing. "The Mormons themselves were not aware of its existence until 1967 when one of their young missionaries, John Welch, discovered the pattern in the Book of Mormon," she said.

"You do understand what chiasmus is, don't you?" Martha questioned in exasperation.

"Yes, I've read of it. What was your question?" Granger asked, confused.

"Where do you think Joseph Smith learned this ancient literary art form?" Martha inquired.

"From the Bible. It is in the King James version," Granger said, still standing his ground.

"Can you identify passages in the Bible that are chiastic?"

"Immediately offhand, no, but give me a few days and I'll show you some examples," Granger said.

"Don't you have a book in your publishing house that deals specifically with this ancient form of writing and takes Joseph Smith to task in some enlightened way to illustrate that he borrowed the form from the Bible? Do you not get into the internal structure of the book, where you show that the literary form in the Book of Mormon may not be correct or is poorly written?"

"No, we haven't yet published anything dealing specifically with chiasmus."

"Or any other facet of what I consider the most difficult part of the writings," Martha muttered under her breath. "I have one more comment, then I'm finished with this charade. Do you know that it took Mohammed twenty-five years to do his splendid work—the *Koran*? Are you so ignorant of literature as to believe that Joseph Smith had the native ability to create five hundred and some odd pages of what you call fiction, which includes so many plots and subplots that it would tax a Russian novelist to approach the complexities that I've discovered in the book? Either you have never studied the Book of Mormon, or you must believe that Joseph Smith was a genius to write such a work in a brief period. Actually, I don't care what you believe. People like you disgust me in the extreme." Martha stopped speaking and glowered at Granger. As she finished, Roy quietly entered the dining room and slipped Stephen the copies he had prepared.

"Mr. Granger!" Stephen almost shouted. "I would like to have some clarification on a matter that has come to my attention." Stephen didn't wait for Granger to respond; he simply arose and asked Freddy to give copies of the stapled letters to each participant. Then Stephen moved quickly to the front of the table and personally handed the stapled papers to Granger. Granger took the copies of the faxed letters and glanced down to study their contents, while Stephen returned to his seat.

As he walked to his place, Stephen said, "I thought the group would be interested in copies of correspondence that has been sent to you by the committee that holds annual open forums on the Book of Mormon. They indicate that you have been invited to present your views at these forums on four separate occasions." Stephen thumbed though the sheets. The third sheet was a reply with the photo image of Granger's embossed letterhead at the top. "It is clear, Mr. Granger, that each time the committee invited you to appear and give your lecture on the flaws in the Book of Mormon, you declined. Why?"

Granger took his time, looked over the material for a moment longer, and said, "I think it is explained here in one of my letters. I simply was booked during those times when they invited me to attend."

"Four years in a row? In all that time you could not schedule in a day to meet at one of these forums? The letters of invitation indicate that you had six months advance time to schedule your appearance. Is your schedule so filled six months in advance that you can't accommodate an appearance to speak? After all, you arranged to attend this gathering with less than a ten-day notice. Something is not computing. Why not go to one of their forums? What a rich opportunity to express your views and correct those misled people."

Granger studied Stephen a moment and then spoke in a hushed voice. "I refuse to enter their arena, only to be mocked. Why would anyone deliberately expose himself to ridicule?"

"What do you mean by ridicule?" Stephen wanted to know.

"Obviously, those professors want me to stand before them so they can twist the facts and make me look ridiculous, just as you people have done today."

"Are you admitting that you would not consider entering a debate with knowledgeable researchers with advanced degrees in the very subject you are debasing? Is that what you are trying to tell us?" Copying Bernie's menacing form, Stephen hurried on before Granger could answer. "Is there something to fear? Do they have information that would put you in a bad light? Are they too knowledgeable? Isn't it, in fact, because you prefer to spread your ignorance among those who lack insight into the fallacy of the venom you are spewing out on a subject you know only superficially?"

"I'm not on trial here," Granger protested and looked over at Peter beseechingly.

Peter came to Granger's rescue, thanked him, and ushered him out of the dining room and into the van, where Roy waited to return him to the airport. The six remained to discuss what they had heard.

After a brief silence, Bernie groaned, "Henry, was he the best you could come up with?"

Henry felt his colleagues' ire at the presenter's lack of scholarship. "First, there are no real scholars who will involve themselves in a study of the book," he said in defense of his position. "Why should they? They have nothing to gain from it. There are no grants or endowments offered for exhaustive research of the Book of Mormon. No real scholars will take on the challenge. We are typical—it took cold cash to entice us to make this study. The other day, by phone, I brought up the subject of this woeful lack of scholarship with my friend Dr. Kibbings at Columbia. He insists that to his knowledge there are no academicians who are currently doing critical work on the Book of Mormon. I asked him how long he felt it would be before scholars would take on the study of the book. Do you know what he said? 'About another two to three hundred years. The book is too new.'"

* * *

Peter had stayed in touch with Bill Bennett almost daily for the past two weeks. They had debated by phone whether to tell the group that part of the money was frozen due to a preliminary injunction and that all remaining money would be available only if they could secure the signature of an obstinate second signer. Bennett had assured Peter that even if the participants didn't get their funds immediately, they would after the trial—that is, if Craig lost.

Each time the two discussed the pros and cons of disclosing to the six the status of final payment, they resolved to hold off at least another day. It was now late Monday night of week six.

"Tell me, Bill, what is your gut feeling about Craig finding the location of this estate before the project is over?"

Bill thought a moment, then said, "Peter, I just don't know. I know he hasn't found it yet, or he would be pounding on the gate. You do keep the gate locked, don't you?"

"That isn't the point. You can imagine how I'm going to look if he barges in here unannounced and blows the whistle on this whole thing. If only I could explain the problem to the group without them bolting the project," Peter wished aloud.

"There is the possibility that they would continue until the end, even knowing that they will not be paid immediately. Do you want me to fly over and talk with them tomorrow? It would be easier for me to break it to them than you."

"No, thank you anyway," Peter sighed. "We have another problem, though. The presenters are expecting their final payment within ten days. That was the agreement. Now we can't meet that obligation, either. At least I can't. I have used my savings to pay off the presenters we've had so far. If I have to, I'll go to my credit union and secure the funds. I just hope I don't have to do that."

"Don't get too hasty. You are legally covered. You did not stop the funds; Craig did. One other thing, not a positive item. I called Mary to see if she had experienced a change of heart. No go. Boy, does that lady hate my guts. Poor ol' Tom. Even if he was her boss, he must have kowtowed to her once or twice."

The two hung up. Peter lay staring at the reflection of the pool water that was refracted through the sliding glass doors off the balcony onto part of the ceiling of his bedroom. It had a swirling effect, much like his mind. *How can I go on deceiving these people? They trust me.*

Sleep came slowly to Peter.

Chapter Twenty-Four
Wordprints

Week Six—Tuesday Afternoon

Henry stood before the group and announced that it was time for them to begin putting together their final reports, since less than two weeks remained for their research. He informed them that they still had a final presentation coming up this afternoon. He explained that arrangements had been made with the University of California at San Diego to use one of their classrooms, where three screens were set up for a demonstration of *wordprints* on the Book of Mormon.

Henry indicated that the broad academic community had very little understanding of this science employed by some universities, but he assured them that a full demonstration would be presented so that they would understand exactly what was meant by the term *wordprints*.

"Three independent university statistical analysts will be presenting their findings, using the Book of Mormon as the document of scrutiny," Henry said. "Here again, the presenters do not know the origin of the document. Their assignment is to determine whether the document has multiple authors. I think we will find this presentation enlightening.

"Now, I must place emphasis on the need for each of you to spend all available time pulling your notes together for the writing of your report."

Stephen wondered how Henry could retain such formality

in this irreverent group.

As Henry mentioned the report, he caught Martha's eye and smiled. "I don't know if any of you are aware of it, but Martha has already done a preliminary draft of her report, and except for the presentation today and some follow-up material, she is well on her way to completing her report. We commend you for your diligence, Martha."

Martha nodded in response.

"Hear, hear," Freddy shouted, "a jolly good show, old girl."

"Way to go, Martha," Bernie said from his end of the table. "Maybe I can look it over and get some ideas, or better still, I'll entertain any desires you have for me, and maybe we can cut a deal. You write my paper, and I'm yours for a full week after the project."

"I don't think we have to bring this commendation down to your level," Henry cautioned Bernie.

"Aw, come on Henry, lighten up," Judith said as she smiled at Bernie's coarse ways. "If Bernie here wants to cut some kind of deal with the lovely Dr. Martha, that's his business."

Henry could see that the group was in a playful mood. He glanced at his watch and said, "Ah, it is 1:30 and time to leave for the university. Please gather out in front, where the van is waiting."

* * *

Noting the deserted campus as they walked into the science building, Freddy commented to Stephen, "With the beach out there and the California lifestyle readily available, who wants to study? At this time of the afternoon, you could fire a shotgun in any direction and not hit a soul."

There were three slide projectors at the rear of the small amphitheater and three large silver screens down in front. The chairs were bolted to the floor six rows deep. Bernie surmised that Peter must have a friend on the faculty.

The first of the three presenters was a full professor from Virginia Polytechnic Institute, his field being statistical analysis. Such a technical subject would normally have been boring to someone like Stephen, but even with his emotional distractions, he found that his mind was immersed in the presentation. The speaker had just explained the concept of *wordprints,* or the science of stylometry. He assured his audience of eight—the six participants plus Peter and Roy—that the document he had been asked to analyze had been sent to him by a Mr. Bennett of Phoenix. "My assignments? They were to determine whether the document was written by more than one author, and to compare this document with the writings of certain nineteenth-century authors to discover if any of them could have written it.

"First, to familiarize you with the science of wordprints, I'd like to show you the results of analyses that have been done on other documents," the professor said as he flashed a cluster of symbols—crosses, dots, and asterisks—on the screen at the far left. "Here you have a wordprint pattern of the authors of The Federalist papers. If you recall, these historical papers were first published anonymously—I suppose for political reasons. At any rate, the identity of authorship of some twelve of the papers has remained a point of debate for over two hundred years. The disputed papers were compared by two renowned statisticians, Mosteller and Wallace. By using a method based on 'frequency of usage' of the small filler words—such as *and, the, of, that, to*—Mosteller and Wallace determined to their satisfaction that the evidence pointed to Madison as the author, as indicated on the screen to your left. Notice the cluster of crosses that represents the writing pattern of Madison, as opposed to that of Jay or Hamilton, the other two Federalists, who have at times been credited with having written some of the papers."

The professor twirled his index finger in the air as he spoke and commented further, "Other wordprint studies have been done on such authors as Shakespeare and his disputed works. We now know that Bacon wrote none of the works attributed to Shakespeare, despite the theories of scholars who would convince you otherwise. Wordprints indicate that they are all the works of Shakespeare."

The presenter described his understanding of wordprints and gave other examples that included background information on the science of wordprints. He said that he and his staff used the method frequently to determine the true writer in some of the world's knottiest authorship problems. He explained that the Huntington Library and other institutions frequently submitted copies of original documents for analysis to determine if, in fact, the writing of a particular manuscript was authentic to the purported author.

The professor soon convinced his audience that there was a reliable method of determining authorship of a work. He reminded them that it had not been possible prior to the advent of the computer. The professor waxed technical when he began telling the group that a system called *multivariate analysis of variance*, which he called MANOVA, was a method used to determine the authorship of a written document.

"MANOVA is a technique that tests for homogeneity of groups, the similarity of the wordprint patterns from one author to another," the professor said.

Stephen had to stretch his powers of comprehension to stay up with the presenter. *In essence, what he is saying is that a person habitually uses these sort of "filler words" and in a characteristic word pattern, and that no two writers use the same filler words in the same ratio. At least, I think that's what he's saying.*

"Let me give you a simplified numerical example to demonstrate the meaning of frequency of the word. Say we have two authors and are using three different passages from each author. Keep in mind, we are examining the frequency of the word *and*."

The screen displayed the following:

Authors	Passage 1	Passage 2	Passage 3
A	.032	.031	.032
B	.063	.065	.064

"These figures on the screen mean, for example, that Author

A used the word *and* 32 times per 1,000 words, while Author B used *and* twice as often in each passage examined. Clearly, the authors differed in the average frequency with which they used the word *and*. We can clearly see that there were two distinct authors.

"Still, if the results were as follows, we could not discriminate between these authors on the basis of the word *and*, because the difference was so slight. This is what I mean.

Authors	Passage 1	Passage 2	Passage 3
A	.032	.055	.068
B	.042	.058	.061

"If we were to use the information I've displayed alone, we could not rule out the possibility that A and B were the same individual. Then we would compare the usage of other filler words."

The presenter continued. "Before we examine the results of tests on the document of focus, let me say that authorship in the document is very complex. There are 1,500 changes in authorship. That does not mean that there are 1,500 authors; but as one passage flows to another, alternating authors interject their material. This text was provided to those of us who researched the document with authorship of each section indicated by initials. One writer was designated as "A," another as "N," another as "M," and the last was "Mi." A scholar named Dr. Rencher did this work for us."

On the desk in front of Stephen and the participants was a copy of the document, plus the letters corresponding to the disguised authors. Stephen noticed that the key authors were Alma (A), Nephi (N), Mormon (M), and Moroni (Mi).

"Now we will look at the document that I have studied for this presentation." The professor began with a series of tests using the MANOVA method. Then he explained that he had assistants working with him, indicating that their credentials were on the handout sheet.

Beginning with blocks of words from the document, he told the group how he first compared twenty-four authors in the document and how he excluded Jesus Christ, Isaiah, and a person called "the Lord" since these authors closely agreed with the Bible.

He then said, "We compared the twenty-one remaining authors by using the ten most frequently occurring words in our list. Statistically, the differences between the authors are highly significant. Differences as large as these simply could not occur if a single author wrote the document. The statistical odds that a single author wrote this document are less than one in a hundred billion." The professor paused to give weight to his statement.

Eyes sought eyes as the group of scholars sat stunned by the evidence presented. They could barely grasp the scope of the technique, but all could see that the work of this man and his colleagues represented a major scientific breakthrough. All their hassles over the credibility of Joseph Smith seemed inconsequential at this point.

The professor continued. "As I mentioned, the words we compared were filler words such as *and, the, of, that, to, unto, in, for,* and *be.* Only one word, in, was not significantly different across the twenty-one authors. Seven of them were significant at less than the .0001 level; that is, the probability that a single author would produce such disparate results is less than one in ten thousand. In a typical research study, a difference would be labeled significant if its probability level were .05 or smaller, less than one in twenty. Most of the differences we found in the document we were given were so large that the associated probability level was very much smaller than .05."

Stephen could tell the presenter was getting into the meat of his exciting findings when he said, "We moved up to thirty-eight filler words instead of ten. The results were even more conclusive. We then compared the key writers of the document, namely, M, N, A, and Mi. The most words in the document came from author M. This author wrote 97,777 words or 36.5 per cent of the document. Author N wrote 10.9 per cent; author A wrote 7.4 per cent; and author Mi wrote 7.2 per cent. Our results were much the same as before.

"Then we compared the writing from the document with some nineteenth-century writers: a Mr. S., Mr. C., Mr. Sp., and a couple of others." Stephen saw immediately that Mr. S. was Joseph Smith, Mr. C. was Oliver Cowdery, and Mr. Sp. was Spaulding.

"We did a study of frequency by comparing the document writers with the nineteenth-century writer, Mr. S. We used all thirty-eight words that I previously noted," the professor said.

"I would like to explain to you what we learned about the document and its writers. First, the most salient result of our test was that none of the document selections resembled the writings of any of the suggested nineteenth-century authors." The presenter paused long enough to allow what he had said to have impact on the minds of the scholars. Then he said, with the smugness of a professional who knows he's right, "The document itself offers the strongest evidence for a clear, scientific refutation of the proposed theory that it was written by one of these nineteenth-century authors." The professor paused, picked up his notes, and said, "Thank you for your attention." He walked out of the room.

The group was speechless for a moment.

Freddy was the first to complain. "What? Henry, no follow-up questions?"

"Just remain seated. We have another professor from Texas A&M who will be presenting shortly. He will show you a different method of evaluating wordprints."

Stephen was impressed with the findings, though he no longer approached the Book of Mormon searching for empirical evidence. He was committed to the spirit of the book and saw far beyond any word proofs. But he did feel excited about what he was witnessing.

How he wished for Anney. *Oh, Anney, my dear, dear Anney! Why can't you share what I'm experiencing? Maybe I should have explained the whole book the first night at the hotel. Why did we waste our time on fun and food when we could have enriched our souls on what I have discovered?* Stephen knew the answer as he formulated the question. *If I had sprung it on her Friday, she would have left for home that night, and no one would have enjoyed the weekend. But did they really enjoy the weekend anyway? Now she can say I held out on her. This is a Catch-22 situation. How am I going to win her over?*

The next professor went through similar preliminary material, explaining that a Dr. Morton in England had developed this concept of linguistic investigation and had done the pioneering work on it in the late sixties and early seventies. He also confirmed that the science of wordprints is relatively new and that it is gaining credibility in many circles to verify authorship.

He demonstrated a second method of classifying wordprints called *cluster analysis*. "Cluster analysis takes a series of measurements on a set of observations and identifies which observations are closest to each other. In this study, the series of measurements would be the frequencies of thirty-eight words that form the wordprint profile, and the set of observations would be the thousand-word blocks."

A switch turned on, causing the second overhead projector to illuminate the middle screen. "May I direct your attention to the screen in the center? Please notice that the nineteenth-century author, Mr. S., does not cluster with the four key authors of the document, as I have already indicated. You will note that the four key authors of the document overlap and cluster quite nicely."

"On the screen, in the center, you will see the writers of the document clustered, while the nineteenth-century Mr. S. is not part of that cluster. We concluded that an analysis of the four principal ancient writers of the document, no matter which definition of wordprints we selected—letters, common words, or uncommon words—yielded the same results. Mr. S. did not fit the cluster pattern as you see. I've shown you one example of clustering, but we have more, and you are welcome to study them afterward, if you wish."

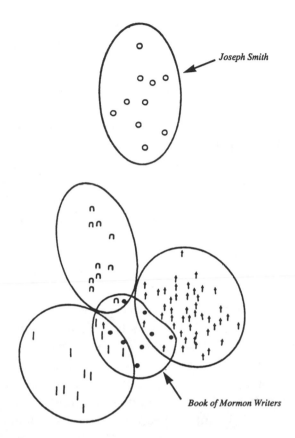

Joseph Smith

Book of Mormon Writers

A third professor, a woman from the University of Southern California, presented her findings using yet a third method of word-printing, which she labeled *discriminant,* or *classification analysis.*

She launched directly into her subject. "I consider this method of identifying authors to be the most powerful technique available. Discriminant analysis is self-verifying. Let me explain."

She had everyone's attention. "The discriminant analysis I used was performed in steps. The word that best separates authors was entered first, the second best-word next. This process contin-ued sequentially until a designated critical level was reached. I did a classification analysis where each block of words was classified with the author whose wordprints it most closely matched. The percentage of correct 'hits' is a measure of how well the authors can be separated and how unique the profile of word frequencies is for each author.

"In the computer run, with 2,000-word blocks and 18 words selected, 93.3 per cent of the blocks were correctly classified. This is a very high rate for a situation such as this, where the number of groups, or authors, is so large.

"I wish to inform you that this profile of usage habits by authors can serve to identify a piece of writing as belonging to a particular author, just as a fingerprint or voiceprint can be traced to its owner or originator. According to the results, I must tell you that there are multiple authors in the document and that it is a translation. Even when a document is a translation, it makes little difference to wordprints. The author's writing still slips through and leaves an identifiable pattern."

She looked out at the attentive group and said, "In conclusion, I would like to say that it does not seem possible that Mr. S. or any other writer could have fabricated a work with several discernible authorship styles. The twenty-four authors do not appear in twenty-four separate blocks of connected words but are shuffled and intermixed in an arbitrary manner throughout the document. How could any single author keep track of thirty-eight word frequencies and vary them, not only randomly from one section to another, but also according to a fixed, underlying pattern, particularly more than a century before scholars realized that word frequencies might vary with authors?"

That's incredible, Stephen thought. *She believes that the Book of Mormon is a translation and that each individual author's style has been preserved.*

The professor summarized her findings by declaring, "The document authors, taken individually or collectively, do not resemble any of the nineteenth-century authors that I have considered, taken individually or collectively. Thank you."

Before she could exit, Bernie shouted out, "Would you stake your professional reputation on that last statement? Don't just walk out on us. We have all kinds of questions to ask you. You come in here and throw all this jargon at us like we're supposed to know what you're talking about. I don't think I got half of it."

Bewildered, the woman looked from face to face for direction. Henry took command. "Thank you," he said to the presenter. He then turned to Bernie, his voice edged with irritation. "I'm sure you have questions. The presenters will now return."

Henry brought all three professors back to the front of the room, explaining, "We weren't intending to let them leave without you having an opportunity to question their findings. So please, go ahead; the time is yours to ask questions."

"To answer the gentleman's question to me," the final presenter said, "indeed, I feel confident that my findings are correct. I have no way of knowing where the document came from. The request I received from a Mr. Bennett was to do a wordprint study of the document and to determine if there is strong evidence that it was written by multiple authors. I feel I have completed my assignment in the tradition of the best scientific methods we have available today. Of course I stand by my conclusions. I identified major differences among the authors of the written document, and they are not even close to the nineteenth-century authors in style, word usage, or several other indicators."

"Thank you," Bernie smiled, convinced he had tapped a sensitive nerve. He still had a hunch that she would not be that adamant about her certainty of her analysis of the document once she learned that she had done her work from the infamous Book of Mormon.

The first professor spoke up, "I would also like to make a definitive statement as to the study I did, using the latest wordprint methods. My analysis, as I have shown, indicates conclusively that many authors wrote the document. I think you will find that all three of us who have given presentations are in agreement on this point."

"Have you any affiliation with any religious, political, or social group that could sway your findings? Any of you may answer my question," Martha said in a booming voice.

"I'll respond first," the second professor said. "My personal affiliations had nothing to do with this. I approached this assignment in a purely professional manner. I was asked by a Mr. Bennett to do a wordprint study of a document he sent me. I was to determine whether there was more than one writer of the document—I found over twenty. And whether a nineteenth-century writer could have written it. I, too, would have to say that it would be an impossibility for someone of the nineteenth-century to write an ancient document and fabricate over twenty authors."

"By Jove!" Freddy exclaimed. "You have catapulted us into the twenty-first century with your word science. None of us will ever make the mistake of plagiarizing again. Good show! You've convinced me that Joseph Smith couldn't have written the Book of Mormon."

"Freddy," Judith scolded, "they weren't supposed to know the source of the document."

"Who cares?" Bernie concluded.

The group laughed and hurried to the front of the room to compliment the professors.

Chapter Twenty-Five
The Unnatural Son

Week Six—Tuesday Afternoon

Craig wondered if the Los Angeles investigative agency could be relied on to follow through with the information Moore had provided. But they had been quick to contact their sister agency in San Diego to request that they check out the address listed only as Fairbanks Ranch. The phone number Craig had been given by Moore was an eight-hundred number, and the person who answered refused to disclose any information. The San Diego agency had dispatched an agent to Fairbanks Ranch immediately, while Moore waited with George in his hotel room.

When the agent pulled alongside the young security officer at the gate to the exclusive ranch, he smiled. "I'm looking for a Stephen Thorn who is with that group of Mormon scholars," he probed, not certain what to call the group.

"Ah . . . you mean that group at the Claybourn estate?" asked the guard. "The only person I have listed for that group is a Dr. Polk."

"Hmm . . . I'll need to pull around and call my office to check on the name, okay? Thanks." He lifted his cellular phone as he drove away.

The San Diego investigative agency reported directly to Craig. Craig was elated, certain that he had found his target. All he had to do now was to figure out how to get inside the locked community and locate the exact house without alerting Polk.

Craig called in his father's former secretary, Mary, to help his staff work out the latest maze. Craig knew that when his father had needed a good, competent mind to help him work out a knotty problem, Mary had been the best.

He explained to those he had assembled that he had to reach someone who lived in Fairbanks Ranch who could clear him through the gate and direct him to the estate where Polk was staying. The staff went to work on the problem immediately, while a receptionist in the outer office booked Craig a seat on the six o'clock flight to San Diego.

After forty-five minutes of searching among friends and associates who were spending the summer in San Diego, as was the custom among some of the affluent of Phoenix, the staff found a lead, a man who had formerly done business with the Kline company and who now lived in Fairbanks.

Mary put in the call to the former Kline associate at his San Diego Golden Triangle office. She reached the man at his desk and buzzed Craig's office. Craig got on the line.

"Mr. Farley. I'm Thomas Kline's son. I understand you did some business with my father. I wonder if you would be so kind as to help me with a little problem."

Within five minutes, Craig had been instructed to give his name to the security guard at the gate. The guard would direct Craig to Farley's home, and Farley would then help Craig find the estate he sought. Mr. Farley said that he would be more than happy to permit any son of Tom Kline's into the locked community. Craig told him that he didn't know the exact location; all he knew was that a group had leased an estate inside Fairbanks Ranch, and it was imperative that he talk to a person within the group. Farley thought he knew just the estate Craig was referring to. He mentioned that there weren't that many estates on the south side, and he had heard two days ago, while on the golf course, about a group of professors who were spending the summer there. He would be pleased to show Craig the estate this evening. "I'll leave your name at the gate, and security will let you drive through."

Across the room, Mary was picking up the phone books, preparing to return to her desk. She overheard Craig's conversation from the start and could see that he intended to fly to San Diego and personally stop the project. *I guess that is business. Is it my affair, anyway?* But it still struck her as odd that this son was so different from his father—the father always helping others, the son so wrapped up in himself. She was troubled by her feelings of animosity toward Craig. *How can I go on working for a man I dislike? But if I were to retire early, I'd lose about five percent of my retirement. Is the extra retirement money worth all this?*

* * *

The lesson that the young missionaries had presented earlier at Bishop Oren's home was simple and direct. Stephen had left the house and told the small gathering, including the two young missionaries, that he wanted to walk home alone and think about what they had been telling him.

They explained how the true church should be organized, told him about a *living* prophet, twelve apostles, and a complete organization like the church in the time of Christ.

Yes, he had heard that the Mormons believe in a living prophet, that the Church of Christ had been restored. He had discovered that and more at Palmyra. Somehow, coming from slightly awkward young men who were little older than his son, Todd, the message should not have been as impressive as it was; yet it was moving and seemed right to Stephen.

Stephen heard the prayers offered for him by Martin Orens and his wife. It had come so naturally, as if the Orens knew they were speaking directly to God. Martin had offered the first prayer. It was simple and sincere. His wife, Betty, had offered the second prayer when the meeting ended. She, too, had a sweetness in her voice. The only thing missing for Stephen throughout the evening was Anney and the kids. He ached for them to hear and believe the things he was beginning to understand and, yes, believe.

It was one of those rare, warm evenings. The moon was a sliver; the street lamps cast a mellow glow over the surrounding grass and shrubs in the peaceful neighborhood. A surging awareness of life's true meaning surfaced again in Stephen's mind. With

Roy's help in the library, he had learned that variations of the tree-of-life story were found in the doctrines of many religions throughout the world. And he knew well by now the story of Lehi tasting the fruit of the tree of life. Stephen knew that in Lehi's dream, the tree represented the pure love of Christ. *That is exactly what I'm experiencing. It is the taste of the fruit from the tree of life.*

Stephen had reread the story only this afternoon. It told of Lehi feasting on the fruit of the tree that was most precious and most desirable. He was stumped on the remainder of the verses, but he recalled vividly those words. *Am I experiencing this feast? Am I eating from the same tree as Lehi? Anney, don't you hear me? Come and share the fruit. Touch it. Taste it. Enjoy it as I am enjoying it.*

Stephen stopped walking. He looked about, wondering if someone had heard him. The street was empty. So was his hope that Anney would come and share the fruit.

Nearing the estate, Stephen noticed a shiny new Lexus and a Ford Taurus. They had stopped at the entrance gate to the estate. He had never seen either car. *What visitors were expected at nine o'clock at night?*

A man stepped out of the passenger side of the Ford. He spoke to the driver of the Lexus, and the Lexus pulled away as Stephen neared the gate. He held the electric opener in his left hand, about to engage the signal.

"Excuse me," the man said as he saw Stephen approach. Stephen paused and said, "May I help you with something?"

"Yeah, you sure can. I'm looking for a Stephen Thorn. Someone told me he is living here for the summer."

"I'm Thorn. How may I help you?"

The man looked startled. Then he narrowed his eyes and with an embarrassed smile, said, "Well, actually, it isn't you I'm looking for. It's just that your name popped up as a participant at this place. I would really like to speak to Dr. Polk."

"He's here. Come in. Does your friend want to come in, too?" Stephen asked, noticing a driver in the front seat of the Taurus.

"No, I just need a minute with Dr. Polk."

"Sure, I'm certain he wouldn't mind," Stephen said as he punched the gate opener.

"Is Peter around?" Stephen asked Judith, as he walked into the foyer beside the stranger.

Judith, wearing a long evening robe, was ascending the curved staircase. She stopped, turned around, and said with a smile that was not lost on Craig, "He's in the kitchen having a snack. I paid my bet to those hungry animals in the kitchen. I made my famous Judith brownies. And who is this?" she asked.

"I'm sorry. I didn't get your name," Stephen asked, turning to the man, certain that he had not given it.

"Craig Kline."

Stephen took Craig down the wide, well-lighted corridor, past the dining room to the immense kitchen. The aroma of Judith's brownies was still fragrant in the air.

"Dr. Polk, I have someone here to see you," Stephen said, getting everyone's attention.

Freddy, Bernie, and Peter sat at the bar, sampling the warm brownies. They turned their heads as Stephen spoke. The color drained from Peter's face as his eyes locked with Craig's. He sat frozen in place, facing his nightmare. He had not thought that he would have to grapple with feelings of hatred toward another human being so late in his life. The very sight of Craig turned Judith's brownie into bile.

"So, Peter," Craig sneered, "I'm sure you're not pleased to see me. But I've gone to considerable expense and trouble to find you. Are you going to introduce me?"

Stephen sensed immediately that he should never have brought this arrogant man through the gate.

"I will not play your game, Craig," Peter said finally, with no intention of introducing Craig to the group. "My only hope, at this very moment, is that your father is not looking down on this scene. He would be most unhappy."

"Come now, Peter, my father is dead." Craig's voice was cold. "I don't think he's looking down on anything. But since you are going to be difficult, either I speak to this illustrious group in the main room of the house, or I will go from room to room and set them straight. And if you try to have me thrown out by security, I will prove to them that I paid the lease on this place. I want your whole group in the main room, now! I think they will be interested in what I have to say."

As soon as the participants gathered, already distraught by what they had heard from the men who had been in the kitchen, Craig began his theatrics. He spread his right arm and hand in a sweeping motion. "Ladies and gentlemen, I happen to be paying for the luxury of your spending the summer here, plus the money you have already received for your participation. The balance you have been promised by Dr. Polk will not, I repeat, will *not* be paid! For your information, your kind Dr. Polk has been deceiving you. He has known from the start of this doomed project that I was opposed to it; he has also known for some time now that I have a court injunction on funds earmarked to pay for the remainder of this little folly you people are involved in. I said it before; I'll say it again: The money will not be coming to pay you another dime, and if it were practical, I would sue every one of you to get back the money that has already been spent on this insane project."

Craig stood on the steps leading from the foyer to the salon. He stepped back two paces, took out a letter, held it up, and said, "This letter is addressed to you all. I will leave it here on the table." Craig motioned toward the small table in the foyer with the envelope. He smiled a twisted, thin-lipped smile that mirrored his self-satisfaction. It was an expression that Mary had come to despise in the man—and one that the six members of the group would recall with bitterness.

"Each of you would be well advised to read this letter and act appropriately. Good evening." Craig turned from the group, dropped the letter on the table in the foyer, flung the front door wide open, and then turned back to shout across the foyer into the salon. "Oh, and Dr. Polk, do not encourage them with the hidden funds that you and Bennett have stashed away in some other bank. My attorney and I believe that those funds require two signatures; that was the way Dad did business. We are convinced that one signature required to draw on those funds is my father's, and he is dead." With that, Craig stormed out the door and slammed it hard behind him.

For Peter, it was as if the Mafia had entered the house and sprayed the room with machine-gun fire. The destruction was almost visible. Craig's shattering spiel was like the German blitzkrieg; it left destruction everywhere.

Within moments, the doorbell sounded. Stephen went to the door. Craig stood framed in the ornate doorway, his face twisted with anger. "I want that entrance gate opened, now!"

Stephen didn't move. He gave no sign that he intended to budge at Craig's command. "Sir," Stephen said in a slow, deliberate voice, "I don't know who you are. I've never heard of you before, but you do not order me around." Stephen glared at Craig with disdain, "You deceived me in the first place to get through the gate. Do not give me orders now!"

"Well, wise guy," Craig shot back, not fazed in the least by Stephen's anger, "I could care less what you think. You needn't try to pull a 'holier-than-thou' attitude with me. I'm not buying it, especially since it was your daddy-in-law who came to see me in Phoenix yesterday and demanded a lot of cash to tell me exactly where you were hiding. Maybe you should save your contempt for him."

Stephen was not sure he fully understood what this bully meant. Then, trying to comprehend what he had heard, he couldn't believe it. *Bob had taken a payoff to help this savage man achieve his vicious goal?* Stephen did not move. Finally it was Roy, who was standing in the hallway, quietly observing all, who ran to the button near the front door, depressed it, and released the metal entrance gate.

Craig saw the gate begin to open, whirled from the door frame, and disappeared.

"Would somebody please tell me what is going on?" Judith asked in a loud voice that demanded an answer. "Did he say that we're not getting paid when we finish? I don't believe it! I hope I didn't hear that right." Judith waited a moment for a response from Peter. None came.

"Did the rest of you hear what I heard? If it's true, then each of us has lost seventy thousand dollars. I don't believe this," she shouted in a frenzy. "This is outrageous. Peter, tell me it isn't true. This is some kind of joke, isn't it? Have I been conned into some kind of scam? Peter! What's going on?"

Peter had not yet gained voice to express himself.

Everyone watched as Martha hurried to the foyer table and retrieved the letter. She was certain she had heard right. She volunteered to read the dreaded message aloud. Stephen had not noticed before how much drama Martha had in her voice. The letter was terse and to the point. It indicated that the group's chief benefactor had died two days before the project commenced and that he had been failing in health for several years. The Kline family believed that their father had taken up a foolish, expensive project when he was not of sound mind, and they intended to rectify the error through legal recourse.

The letter went on to warn that all known funds were frozen. No one would be paid, not even the people who were offering services, such as household help and instructors. It also stated that those who left the project by the following day could request a five-thousand-dollar reimbursement for travel and expenses. They would, of course, have to sign a waiver, releasing the Kline family from any liability, before actually receiving the funds.

The letter divulged more information, but Peter didn't hear any of it. He was visibly shaken by the ordeal. All six participants could sympathize with his misery, but their concerns were for their sudden loss of funds.

"Peter, did you know about this account being frozen? I'm frankly disturbed," Henry challenged, his voice shaking with anger.

"Yeah, Peter, what's going on? If you knew, why didn't you tell us?" Bernie entered the fracas.

All had turned to glare at Peter, who stood uncertainly near the doors that led to the terrace, as if he were ready to bolt the room. He stood with drooping shoulders, his face dejected, for the moment unable to speak. At length he swallowed and began, his voice barely audible. "Yes . . . I'm so sorry. I have known about the injunction for a couple of weeks. . . . You don't know how this situation troubles me. I had hoped that we would get hold of the other funds that are hidden from Craig Kline, the man who was just here. I need to ask for your cooperation while I explain the entire situation."

Nerves were frayed. Bernie refused to sit down; Judith wanted to know how much time it would take. "Because," she said, shaking with concern, "if I don't get the right answers, I will pack my things and leave here tonight. Tonight! Did you hear me?" Her eyes flashed with anger.

Peter explained how he and Kline senior had planned the project, had looked forward to it with enthusiasm. He told them that Kline was a wealthy man who had set up the funding through his attorney but that, as it was about to begin, Kline had suddenly died. Peter admitted that the son, Craig, had disapproved of the project and had spent the last few weeks trying to locate the trust fund and the group so that he could slap an injunction on the funds and cancel the project. In an effort to encourage the six, he also told them that another deposit of one million dollars was still available, if the second signer to the account would consent to sign a check. He would not divulge Mary's name. At this point, Peter felt he could trust no one in the room with that kind of information.

"Well, that does it," Judith moved toward the door. All she could do was shake her head. No one tried to stop her. "I'll need a ride to the airport," she called out imperiously. She did not so much as look at Peter.

The group was decidedly hostile. They interrogated Peter unmercifully about why they would not be paid. The surprise and loss of so much money struck at their sense of security and suspended rational behavior.

"Peter, I intend to determine just whose fault this is," Freddy said in a most intimidating manner. "But I must have more answers. I shall go to this Craig and wring the money out of him. What are my rights? Should I retain a barrister, or should we secure one for the group? I intend to stay right here until we have worked out a plan or at least have all the answers possible."

"Freddy's right," Bernie exclaimed.

Martha seemed puzzled as she moved closer to Peter to ask, "How have you managed to pay all these servants if the money was frozen two weeks ago? The maid, Sergia, told me that she has been paid every week and sends most of her money home to her family in Mexico."

Peter was close to collapse. He leaned on an upholstered wing chair and sighed. "Well," he answered, "I've drawn from my savings; and now that they are gone, I've had a loan approved at my credit union. You have to believe me. I don't think Craig can stop the payment of funds permanently. We all have legal agreements. We had already paid the initial thirty thousand to each of you before my friend Thomas died. I don't think a court in the country would halt something that was in progress while Thomas was still alive. Please have a little patience. I believe you'll get your money. The project is vitally important. I *can't* let Thomas Kline down."

Martha said no more. She sat down on a sofa, deep in thought. The men exchanged glances but were not about to let the matter rest.

Stephen was more concerned about Bob's actions, wondering exactly how they contributed to the disappointment permeating this room.

Another half-hour of hot tempers and recriminations flew about the room. Stephen looked up to see Judith carrying one of her large suitcases down the stairs. He jumped up and offered to carry her luggage. Roy hurried over and asked if he should bring down the rest of her things. Judith silently nodded her permission. She turned and gazed directly at Peter. "I guess we have our evidence of Mormon truth," she declared regally. "I'll see you in court, Dr. Polk."

* * *

The Mercedes 500 SL sped along I-5 where it paralleled Mission Bay on the right. It passed under a freeway sign that indicated *Sea World Drive*, with an arrow pointing to the right. Stephen continued south toward Sassafras Street, the airport off-ramp.

Judith had said nothing after getting into the car. Stephen had firmly overridden Roy's protests, insisting on driving Judith to Lindbergh Field himself. He hoped to talk with her, but he was also anxious to get away from the estate for a while. He needed a breather—a chance to sort out his thoughts.

The wind noise around the soft top of the car covered the faint sounds of Judith crying, but Stephen saw the tears under the freeway lights when he glanced her way. She was rummaging through her purse, for a tissue he supposed.

"I think there is one of those little tissue boxes in the pocket of the door."

Judith retrieved the box, pulled out a tissue, and blew her nose. She no longer hid her sorrow from Stephen.

"Oh, Stephen, Stephen, Stephen," she said bitterly. "This has been my life over and over, except for a couple of good things. I have a good education and some peer recognition, but not much else. I failed at marriage, and now just when I get close, I lose the big money. Why do I get my hopes up? I need to face it. I'm just a black girl from the south side of Chicago, and that's all I'll ever be."

Stephen hit the steering wheel of the Mercedes with the heel of his hand. "How can you say that? You're just feeling sorry for yourself and want to unload on me."

Judith patted her eyes carefully to keep from smudging her mascara and snapped, "Well, I didn't ask you to drive me to the airport, Mr. Right."

"Come on, Judith. You have a doctorate degree. You have a great job with one of the better universities around. You're published in several journals and have a book to your credit. Hey, I'm sorry, but from my vantage point, you have it made. So you lost your seventy thousand. So did the rest of us. How does the color of your skin figure in here?"

"Stephen, why don't you just shut up and get me to the airport or a taxi stand—I don't care which. I don't want you telling me that I'm wrong to feel like I've been taken."

Judith's head was shaking with rage as she took a deep breath to control her anger. "If you're not as upset as I am, then maybe you've got some rich family to fall back on. I know all about your father-in-law. He's probably the richest preacher in San Francisco. And don't tell me he isn't. I've heard about him from a friend up there."

"That isn't true, but forget about me. I'm concerned about you."

Stephen took the airport off-ramp and drove in silence to the first stoplight. He turned in his seat and looked at Judith. "I think you need to come back with me and tough it out for another week. Judith, if you leave now, you will have played right into the hands of this Kline guy. And what's worse, you will live out your life, forever asking yourself, 'Why didn't I stay?'"

"Ha!" exploded Judith. "No way, man," she insisted, slipping back into the jargon of her youth.

Stephen grimly pressed the accelerator, turned right at the next intersection, and drove smoothly past the rental and parking vendors that were closed for the night.

"May I ask you a question about the project?" Stephen was determined to get to the subject he wanted to discuss with Judith. "Do you have any feelings that what you've discovered about the Book of Mormon rings true? Honestly, do you?"

Judith didn't want to answer. Yet she had liked Stephen since the first morning they met. He had an openness that few men in her life ever possessed. She knew he deserved a straight answer.

"Sure, I've had stirrings inside me. But I'm a lot like Freddy. I don't give in to my emotions too often. I know the book is inspired. I'm the one who discovered the outpouring of love in it. What do you want me to say? I don't intend to do anything about it, but it's there, all right."

"If you've found love in the book—and it was Peter who, in reality, brought you to that awareness—why can't you show him a little love and forgiveness and return to the estate with me? All I'm asking you to do is see it through to the end. Is that asking too much?"

"Yes! Yes, yes, yes. I don't want to go back. I do . . . but I don't. I mean, it's not my style to leave a project half finished. I had my agenda, and . . . until tonight I intended to keep it. Why would I want to go back now, anyway?" Judith vacillated.

"For your own best self, come back with me. Besides, if by some slim chance we do get the balance of the money out of that other account, then you may have put your share in jeopardy."

Stephen eased the car up to the curb next to an outside luggage check-in counter. Judith turned to face Stephen, extended her slender, elegant hand, and said, "Stephen, . . . almost thou persuadest me to return with thee. . . . Thanks for your help." She opened the door, put one high-heeled foot to the pavement and held it there a moment, clearly struggling with herself. She started to shift her body out of the car, and then she slowly replaced the leg inside, closed the door, turned her tear-streaked face to Stephen, and said, "Stephen, . . . lie to me again, and tell me you think we're going to get paid next week out of that other account."

Stephen grinned and gave the Mercedes its head.

The estate seemed strangely silent. Judith fled to her room as soon as the two returned from the airport, and Roy, who was still up, patiently carried her things upstairs behind her. Stephen's heart was heavy; he felt responsible for their loss. Rationally, he knew that their repulsive visitor would have gained entrance to the estate without his help. But, worse, he felt responsible for Bob's unfathomable behavior. *How on earth had he connected with that disgusting Kline fellow? Surely he was mistaken that Bob had taken money for information. But the man seemed to know what he was talking about. Boy, I will check that one out, and soon.*

Stephen did not for a minute regret coming. He felt sorry for Bob because of the loss of funds. But apparently Bob had created his own set of problems. *Do I really know my father-in-law? He's been doing some strange things lately.* He knew Bob was depending on the seventy thousand to pay off the loans, or at least pay on them. *Does Bob realize the havoc he has wrought?*

Stephen, for his part, knew that he would never return to the ministry. He would immediately begin looking for another job. He had decided that last week on the return flight from Israel. That was another thing he hadn't discussed with Anney. *So many things to talk over.* It was a sweet-and-sour dilemma for Stephen, though he knew that the sweetness of the gospel overpowered the sourness of the situation. *What a strange mix of events.*

Chapter Twenty-Six
The Colleague

Week Six—Wednesday Morning

Peter had arisen, exhausted but determined, the day after Craig's invasion. He had spent a fitful night, concerned for the participants. It was now clear to him that they might not get their money. Some had finally accepted it as one of life's twists; a couple were still very distraught. Henry had served notice that he was leaving this morning.

Earlier, Peter had given Bennett a debriefing of the conflict and a body count. Craig had inflicted some damage on everyone in the house. Bennett repeated that all was not yet lost, and then he encouraged Peter to get them to remain at the task of finishing the project, if possible. He said that there was still a slight chance that he could talk Mary into flying out to Beverly Hills to sign her name to a check. But Peter detected that the old spirit of conviction was lacking in Bennett.

Stephen had come up to Peter's room before midnight to report that he and Judith had talked, and that, after she had cooled off, she had decided to "tough it out" until the project was completed.

Peter faced each of the participants throughout the long day. He apologized for not being candid with them about Craig's threats and tried to encourage each of them to submit their report.

Peter appreciated the way Freddy had responded. He was disappointed but held onto the hope they could still get the funds from the other account Peter had mentioned. "Peter, if it is simply some lady who is holding up signing the check, why not send me to her and let me woo her into signing?" he had offered. "I'm really quite a ladies' man, you know."

Laughing at the irrepressible Freddy, Peter explained that Bennett was on top of that problem, and he didn't dare interfere. But Peter would keep Freddy's suggestion in mind. In fact, it occurred to Peter that it wouldn't be all that far-fetched to take the whole group to Phoenix to plead their cause—except Peter knew Mary. Mary was not easily persuaded to do anything she didn't want to do.

Henry decided to pack it in and leave. It was the principle of the thing that swayed his decision. He refused to remain and, as he saw it, make a mockery of his research. He had been on the phone early that morning with his wife, who encouraged him to come home immediately. She had expressed relief that at least the entire summer hadn't been wasted, since they had received thirty thousand dollars before the project collapsed.

It was exactly for that reason that Martha stayed on. Not at all pleased about losing so much money, but willing to admit that thirty thousand was more than she would otherwise have earned, she threw in with the others who voted to finish the project.

Bernie was not happy with the turn of events. In fact, he was furious. He debated whether to leave and get an early start on a trip he and his brother would take as an alternative to the one he had planned to take to Crete. It was hard for him to adjust to the loss of so much money. With the funds he had intended receiving, he had planned to take a year's leave of absence in the spring and visit sites in Crete where, anciently, major battles had been fought.

Now he would have to scrap that plan for a year or more. He had lent his brother twenty-five of the thirty thousand dollars he had from the project. His brother had already made a down payment on a highly patronized, dusty bookstore near the Met in Manhattan.

Angry though he was, Bernie decided to stay with the project. Beneath the tough-talking, hard exterior, Bernie was a true scholar. To leave what had turned out to be a fascinating research effort before completion would have been tantamount to a mother abandoning a child. Still, Bernie made a mental note that he was abiding by no more house rules. He'd have Miller Lite for breakfast if he wanted it. He grumbled to Freddy about chucking the rules, and Freddy reminded him of the possibility that they would yet see some cash.

"Remember, Bernie, my wicked little friend," Freddy said, "if you fail to live up to the rules, Peter can still zap you and toss you out on your shiny little posterior. So don't tempt him with overindulgence or with your dirty little phrases, which personally bother me not in the least. Just a word of caution from a friend. Think about it, my good man. Is it worth unleashing your habits for a mere ten days?"

The money was not an issue with Stephen, and he told them so. If, in the long run, he got the remaining seventy thousand, so much the better. Remembering the lien Bob had placed on his home, he knew that losing the twenty thousand that his father-in-law had promised him could result in the loss of his home and cars. But that didn't matter as much as it would have under different conditions.

Each day Peter mustered an inner resolve to forge ahead, no matter what walls were thrust up. The project had already been a fair success, at least by his standards. Though the reports had not come in, it looked favorable for Joseph Smith. All indications seemed to point to the group's united, learned opinion declaring him to be the translator and not the writer of the Book of Mormon. After all, that was their challenge—to determine the antiquity of the Book of Mormon.

In spite of Peter's efforts, the week was drudgery for most of the participants. Much of their enthusiasm for the project had diminished. He tried to reassure them that, in time, he felt sure they would receive a fair compensation for the work they had already put into the project.

One bright spot in the week had come when Peter asked Stephen if he would like to attend the local Mormon church with him. Peter had attended the Del Mar chapel of the Mormon church only twice during the past six weeks; on other Sundays, Peter had gone to La Jolla to attend services with an old missionary companion.

The large new Del Mar meetinghouse was alive with families, young adults, and a few older couples. The atmosphere seemed more like that of a family reunion than a somber church service. It would have startled Stephen had Peter not primed him for the "Mormon shock."

"Don't be alarmed if people reach out and shake your hand on the way into the chapel," Peter had warned. "The Mormons are family oriented and gregarious to the extreme, so don't make any quick judgments. They bring their families, and there is no child care provided during the main meeting, which is called sacrament meeting. Remember that the noise level in the chapel is a result of love and not disrespect.

"Your friend, Martin Oren, will likely be at the chapel door with his arms wide open. He was bishop of the congregation a few years ago. You see, the clergy in the Mormon church is not paid. All the leaders are *called* to their assignments. After they have served for a time, they are released and others are called to serve in their place. In fact, all of the active members have an assignment of one sort or another, for example, teaching Sunday school classes, or working with the youth, or serving in the women's organization. Anyway, Oren is now the scoutmaster and doing a terrific job, I understand. The current bishop is Jim Maxwell. He knows you're coming today."

"So *you're* Stephen Thorn," an enthusiastic man beamed, reaching out for Stephen's hand as he walked into the foyer of the church. Peter introduced the man as Bishop Maxwell. Stephen was drawn to him at once. *He gives me the impression that he's hugging me with his eyes.* "Martin told me you've had some incredible experiences this summer," Bishop Maxwell was saying. "We're so glad you're here." From the warmth of his manner, Stephen knew that he meant it. Other men shook hands, introducing themselves, as they made their way into the chapel. And, sure enough, there was Martin just inside the chapel door. He grinned at Stephen as he grabbed his hand in welcome and ushered the two men into the pew alongside his family.

Peter was right—these people are very friendly and a bit noisy, too. Peter's prior warning notwithstanding, Stephen still found it somewhat disconcerting as the meeting began, with babies fussing and parents traipsing in and out with their children. But as the meeting progressed, the noise and commotion faded from Stephen's conscious awareness.

He was caught up in the remarks of a young man who had recently returned from a mission to New York's Harlem. As the speaker reported some of his mission experiences, Stephen could feel his love for the people he had taught, his devotion to the Lord, and his appreciation for his supportive family. As the young man sincerely expressed his firm belief in the divinity of Jesus Christ, Stephen's imagination soared.

Oh, that I had had such an experience when I was about twenty. The young man speaking lived in Fairbanks Ranch. He had been raised in unspeakable luxury by Harlem's standards, yet he worked among those people just like Ammon and Aaron, taught them, and grew to love them. *If only my Todd could have this experience. I wish my family were here to feast as I am feasting.*

* * *

It was missionary lesson five for Stephen on Tuesday of the seventh week. He had absorbed the missionaries' instructions, even offering a prayer when asked. They had skipped the Book of Mormon lesson, naturally; Stephen knew more than the missionaries about the subject. Instead, they explained about tithing and the operations of the Church. The lesson impressed Stephen with the thoroughness and organization of the Mormons.

Other members of the local ward had called Stephen, aware that he was receiving lessons from the missionaries. He had accepted an invitation to dinner from Bishop Maxwell's wife, a charming lady. He had enjoyed meeting two of their four children and playing with their Dalmation pup, a gift to the bishop from his son who was away at Brigham Young University. Stephen was amazed that so many people took an interest in him.

After lesson five, Elder Beesley introduced the topic of baptism. "You know, we are having a baptism Thursday evening. Do you think you will be ready to be baptized?"

The question haunted Stephen all the way home that evening. He was undecided up to the moment when he opened the electronic gate and entered the estate. There was nothing he wanted more than to become a member through baptism. *But what about Anney? How would it affect her attitude toward the religion if he were to be baptized without her?* And yet he knew himself. He had stood firmly at the airport and had not left with her. He knew in his heart that if it had been for any other cause, he would have grabbed the ticket from Todd himself. But this cause was too great. So much was at stake. If he didn't stand firm, there would be no eternal family in the Thorn household.

Stephen wondered if he had the tenacity to withstand the onslaught of his family once he returned home. He had always been influenced by his father-in-law and in turn by Anney. Could he walk back into the same environment and resist being his old, accommodating self? If he were baptized, he would have the force of commitment on his side. He needed everything he could get on his side. Yet, he must be fair to Anney. *Martin is right. Don't drive a wedge any deeper than it is.* He would tell the missionaries that he couldn't be baptized, not at this time, not without Anney.

* * *

It is early in the morning for Craig to be in his father's office, thought Mary as she responded to his request to come into a meeting. Half past eight, Mary noted. If Craig were at his desk by nine-thirty, the staff considered it early. Walking into the office, Mary observed that the room that had once been Thomas Kline's office now seemed empty of life. The Remington had gone into safe storage, and the western pieces had been packed away somewhere. The room was a shell. It had lost the soul of Thomas Kline.

"You wanted to see me, Mr. Kline?"

"Oh, yes, Mary. Thank you for coming in. I've been up since dawn working out a little problem. I'm faced with this thing about the trust my father left—you know, the Brigham Young University donation and the other project.

"I really believe I have the project licked. The judge slapped an injunction on that Finley & Southam account, and my attorney and I believe that my father was the first signer on the other account, wherever Bennett has it hidden."

"Why do you think that? You don't know for a fact," Mary said with an air of condescension that she hoped Kline would sense.

Craig looked at her, a little startled for a moment. "Well, you knew him as well as any of us. Did you ever know him to put away large sums of his own money into bank accounts and not be one of the signers? I think I asked you that before."

"I'm sorry; I don't recall that you said any such thing to me before this very minute," Mary hedged, knowing she had been asked that question and had responded that Mr. Kline had always been one of the signers. For some strange reason she did not want him to think he could use her experience, her understanding of his father, or for that matter, her expertise, either. She wished that he would get on with what he had called her in to discuss. "Is that all, Mr. Kline?"

"No, oh, no. I just thought you would recall having told me about my father's banking habits. Anyway, I am still convinced that we will see that Dad's name has to be on the checks before money can be drawn. At any rate, that account will surface when we settle the estate."

Feeling a sense of suffocation in the same room with Craig, Mary desperately wanted to leave. "I'm sorry, but if you have nothing else to discuss with me, I do have a stack of work to complete."

"Please, would you sit down? Your work will wait; I will see to that," Craig said, with a slight edge to his voice. "What I really want to talk to you about is . . . I want you to do me a favor. My attorney is going to begin taking depositions in this lawsuit against the museum and the trust that Polk is misusing. He'll start in a couple of days and—"

"A deposition? Why am I being brought into this?"

"Because you were as close to my dad as anyone. The attorney needs your deposition. Mary, I'm sure you got some type of notice that he would be scheduling a time for you."

"I don't recall."

"You what?" Craig bit down on his lower lip, holding in his

mounting frustration. He couldn't afford to alienate Mary. He needed her to testify his way. With forced patience, he said, "Maybe we just need to start all over again."

Mary took a deep breath. She had pondered late into the evening just before a fitful sleep whether or not to quit this job and take early retirement. Now she saw clearly that it would be the wisest course of action.

"What is it you are trying to get at, Mr. Kline?"

"Okay, okay," Craig growled. "I need you to say in your deposition that you feel strongly that my father was not himself during the last two years you worked as his personal secretary. There, can I be any clearer in this matter?" Craig's eyes burned in his scowling face.

Mary said nothing.

Craig went on. "Now, you know and I know that he did some strange things these last couple of years. I personally feel he was mentally ill. Don't you agree?"

The dam burst inside Mary's head. It had held back a flood that crested at last. Its concrete pilings could no longer resist the weight of backed-up anguish. Mary knew she was quitting. She had nothing to lose, but even if she had, it was time to let him know exactly how she felt.

"Listen to me, Craig, and I only say Craig because you do not deserve the last name of Kline—you have sullied it to the extreme." Mary was just warming up. "Your father was a saint—a saint, I tell you. I was with him up to fifteen minutes before he died, and he was as alert as the day I walked into his small office on Fourth Avenue and asked for a job. Don't you stand there and ask me to lie for you. I loved your father. He was the most honorable, kindhearted, sensible man I ever knew. You have no right to even imply that he was not mentally competent. How dare you? You never *were* his child."

Mary made a deliberate about-face and stomped out of the office. Stopping at her desk, she picked up her purse and asked Alice, a new employee, to arrange for her personal things to be shipped to her home. Then she took the elevator to the lobby, walked to a pay phone, inserted a quarter, and dialed Bill Bennett's office.

"May I speak to Bill Bennett? Tell him Mary is on the line. He'll know me."

"Mary," Bill said, canceling a call on the other line.

"Mr. Bennett, I'm ready to sign the check."

* * *

The bank officer at the California Bank and Trust had taken twenty minutes to check out Bill Bennett and Mary Ellis to be certain he was dealing with the correct signers on the account. After a call to Arizona for verification by Valley National that both were excellent customers with high personal credit ratings and an additional call to his superior in Century City, the bank officer came back all smiles and reported that he had found everything in order.

Bill instructed the bank officer to make up seven cashier's checks amounting to seventy thousand dollars each. "Here are the names that are to appear on the checks. Then I would like the balance to be paid jointly to us, also in the form of a cashier's check, if you don't mind."

The officer took the check that Bill and Mary had cosigned and carried it to a clerk behind the counter who then quickly made up the cashier's checks.

While Mary and Bill sat at the desk waiting for the officer to return, Bennett said, "You do know that one of those checks is for Dr. Polk, don't you? Thomas insisted that he was to accept a fee equal to the amount the participants received. So one of those seventy-thousand-dollar checks is for him. Plus, I will have to draw additional funds from those we will deposit into the account we arranged in Phoenix this morning. It will be to reimburse Dr. Polk for personal monies he has already spent to keep the project alive. I would add that amount to his check now, but I don't know how much he has spent. The staff will have to be paid for the last two weeks, and the lease on the estate must be settled. Surely you can understand that we have to tie up all the loose ends."

"Don't discuss these things with me. I'm in no mood to talk about any of this," Mary snapped. "Yes, I will sign if you send someone around with the checks, but I don't want you coming to my home. I'm so upset with this entire business that I could cry."

Well, cry all you want, Mary. Just so long as I get the money to Peter. That's all that matters now. Bill's face remained impassive.

After the transaction, Bill and Mary stepped out into the late afternoon sunlight on the sidewalk in front of the bank. Fashionable people passed by, oblivious to the drama before them.

For just a moment, as Bennett checked his briefcase, containing the checks, to make certain it was locked, he and Mary stood together.

"Would you like a ride back to the airport with me?" Bennett asked, pointing up the block to his rental car. "I'm going right by there on my way south to see Peter."

"Bill Bennett, I will call a cab. I don't want to ride back in your car. I can do very well on my own."

Without warning, Bill grabbed Mary by the shoulders, pulled her to him, and kissed her squarely on the mouth. Mary jerked back and caught herself. She glanced around quickly and then fixed Bennett with a shocked look.

"Mary, don't worry. These people think we're married. Besides, I just wanted to show you a little appreciation. I don't think it would hurt you a bit if a man kissed you once in a while. Thank you, Mary, for all of your help."

Bennett looked up the street to where he had parked the blue Chevy. He waved to the speechless Mary and then moved quickly in that direction, holding his briefcase with a firm grip.

* * *

"Tell him it's Mr. Bennett at the gate," Bill said to the guard. He waited while security phoned the estate. He had not called Peter to tell him Mary had consented to sign the check, because if there had been any glitches, he did not want to traumatize his associate again.

"Here you go, sir." The guard handed Bennett a yellow slip with the lot number, gave him directions to the estate, and then said,

"Have a good evening, sir."

Bennett had been to Fairbanks Ranch once before. He noticed that, even in the dark, it looked manicured and expensive. He knew that he would probably never drive through these streets again, but he felt satisfaction that he had been able to come once more. His heart beat faster as he pulled up to the metal gate of the estate. It swung open automatically as he approached.

The front door to the estate was open, and the lights shimmered from the corners, illuminating Peter on the steps. As Bennett emerged from the car, he flung his arms out wide and shouted a jolly, "Ho, ho, ho, my child! It looks like Santa came early this year."

Peter understood . . . and wept under the glowing lights of the portico. He had been absolved.

Chapter Twenty-Seven
A Consensus

Week Seven—Thursday morning

Dr. Henry Syman stood before the group. He had shown up at breakfast without any explanation or apology. Henry had expressed those earlier when Peter met his 8:15 flight from Chicago at Lindbergh Field. Henry saw no need to bare his soul to the group, and no one had asked any questions.

Peter had called him the evening before and begged him to return. He had informed the professor that he had a seventy-thousand-dollar cashier's check waiting for him in his room. Peter said he was even willing to give him an extension on the final report, if he needed more time to finish.

"Please come back, Henry," Peter had said. "I need you here to lead the summation. It would be too biased if I directed it—you know that."

Henry had managed to catch the redeye out of Chicago. He had arrived before dawn in Los Angeles and had taken a shuttle flight on to San Diego.

Though he had not slept much on the plane, Henry was in high spirits, glad to be back with the group.

"Peter, thank you for allowing me to conduct this summary session, which we have all anticipated," Henry said as he began.

Peter nodded from the rear of the dining room.

"As you all know, we started our little venture with the expressed intent of trying to discover evidences of antiquity in the

Book of Mormon. I personally feel that we diligently went about our assigned task, and now we will see if the consensus of the group is, in fact, that there is evidence of antiquity. I know you have labored for the past two days to put together a summary report. I appreciate your efforts. This has not turned out to be the grand, three-day series of presentations we had envisioned, but now we have time to express our individual opinions and attempt to agree on a joint statement or summary of our collective impressions of the work."

The three-hour discussion commenced. Bernie spoke first, with his impressions that, after intensive research, the portrayal of warfare in the book included all the earmarks of an earlier culture at war. He strongly *felt* that it was along the lines of Mesoamerican warfare, but he stopped short of committing himself.

Picking up a sheet of paper, Bernie looked over some notes before commenting. "We have touched on this subject before, but a major area we have not discussed enough, to my satisfaction, is the book of Ether. This is an aberration to the rest of the work, if you ask me. I read it. It is so general in the telling and so broad in scope that I have no idea where to classify it in my research. If I had to say that Joseph Smith wrote any part of the Book of Mormon, it would have to be the book of Ether. It reads as if an ignorant man sat down and, in a weekend, tossed together a condensed history of an ancient period. To me, it's like the old Victorian sweep of history, all done in generalities. I will say this much, though. I came across a new study on warfare in the steppe regions of Central Asia. I think there is a similarity between the two."

Henry accepted Bernie's evaluation, and then Martha commented. "Let me interject a thought into Bernie's time slot, if you don't mind. I have made a point of looking into research on Ether. I don't share Bernie's opinions. I think I mentioned a week ago that this section is the most easily identified, a unit with little interference from Mormon, whom I've come to regard as a compulsive meddler into original documents. Let's face it. You can tell when you're reading Mormon's opinions and interjections, and when it is the original writer."

Judith commented on the appearance of Christ in the book

of Ether and that the group had discovered some interesting aspects to the book of Ether early in the project. She reminded everyone that they had unofficially agreed to set the book aside because it was more complex than they could tackle in seven weeks.

The discussion moved to Hebrew influences in the Book of Mormon. "Without question," Henry insisted, "to be candid, in my opinion, virtually no original document in America is more qualified to stand on its own merits as a piece of translated Near Eastern writing."

Chiasmus came up. Since the presentation, Judith had read every article and book available from the estate's library and done a computer search of all files on the computer compact discs, with Roy's help. She had found examples of the inverted poetic form in two books of the Book of Mormon, examples that no Mormon writer had yet found, including Welch.

"I have come to appreciate the great contribution the book is making to an understanding of this ancient writing form," Judith said in summary. Then she presented her thoughts on the literary aspects of one of the books.

"There are parts of the book that I have no interest in; yet when it comes to the poetry that I have researched, I'm pleased with what I have discovered. For example, it was Richard Rust, a Mormon intellectual, who directed my attention to the beauty that is in the book. I spoke to him by phone maybe two hours one evening about how he has structured verses to give them poetic impact." Judith thumbed through her notes and retrieved the poetry she wanted to share. "Here, I ran off some photocopies for each of you. What I have handed you Rust calls the *Psalm of Nephi*. Here it is laid out in verse form for you to see the beauty of this cry to the Lord. It's from 2 Nephi 4:28-33. Just listen to it:

> Awake, my soul! No longer droop in sin.
> Rejoice, O my heart, and give place no more for the
> enemy of my soul.
>
> Do not anger again because of mine enemies.
> Do not slacken my strength because of mine
> afflictions.

Rejoice, O my heart, and cry unto the Lord, and say:
O Lord, I will praise thee forever;
yea, my soul will rejoice in thee, my God, and the
        rock of my salvation.

O Lord, wilt thou redeem my soul?
Wilt thou deliver me out of the hands of mine
        enemies?
Wilt thou make me that I may shake at the
        appearance of sin?
May the gates of hell be shut continually before me,
because that my heart is broken and my spirit is
        contrite!

O Lord, wilt thou not shut the gates of thy
        righteousness before me,
that I may walk in the path of the low valley,
that I may be strict in the plain road!
O Lord, wilt thou encircle me around in the robe of
        thy righteousness!

O Lord, wilt thou make a way for mine escape from mine
        enemies?

Judith's voice rose with excitement. "Now look at this next passage," she said. "Watch the opposition and the repetition of an idea in reverse order. I would never have seen this without Dr. Rust."

Wilt thou make my path straight before me?
Wilt thou not place a stumbling block in my way—
but that thou wouldst clear my way before me,
and hedge not up my way, but the ways of mine
        enemy.

"Isn't that a marvelous example of a plea to God—please don't put any object in *my* path, but *do* hedge up the enemy?"

Judith paused momentarily to allow the group to reread some of the verse, and then she said, "I know I'm taking more time than I should at this stage, but one characteristic is significant in most scripture, and that is the correlation between poetry and prophecy. In the Bible, poetry is used effectively to magnify the utterances of the prophets. Usually, when a prophet speaks for the Lord, the passages are more memorable to the listener because of the poetic method of expression. Rust told me that poetry was not used by the prophets of the Book of Mormon for ordinary events of life; rather, it was reserved for divine interpretation, which is also common in the Bible." Judith reached over a small stack of books and retrieved a computer printout. "The following excerpt is from *The Art of Biblical Poetry*, where Robert Alter says, 'Since poetry is our best human model of intricately rich communication, not only solemn, weighty, and forceful, but also densely woven with complex internal connections, meanings, and implications, it makes sense that divine speech should be represented as poetry.'

"For years I have been a student of Biblical poetry. I have discovered poetry in the Book of Mormon, as I did in the Koran— not just simple verse, but a profound, intricate array of verse. What I will do with this newfound source of rich verse, I don't know, but I am impressed." Judith deferred to Freddy.

The discussion moved to Freddy, who made it clear that "no ignorant frontiersman wrote this work. I repeat what I have said for the past few weeks: Joseph Smith could not have written the book. My biggest dilemma is how he ever pulled off a translation of the original document, whatever it was." Freddy continued for several minutes, documenting the early life of Joseph Smith, pointing out that it was preposterous that anyone could entertain the idea that Joseph Smith wrote the book. "I say, chaps, this has been a stimulating round, certainly equivalent to a good refresher course in American History, with a touch of the Old World thrown in to boot."

Stephen brought up his assignment, the Allegory of the Olive Tree. "You know I'm convinced that the book was translated from original documents. I need not say any more. I have bored you all with my views since we returned from Jerusalem. I'd like to reiterate that I walked through a Samaritan olive vineyard with a farmer whose family has perpetuated the ancient method of farming the olive tree through unbroken generations. I saw the grafted wild olive branches and the old trees that had been revitalized. Joseph Smith could never have known about the horticulture of olives. On another matter, I would like to say something else before I—"

Henry sensed the religious fervor in Stephen's manner and interrupted. "Stephen, you'll have your voice in a minute. We've got to wrap this up. Let's move on to other evidences."

Martha spoke next. "I suppose of the array of presentations we've had over the past several weeks, the wordprints impressed me the most. I had heard of this science in relationship to Shakespeare's works. I'll have to admit, unless we have been manipulated in some manner by a devious mind—and I personally think Peter is incapable of such methods—it is absolutely astounding that anyone could believe Joseph Smith was the author of the Book of Mormon. The scientific applications of wordprints show that there were multiple authors, and I for one have performed an investigation on the professors who presented the wordprints. They are of sterling reputation. What else can I say?"

The discussion continued through the noon hour. The group skipped lunch, had fresh coffee brought in, and kept pouring out their findings.

By two in the afternoon, they were ready to issue a joint statement. They had worked over it for an hour before agreeing to the exact phrasing to convey their consensus opinion. Henry read the rough draft aloud, and then Roy typed it and returned a finished copy. As the group gathered around to proof the statement for errors, most wore smiles. It sounded pretty good, they had to admit.

Position paper submitted as a statement of findings by a committee specially convened to investigate whether the Book of Mormon qualifies as a document of antiquity. . . .

The final draft of the statement encompassed two single-spaced sheets of computer paper and expressed the overall findings of the group. Henry asked Martha to read the final statement aloud, again, before they signed it.

The statement explained the time constraints, the limited scope of the project, the presentation of material, and the methods of research used by the committee. It also detailed the intricate patterns of ideas in the Book of Mormon and its history and writing style. It pointed out that the complex accounts in the book consistently supported each other. It affirmed that an inordinate number of Hebraisms and Near Eastern writing patterns were uncovered, with such styles of expression as were prevalent in Near Eastern writings two to three thousand years before the time period of the document.

But the united statement fell short of confirming that the book was a translation. A disclaimer noted that the committee had not found proof of an original source from which the Book of Mormon could have been translated.

The summation of the statement indicated that the Book of Mormon appeared to be outside the framework of written works of the nineteenth century, and therefore, based on the committee's limited research, appeared to be a much earlier document.

The committee did include one emphatic statement: "We do not accept the prevalent opinion by unaffiliated individuals that Joseph Smith wrote the Book of Mormon. Since scientific evidence indicates that more than ten writers contributed to the text of the Book of Mormon, we feel that none of the nineteenth-century authors we investigated could have fabricated such an extensive work."

When Martha finished reading, Henry asked the participants to sign the consensus report. Stephen exchanged a solemn look with each of these men and women. He sighed, adding his signature to the paper beneath theirs. No, it wasn't the glowing, fervent witness that he would have framed; still, for scholars such as these, it conceded a great deal.

As Henry handed the report to Peter, he remarked, "You have not said one word, Peter. I think it is time that you give your 'biased' opinion of how you view what has transpired. This was your brain child, you know. Tell us, what do you think?"

Peter sat for several minutes, gathering his thoughts, while the group respectfully awaited his response. He stood and walked to the head of the table. Peter began speaking hesitantly. He voiced the anticipated response that he had appreciated all their efforts, had enjoyed getting to know them, admired their scholarship, and was grateful that they had stood by him when the funds were cut off. He stopped and looked down at his hands, which Stephen noticed were buttoning and unbuttoning his coat.

At last, Peter looked up and opened his mouth to speak again. "You have asked my views of this exciting experiment. I have to say . . . that for me, it's a failure."

Puzzlement showed on every face. Peter spoke more boldly. "The only one who has caught the true meaning of the Book of Mormon is Stephen. I have watched each of you closely. Stephen has looked and found the more precious parts of the book, while the rest of you have contemplated the evidences. I am not belittling anyone. It was my mistake. You have performed beautifully to specifications, and I appreciate it, but for what purpose? So you and academicians like you, teachers and researchers on college campuses, can pick at these marvelous scriptures and say, 'Yes, this appears to be Hebrew,' or, 'Oh, I see there is style and poetry in the book—marvelous,' or, 'No lad could have done what Joseph Smith claimed to do. He was not steeped enough in the learning of men.'"

Peter stared at Freddy for a long moment. Then he said, "Freddy, I have done you a grave disservice." Next he looked deep into Bernie's face and said, "Bernie, I've done you a grave disservice."

Peter went around the table, picking out each face and repeating the phrase. Then he paused, looking at Stephen. He said, "Stephen, Stephen . . . of all in the group, if you fail to act on what you feel and know now in your heart, you, of all who are gathered here this day, at this hour, will be most miserable."

Peter pushed his fists onto the tabletop with all the strength he could muster. Then he concluded. "I did it all wrong. I should have had you find evidence of the gospel of Jesus Christ in these precious pages. I wonder if your hearts would have been touched." Peter then walked away from the front of the group.

Stephen had the strangest impression as he watched Peter return to the rear of the dining room and continue into the salon and from there to the outdoors. He realized that he was a witness to a great baring of the soul. *Will the same kind of witness be required of me?*

Stephen waited quietly, glancing curiously around the group. Henry did not return to the head of the table. He stood up and walked away to his room. Freddy left, and then Judith, and soon the room was empty. Everyone left without comment. Of all Stephen had experienced in these past few weeks, this silence was the strangest. *It is as if someone passed away, and there is nothing more to be said or done.*

Chapter Twenty-Eight
A Rare Commitment

Week Seven—Friday morning

The phone rang at the Orens' house; Stephen waited, holding his receiver. After three short rings, one of Martin's daughters answered and called her dad to the phone. *Martin is such a warm person*, Stephen thought. He wondered how anyone could project such friendliness all the time. *If only Anney knew them. Anney would love the Orens.* But Stephen knew he was dreaming of a relationship that might never happen.

"Hello?"

"Hi, Martin. Stephen Thorn here. I just wanted to call and thank you and your family for the great help you've given to me."

"Well, it's nice to know we've done a little service."

"I sure hope those fine missionaries are not upset with me for not going through with the baptism. I *have* to bring my family into the Church with me, at least my wife. It wouldn't be right any other way."

Martin agreed. The two spoke for another five minutes; Stephen assured him that he would come down before Christmas. He wanted to stay in touch.

Peter had talked to each participant individually throughout the morning to thank them for being part of the project and to wish them well. At breakfast he had asked Stephen to come up to his room to say good-bye before leaving.

The door was closed when Stephen got to Peter's room. He knocked, and the door opened immediately.

"Do you have a minute?" Stephen asked, with one hand on the door frame.

"Sure, come in." Peter stood aside and let Stephen pass into the suite. "Have a seat over there," he smiled.

They had talked before in the suite. This room felt familiar and comfortable to Stephen. He eased his body into an overstuffed chair facing Peter.

"It must have been hard for you to say the things you said to the group yesterday," Stephen said, not sure how to broach his new convictions. He wanted direction from this man he had come to admire. Stephen knew he had Martin Oren as backup, and he had been super, but Peter knew firsthand the process of Stephen's conversion. Stephen felt he needed Peter's directing hand.

"You know, Stephen, there are some things I feel are essential for people to know. I had their attention down there yesterday, and I felt compelled to say what I said. I don't regret it."

"Nor should you," Stephen agreed.

Peter studied Stephen's face for a moment and then said, "You have caught that witness of the book. None of the others in the group have attempted to achieve, in their brief study, what you have. I commend you, Stephen."

"Thank you. I appreciate your confidence in what I am learning, but it is for this very reason that I have to talk to you. I'm ready for baptism, but my family is not. This is why I'm so troubled."

Stephen hesitated a moment, and then stretching out his hands with palms up, he said, "What do I do, Peter? I'm on my way home." With a shrug he continued, "Come to think of it, I may not even have a home to go to. What do I do?"

"What is it you personally *want* to do, Stephen?"

Stephen pulled his hands back and gripped his knees as he spoke. "I want to go through with baptism, of course. Yet my heart is attached to my family, and I can't do it without them, or at least without Anney."

"Then don't," Peter advised.

"I'm scared, Peter. I'm afraid my life will sink back into what I had before, and I can't allow that. Do you understand?"

Peter scratched his large nose and rubbed the palms of his hands over his chin and face. He had possessed the mannerism since he was a child, and it would forever be a habit. "I think you need to go home to Anney and teach her the gospel."

"It's not that simple. . . . Oh, that it were. I don't want to step back into an old life pattern that will pull me down."

"Then don't let it happen." Peter's voice grew forceful, as it had the prior afternoon. "You are the man who must take charge of your soul. It is uniquely yours. You are the person who has to stand for the right—and the right thing to do here is to lead out. Go home. If in a year Anney is as strongly opposed to you joining the Church as she is now, you must make a decision. But at least give her the option of coming into the Church." Peter took a breath. *I've certainly become free with other people's lives.*

"I'm worried," Stephen said, openly concerned. "My job is tied in with my father-in-law's ministry. I have to quit and find another job, fast. I think I told you a while back that most of the hundred thousand was not mine. It went to the ministry."

"Yes, you told me," Peter said. "I don't see how you can work for the man, either." Peter leaned back in the chair and said, "Stephen, you don't need me to tell you what you have to do. You already know in your heart that there is no turning back. If you do, then all I can say is that you will lose more than you can possibly imagine. I warn you of that."

"You're right," Stephen agreed, "but I wanted to hear it again."

Pondering a moment before speaking, Peter then said, "I've been thinking; why don't we cut a deal?"

"A deal?" Stephen asked, taken aback by the phrase.

"Yeah, a deal. What would you think if I were to ask you to call me every week, without fail, for the next six months? During that call we would review your progress each week."

"I'm for that."

"There's more to the deal, though. When I was a bishop, I frequently counseled with people who sincerely wanted to change their lives. In time, I worked up a little plan of action that, if they followed it to the letter, worked."

"Tell me," Stephen said with anticipation.

"Here's what you have to do, and these are the things I'll be checking on when you call me from week to week." Peter rolled out of the chair and stepped to the night stand, where he picked up a pen and a blank envelope and handed both to Stephen. "Here, write down these vital guidelines."

Peter began, "One, you must get down on your knees at least twice a day and offer up a prayer for guidance, and pray that Anney and the kids will come into the Church." Peter waited for Stephen to write the words. "Two, you must read the Book of Mormon for fifteen minutes each day—no exceptions. Three, you need to fast at least twice a month. I'll explain this in more detail later. And four, you must attend church meetings every Sunday, without fail. If you do all four of these, plus report to me every week—and I mean *every* week—you'll have a fighting chance. If I don't get a call, then I'll figure something is wrong. Is that fair? Now remember, I want you to review those four points every week. They work."

"I'll do it, Peter. I'll do it," Stephen said without any hesitation.

Stephen was about to arise, when Peter reached over and touched his shoulder with his hand. "Wait. I have something I would like for us to do first." Stephen nodded his head with approval, perplexed, and then Peter said with the most tender voice Stephen had ever heard, "Would you mind if we paused here to have a word of prayer? I would like to offer it. We both need strength to go through with this resolve."

Stephen's smile expressed his appreciation to this man he had come to love.

It took the remainder of the morning for Stephen to complete his thirty-page report to Peter. Though he had written it, documented it, and had it all in the computer two days earlier, it was not quite what he had wanted to say. Scholarly, it was not. Bernie had sat at the computer next to him and coached him on how to phrase things without commitment and how to document it so that others would say that he had done his homework.

Stephen added his personal feelings about what he had discovered concerning strong evidences of antiquity. He wanted whoever read his findings to realize that he had undergone a spiritual change by studying the book in detail. He knew it lacked the finer points of good scholarship, but it made great sense. Roy accepted the report and filed it.

* * *

At length Anney took the call from Stephen. She was in her office when it came in. Confused about how she should respond, she waited a full two minutes before lifting the receiver.

"Yes, Stephen?"

"What's this, 'Yes, Stephen?'" he asked gently. "Anney, sweetheart, we need to talk. I'm coming home. . . . I love you *so* much, but I'm a different person." He spoke slowly, hesitantly, afraid he might say the wrong thing. "I have not changed my mind since we last spoke. But we need time together."

Anney's eyes began to well up with tears. She had cried so much in the past two weeks that she wondered how she could shed yet another tear, but she managed it.

"A phone conversation is not the way for us to discuss our problem, Stephen."

"Did you receive my letter?" Stephen had written a long letter explaining why he could never turn back and that he could not give up the truths he had discovered, and pleading with her to keep her mind open, to listen to what he had to say to her.

"Yes," Anney managed.

"Then you understand that things can't be exactly as they were." His voice gathered strength as he spoke. He thought about how he must sound and softened his tone of voice. He became kind, as he always was, toward this woman that he loved. "I have never stopped loving you, Anney. My love for you has increased, if anything. It is just that . . . I can't come home and go back to our old lifestyle . . . I mean, working with your dad and all. It will no longer work for me."

"Stephen, I don't know how we can ever work this out." Anney's voice betrayed the anguish she felt.

Stephen held the phone tight against his ear and could hear Anney's nervous breathing. *She does want us to work this out; she really does, I think.* "Sweetheart, I'm flying home this afternoon. I will arrive in Oakland at 5:25 on Southwest. If you're not at the curb to meet me, I will know to make other arrangements."

"Don't put these ultimatums on me. I don't understand," Anney's voice broke. She felt the tears streaming down her cheeks. She could not speak.

"Please. Just listen. I will come home. I will be there. It is up to you if I'm still welcome. I love you, Anney. I love you."

Stephen quickly hung up. He felt that if he continued to speak on the phone, it would open the wound further and nothing would be solved. He sat on the edge of the bed, looking out at the pool, and felt as if his whole world was slipping away from him. In time, he made his second call. This one was to his father-in-law.

* * *

Bob lifted the receiver with a cheery, "Well, well, well. How's our conquering hero?"

"Dad, I'm about ready to leave and catch my flight home," Stephen said. "I would like to meet with you this evening, if you're going to be around. Let me rephrase that: We *have* to meet tonight."

"Of course. We've got a lot of catching up to do. How about dinner? You, me, and Anney. I'll make reservations as soon as we hang up."

"No, Dad; I think just you and me. I don't think I want to do it over dinner. I—"

"Hey, I see you deposited the seventy thousand. Now we can breathe a little easier. We're not out of the woods yet, but we can sure see some light."

Anney heard her father on the phone from the hallway as she approached his office door. She, too, wanted a word with her father. She hoped he could help her with this tangled problem with

Stephen. She paused in the doorway of his office. She could tell he was talking to Stephen by the lighthearted tone of his voice.

Bob glanced up and waved his daughter into the room. He put his hand over the receiver as Stephen continued to talk to him.

"It's your hubby." He motioned with his hand for Anney to take a seat. Then he punched the speaker phone so she could hear the conversation.

"Stephen, uh," Bob started to tell him that Anney had just stepped in, but Stephen went on speaking.

"I don't know if Anney has said anything about what happened here when she and the kids came down, but I—"

"Son, Anney and I have been running in different directions for a week and a half. We haven't had a minute to talk," Bob said, as Anney listened. "I did tell her about the seventy thousand that is tucked away in our account."

"Okay, since we're on the subject, I may as well ask you about that now. Did you receive extra money from a Mr. Kline as well? And what was it for?"

Bob froze. He wished with all his heart he hadn't motioned for Anney to come in, and more to the point, he wished he could cut off the speaker phone without being obvious. His answer was a long time coming. "Well, I really haven't had a chance to mention that to either one of you. As you know, we had a large interest payment to make last week, but fortunately, Mr. Kline was good enough to make a sizable donation to our ministry."

"How much of a donation, Dad?" Stephen probed, not knowing himself the amount.

Bob paused, thinking fast. He knew that it would be easy for Stephen to go in tomorrow and talk to Clifford about the payment; after all, Stephen did as much of the financial banking of the ministry as Bob. Clifford was accustomed to working with Stephen as well. Bob also knew that he had paid the exact amount that Kline had given him.

"I believe it was about twenty-five," Bob said quietly.

"You mean twenty-five thousand? Is that right, Dad?" Stephen was nearly shouting.

"Yes, why? It was a donation. We need to send him a special thank-you letter. You know, one all done up in gold bordering."

Twenty-five thousand? Anney had never heard of her father receiving such a large, single donation. She listened to Stephen's voice. Something was edgy in the tone.

"This is why we need to talk," Stephen said flatly, still not aware that Anney was in the room. "I was told by an angry Mr. Kline that he had given you the money in return for information to enable him to find the location of the estate, so he could do just what he did. He closed us down for a while, or at least he thought he had."

Anney caught her breath, remembering her father's casual question the other day: *"Honey, how can I get hold of Stephen? He gave me his address and phone number, but I don't recall where I put them."*

Stephen was just getting warmed up. "Did you know that he tried to prevent us from receiving our final payments of seventy thousand dollars? Did he tell you that you were helping him cut your own lifeline?"

"What?" Bob was incredulous. "Let me tell you something, Stephen," he said defensively. "When I accepted the donation, I had no idea what he was going to do with the information."

"Did you *ask* what he intended to do with it?" Stephen pressed the issue.

"I don't like the tone of your voice, son." Bob had always known that the best defense is a good, strong offense. "You seem to imply that I was paid off in some way."

"You were, Dad. Face it. They suckered you into divulging information for twenty-five pieces of silver. What else can I think at this point? That's why we need to talk. This Kline guy either came up with a large figure because he was desperate for the information, or you inveigled him to pay a large amount because you were desperate for money. Either way, I'm not at all happy that you gave out information regarding my whereabouts without checking out the facts. Didn't it occur to you to wonder why that information was worth so much money?" Stephen's voice was sharp.

"Oh, Stephen, I think you are being entirely too dramatic

about this whole thing."

"Am I? Any time someone pays that much money for information, he's a serious player. No, Bob, I don't think I'm too dramatic."

Bob? Bob? When has Stephen ever called him Bob? It has always been Dad. What has happened for Stephen to be so angry with Daddy? Anney sensed the relationship between the two men was deteriorating, but then, no wonder. The same thing was happening with her and Stephen.

Glancing at Anney, Bob saw the shocked expression on her face. "Stephen, if you don't mind . . . we can pick up this discussion when you get here. I owe you a debt of gratitude, and I want to make it up to you somehow, but not on the phone and not now. I have another call to take. I'll see you this evening."

"*Maybe* you'll see me, Bob," Stephen said and hung up before Bob could learn what he meant by this final statement.

Anney sat staring at her father. He said nothing for at least a minute. She could hear the dial tone when the line disconnected. At last her father noticed and hung up the phone.

"Daddy, do you make it a habit of lying to your son-in-law?" Anney asked, her mind weary from so much contention.

"What are you talking about?" Bob countered.

"A moment ago, you told Stephen you had someone else on the other line. But you don't."

"Are you going to sit there and berate me for trying to get off the line with your husband, when you could clearly hear that we were about to get into an argument?"

Anney got up out of the chair. She was not ready to talk to her father about Stephen. It would not be a good time. She started to leave the room, and then she said, "Daddy, Daddy, you always have a good answer for every situation."

"Would you mind not dropping casual comments as you leave?" he snapped. "I can see that you are not happy with me, but I have a big job to do, just to keep this ministry funded. I think you and Stephen lose sight of that."

"No, we don't." Anney returned to the chair. "My concern is with you as much as anything. You told me when you called last week from your hotel in Phoenix that you were staying to get a check from someone who wanted to donate to the ministry. Then, in the same breath, you casually asked me for Stephen's address and phone number, knowing all along that someone wanted to pay you a large sum of money for that information. What kind of money would you call that?"

"He did donate. It *was* a donation."

"That is not what I would call the normal way donations come to the ministry. It sounds more like you extorted the money out of him."

"How can you say that? Don't forget who you're talking to," Bob demanded.

"Okay, so you landed a hefty donation," Anney said with resignation. She ran her long fingers through her hair, taking deep breaths, on the verge of tears. Finally, she went on. "That is not my main concern right now, anyway."

"What is?" Bob asked, his voice slipping back into its accustomed conciliatory tone.

"Stephen, . . . I can't," she stammered. "I don't want to go into all the details of what happened when we were in San Diego." Anney blew her nose. Bob waited for her to go on. "But I do know that I may lose Stephen."

"Lose . . . what do you mean *lose*?"

Whether she had intended to or not, Anney poured out her distress about the whole attitude change in Stephen. She told her father that her worst fears had come to pass. By now she was openly crying, hardly making sense to Moore. She related the entire weekend as it had unfolded, including how she had made a scene at the airport.

"Then are you saying you don't think Stephen will come back to the ministry?" Bob asked, dismayed. "Is that what you are telling me?"

"I'm saying he wants to join the Mormon religion," she grieved. "I don't know but what he has already joined, except that Stephen has always told me before doing anything drastic." Anney dabbed at her eyes, hiccuping softly, as she searched back in her memory to recall when, if ever, Stephen had been disloyal to their relationship. None came to mind.

"This is almost impossible to believe." Bob was stunned. "Why didn't Stephen come to me, or at least call me? I could have prevented this from happening," Bob said. "I can still salvage this thing. We are very close."

"No, Daddy. This time you are powerless to salvage anything. Didn't you hear the change in Stephen just now? He is his own person—at least, he is not *our* person any longer. I have to deal with this in the next couple of hours, and I don't think . . . I don't think I'm prepared." Tears flowed again as Anney desperately sought for a solution.

"What can I say? This seems to be a problem the two of you will have to work out yourselves. If Stephen decides to leave the ministry—and, mind you, I'm not encouraging it—then he'll just have to leave." Moore's face brightened. "Believe me, there are lots of young men who would leap at the opportunity to do public relations for my ministry."

"Daddy, what are you saying? We are not talking about some job. We are talking about Stephen. Don't you see? He is joining a cult. You have given lectures on the Mormons. You must cringe when you think of a member of your family getting wrapped up in Mormonism. How can you not be worried?"

"Maybe we ought to discuss this later, when you are more yourself, honey. It's getting into some rather complex issues."

"I'll say it is," Anney cried. "Daddy, you don't seem very troubled that your son-in-law is going over to the other side."

"Don't be so dramatic, Anney. You make it sound like he is about to be tortured and killed."

"Spiritually, I think he is."

"I don't. He's a big boy now. He will have to live with his decisions. Frankly, I believe in an all-loving Maker who will correct all the wrongs and accept all of his children back into his bosom. Have I not taught you this through the years? Anney, take a little time to think about this. As far as the ministry goes, I would not want Stephen to broadcast what he is doing, but if he and I can sit down and talk, man to man, I think I can convince him not to make an issue of his new beliefs. I would hate like the devil to have him get up before my group and confess anything, especially if it would harm the ministry. I just happen to believe that—"

Anney jumped up. "Harm the ministry? What about harm to your daughter and grandchildren, let alone what this will do to Stephen? I can't stay in this building any longer. I can't breathe in here."

Anney was out the office door and on her way out of the building before Bob could speak. He overtook her at the elevator, urging her to come back and compose herself, but she would not listen. At length, Bob returned to his office to do some quick planning. *Why are things suddenly going so wrong? I can't understand. We've met our immediate financial crisis. Things should be right. Why aren't they? Maybe I can use this in my Sunday sermon to show how life's little conflicts can pull one down. That's what I'll do. I can use this as a springboard into hope—calling on the powers of heaven to conquer. My people will love it.*

Chapter Twenty-Nine
Introspection

Week Seven—Friday Afternoon

Anney sat for a long while in the driver's seat of her BMW in a pleasant middle-class neighborhood. She had parked in a marked space in front of the nursing home where her mother had been a resident throughout Anney's adult life. Instinctively, she yearned to turn to her mother for guidance, knowing rationally that it would be meaningless, yet somehow hoping she could communicate with her. She peered at the shady, green lawns through the open window of the car. Three little boys whizzed along the sidewalk on their roller blades but paid no attention to her. Fleetingly, Anney wished she were a little girl again, without a care in the world.

She wondered momentarily about the children, not that they weren't old enough to take care of themselves if she was late getting home. She knew that she couldn't worry about them, not right now. She needed space and time to think through her problem. Now her mind raced.

Why am I not getting a clear signal in this whole tangled mess? What have I done to be victimized by this religion—first Chip and now Stephen? Why has he felt the need to turn to something else for solace? Haven't I loved him as I should?

Anney reviewed her relationship with Stephen. He had always been so good about what she wanted to do. Had it ever been his desire to join the ministry? Had he really wanted to work for her father, or did he simply do it to please her?

She remembered that not long ago Stephen had wanted to take a job in Southern California for another televangelist. She had resisted. Why? She knew why. It would have hurt her father.

Have I been my father's child more than I've been Stephen's wife? She pushed the thought from her mind. She wondered how she could think such a thing. Of course she was more loyal to Stephen than her father, she reasoned.

Then slowly, slowly, she allowed herself to ponder the relationship she had always had with her father. To her, he was a holy man of God. But was he? She thought of the conversation she had overheard today and wondered.

She recalled the phrase Chip had used when they were dating before their break-up. When he had begged her to go to church with him, Anney's response had been negative. She had told Chip that her father represented the finest form of Christian religion. After futile efforts to teach her about *his* beliefs, Chip had finally vented his frustration. "You've been raised on a *feel-good* religion, Anney. Preaching on television is just one big ego trip for your dad." That had led to a definite change in their relationship.

Now Anney thought about what Chip had said. How quickly her father was willing to replace Stephen, if it came to that. *Why? Isn't his soul as precious to the Almighty as any other soul?* Was her father truly that interested in the destiny of individuals and their search for the right way? *Or is the ministry just a business to him or an ego trip? And what had transpired between him and that man in Phoenix?*

Suddenly, Anney could remain in the car no longer. She felt that she was suffocating. She got out of the car and mechanically walked into the building. The attendants at the desk knew Anney well and greeted her kindly as her heels clicked past them on the solid, shiny floor. The nurses exchanged a look, a bit surprised that she had not seemed to notice them at all. When Anney entered her mother's room in the far south wing, her heart leaped within her. Sometimes she felt as if her mother were going to murmur the endearing phrase that she had tenderly spoken thousands of times before, while Anney was growing up.

But no such words escaped her mother's lips. Nadia Moore had not said a meaningful word in twenty years. She had undergone a hysterectomy while Anney was in her first year at Berkeley. She had seemed so healthy; the surgery was a routine procedure, the doctor had said, to remove benign fibroid tumors. Without warning, her heart had stopped in the middle of the operation. The frantic efforts of the whole surgical team had finally revived her. But too much time had elapsed. . . . Too many brain cells had been deprived of precious oxygen. Bob's lighthearted Nadia, Anney's tender Mama, was gone. Even this frail shadow of the woman she was had never returned home. She had been taken by ambulance to the nursing home.

Much like her father, Anney had visited her mother for a few minutes each week for the past twenty years. Years ago, when the finality of the prognosis had become clear, Anney had been devastated. Those first years of visiting her mother—seeing her eyes so vacant, her once expressive face listless—had been hard. Mama had been so alive and loving. Now her mother had slipped into a near coma, not knowing anyone.

Anney approached her mother's bed more slowly than usual, searching the pale face for some sign of awareness. As she had done for the previous twenty years, Anney forced herself to be cheerful. "Hello, Mama," she said brightly as she stepped to her mother's side. "It's Anna," she said, calling herself the name her mother had given her, the only name her mother had ever used. It was Anney herself who had chosen her nickname and its unique spelling.

Nadia was propped up in bed, wearing a soft pink robe with a white satin collar. Anney noticed that her mother's hair had been done that morning. Her father had arranged with a nearby beauty salon to shampoo and set Nadia's hair once a week. Her white hair looked soft and lovely, but her skin had a gray pallor and her eyes were focused on nothing—straight ahead. There was no response to Anney's greeting.

Anney kissed her mother's cheek and, as she had always done, adjusted the pillow behind her mother and patted the frail hand that looked almost blue from so many veins visible through the skin. Anney pulled up a straight-backed chair and sat next to her mother, still holding her hand.

"Oh, Mama, I need you so much," Anney pleaded softly. "I need you to tell me what I should do. Tell me, as you did when I was a little girl, what I must do."

Her mother's face remained impassive.

"I've been so hard on everyone. I don't want to think of Daddy the way I've been thinking today." Tears began forming in the inside corners of Anney's eyelids. "Really though, Mama, the problem I have is with Stephen."

Anney put her head down on her mother's hand and thought of Stephen—his strong, good looks; his interest in sports and exercise; his concern for her and the children; his even-tempered nature; his genuine desire to do good works. *What was it he had said to her at the hotel? "Anney, the Spirit has told me that this is the true gospel of Jesus Christ. Please try to let the Spirit of the Lord whisper to you, too."* Anney lifted her tear-washed face to look closely into her mother's eyes. "But my father has always told me that the Mormons are a cult," she said aloud.

"Mama, I have to decide if I can endure living with Stephen when I will hate his new religious convictions. You don't even know about his new beliefs, Mama. He has changed. How will our lives ever fit together, me with Daddy and Stephen with the Mormons? It won't work. But I'm his wife. I love him." Her anguished voice broke. Anney raised her head up with a start. *That is really true*, she thought. . . . *I do love him.*

"Mama, what should I do?"

Her mother's pale lips spoke no words of counsel.

* * *

Craig was at his Paradise Valley home for the afternoon. He had decided to take a dip in the pool. The sun beat down as he lay back in the floating armchair, covered with thirty-plus suntan lotion, with a drink secured in the slot of the wooden arm of the chair.

Sharp walked slowly over to the pool's edge. He thought

how much Craig looked like a real estate ad he had seen recently on television—his fat stomach overlapping his swim suit, while his thin hair was bleaching in the sun. The whole scene was comical, though what he had to tell Craig was not funny in the least.

"Hi, Craig," Sharp shouted across the water. This pool was twice as big as his. But then everything Craig had was twice as big as the next guy's.

"Why are you here this time of day? Don't you have to work?"

"I am working. I've come to bring you up to speed."

"Okay, shoot," Craig said, leaning back to let the sun shine directly on his face.

"It doesn't look good, Craig."

"What do you mean?" Craig jerked his head up and looked over at his attorney.

"I mean we lost the preliminary injunction on those funds administered by Finley & Southam."

It took a moment for Craig to feel the blow, but in about twenty seconds the full impact hit him.

"What do you mean, we lost it? They can't do that. I have a right to my father's estate. How can they withdraw the injunction?"

"Because we lack evidence to warrant a judge enforcing an injunction. I can't get a soul to say that your father was not in his right mind when he decided to give his money away. It looks bad, Craig. If we can't sustain a preliminary injunction, I really doubt if we can pull off a full-court fight. That's it. We are not in a good position."

Craig felt the numbness in his brain. He wondered to himself how he could ever sustain himself and his family without hefty funds, well secured and in his possession. If he didn't win back the money his father had earmarked for Book of Mormon research, what would he do? He knew there had to be a way. There *had* to be.

* * *

Freddy and Bernie appeared in the doorway of Stephen's bedroom as he was closing his suitcase.

"My boy, my boy. We were hoping you hadn't left yet," Freddy grinned as he sauntered into the room.

"Yeah, we both want to say good-bye," Bernie chimed in, leaning against the doorjamb. "I see where Henry is about to leave, too. We're just making the rounds. We're checking everybody's luggage to make sure there are no towels or silverware tucked away. We can never be too careful in these matters."

"Will you knock it off, Bernie?" Stephen laughed. "I'll bet you stowed some in that box you shipped out yesterday. I wouldn't put it past you."

"No, not me, Stephen. I am a simple man of simple tastes. Freddy on the other hand . . ."

Freddy turned and said. "No, Bernie, you misphrased that. You mean you are a man with a simple mind."

Bernie stepped into the room, gave Stephen a high five, and said, "Stephen, I've got to get back to my report. Have a good one."

"You too, Bernie. If you're ever in the Bay Area . . ."

"I know, drop in and see you."

"Seriously though, Bernie," Stephen said, "one of the greatest evenings I ever spent was at your aunt's dinner party in Jerusalem. Besides being fun, there was something moving and . . . I guess I felt close because of my wife's Ukraine heritage. I told her all about it. She would love to have more contact with her mother's family."

"It was a great evening, wasn't it? But for me, maybe it was because I had a little too much wine," Bernie laughed, not one to allow himself to get sentimental. "Got to get back to work. . . . See ya." He waved and ambled out the door.

"Where have you been for the past hour or so?" Stephen asked Freddy. "I see that you're not packed yet."

"I'm just in there writing my bloody report," Freddy said, "though Peter says that I may finish it tomorrow if I wish to stay on another day. Bernie is still working, too. It looks like the two of us will be burning the oil tonight. But then that's the way procrastinators like us live our lives."

Stephen and Freddy prattled on for a few minutes, telling each other that they really should get together in the future, but they made no firm plans.

Stephen turned and met Freddy's cheerful face with a smile. "You know, I'm glad you came back to our room, even though we all said our farewells this morning in the dining room. I wanted to tell you what it's meant to me to have you as an ally, you know, to put the stuffy intellectuals in their place when they were too impressed with themselves."

Freddy shrugged. "Well, my good man, for an aberration, you turned out rather competent at the game."

"Freddy, what are you going to do now?"

"What do you mean by *now*?" Freddy asked, a little puzzled at the question, though sensing something uncomfortable was coming.

"I mean, about the facts we've uncovered. I guess you know I've taken a stand on the issue of the truth of the Book of Mormon."

"Truth, Stephen? What do you mean by the 'issue of truth'?"

"Don't joke with me. You know what I'm referring to. Peter phrased it well yesterday. I'm just curious about where you stand on what you have discovered about the book. I mean, if Joseph Smith told the truth about the origin of the Book of Mormon, then wouldn't it follow that he told the truth about everything else he said? Surely you can see that you have come face to face with these marvelous teachings that can lead you to a knowledge of Christ."

"Stephen, please." Freddy had a forlorn look on his face that Stephen had not seen before. "I'll not jest, nor will I pretend that I don't understand what you are getting at. You may think me insensitive, but I am not. Don't you think I read the same book you did, went over the same passages? I listened to the warnings and encouragements of those prophets in the Book of Mormon . . . and they will haunt me forever if I don't expunge them from my conscious thoughts."

"Why are you fighting it?" Stephen asked.

"Because I didn't ask for it. I know myself. I could never measure up to the ethics and ideals that would be required of me to follow Christ. Stephen, it is that simple." Freddy spoke with an understanding that Stephen had not realized he possessed.

"I see that the book has been put here for us to follow." Freddy shrugged. "But I choose not to follow it."

Stephen was engulfed with sadness. He had come to love this unusual friend. He bit back the words he was about to speak, deciding instead to say good-bye. "Well, Freddy, I have to tell you that you made being here a fun experience and I'll miss you."

"I shall miss you also. Please don't fret over my soul. It is not worth the effort. Cheerio, lad."

Stephen sat with Roy in the front of the van, while Judith and Martha occupied the rear seats. Since leaving the gates of the estate, Judith had been giving a detailed account of her plans to spend part of her money. "I'm going to get off that plane in Los Angeles and take a cab straight to Rodeo Drive," she bragged. "My layover is going to last for as long as it takes me to spend ten thousand dollars—not a penny more, not a penny less. I'm going to sit in one of those expensive dress shops and have them wait on me hand and foot." Seeing Martha's puzzled face, she explained, "You know they serve you champagne while their models stroll by in those elegant threads. Mmm, mmm! Then I'm going to have them send everything I buy to my hotel, while I sit by the pool and drink something nice and refreshing. When I've spent the entire ten thousand, then I'll go home, but not until I do."

Judith looked radiant in her white summer suit and dramatic white hat. Stephen thought she already looked the part of some wealthy lady who knew her way around Rodeo Drive.

"I've tried to talk Martha into coming with me," Judith taunted.

"Hey, why don't you?" Stephen encouraged, turning around in his seat. Roy sent the van speeding off to the right at the junction of the 805 and 5 freeways—toward Lindbergh Field.

"It wouldn't be me," Martha said. She hunched her shoulders and looked out the side window of the van.

"What do you mean, it wouldn't be you?" Judith asked. "Who cares if it's you? Live a little, Martha honey. Life is too short not to have a little fun. Besides, what are you going to do with all that money you've got stashed away? Sweetheart, I know you have at least seventy thousand, 'cause you haven't spent a dime since we've been together," Judith laughed, feeling lighthearted about everything.

"May I ask you a question, Martha?" Stephen inquired. "You have a daughter, don't you? That was your daughter I met at the hotel, wasn't it?"

"And a husband," Martha said, turning her head away from the window to meet Stephen's inquiry. "And a mother and two cats. Since you ask, I'll tell you. In St. Louis, where we live, I am the only one who is working. My daughter is staying with us. She's trying to break out of a bad marriage. My husband is ill—he's twenty years older than I am—and my mother is as unhappy as she's ever been. So there you have it. These seven weeks have been like a vacation for me. I'm not really happy to go back. But at least I now have enough funds so that if I don't want to teach an extra night class or summer session, it won't be absolutely necessary."

"So you think our little project was worth your time?"

"I would have come without getting paid. I've needed this time away from my family. Now, I'll go back. But I feel like I've lived a little, and I've had a definite change of environment."

"What about what you've discovered?" Stephen asked, wanting to know how Martha would use her newly gained knowledge of the Book of Mormon.

Roy reached over and tapped Stephen's shoulder. "Look up the freeway on the left. Do you see that magnificent building, the white one with spires? That's the new Mormon temple."

They all stared as the van approached and then sped past the intricate white building. "It almost seems to be jutting out onto the freeway," Stephen commented. "Freddy and I came over one evening when we were out cruising in the Mercedes. Too bad we didn't come over here as a group." *According to Peter, the temple represents a more complex level of Mormon worship. Magnificent.* He had seen the temple in Oakland, but this one was even more regal.

"Sorry I interrupted," Roy said and returned his attention to the highway.

"You didn't answer me, Martha." Stephen inquired a second time, "How are you going to use what you've found out?"

"Well, I'm sure not going to join the Mormons, if that's what you mean."

"Maybe that is what I mean," Stephen thought aloud. "It puzzles me how we could sit through the same sessions and not one of us come away with the same insights or impressions. What would it take to convince somebody like you, Martha, or you, Judith, or even Roy here, that there is a God and that he directed the translation of that book we took apart? What does it take?"

"I'm sorry, Stephen, but you are getting entirely too deep for us. We're on our way to have some fun. Don't plant a guilt trip on us. We're not buyin' it," Judith said, chiding him in a light, easy manner.

Stephen knew he had tried to scrutinize their deepest feelings and had come up empty. He knew too that they didn't want to be reminded of their new findings. Even Roy, who seemed to want to say something, kept his eyes focused on the freeway. Of those in the van, young Roy had spent the most time and had gained the greatest insight into the documentation of the Book of Mormon.

Drop it. It's going nowhere.

"Well, Stephen," Martha asked, "is that darling wife of yours going to meet you at the airport? You have a beautiful family. It was nice to get to know them at the hotel. Be sure and give her my best."

Stephen felt that Martha was speaking fast in an attempt to change the mood. "Yeah, Stephen, give her my love, too," Judith added.

"I'll be sure and do that," Stephen said. *But will I see her again? Will she come to the airport? Do I still have a wife? Oh, Anney, I pray that you'll come. I pray that we can work out this problem. Please, God, please help us.*

"Well, it looks like we're here," Roy said in a flat, matter-of-fact voice. There were hugs all around as their luggage was unloaded. As soon as he could break away, Stephen checked his luggage at the curb and made his way alone to the Southwest gates. He walked through the detector, cringing inwardly as memories of the scene with Anney two weeks ago flooded his mind.

I've got my ticket this time, Anney. Please be there when I get off the plane. Please, oh, please.

The flight took a long hour and fifteen minutes. Though it was on schedule, it seemed slow to Stephen, who spoke to no one in flight to Oakland. He could think of nothing else but Anney.

Anney. What was there about her that had attracted me in college? A pretty face? A full, firm body? That was physical, but it was more than that. I dated other girls who were physically alluring. No, I felt from the moment that we sat together in that philosophy class, listening to that dull, dull professor, that I had known Anney somewhere before. She seemed so familiar.

What was there about her that was so irresistible? Her smile? Her eyes glistening with excitement and wonder? It was more, much more. The qualities that attracted me to Anney were her frank and open self. Her sincerity, a depth I had not discovered in anyone else—such a rich vein of pure gold. I wanted her then as I want her now. She must, she must, she must come to me.

I'm trying to go to her. But on my terms. Is that the way it has to be? No! It is not one or the other. I now have the gospel of Jesus Christ. I must carry it to her and the kids. But how? I must do as Peter instructed. I have to stay close to whatever it is that brings others to an awareness of the truth.

Stephen stirred as the flight attendant reached across him to hand his seatmate a drink. *Where did I go wrong with Anney? I rushed her into something she wasn't ready to cope with. She has a right to study these things. I've been pushing her beyond her ability to grasp these marvelous truths. I must be patient. That is what I will have to do. Remember our wedding night?*

A wistful smile crept over Stephen's face. *She was so frightened. So was I, but I refused to let on. Her face was pale, and she finally told me that she had never been to bed with a man. I remember saying to her that I had never been to bed with a woman, either. Then I suddenly realized that I had to be patient. We fell asleep in*

each other's arms because neither of us wanted to hurt the other.
There were three days of that on our honeymoon.

If I was so patient then, why can't I be patient now? I can.
I will. Oh, Anney, just be there. Be there, darling. I love you so
much. I will be patient. Trust me. I will gently lead you, and I will
not assault you with my newfound beliefs. Please, Anney, just be
there . . . please. The sound of skidding wheels on the tarmac jarred
Stephen back to reality.

The plane landed and taxied to the extended ramp. The
flight attendant announced over the intercom: "For those of you
who are already up, please notice that the 'fasten seat belts' sign is
still on." Stephen didn't care if some flight attendant was displeased
that he was on his feet before the plane had come to a complete
stop; he wanted out. Now.

Stephen hurried off the plane and dashed to the escalator in
the terminal. In his rush to get to the street, he bumped into two
older women who stood, dead center, in front of the escalator, talking. "I'm sorry," he said, darting past them. He couldn't yet see over
the heads of the passengers moving along toward the baggage claim
carousels. He was not concerned about picking up his luggage. He
kept his gaze on the glass-fronted terminal as he quickly moved
around the crowd and walked with long strides toward the entrance.
Then he saw it. From where he stood, he immediately recognized
the silver-gray roof of Anney's BMW.

She's here! She's here! Then he said it out loud, not caring
who heard him, "She came! She came to get me!"

To Be Continued

About the Author

Keith Terry is a popular and prolific writer who has authored a number of fiction and nonfiction books for the LDS market. *Out of Darkness* and *Into the Light* are his first novels to be published by Covenant.

A perpetual student and researcher, Keith has earned bachelor's and master's degrees from Brigham Young University. He has also pursued graduate studies at the University of California. Along with his busy writing schedule, he enjoys scuba diving, jogging, and family history research.

Keith and his wife, Ann, live in Provo, Utah. They are the parents of nine children.